MY GUN WAS AS TALL AS ME

Toni Davidson

MY GUN WAS AS TALL AS ME

Toni Davidson

**FREIGHT
BOOKS**

First published in the UK August 2012
By Freight Books
49-53 Virginia Street
Glasgow, G1 1TS
www.freightbooks.co.uk

A CIP catalogue reference for this book is available from the British Library

ISBN 978-0-9566135-9-2

Typeset by Freight in Plantin
Printed and bound in the Czech Republic

the publisher acknowledges investment from
Creative Scotland toward the publication of this book

Toni Davidson was born in Ayrshire, Scotland, in 1965. His novel *Scar Culture* (Canongate, 1999), about child psychiatry and abuse, was published to international acclaim and translated into nine languages. It won an Scottish Arts Council Book Award. He lives in, Switzerland with his wife, the writer Kate Orson, and daughter Ruby.

Praise for *Scar Culture*

'Like William Faulkner's *The Sound and the Fury, Scar Culture* is a book not to read, but to reread' *Sunday Herald*

'Compelling… A novel of ideas that is also humanly compelling' *Times Literary Supplement*

'Toni Davidson's first novel is a clever, well-executed work' *Independent on Sunday*

'A macabre, disturbing and bitterly funny look at sexual abuse and psychiatry' *Dazed and Confused*

'As an account of pure, undiluted wickedness, it is hard to imagine this novel being bettered - but perhaps it is just a question of waiting. Davidson's novel is a deeply pessimistic work, but also a timely and necessary one.' *Daily Telegraph*

'Veering between the poetic and clinical, human and monstrous Scar Culture is a brave, highly filmic, and complex book displaying a real intelligence prepared to tackle taboo territory with imagination and subversive humour. It could well be destined for cult status.' *Herald*

'Toni Davidson's first novel is disturbingly mesmerising, complex in its construction and devastating' *Observer*

'As riveting as vehicles colliding, powered by aggression and elegance… The writing… is completely harrowing, transcendently beautiful, and remarkably discreet' *National Post (Canada)*

'Like Ken Kesey's *One Flew Over the Cuckoo's Nest* slugging it out with Dorothy Allison's *Bastard Out of Carolina* – Davidson has crafted a work of spellbinding contemporary fiction' *Uncut*

'Sentence by chilly sentence, Davidson is a fine writer, proud of looking where others would turn away' *Publishers Weekly*

'And from the way *Scar Culture* reads, he could be a worthy successor to his more famous novelist namesake, Toni Morrison' *The Torontor Star*

'Dévasteur... Toni Davidson brosse avec intelligence le portrait d'un monde dérangé, où les soignants sont aussi tordus que les malades' *The Face*

To all
Internally Displaced Peoples

'What is wrong with peace that its inspiration
doesn't endure and that its story is hardly ever told?'
Wings of Desire

Je Lin did not see the man who gave her Lynch and Leer.

He spat into her eyes as he swore at her for everything she was. She saw his gun though leaning against a rock; saw the jade green of his uniform, felt its rough fibres and the touch of his rank embossing her skin. He shuddered then dripped his lust leaving her bruised and bleeding.

Je Lin burned her clothes in the embers of the fire; burned the soldier's stains, as sudden flames, jagged in the night. In the fire she saw two writhing, wriggling children emerge into the humid air, their tongues unravelling, lashing her with venom then words. Such words! Vicious, revolting words – taunting her, filling her ears then her mouth, making her choke as the smoke puffed clouds into the forest night. Their skinny arms were not held out for comfort nor embrace but were strangely straightened in accusation, their fingers pointing parallel at her.

With rage she stepped into the fire to reach them, to silence them, singeing her feet, burning her soles. The heat simmered their anger, boiled it over in fact and they screamed the story of their violent conception for all to hear. It was the dissonant harmony of their truth. No one could stop it but Je Lin did not want to hear, did not want anyone else to hear and she reached into the fire's heart to wring their necks, to squeeze their apples until they popped.

As she writhed in the dark lit by flickers and ash fire-flies, the villagers looked on then looked away, their heads shaking. This had happened before.

Even when the flames had died down, the boys like melting shadows, Je Lin could still hear them, spitting sparks of insinuation, of accusation that she had encouraged the vicious act, that she had led herself into darkness to wail to be wanted. Soon enough these fiery boys would be reduced to ashes and glow, all but flecks of red heat splintering the black air. When the time came who would believe her? No one would believe her and everyone would believe them. She spat her promise at their fading forms.

'You will have nothing to say. I will silence your story.'

Espirit and Tuvol

Espirit was old now, his breathing shallow but the occasional sighs were deep as though all the burden and responsibility had caught up with him, a late arrival before dying. The seamless operation of care glided around him because footfall might have roused him out of his sedation and the senior nurse was careful to make sure the eye mask was still in place. Now that he was near death, he could no longer bear light.

Old Hope, as the nurses had nicknamed his father, was dying and Tuvol was just beginning to realise that this bombastic, brilliant man would not be alive for much longer. It was not a shock; the slow reveal of illness, loss of mobility, lessening of mental agility all indicated that days were numbered for Espirit. With a strange mixture of sadness and excitement, Tuvol found it thrilling to count the days. He did not exactly tally on the wall of his room like a jailbird waiting to be sprung but he could not deny there was a calculation to his father's inevitable death. There was a past to account for and a future to assess.

On lucid days, Espirit liked to sit up in bed leaning forward just long enough for two pillows to be placed behind him. He regaled all those who would listen – nurses, doctors, the occasional distant relative, his wife and his son – with his own eulogy, which seemed neither premature nor inappropriate. Those who knew Espirit could think of no one more suitable to deliver the account of an extraordinary life.

Espirit had created a socially aware empire; a vast network of *Homes for Peace*, built for refuge and love that few apart from *Barnardo* could lay claim to matching. He was the doyen of life-building charity, a post-war leader in social salvation and moral engineering. Critics, politicians and religious leaders had stood side by side with him as he spread his bricks and mortar, his love and family message across the world. He was to put it finely *that* big. Not so much rich – although they were hardly poor – but respected, influential and renowned. But there was always a common denominator to such things, to such people, a leveller say and always that moment of honesty away from the glare of other people. When he returned home, his father would light a pipe, curse the world and disappear into his own cloud. The great communicator would slam his study door and hide.

The most important moment in Tuvol's life was a fossilised tale, as old as the stone of the mountains and which was deliberately titillating, and yes, a little shocking. Espirit delighted in telling it like an announcement, a rude flourish to some after dinner speech. An icebreaker.

'Our dear son was conceived in a snow-hole, a temporary dugout in compacted ice as my wife and I sheltered from one of the many avalanches in the mountains. It was a bad year for avalanches but a good year for babies.'

When he was younger Tuvol would wonder why grown-ups patted him on the head, or pulled at his rosy cheeks and let out air in a long aaah as though they were checking their voice for health. When he was older smirking adults would pat his buttocks with maybe a tweak and certainly a wink and ask if he was a chip off the old block. When he was older still he imagined his father frozen with his mother, as rigid as the ice they lay in and Esta, his mother saying nothing, expressing neither joy nor pain; a plateau of non-reaction as the swirl of Tuvol's imagination would have him be a red, bloody ball, rolling down the mountain, a smeared trail of possible life left on the white.

Tuvol understood what Espirit got out of that quirky anecdote told to wineglass-holding acolytes with minds as thick as their wallets. His father loved to be centre of attention, thrived through communication and Tuvol understood what his unusual conception meant to his father. Tuvol was the product of his father's sense of fate or rather his impeccable sense of timing and he came along just as he was empire building his charity. Such fate was feted when he was young; he was symbolic of grabbing the moment, seizing opportunity and throttling it until it spat out what you wanted. So Tuvol entered the world.

When he was barely two years old, Espirit, flushed with brief, fatherly pride, brought his son to one of the community meetings that he was fond of holding, with him as chair of course. With a flourish and an inaudible fanafare he led the young Tuvol on to the stage and introduced him. Tuvol sat on his father's vacant chair, swung his already long legs and said nothing. Espirit smiled nervously and held out his hand to him, 'Here, let me introduce you to your extended family.'

Tuvol refused his father's hand and shut his eyes as though falling into some kind of trance. It was the first of many refusals and Espirit did not take it well. The great showman had expected at least a hello, a smile or some kind of animation, a sign that Tuvol would react to a crowd like his father, harvest energy and brilliance from their attention but on that stage were sown the seeds of dullness as far as Espirit was concerned. He had been shown up by an amateur and the rot in their relationship was firmly established. Returning home, Tuvol the young child was shoved into his mother's arms and the house would rattle to the slamming of the study door.

'For a son of mine, you are remarkably selfish.'

This was sung as much as it was shouted; an unexpected tune to his tone and while Esta and the young Tuvol listened at the door, the tune belched and grew operatic, flooding through the crack below the door. This was Espirit defusing himself, anger ricocheting into the ridiculous. Tuvol imagined him strutting around his study in a feathered hat, king of that world too.

Espirit was both efficient and eccentric; competing characteristics that somehow worked, that made him by any judgement memorable. He took situations that politics or religion or other world events had made complicated, that the powerful elite of corrupt and vicious cliques had imbued with hopelessness, and made them simple. It was a winning mixture of back to basics morality and love-is-all-you-need philosophy that was neatly homespun for the people. And the people liked it. Captains of industry, gurus, moguls and philanthropists all lapped it up. But there was business there too, make no mistake about that. At the beginning everybody was a volunteer but it couldn't grow without money, without a sense of being employed. If people had to do other jobs in order to survive it took them away from where they were needed and Espirit quickly realised you have to fund good intentions.

Even now, as his eventful life was drawing to a close, he was still in charge. Not so much technically but figuratively. The business had progressed so far and his health and energy deteriorated so much that it had been a long time since his signature was actually needed. The charity's board recognised that his history was his value in the present and gradually they reduced his public contact, sidelining the great communicator now that his long speeches were bracketed with songs or poems that he had written. The board members winced when they saw the ordered index cards with his elaborate handwriting covered in verses with titles such as 'To The Universe With Love.'

Homes for Peace built its first official children's home in downtown Bente, a small town close to the border. It was a sleepy, socially conservative town and not the most likely stepping-stone for a caring empire that would decades later stretch to five continents. Espirit had various family connections there and this helped, at least a little, to prepare the town for not just a small invasion of ragamuffins but also for what many considered to be an eyesore of a building complex, an ugly blot of modernism camped on their rural landscape.

Espirit employed a young and upcoming architect Fritz Fuege to create the homes in Bente. Not, you understand, a children's home. For Espirit and his small band of dedicated followers, friends and students, the last thing they wanted was to recreate workhouses or brutal orphanages that had been set up in other countries to cope with the dirty stream of children from the disinherited, the displaced and the dead. Theirs was a modern view, a modern idea not of care but of restructured family.

Tuvol thought of his mother, Esta, mute and irritable, hiding in her kitchen, rattling her utensils like a cup on prison bars.

'There should be a nurturing, facilitating mother in the home along with brothers and sisters and there should be a village, a community of a finite number of dwellings that house the mother and her children. We shall seek to eradicate words like foster or adopt and use only the words son and daughter. Childhood shall be re-established within the walls of both the home and the village.'

Even as a young boy Tuvol knew this speech and others by heart and he would lip-sync when he had heard it, standing close to the bathroom door, stifling his laughter and imitating his father as he preened and keened. Espirit rehearsed his words, quietly intoning some phrases then wildly singing key sentences, his arms flung wide in front of the mirror, his lips curled around his thick moustache and chunky vowels as he made sure to annunciate every syllable.

The young Tuvol toured these Fuege-designed homes with his father on a regular basis. The caring empire was flourishing in every major city as need surfaced from hidden squalor and Espirit drove straight into the heart of it all. Tuvol recalled being stuffed into his father's huge car, squashed against the door, his sweating skin sticking to the upholstery while Espirit held court on the back seat, gathering Fuege, his lawyer, local politicians together for a meeting on the move. He captivated his invited audience, his big voice booming over the throb of the engine.

Tuvol rarely saw his father alone. He was always in the middle of a group, at the head of table, or on stage in front of hundreds then thousands. In the beginning while he was still trying to instill verve in Tuvol he would search out his son sitting bored in the car and force him on beaming benefactors. By the end of the day Tuvol's jaw ached and his hand had the grip of a dozen people on it. He looked at his palm expecting to see the layers of their skin.

Tuvol was full of physical tantrums that would have him kick anything that moved and though there were few words there was the howl of his tender years, a rush of sound and fury that dampened as he grew older, taller. In such situations, Espirit would usually completely ignore the mood and carry on with the task at hand. In the middle of some crying fit, he made Tuvol model the uniform for the children of the village, trying out different styles, different materials. Whatever mood Tuvol might have been in was mutated by this catwalk as his father gushed and pinned thin cotton shirts and thick velvet trousers. Nor did Espirt just try out the boys' uniform and Tuvol's long legs were soon to be seen protruding gangly and awkward from the prettiest of girlish patterns. Espirit had an eye for such things.

When Espirit grew too busy to be involved, he simply let Tuvol run around the Homes for Peace compound, hurdling bushes, scraping the bark off trees, spinning then kicking up tufts of grass, a scream pitched to break glass, to shatter ice.

'My son.' On tour, Espirit would openly gesture towards a wailing Tuvol. 'He's setting fire to himself and expects me to put it out. He doesn't know how lucky he is.'

This audience-pleasing remark, his carefully worded put-downs and having-to-put-up-with-a-lot sighs, usually won over his companions, wooing them with humour and self-deprecation while casually alluding to his commitment to the cause of other people's suffering.

The fire died out when childhood gave way to the hormonal rush. Tuvol quietened where others got busy with their bodies and the bodies of others. His father took him less on his compound tours and there was little doubt – at least in Tuvol's eyes – that once he had started to grow and grow tall, he was less cute and ironically less noticeable. Espirit seemed happy to leave him at home as the business trips grew longer.

When body and mind changed for Tuvol, his gangly limbs got in his way; his awkward voice that was already too soft, broke and then no one could understand him; he muttered – 'You're a mutterer,' his mother cried. 'Speak Up.' Espirit chastised. Tuvol was also less inclined to step into the foster homes around the compound where once he had been welcomed in, a curiosity, the odd looking offspring of the Founder. The mothers seemed to be keeping a watchful eye on him now, checking his crotch, his eyes. He was becoming a man and men had already done so much damage. But Tuvol was not of that ilk, his hands didn't find himself until many would say it was too late. As a young man he was expected to behave in a certain way that he didn't know. His birds and bees had been frozen in the snow and served up as a canapé at fundraising functions. This was how he learned life was brought into the world. Hasty, icy copulation in the cold mountains.

Tuvol became housebound without any injury; put himself under house arrest without any sign of authority. And no one with authority stopped him; he was free to imprison himself. While the adolescence of compound children thrust them through the tunnels dug under the compound wall to meet local girls or fight with local boys, Tuvol listened to their shrieks and cries as though it was his first taste of a jungle listened to from the safety of a hideout. And with Espirit away much of the time Esta was left in charge of the house which meant nothing at all. Fuege's heralded design had been muted by bursting pipes and creaking floors. She stayed in the damp kitchen and he stayed in his room. The food tray became their intercom. Hungry? Yes. Finished? Yes.

The doctors said there was nothing to be gained from staying at Espirit's bedside. No doubt they had observed how silent the vigil was, how utterly lacking in communication these last moments were.

It wasn't strictly a medical intervention but it was a human one.

Give yourself a break, they advised. So Tuvol went in search of the snow-hole.

From 18 years old, the age when the children were getting asked nicely to leave Homes for Peace to fend for themselves in a job or in the state system, Tuvol became what he was always meant to be; the inheritor; the chip off the old block who would take over the reins when necessary, reign when it seemed appropriate. There was a legacy to be continued and although Homes for Peace was both a company limited by guarantee and a registered charity with the relevant authorities, he was the obvious choice. He was the son of Espirit. He was the son of the man the compound kids dressed up as on Founder's Day; miniature Espirits in breeches and embroidered velvet, bumping into each other with their chests pushed out squawking as loud as they could.

In his reluctant role he kissed children on the cheek and wished them all the love and hope they needed to hear when they first stepped foot into the Homes for Peace compound. Tuvol made sure no one could feel his pain or hear any kind of howl. He took all of it, balled it up. He fell asleep dreaming like he used to as a child of his own death; a spiralling, sparkling unfolding of life laid bare then quiet, smothering darkness. The next day, always the next day, there were administrative duties, public duties and openings along with media duties and further admin chores. Then he would kiss more children on the cheek and wish them all the love and hope that *he* needed to hear. He fell into bed wondering if his sex would rouse itself for possible, fleeting imaginings, a loose grip on lust but found that the alcohol he was increasingly keen on had numbed more than his mind. Everything had gone green. He found nothing in his life that wasn't obscene.

In the Snow

Tuvol's feet were sinking into the fresh snow on the Anvil. With the doctor's advice still hanging like vapour in cold air, he had grabbed only his jacket and a Styrofoam cup filled with black coffee from the hospital canteen before climbing in to his car. Now that he was on the mountain slopes the coffee seemed ridiculous and his jacket inadequate. It was also later in the day than it should be for such an excursion and when he met a few other geared-up walkers on their way down, their muffled *tchs tchs* confirmed his irresponsibility.

He did however have a pretty good description of where the snow-hole had been. Conveniently his father had a quality print of the Anvil on their living room wall and Espirit in his typically extravagant manner had wanted to pinpoint on a regular basis to whoever was there to listen, the exact gully on the mountain where the deed was done. Maybe Old Hope lying gurgling back in the hospital would have actually approved, would have applauded Tuvol's spontaneity and declared it a personal Zeitgeist to be pulled up the mountain in search of something one was yet to discover.

Tuvol knew his destination but he had no idea why he was going there. He felt like a city hiker on the slopes in flip-flops. He grew up near here, he knew the allure and danger of the mountains and had learned off by heart a code like all children in Bente had to learn when it came to mountain safety. Caution had been thrown to a wind now picking up speed as the light of the day began to fade and a muted throw of colour descended on the mountain, the angular setting sun finding well worn crevasses to brightly light; a last salvo before the mountain was gently covered by dusk then smothered by darkness.

It was ridiculous and yet he kept going. Was he going to light a candle for his place of conception; was there a ceremony that would suit the occasion? It seemed unlikely but then it was an unlikely place for sex. Tuvol couldn't shake the impression that this was his father's only sexual interaction with his mother; sex was simply procreative and having decided on just one child that was it. Tuvol doubted Espirit attached any religious significance to sex and how it was conducted; he was a businessman not a religious man. Having sex once and Esta getting pregnant was an efficient use of resource. Job done and, as it transpired, he had no further needs. At least not at home.

All his life Tuvol had felt there was something wrong. Missing. Or taken. Sometimes it was an ethereal background feeling; a draught working its way into the house from some crack unseen. At other times it was like a sledgehammer working on his confidence so that he felt crippled by everyday actions; the mechanisms of a normal life. That was hard but ignorable as a child; difficult but easily masked as an adolescent but as an adult it creaked and wrecked his body in so many ways he could only manage to crank lifeless smiles and limp on to the next day. Tuvol was being put to death by doubt.

This was what Espirit would have hated to hear. While his father cracked on with charity, *bon homie* oozing from every pore, Tuvol made sure he indulged in aggressive introspection. A *fuck you* to a busy man was to do nothing; for a man on the move malaise was two fingers upright and insulting. Sometimes he felt strong enough to do that but at other times he would be pestered by shadows, not people as such, nothing as spectral or corporeal as that but by accompanying shades of shadow and light; a sense of expectation and the lure of the void. The truth was he couldn't describe to anyone what was truly wrong. Tuvol didn't know. And how exactly could he describe the sense of morbid doubt to people looking after kids who had seen their parents disappear before their eyes; to children who had simply not been wanted and left to fend for themselves on the street? His pain was a luxury few could afford.

At night Tuvol would walk for hours along the paths of the village, past houses where families were sleeping soundly, where there would always be somebody's snore leaking out of Fuege's thin walls. It was strangely comforting to hear the sound of other people sleeping as though there was a possibility of second-hand sleep, a catching condition that would see him narcolpetically fall on to one of Fuege's strange flat bridges that crossed the small stream that weaved its way through the village. Sometimes he would stop on a bridge and look down into the black water listening to the sounds of the village at night. It wasn't sleep but sometimes it got close to rest.

On the mountain in the fading light, Tuvol half-expected there to be an X that would mark the spot; he thought there would be relics of Espirit's desire still lying around, frozen to the spot, cryogenically preserved. The gully was barren; just more white on white with a nasty looking crevasse for walkers to avoid a few metres away. It didn't seem ridiculous to expect a sign; a signature that Espirit and Esta made love here, a stony heart carved into the rocky outcrop a few metres up the slope towards the summit.

It was here that Tuvol made a simple decision. It might be expected that such a decision would be dramatically reached with much howling and wailing. It wasn't. It seemed both clear and frightening.

Close to where Espirit and Esta must have been nearly 35 years ago and just under a small outcrop of rocks that pointed west towards the setting sun, he managed to squat into a relatively comfortable position. The wind was continuing to pick up speed and what was left of the light showed gathering clouds further down the valley. Townspeople said that bad weather that started there would always come by way of the Anvil. Tuvol wouldn't be alone.

He remembered what one of the hikers said as they passed him, more to his friend than directly to Tuvol.

'People are ill-equipped these days. This isn't a walk in the park and yet people blithely…'

The wind took the rest.

Tuvol remembered what his father said too, as though continuing the climbers' conversation.

'Some people expect life to be easy, served up to them beautifully presented and pre-digested. Yet I have seen how people survive the worst that life can devise. It is in suffering that we find out who we are and it is in privilege and comfort we lose perspective on our own souls.'

So, the son of Old Hope made himself comfortable underneath the rocky outcrop looking towards the last embers of light. When darkness descended on this mountain, any step could be a treacherous one and so Tuvol could not move now should he change his mind. Soon it would be too cold to think and his eyes unable to see would close gradually, like the rest of his body, becoming closer to the ice and snow. Then he would sleep.

Village Life and Death

Verlaine, a little stooped now at 50 years old but still strong, still working a full day, made his way through his home to the veranda to see how his boys were doing. He could hear the drone of a plane high above the village.

'What you got there, Lynch?'

Lynch and his brother were sitting on the steps of Verlaine's aged bungalow, the split bamboo splintered in several places where footfall had been too heavy; where the rain and heat had taken its toll year after year. He'd built this bamboo home with his own hands before these two scrawny boys had breathed air.

Lynch held up some charred pieces of paper and shrugged. There was a pile of such paper beside him. This was Lynch, give him paper or old plastic and he would try to make something of it.

Verlaine nodded.

'That's right. That paper is better off as ash. Comes from planes like that one.'

Leer held one of the brittle, ashen papers to the sunlight, squinting his small, hazel eyes.

'There's nothing worth reading there. You haven't been taught to read so you can look at that. Nothing but lies. They drop information like they drop bombs.'

Lynch let the pieces of paper he had been tearing for the past half an hour fall on to the dirt in front of the hut. They were joined by loose bits of thatch that Leer was absentmindedly tearing out of the roof.

Verlaine cuffed Leer on the back of his head.

'If you keep pulling at that, our home will no longer be a home and you will be sleeping with the pigs.'

Lynch laughed and spat into the dirt.

'You too.' Verlaine reminded him, half-sternly.

Above them Verlaine watched the trail of the airplane through the thick canopy of the forest. He shook his head.

'Nothing but lies. They think that words will be enough to make us give up.'

Leer grabbed a large handful of the dried grass and shoved it down his shorts, the spikey fronds pricking his skin.

Lynch laughed but shook his head pointing at Verlaine who still was still watching the sky. Oaths were slipping through his lips.

Leer gyrated, his hips pushing the dried grass out over the waistband of his shorts.

Lynch leapt up, grabbing enough dried grass to make a wig for his head but when he attempted to make one for his brother they both lost their balance and hung giggling over the rickety rail of the veranda, their laughter echoed by a few villagers who had come to see what was happening.

Verlaine turned his head and then stroked his greying stubble in mock consideration.

Leer pulled out the dried thatch and threw it to some of the people who had been drawn to their squeals. With their backs to Verlaine they behaved like actors, the veranda their stage.

Verlaine stepped forward and interrupted the performance by lifting up each of the boys and dangling them over the veranda, to their delight. The boys were small for 11 years old even by local heights and there was little extra flesh or muscle on them. Their dark skin was stretched tautly over thin bones. Lynch had a more rounded face with Leer's angular, sucked in cheeks and thin lips. They were children of the country, it was there to see. There has been no city fattening or whitening for these two. Their mother, dead now, her last breath taken after their first, had little to her but Verlaine was strong, a mountain of a man and easily the tallest in the village – even with his stoop. Perhaps they would have his muscle when they were older but for now they were reeds dangling in the wind. Their long hair made them like young girls, different from other boys in the village.

Verlaine liked it that way and the boys saw no reason to disagree except when ticks clung to their scalp and time had to be spent searching each other's hair for unwanted guests.

But the boys had no voice – at least not a voice that made words the villagers could understand. It wasn't clear in their infancy, when their gurgle and shriek was like that of any other baby but when people tired to coax words out of them they heard mutant sounds, vowels truncated where they should be elongated and the growing absence of complete and rounded consonants. Their words were cut short and soon a queue formed as villager after villager looked into their mouths and shook their heads. The elders looked deeper, beyond the mouth and into the throat. The animals who had taken half their tongues seemed to have left everything else. Verlaine watched in silence.

It was thought Verlaine and Je Lin had finally achieved what whispers had denied them. A childless couple would have been an unfortunate state of affairs but even damaged children were better than none at all and they appeared otherwise equipped to be boys and then quickly men. At their naming ceremony Verlaine got carried away with the moment, by emotion and raced back the *Kasheen*.

Inevitably he said what he thought and listened to what he believed. A few friends, confirmed rebel sympathisers, urged Verlaine to dedicate the celebration, this special twin birth, the death of their mother, all of it to the cause of first defence and then liberation.

Verlaine nodded and held them up into the humid night air.

'These boys, Lynch and Leer, are the sons not just of Je Lin and me but of all the village; their birth is a sign of hope, strength and determination for all of us.'

It was a grandiose claim but no one flinched, no one spoke against such a statement. Verlaine's was a quiet authority that had been challenged only by his time with Je Lin, where he acted as a weary restraint to her wildness. With Je Lin's passing into the spirit world many believed she was already part of, Verlaine was able to lead again and when he spoke people stopped to listen. He wanted them to believe that these two squirming boys could solve the problems of encroaching government violence, crop devastation and poverty. Their birth was an injunction served on the slow decline of the village. Their birth was something that fate must respect.

Far from being ashamed of their voice deformity, their cut-off tongues, there were many times when Verlaine enjoyed the boys' quiet, saw in them a reverie that was trusting, contemplative. He was able to harbour dreams. Theirs was a hush waiting to be a noise. They would explode. There were other times when he caught villagers looking oddly at their near-silence, shaking their heads at their hand signals and twitches and quirks of mouth and eyes. This was not what they expected – Verlaine shooed some, the more respected, away with a knowing nod but chased others away with a shaking fist. Gifted or cursed they were his sons and he would bear no ill stare or intent.

The peace of their childhood, the quiet of their home was welcome too after Je Lin. Their marriage had been residual; they were what was left. Desire had evaporated over time and monthly hope drifted into years of gathering despair, inevitable distance. Verlaine would tell no one she was not missed, would not allow talk of her near him. When he suspected whispers were about her, or about them both, or the late arrival of children; any such rumour or tittle-tattle he could not bear and threatened all with his temper that few had seen and none wanted to experience.

For most of the time he had kept her at a distance as he tried to protect himself from her incessant torrent of words. Her babble jangled his nerves, her incantations irritated his rationality. What would the spirits want with her? With them both for that matter. On the balcony swinging in his hammock Verlaine would shut his eyes and listen. The sounds of children playing were like whispers in the sun compared to her incandescent conversation. Je Lin had filled their bungalow with endless chatter about magic and rituals; totems and superstition. She scared most people off, even the few that were left who believed in such things. Verlaine lost no time after her death in ridding their bungalow of all the trappings of her belief. While she was alive it had been not just her delusion, it had been his.

As he watched the boys acting up for their audience in the stifling shade of his home, Verlaine would not allow himself to dwell on Je Lin. Even she, especially she, would have agreed that her fate was sealed when these two boys were born. What had taken their tongues, had taken her life.

The boys screeched like Shinla birds hunting and their stunted tongues allowed for the call to be pitch perfect. As the villagers applauded, delighted at their accuracy, a wind suddenly started but it was not the wind that came out of the jungle sometimes felling trees and ripping up roots, not like that but a vertical wind, a downdraft, like the woosh of a hand through the air.

But not a hand.

A metre from Lynch. Two metres from Leer and some six metres away from the veranda of Verlaine's house a body fell with a loud thump into the dirt less than half a metre from young Salva. Most of the group screamed, a collective howl that rushed into the cloud of dirt that had risen from the body. It was impossible to see for a few moments and this brought on a secondary rush of shouts and cries; feet could be heard to scramble on the ground and thumps of body into body could be felt as people panicked and tried to run in all directions. Somebody shouted, 'It's an attack!'

As the brown red dust cleared a little it was possible to see Lynch and Leer rooted to the spot as they stared at the body that had fallen from the sky. The body outwardly remained intact but the form of the man, his length and breadth, had folded as though his outer skin and skeletal frame had been sucked in. The force of impact had pushed the man underground. He had made his own grave.

Verlaine walked through the clearing dust and stepped over the fallen body to Salva who was twitching and trembling. The young boy was in shock and when Verlaine bent down to take him into his arms he noticed the boy's right arm had been broken to some terrible angle. Instead of standing him up, he sat down with him, telling him with a whisper close to his ear that everything would be all right.

As the dust lifted and the other villagers ran further back, it was only these four and Jel Unw who remained close to the silent, sunken body. The sound of the plane could still be heard but it was far in the distance and nobody was looking up.

'Do we know him?' Jel Unw asked, searching around him for a stick.

Lynch and Leer shrugged in unison, each of them searching around him for stones.

Verlaine shook his head. 'It doesn't matter, Salva's hurt, this body… this man must have hit his arm before he hit the ground. It's badly broken.' Salva was whimpering but not loudly, the shock numbing him for the moment to the pain.

'I think I know him.' Jel Unw found a stick and stretched for it. 'He could be anyone but still…' Jel Unw poked at the body with the thin stick. 'He looks kind of familiar.'

Leer nodded and made a cross sign to Lynch who nodded and made the same sign back. It was their way of saying danger.

'Boys,' Verlaine stood up with Salva in his arms. 'Find Root. Now. No playing around, just action. This young boy needs our help. Where this body is from doesn't matter. It's Salva we have to help now. So move your scrawny bones!'

Later, when it was dark, Lynch and Leer crept back to the body that no one had moved or even touched. A few dogs had nosed a leg or an arm but something frightened them off. Perhaps he wasn't dead long enough or perhaps like Jel Unw they thought they knew him.

There was no moon so the jungle around them was a black wall, impenetrable yet patterned; the wreath of vines and roots undulating even in the dark, adding texture to the black, giving depth to the night wall. Around the village were a few oil lanterns hanging on bamboo poles as families talked in hushed whispers, a few eyes glinting towards Lynch and Leer.

Lynch passed the light to Leer. This was their job. Verlaine encouraged it. It was an honour, spades at the ready. But it been done only once before, when the village's oldest woman had died and they had carried her skin-and-bone body to the grave they had dug and laid it as gently as they could into the hole. Leer had been fascinated by her death mask, peaceful, pain free, while Lynch could only look away, pale. He remembered her alive, saw her alive just a day before. It was hard to reconcile and difficult to believe there could be breath one moment and not the next. He started to count his own.

Leer squatted close to his brother and pulled the light between them so their eyes met in the dark. They blinked three times. Leer waited for the tears to fill his brother's eyes and then shed a few of his own. They were twins of equal height and although they were not identical they were inseparable. Close up the resemblance was unmistakable and their voices, although only in squeak and scream, cried and groaned, laughed and grunted sharing the same intonation.

Leer took the spade out of Lynch's hand and laid it on the ground beside the shallow grave. Without sound he levered a stick underneath the corpse and then began to push. The body was heavy for him and seeing him struggle Lynch reluctantly retrieved his spade and helped his brother turn the body onto its back. It turned with a soft thud. They both gasped and turned away from what was once a face but which had imploded. There were no distinguishing features except for the mound of grubs and bugs that were assembling around the mash of skin, bone and blood.

Lynch let the stick go and curled in on himself, pushing the palms of his hands into his eyes.

Leer proceeded to make the hole deeper for the body to be properly buried where it fell from the sky.

Lynch raised his head from his knees, sniffed and wiped his eyes with his bony arm. Another body without breath. He held one hand up to his mouth making sure he could feel his own hot hair and with the other he drew, in the mud, a small outline of the body, a tiny replica of the corpse slowly disappearing into the earth.

When it was finished, Leer reached for his brother's hand and pulled him back to standing.

Jaffe

When Jaffe came back, he didn't fall out of the sky but fell out of the forest. He just appeared one morning when the villagers were readying their labours' worth for the market, everybody busy. Even the children had been told to stop playing and help load and tie sacks of vegetables and fruit, although one or two of the youngest were free to chase after the cockerels who scattered to hide below the bungalows. This bustle stopped almost in unison when they saw Jaffe. He didn't walk through the clearing in the trees but tumbled head over heels like he had taken a dive or was rolling down a hill, like the children all used to up in the Papen Hills before soldiers started to lay mines. Now the children didn't roll anywhere outside the village.

Except Jaffe. He was like a wild thing, like the forest had just given birth and here was its child; smeared in dirt, soil pushed dark and brown into the eyes and mouth and a long green vine stretching from his stomach back into the trees. If someone didn't cut it quickly he would strangle himself as he rushed into the village. Jel Unw acted quickly and used his panga to cut the forest away from Jaffe and when a scream went out some thought maybe the boy had cut Jaffe but it wasn't that. Verlaine knew it. It was just the letting go. If someone has been held tight, just the letting go can cause a scream like that. Verlaine could see with his own eyes the forest's fingers slink back into the green and the boy sink into the mud which had once been his home.

The twins didn't know what to do at first. No one did. They didn't know who this screaming ball of mud was. Those who caught the moment when he fell onto the ground thought an animal had come into the village and they were reaching for their pangas to cut more than the forest. Lynch and Leer didn't know who it was either and hid behind Verlaine's legs who in turn pushed them gently in front.

'You must always show courage. It is expected,' he whispered into their ears.

When Jaffe let out the scream it was a sound they didn't just hear. They felt it and it was familiar to some of the men and a few of the women who'd had their eyes opened and distracted from the old ways by the war. There had been fighting before of course, angry shouts and quick cuts from pangas, but that had been family and it was different now, now it was a fight brought by strangers. Now when they looked into the forest they wondered what would come next. With Jaffe's scream came recognition, that this ball of mud and angst was one of them. Or used to be.

No one had forgotten Jaffe but most it must be said never expected to see him again. He was not the first to be taken nor was he the first to disappear. He was the first to have come back. One moment he was one of strongest boys and best workers and the next no one could find him. He had gone to the market in Mae Rot with money he had from working in the fields and that's where he had been taken. He was 14. This was a popular way for the army to recruit. In the towns, at bus stations, at train stations, anywhere where there might be a crowd waiting. Until this, the village had been lucky none of their boys had been taken when nearly every other village in Papen had been stripped of their young males. A bitter harvest for all mothers and fathers, Verlaine would remind them when security got lax and the children started to wander. Even Lynch and Leer took fright sometimes and would stop at the edge of the village looking into the green but Verlaine would whisper into their ears, 'Not you boys; you are special. You are stronger than anyone else.' The boys nodded and put their fingers inside each other's mouths. This was their sign of togetherness. This was what made them the same.

When the brothers recognised their old playmate, they rushed to pick him up and hug him. They brushed off some of the mud from his body and pulled the twigs and leaves from his hair. They saw how different he looked but did not meet his wild stare. While some of the villagers put down their pangas and sharpened sticks, others slowly emerged from their bungalows and the twins, with Jel Unw's help, lifted Jaffe on to their shoulders and carried him ceremonially into the village. It was then Verlaine noticed how thin Jaffe had become with arms and legs like sticks and much of the skin on his legs scarred with fine raised lines, some still swollen. He noticed too that apart from the scream Jaffe had said nothing. Verlaine felt hairs on his body rise.

When they brought him past Verlaine, like a captured prize, with a few of the other children running alongside, Verlaine looked for and found Jaffe's eyes through the smeared dirt. He found his eyes but didn't find him. His own father had told him what he already knew, to look for the eyes in both friend and enemy; young and old. Everybody knew that and Jaffe's eyes still moved, still blinked and stared straight ahead but Verlaine could not tell what he was seeing. As Lynch and Leer moved around, each hut celebrating Jaffe's return, it was the same, it was not just Verlaine who held back, who kept celebrations for another time. Most of the adults and all of the elders stayed where they were and looked keenly at Jaffe and then slowly, warily, at the forest he had come from.

When it got dark, the village gathered at Verlaine's bungalow and those young ones who couldn't see or hear crawled forward on their bellies so that they were right under the bungalow, with just their faces showing level with the floor. Never had there been so many people in or outside his home but then never had some one come back from the dead like Jaffe had.

When the villagers saw him close up he told his story. Verlaine saw it wasn't only his legs that had scars, his chest, arms and face all had recent rips and still suppurating wounds. He was 15 and his voice was lower now and there was none of the quick excited movements of youth, just the nod of an older age.

'They took me at the bus station. I had done what I was told, got most of what people had asked for but there was not enough money left. I met Jyi, some of you know him, he has a truck and his son was in our school, the last one, the one that the army burned down. I saw a few soldiers and an officer come in to the bus station. I saw a few kids run away at the far end of the station but where I stood there was nowhere to go. I would have to have run past them. That wouldn't have worked.

'They asked me for ID but I don't have it – who does? – and they know that. They said, "If you don't have ID then you have to go to jail or join the army." When I said that I didn't want to join the army the youngest soldier only a few years older than me said, "Fool. That's not the right answer. What's the right answer?" When I didn't say anything the NCO kicked me in the stomach and I fell on to the ground being sick and coughing.

'Soon enough they heard what they wanted to hear and I found myself at what we all know as the Gathering Place, *Sa Sun Tay*.'

Jaffe had to stop because several of the villagers exclaimed so loudly that they had to be sshed by others and, if it were possible, people pressed closer to Verlaine's home so that he thought something would break under the weight of everyone.

'I know everybody's heard about *Sa Sun Tay* camp. Nobody knows where it is exactly, all I know is that it was deep in the forest in the valley, somewhere, but all of us on the truck knew where we were going. It was the place they take boys to; it's where they make boys into soldiers.'

The word soldier didn't fall easily from Jaffe's lips nor did it find an easy home in any of the villagers' ears. The soldiers, the army, the Tat, these were all words they had long associated with the regime, those in authority far away who sought to destroy them where they found them. Once found the villagers would be made to leave their crops and go into hiding high in the Papen mountains where little could grow and few could live. The talk amongst the villagers was that the soldiers were close by now and Jaffe being back amongst them was not the joyous occasion it should have been. Several of the older villagers stepped back from the throng and kept their eyes on the forest.

Jaffe continued, 'When I got to the camp, I wasn't the only one who had been recruited that day. They put me in a lock-up with 30 other boys, the youngest was maybe 11 or 12, all of us in a room squeezed with bodies. Nobody could lie down. We stuck to each other, a stinking mess. The guards said we could eat but they gave us a small bowl with rice and stones in it. It wasn't enough. I don't know how long I was there. I just tried to remember where I came from and not to cry. If you cried the guards would come in and beat you. If you got beat you would bleed and there was no medicine. Wounds just got worse and some of the kids got really ill. Two died. I don't how long they had been there. Their bodies were passed from one to another from the back of the lockup to the guards at the door who bundled them away. I knew one of the kids, he was at the school too, the one we had before it was burnt down. I knew him…'

Jaffe didn't break down or run off or do anything apart from close his eyes. Many of the villagers closed their eyes with him. With his eyes still closed he went on.

'They told me it was good that I was big for my age. It got me out of the lock-up quicker than some of the others I had been taken with and into a room where they made me fill in some forms. On the form I wrote that I was 14 but the officer just smiled and scored it out and put in 18 instead. The next day me and maybe 30 or so others were put on a truck and taken to the army base. The soldiers on the truck said we should be proud, we were *Ye Nynt*, the Brave Sprouts, cadets being trained to serve our country. I looked at the faces of the soldiers, but I didn't see my country in them, none of us did. They were from another place. They wanted us to fight their war against our own people. One of the boys spat on the floor when they said this and three of the soldiers just pounced on him and beat him until there were two of his teeth on the floor of the truck.'

A woman on the veranda sobbed quietly. Jaffe's mum was a striking looking woman, taller than most with beautiful eyes and a wonderful laugh that would always set others off until she could get a whole group laughing without any of them knowing why. But now she was leading everyone into crying and this proud woman had doubled over the bamboo rail, her body shaking with all kinds of tears coming out of her. Relief, joy, fear, anger, horror. It was all there in every heave. Verlaine held her as she fell back, her muscles giving up the strength to grip.

Jaffe ran a hand over his stubbled head.

'When we got to the army camp they shaved our heads so that if we tried to escape everyone would know where we came from – if they knew no one would help. Then they made us sit cross-legged in the yard in the sun all day while they took us one by one and filled in more forms. Several boys fainted from the heat and they only gave us rice soup with a few water greens in it. At the end of the day they put us into barracks, which were long, baking hot, outhouses made of concrete with wooden floors. This was where we slept. There were no mats and we slept side by side getting bitten by mosquitoes. I couldn't breathe sometimes. The air was bad and they took all our clothes. They told us that if we were naked we wouldn't run away. It didn't stop everyone.

'Yeah, some boys did try to escape. They made us drill every morning by running round the camp and these two boys found a gap in the fence and just kept on running into the forest. We all thought it was risky but we had all thought about it, all dreamed of it. We wished them well but they had short hair and had only stolen army fatigues to wear. Sure enough a patrol caught them. They hadn't got very far.'

At that moment there was barely a sound from the huddled group of villagers, just the shriek and call in the night forest around them, and Jaffe joining his mum in quiet tears. He cleared his throat and looked only at the floor.

'The two boys were beaten until one of them died. I did it. We all did it. The NCO didn't touch them but they gave me and a few others a stick and we each had to hit both boys in turn. If I didn't hit them hard enough, they would make me hit them again. I closed my eyes the first time and I missed the small one. The stick just kicked up the dust into the air. "Do it again!" the NCO shouted, "Or you will be hit twice as hard." And I got so scared that I hit the boy, not just hard but as hard as I could and he screamed and blood poured out of his mouth. I'm sorry. Then I swung at the other boy who was still standing, I made him fall. I hit him on the chest and the stick cut him, scraped then dug into his skin. I'm sorry. The NCO took the stick from me. I could hardly stand. "You listened well." The first boy had lost consciousness and the second boy was now coughing blood. One of them died later. I don't even know which one.'

The jungle came back to the village, it's screech rushing into the space left by Jaffe. There could be nothing more to say and Verlaine thought it better to stop him. This was a terrible thing to hear and Jaffe was curling further in on himself, the pain of recollection creasing his face. His story could be finished when he had some rest, some food. This was what he was worried about and Jaffe with his words had brought fear one step closer. He tried to get people to go but no one moved, they were tightly locked in, as though they could only be released by Jaffe himself who said quietly, 'Let me finish, please. I want to finish and then never talk about it again.'

No one moved and Verlaine backed off, looking at his two boys either side of Jaffe, ready to hold him should he fall. That, at least, looked right. They were there for him. For all of them.

'I thought this was not the army. I was a slave. There were no soldiers just us boys washing clothes, cutting wood, digging ditches and holes. Then officers came and took some of the younger ones, they liked their hands for massage. The boys had to hold up their hands for inspection. When other soldiers came back there were many beatings. We all got hit over and over. For nothing. For being there when we didn't want to be.'

'Then they gave us guns. This was what we wanted. Then we could stop cleaning. More came, new ones and then they would do the cleaning. It was the way of things. I tried a G3, nearly tore my shoulder off and a lot of the younger boys couldn't hold it and fire it never mind march with it. If any boy got so tired they dropped the gun, an NCO would beat them and make them run round the camp or squat thrust until they couldn't breathe. They gave us real bullets. They told us, "You've got to get used to having the enemy close to you, being fired at from a distance or in an ambush close enough so you can smell some stinking revolutionary." '

Jaffe's mum could no longer sit where she was and she stood up unsteadily and started to walk towards her son. But Jaffe held up his hand and looked away.

'I had nowhere else to go, I'm sorry. I shouldn't have come back. Do you want me back? The army is looking for me. The army is looking for all of us. No one is to be spared, thats what they told me at the camp. They are looking for rebel soldiers wherever they are. Wherever they are hiding. They will burn our homes. Burn us.'

A few of the older men in the village had moved away from Verlaine's bungalow. They had picked up the pangas they dropped and started walking into the forest. 'We will need all the warning we can get,' one of them shouted. Jaffe stood up, adrenalin somehow found, the sweat pouring down his face.

'I escaped when I could. Two other boys were going to come with me, they were from Kayi village. Is it still there? I heard…'

People in the crowd began to talk, their tone turning from pity for Jaffe to fear for themselves.

'I'm sorry, I wasn't careful about running; there were too many tracks to be covered. I just ran and ran until I found the river and a good soul who took me up the river. He saw my army clothes but kept looking at the river. I don't know. I didn't know him. Maybe he wasn't a good soul. I'm not, I…'

Jaffe has reached the end of his strength and the brothers held him as he slipped on to the floor. His mother could be held back no longer and rushed to hold him, crying into his chest while he just looked over her shoulders with that same look; seeing but not seeing.

Two of the elders approached Verlaine and it was clear a decision, in the light and in the darkness of Jaffe's story, had to be made. They had all known that other villages in the State had been burned to the ground by government forces and that every village was a target. Mae Rot was filled with villagers who no longer had a village. Verlaine had been urging the other elders for some time to make preparations to leave. But there was always the crops, the harvest, the food they needed to grow and sell; there was never a good time to leave. But Verlaine could hear the guns even if they could not.

'Where would we go? There's nowhere else. This is our home.' They told him this, they asked him what they would eat, what about the children? They pushed questions at him and he could not answer. He looked at the children, his children playing and laughing; and he looked at the forest beyond the village. There was no place for them to go; this was their home beyond living memory. They had made this their land, the fields had yielded a good rice crop and children had been born just as their grandparents had died here. But Verlaine knew that just because there was nowhere safe to go didn't mean they could stay.

Verlaine said what he had to say quickly and with a heavy heart.

'It's time we left. We will go up because we can't go down. At dawn. Gather only the most important things. Do not take with you more than you can carry.'

He looked over at the twins, who were coiled, waiting for his instruction. They had the energy to save them all. They were Verlaine's Brave New Sprouts.

The Rains Come

There was not silence but sound between the boys. It took a while for the villagers to understand what they saw when they queued up to peer into their mouths. It made them curl their own tongue against their cheeks, sound out words they knew they could say but tried to imagine how it could be done without a tongue. Verlaine the father, Lawe the teacher, did a lot to make everybody aware that words and meaning had not gone, that the boys were simply missing a part of their body like many of the people who had come back from the forest with truncated arms and legs. In the absence of complete limbs there was much to adapt to and in the absence of whole tongues the boys changed spoken words into signaled words accompanied by the splutter and pop of gums and teeth.

They fitted this world to suit themselves and their life in the village. As the boys grew older, from infants to crawling, to staggering then climbing, they were adventurers like any child their age, seeking every possible place in the stilted home, their tiny hands fitting through the roped bamboo stems. Their talk was of course strange at first but Verlaine always listened, bent his head down, nodding then smiling.

'I will know what you need, what you want to say. I am your father.'

Lynch opened his palms upwards and looked at Leer with a slight smile. Leer twisted his hands, fingers pointing limply upwards. This was often the beginning of their conversation just like it was for everybody in the village. A question followed by an answer. Nobody who saw their gesticulations gave them a second glance now. They were all used to the way the twins talked to each other. Although it was their own private means of communicating, Verlaine and Jel Unw had picked up the basics and through a combination of movement, gesture and facial expression most of what they needed to communicate was understood.

In the darkest part of the night, 80 villagers were running around, a few holding battered old lamps, a few carrying battery torches while most squinted their eyes and felt for what they knew to be there. The village had been on these gentle, lower slopes of the Papen Hills for as long as the elders could remember, some of them had cut down the first bamboo and grown the first rice. The children were told, *it's just a stick, a toy, you can make another, don't cry, we will make another together. We will travel with our spirit and our courage. They're ours wherever we go.* Quietly and almost stealthily the villagers prepared to leave. There was little light from the sky but clouds were already gathering. The rains were coming and all the villagers knew if they were to go higher into the hills it had to be now. In a matter of days the paths would be mud, there would be no grip and they could all slide into the sights of the government soldiers.

Lynch and Leer had filled their packs with all the food they could find in Verlaine's hut – a sack of rice, bags of betelnut and cardamon pods, some dried fish. There were few clothes, they wore what they had until it was too torn, but there were favourite t-shirts, faded images of far flung cartoon characters somehow smiling, half erased from the thin cotton. They both had favourite sticks from a storm broken Rawpa tree. They had carved them into points and used them for fish or on other boys in the village in playful but still blood-letting fights.

From where they crouched, they could see Verlaine helping some of the elders with their belongings, pleading with them to take as little as they could. 'We will be back, this is just temporary; this is our home, we will not forget it.'

Jel Unw, two years older than the brothers and growing up to be as tall as Verlaine, joined them.

'Leave nothing you want to see again. There will be nothing left when the soldiers come.'

Lynch and Leer both looked at him, their eyes widening.

'Yeah, I heard they break the cooking pots and shit and piss in the rice sacks; they kill the chickens and eat them and when they have done all they want to do, they torch every last hut and rice store. Burn them to the ground. Bastards.'

Lynch made a roof with his hands then drew in the ground. This was a skill everyone had noticed. From the moment he could grip a stick, the ground – the dust of the dry season and the mud of the wet – was his canvas. Through quick scrawls of words he had learned from Lawe to the drawings that came from somewhere, from head and heart most likely Verlaine thought but certainly from somewhere deep, he could capture with simple strokes the picture of what was in front of him. And as he got older it gave an idea of what was inside him.

Lynch drew a longhouse, an extended bamboo structure that had been built by a proud village, drawing many children to it from a wide area. There were smiling faces on one side of the house, with kids leaning out of the windows with pens and paper waving in the air. On the other side there were more children leaning out of another window but this time there were flames roaring up from a fire below the house and not only the pens and papers were on fire but their heads too. Lynch's quickly flicking wrist captured the twists of flame.

'Yeah, just like what they did to our school.'

Verlaine was shouting something from one of the other huts which none of the boys could hear but they could see him backlit by the first sign of dawn, his arms waving them over.

Lynch and Leer both nodded.

Jel Unw shook his head. 'This is going to be hard, brothers. If the rains start we will be up to our chests in mud, slipping and sliding while watching Grandma Joul wash away to the bottom of the hill. And the little kids will cry so much we will have to wrap their mouths with banana leaves. Then we'll all be crying because our feet will bleed and our heads will ache because we will be tripped up when we run for our lives. Yeah, brothers, you'll wish you can speak so you can howl how bad this is going to be.'

Verlaine came to them, his palms raised towards the dark clouds of dawn.

'Is the whole village to wait for you to finish your conversation?'

Leer picked himself up and pointed towards the evacuating villagers. Lynch nodded and Jel Unw had already moved off, always quick on his feet to avoid the wrath of Verlaine.

For a moment Verlaine saw them both as being much younger than 11 years old. Eleven could seem much older than it was in the forest; village living had many chores that had to be carried out as soon a child could lift or grip a pan or panga. But from what Verlaine had seen of the city this had always been the better place to be a child, to grow up with the sighs of the forest and not the shouts of the street.

Until now. Their forest home was changing and even the youngest carried their deteriorating world on their shoulders.

The brothers unorthodox communication meant that other people often took it upon themselves to speak for them, interpreting their wishes, feelings and needs but Verlaine would not do that. As children it had been hard and there were many tears and tantrums, their heads banging into walls or each other as they tried to express what they needed. But the need to be understood honed their skills and it was something the boys had come to excel at – conveying something to a group of people with the flick of an eyebrow, the turn of a hand. Even their stunted vowels could be used to emphatic effect. No sound was wasted and although no one in the living memory of the village had not been able to speak, Verlaine made sure people realised that they had a gift not an affliction. Lynch and Leer were special because they needed to be.

They looked at Verlaine at that moment, their eyes holding for as long as it took for a mortar to hit, and then the village was turned into a writhing corpse, on fire and twisted with pain.

There were a few seconds after the grenade exploded when there was a silence, not a calm nor a quiet but a moment of vacuumed sound as though the explosion had obliterated all noise in its hot, lethal thrall. Then a rising crescendo then a layered glissando of cries and shouts as those villagers who had been close to the explosion appeared through the cloud of debris and dust.

Verlaine, a big man of muscle and taut strength, had been knocked off his feet, but quickly pushed himself up when he saw the terrible state of the mortar victims. There were three on the ground close to the hole. Each of them had something missing; two legs, one arm and a head. A further four people were staggering wounded, a whole family, a mother holding on to just the arm of her daughter whose legs were buckling as she tried to hold on to her five year old brother who was reeling from a head wound that had split his forehead. The father, still a young man, seemed unhurt with no signs of blood dripping or tissue dropping on to the scorched ground. But when Verlaine stumbled closer to them, his arms outstretched in the hope that he could do something, he noticed the man, Jyaw, had no eyes to see the help Verlaine was offering.

Lynch then Leer shook the dust out of their hair and jumped to their feet; shocked but spiked with adrenalin.

Verlaine, as he gathered Jyaw's family together as best he could, shouted back to his sons. 'That was just the start. To unnerve us. This is what they do. They bring terror from the sky then bring it on foot and by hand.'

Leer took Lynch's hand and they ran to where Verlaine was holding the huddled, broken family. Lynch eyes strayed to the mutilated corpse of Huh Tawn who had been singing the night before, his guitar tones finding resonance in the trees, in the wood it had come from. They had all listened in silence, bodies close and some eyes shut. Another woman, one the brothers did not really know, joined in, her voice light, full night air. Now she was silent, her face a red and black jungle of bone and blood.

Verlaine's voice was strong, but taut and angry. 'It's possible they might be ahead of us, further up but I doubt it. But we must go where we said we would and right now. Look at them boys.'

Verlaine gestured towards all the villagers who were now gathering, edging closer to where the RPG had hit, their hands around their children and the belongings they had packed, ready to leave.

'No one must wait now. If there are things they don't have then they must leave them behind; there is nothing to stay here for except for more of... of this.'

He nodded towards the charred remains of the villagers.

Leer looked around him and asked Verlaine, spelling his name on the palm of his hand, 'Jaffe?'

Verlaine snarled a reply as they all searched the crowd of villagers.

'Jaffe, our son, it is now clear returned only to betray us. If you see him slice him with your panga.'

Leer shook his head and pulled at Lynch's hand, so that they were brought close to each other, their eyes meeting, their breath mixing.

Verlaine growled, 'You have to be stronger than that. It is expected.'

Jel Unw shouted to anyone that would listen. 'They know where we are. It is not a secret. They are here because they have decided to come. It is our turn. We are now part of their war.'

Lynch pushed his head into Leer's chest who cradled it but he kept shaking it as though trying to shake the words back into place. He could feel them falling inside him.

Verlaine let out a howl that seemed to stop everyone; the brothers, the screaming wounded, the sobbing villagers.

'Enough. We're going now. Do not stop for anything. There is nothing to say now.'

'But there is...'

Verlaine looked around to see who had spoken so softly.

'But there is…'

Jel Unw sneered.

'Jaffe.'

The scarred boy soldier, the childhood playmate of Lynch and Leer, had walked from the perimeter of the clearing. In his right hand was a machete he had used to cut at vines and branches; his thin arms and legs had fresh grazes and slashes where the trees had recoiled, where thorns and prickly barbs had rebounded. In his left hand was a gun. He walked toward the villagers who despite Verlaine's clear instructions had all stopped to stare. They had listened to his story of abduction and induction into the ways of war with heavy hearts but these villagers were not fools incapable of thinking beyond the moment. No one survived here without being able to grow food, keep shelter and bring up children but they had wanted to believe that some good can come out of hardship. They had listened with sympathy but their eyes were drawn to the forest.

Then Jaffe stopped still some distance away from them. When it was recalled later, in the depths and height of the jungled hill country, what was talked about was his silence; the seemingly neutral embrace of the inevitable, the brutal training, the mesmerised stance of the indoctrinated, of a soul now lost. Some villagers spoke of his stare, which seemed to go right through them and beyond while others could not describe him as Jaffe the boy – innocent youth was long gone – but rather he had become *Keli*, or Wicked One.

'They are here…'

Of course this wasn't a fair contest; villagers against soldiers; the armed against those who could only grip onto sticks and a few pangas. Jaffe raised his weapon as 20 or so soldiers emerged from the green, their camouflage suddenly unmasked yet still merging with the background, as though the scenery was moving with them as they lumbered forward. They were trees and bushes; they were bringing the jungle to the village. When Jaffe raised his weapon, villagers raised their arms to protect their children, bending their bodies so that the inevitable fusillade would tear into older flesh.

And so it did. With his eyes shut, Jaffe pulled then held the trigger of the rusty foreign gun he had been so quickly taught how to use. While his head remained still, his lips slightly parted, the repeated jolt of the recoil shuddered his body. This was no random shooting. While the other soldiers moved towards the villagers with a sense of routine – another village, another rout and pillage was what they sang – Jaffe knew each of the people his bullets tore into. The greeting *Pewle* was used to greet those you had not seen for some time. It was usually a warm hello full of glad remembrance but when Jaffe's voice, dry and rasping, said its tones, it was a threat, a declaration of violent intent. This was assassination.

Pewle. And so a cousin was greeted, a bullet that shattered first her hand as it was raised to protect her face then her nose which exploded as the bullet came to a halt inside her skull. *Pewle*. The old man who had begun to lose his thoughts while memories danced with him, his smile years back, creasing his face with a just remembered moment, raised his arm as though in some distant class, ready to be educated, raised his arm and a bullet answered him, clearly, through his heart. *Pewle*. The Lew Ya sisters ran loose from their parents when the soldiers first appeared. At eight and nine years old they had already heard what the government soldiers did when they came into the jungle; they already knew that when they saw such camouflage they ought to hide. It was too late. As they started for the other side of the village, up the steepening slopes of the Papen Hills, Jaffe, with poignant accuracy used just one bullet to take both of their lives. The bullet went through both of their necks and as their blood fountained they at least crumpled into a heap together. It was with satisfaction that others acknowledged with horror, the accurate dispatch of villagers as they ran for the forest or shelter in homes, which were already being set alight by the singing conscripts.

There was a systematic movement to the company of soldiers. They knew where they were going as Jaffe must have given them the layout of the village. While Jaffe stood carefully sniping at the fleeing villagers, the other soldiers made their way from one hut to another, bullets first and then fire next, setting the tinder bamboo alight making sure the burning started at the door so there could be no easy escape. The villagers who had made the mistake of running for cover in their home were either burnt or shot as they ran aflame through the village. In the dawn light there were human flares rushing around, zig-zagging with pain, first screaming then silent, as torches doused by their fall to the ground; as target practice for the soldiers irritated by their rattling, piercing deaths.

Verlaine stood his ground. There was some debate later, whispered somethings as to how Verlaine could possibly have survived. All around him was the chaos of instant war, the ricochets of violence, stirring up the debris of the wounded and dying. There were clouds of dust and shredded flesh coating an extra layer on to his glistening skin and he did not move. There were bullets in the air, flames wrapping themselves around the very bungalow he called home for most of his life and still he did not move. On more than one occasion, a red-eyed teenager, still young, still high, chewing betel nut, came right up to him, spitting red saliva into his face, preparing to personally and meticulously gut him with his knife. He would be pulled away by an NCO or by a shout from Jaffe who would simply say, 'Leave him. We can use him.'

Of course that was one version. Another tale that would be told was more creative in its evaluation. The spirits, the same spirits who led some to safety, protected Verlaine, like the brothers Lynch and Leer. Neither bullet nor knife could pierce nor lacerate; no explosion could tear him apart. He stood proudly on what had once been a playground for the children, their beads now scattered across the soil, counting games upgraded now to a tally of the dead who fell heavily, terribly.

Occasionally, a villager would fight back with a machete to hand, swiping as though thrashing the jungle. These were not trained soldiers but scared witless conscripts who fought for no reason other than they were afraid for their own lives. Kill or be killed. These were the jobless, ID-less children who had not paid attention to their all too brief training, who maybe still harboured dreams of returning to their community, who might have lingered too long in the wrong moment, missed a beat in this horrific dance and felt the burn of the villager's knife. In a meaningless instant there would be both desperate defence and motiveless attack.

Not many believed that Verlaine was frozen with fear hidden by the lucky Tamarind tree.

This was just the next village; the next offensive or calculated putsch to coral the rebels and their likely collaborators amongst the poor farmers who were to be seen running aflame into the jungle, their wild arms setting branches alight. Tindersticks. But there were so many children, old men and women amongst them and both their youth and their age slowed them. The government soldiers were quick to kill or capture the more able. The physically strong and those who didn't immediately surrender were dispatched quickly with a gun to the temple or more cruelly a scything cut to the groin and a long slow bleed into the earth.

No one could have prepared themselves for what happened even though it had been feared for some time. How were Lynch and Leer to survive such an attack when friends were losing their lives and limbs all around them? Verlaine believed their affliction gave them powerful mystery and it was true the villagers had never seen their twinned like in living or dead memory. Such duplication, many were convinced, meant the spirits had fueled their soul.

Already they were loved as all the children were but at dusk and into the night, the villagers would cajole Verlaine to pick up his guitar and he would play and sing a song they all knew. Lynch and Leer too, managed harmony without words, and their voices, a strange electric hum, quietened the jungle prattle and the older heads which so often shook with disapproval at their strangeness would then simply nod; eyes closed, the scent of charcoal and rice in the air and songs of Verlaine and his two sons were the only thing that mattered.

Survivors of the attack who escaped, scattering up the slopes, deeper into the forest, higher up into the hills; who looked over their shoulders scarcely believing the horror of it all, scarcely believed their eyes when they witnessed Lynch and Leer suddenly galvanized; unlikely heroes, timely saviours who scooped up tiny, wailing children whose parents had tumbled blood soaked into the earth or who pushed to safety a whole family with their arms outstretched as though they were gathering a flock. A few survivors of what became one of the most brutal government attacks on so-called rebel villages singled out again and again the incredible, unlikely role of Lynch and Leer.

Aweju, one of the elders and not a man given to exaggeration described his escape from the village as miraculous. 'I couldn't move. I saw my wife cut down by a soldier as big as a tree and I couldn't move. I feel terrible. I did nothing to save her. When I saw the soldier turn to me there was nothing in his eyes. Not hatred, not anger, not need.

All the reasons that there might be to cut a woman nearly in two from the crown of her head to the base of her spine didn't seem to matter. There was nothing in the eyes that I could see. I did nothing but wait for the blow from the soldier's panga. It didn't come. Instead one of the boys, those blessed brothers, pulled me with a strength that took my breath away, pulled me not just out of the way of the machete blow, but away from the village and in the blink of an eye I was scrambling up the slopes away from the village.'

Lynch and Leer's actions were instinctive; as urgent as the situation required but they were hardly oblivious to dangers as many characterised them; they were not *venhasa*, to be without fear. Especially Lynch, who had to carry around him the dying pain of Salva. For Lynch and all the villagers of the region, to witness death was to be a part of the journey of the dying. You are their company, their companion; not abstracted but inherently their death throes are felt empathically and sometimes physically. If someone dies as violently as young Salva did then the involvement is strong. Many of the villagers believed that a youthful death released an untamed energy; the kicked up life-force of a soul still to be fired and tempered.

So it was with Salva. He hadn't been the same boy since the body fell from the sky. He had watched Lynch and Leer bury the body and even though he was hurt he went to where the unknown faller lay and kept him company. It was possible that during the course of such a terrible event no one had given thought to who was company for the faller. The talk in the village was that the faller was already dead when he dented the village earth in which case no one could be expected to hand hold an unknown corpse to the next world; better that he be buried without ceremony. While Lynch and Leer mused as to his possible identity, Salva still trembled from his descending touch.

It was not what anyone had hoped for, had dreamed about. Salva still at a tender age, still at a high-pitched voice age, had something about him that all the villagers remarked on, not just his proud parents. Along with Jel Unw and the brothers, Salva was considered a golden child blessed with prodigious birth signs and good fortune. He was striking in his looks, deep set oval eyes, blood red lips and an unusually long face as though he had been slightly stretched from the norm at birth. He was tall for his age, gangly too and as his body grew it was clear he would end up as tall as Jel Unw and Verlaine; a physical presence that would likely match his verbal prowess. He was a talker, an immediate friend to Lynch and Leer and the three of them ran around the villagers, playfully tricking, expertly conning with simple cunning all that they wanted out of them. No one minded. It was playful flirtation; a dance with both the silly and the absurd. Of course, they would push it too far, stretch the joke, belabour the point and they would be scolded but never seriously and their antics reminded the older villagers of their own youth.

He had, everyone agreed, the spirits in his every laugh and movement. 'We have all seen such children,' Lawe the teacher said, 'They light up and flare; they are fired by energy and can hold everything with a simple stare.' So it was with Salva. None of the villagers deserved what happened but there were more tears shed for Salva than anyone else.

It happened near the end of the massacre, as the soldiers began to wind down their operation, lighting up the last few homes and scattering the last bits of fire in the direction of the woods leading further into the hills. They had no orders to pursue and most of the battalion was happy to sit and smoke once their job had been done. It wasn't quite finished and many of them enjoyed this part more than any. A quiet would come into a village after all the hullabaloo, interrupted only by the moans of the injured and the spiraling, greedy flames licking the bamboo, slickened by the rush of sap as the fires added to the heat of the day. In these village routs or inspections or clearances, depending on the terminology you agreed with, there was always the few who had hidden well during the fire fight but who, when the whole village was in flame, had no where to run to while there remained a whole battalion of wired soldiers, their stoned vibrations undulating through the haze, a lingering snare of menace.

Jaffe moved from his commanding position to settle into a slow but triumphant walk through the village, his home that was before he went away, before it was burnt to the ground fueled by the skin and blood of his family and friends. Not that he saw this in that way or in any way that we know but he did see Salva sneak out from the burning hut of his parents whose charred bones were entangled in one last burning embrace, their pain, Salva hoped, brief. Surely that's how it should be. They had showered him with praise; hugged and kissed him with every year that he grew. They never held back from touch or reassurance between themselves or with him. They were extrovert, demonstrative and public with all that they did which marked them as different from the rest of the villagers who kept their expression hidden, their ardor and desires as quiet as the creak of bamboo at night. They encouraged him to step in any direction he wanted. So now he ducked down as low as he could go and stepped away from them for the last time.

The NGOs and human rights groups could and did count numbers of such atrocities, compiling reports based on witness accounts accompanied when possible by grisly aftermath photographs. But they could not possibly be there to witness the intimacy of such a terrible moment; the moment for Salva, the moment for Jaffe. As most of the soldiers rested and got high, Jaffe saw Salva's sleekit movement and quickly aimed and fired, instinctively knowing that it was not one of the battalion but an enemy combatant, an insurgent, a rebel who without a second thought would raise a weapon to him.

He cut Salva down with a single shot that pierced his slender neck and while the last life thrash was enveloping Salva's body, Jaffe grabbed a flailing arm and hauled the corpse-to-be across the earth giving the now sedated soldiers something to cheer or whistle through burnt lips. He brought the still gurgling Salva together with his parents, who he dragged from the entrance to their home, and then laid them side by side, a fetid steam already rising from the parent's bodies as mosquitoes swarmed around them.

While the soldiers rested they watched their conscripted progeny set to work. Some of the older NCOs had seen this kind of thing a few times. When the soldiers joined – or were abducted into – the army they would be subjected to a strict (in their eyes) regime of training and often used strong narcotics both to numb the terrible reality of killing one's own and to provide a chemical energy that would see the child soldiers march and kill while all around them adult soldiers dropped from fatigue. Above all, it was well known there was an innate viciousness to the way boys would fight. Although, obviously, they could not be used to fight hand to hand combat, the more astute commanders would use them as guerillas, springing ambushes where few would expect to see a child with a blazing gun and using boys where there would nearly always be hesitation.

The split second it took to decide whether to kill a child was usually the last moral dilemma someone faced. There were few places to go after such an act but Jaffe must have been pushing himself, testing himself and others. It was typical of such units. Who could be the most extreme, who could impress, distress and appall; the camaraderie was the key, there was an audience for his cruelty; willing applause that egged him on. If Lynch and Leer won plaudits for their raw courage and touching care then Jaffe won the respect of full-time soldiers. He relished the opportunity for cruelty.

So many of these new recruits, the ones stolen from their mothers' clutch or snatched from bus shelters, so many of them were ill-equipped in body or mind to cope with the stress and vigour of life on the front line. Most commanders thought it was better to use them as skivvies – cleaners and cooks; dogsbodies who would be at the beck and call of the regular army. This was what was thought until they saw some skinny ferret of a boy sneak behind rebel lines because he was ordered, because he was full of *brown* or *red* or the thing that made him go and go. When they saw the tenacity, the willingness to keep going after the first few shocks of combat that broke many grown men, when they could take the blood of their first kill and let it dry on their skin without wiping it off with horror, then soldiers began to see them in a different light. Opened mouthed they saw them blaze their guns, their voices raised into an animal howl and show absolutely no mercy for screaming wounded or trembling toddlers, there was no doubt they were to be respected.

Jaffe unwound the rope he had found in one of the huts and knelt beside the mother's corpse. Carefully using his long fingers he opened up the wound in the woman's neck, pulling at the side of the hole, stretching the skin just wide enough for him to push the rope in. It took a few attempts but eventually he found the hole at the other side of the neck where the bullet had made its exit. One of the other young conscripts moved forward to help Jaffe but he brandished his semi-automatic towards him and he soon backed off. This was Jaffe's show after all. There were no other parts to be played.

Jaffe bound the husband and wife in death, linked by rope which carried their gore from one body to another; through the neck of the husband and on to Salva. The freshest of kills, some of the soldiers thought they saw the child burst into life, a fibrillating leg or a jerking head were enough for them to twitch into action. But this was a trick of the light, shards and shadows of memories and expectation, of battle trauma and drug addled imagination. They had already won their battle. Bring on the entertainment.

Jaffe didn't disappoint. With slightly more difficulty threading the now sodden rope through young Salva's neck – the thinness of the boy's trunk proving momentarily awkward for Jaffe's suddenly outsize hand – he was eventually ready. There was no shortage of volunteers and he took the first two he saw and the three of them dragged the neck-tied bodies to the two strong Yurla trees which the villagers had always thought as guardians; keepers to the village, their thick, twisted trunks having stood for so long. They were witnesses to this latest abomination, this betrayal of all things nearly every soldier or villager had once, in more peaceful times, held close. These solid, ancient trees held steady as first the parents were hung up and then the young Salva whose body only needed one solider to lift him. The soldier spat out some betel saliva and let Salva go with the palm of his hand and suddenly all three found movement as they swung in time to the drum of the rain.

As the soldiers began to leave the village, there was still the occasional shot to be heard. There was nothing moving now among the huts except for the flames which were fighting back against the inevitably dousing rain. A few stoned soldiers were shooting at shadows as though their life depended on it and one had even cornered a monkey who had been set free from its cage into a cruel freedom. The soldier, eyes wide and red, hands shaking on his gun, didn't even wait for plain sight; it could have been anyone, but when a trigger can be pulled with the slightest touch then a bullet will find its way into wood or flesh, human or otherwise. Not a sound was heard as the monkey tumbled into the quickly forming mud.

From just beyond the fringe of the jungle, the trodden scrub of land they had been clearing for crops, Leer closed his eyes and swayed slightly in the damp night air, allowing himself just a moment as the cries of the soldiers lessened. Beside him, Lynch was ushering the last few survivors, urgently beckoning the remaining villagers who limped and stumbled their way into the green.

Leer was the last to leave of those that could. He could see from the edge of the green a few villagers, including his cousin, Salawin, remaining behind in the smoke that billowed from the ashes of the huts and rice stores. With each passing moment the first rains spat their threat on to the sizzling fire of the village. While the soldiers whooped their victory songs, the dying villagers sunk further into the mud. Salawin tried a few times to raise himself from the ground, but his hacked limbs had no possible strength in them and he fell face first, a terrible and sad plop of motion into the slime. He managed to turn his head sideways just enough for his mouth to gasp for air. Leer waited to see his prone death, hoping the last breaths would be mercifully short. While his cousin had been quiet and brooding yet so skilled at weaving and other crafts, Leer and his brother had troubled him with jokes and teasing, seeing themselves as better than the quiet boy just turned 14. Leer choked on his tears. He should have been better but there was no going back just as there was no way to help Salawin now or any of the others.

Leer could hear his brother hiss at him from a few metres away, Jel Unw too urging him to move. This was all just a dream that had gained animation, ammunition in the febrile heat at the beginning of the wet season. Indeed the rain could create shadows just as much as the sun; darker shadows, murky and blurred and sometimes mere silhouettes of undistinguished forms. But there was the rise of something else; a surge that took him out of his reverie. Over and over again, the words in his head continued, *he's gone. Everything he was is gone.* When the words came out, their form mutated from clarity, the feeling was clear. It was already said before it was spoken. This was the rise of something. When Leer stood up he managed to break free of supporting hands, of the palm that tried to cover his mouth and with all the air in his lungs he broke any sense of calm and let loose a violent oath, a growl fortunately camouflaged from the army by the possibility of wild animals. This was the rise of an ageless anger. Verlaine hugged him while moving him quickly into the green, saying softly but intensely, '*Ma Kan Kyin Seit*. This outrage will be remembered and avenged.

You will avenge it.'

The last of them disappeared into the protection of the forest.

At the other end of the village, Jaffe turned for a moment, his finger twitching on the trigger of his gun and listened for more. He smiled when all he heard was the rain and the sizzle of flame turning into smoke. As he walked he kicked out of the way the debris of the fire, the embers of the village, and paused only when he thought he recognized some charred face. He didn't.

Tuvol and Introducing Dominique

It had been a dramatic rescue. The people who found him, deep in drift and hypothermia, were early climbing types hurrying up the slopes to the Anvil's jagged summit. Typically ardent climbers who felt the need to rise before dawn to challenge themselves to be in thin mountain air with sleep still in their eyes. The mountain attracted such enthusiasts and many would 'bag the Anvil' on their way to climbing other summits, conquering if not the stalwart geography then at least their own sense of endurance. The mountain ranges around Bente were populated nearly year round by such people and on a few of the steeper slopes there were makeshift markers, frozen floral tributes of iced roses and climbing accessories of mountaineers whom the mountains had claimed.

Of course Tuvol would have been a less celebrated victim of the cruel vagaries of nature. While fallen mountaineers were commemorated with ice axes slammed into rock with trailing, tribal-style ribbons of dedication, he would have been barely recalled by a punctured Styrofoam coffee cup lodged carelessly on the rock where he was found. It wasn't quite the same thing he knew but the energetic young NGOers on holiday from the heat concentrated on rescuing rather than condemning. He was well aware of how the amateur climber would irritate locals and professionals alike by sauntering up the Anvil in sandals and with a bottle of cheap wine, treating it all like a jaunt in the park, a swalley up some local hill that of course went better with booze. Tuvol understood that but in retrospect from the distance of tropics to drizzle; from a warmed up heart to a frozen, cyrogenic soul, it was hardly the same. The drunken bravado types who had staggered up the hill to prove themselves impenetrable to hazard, to cock a snoop at human frailty and piss on fear like it was some threatening fire needing to be doused were, generally, complete idiots. The son of Espirit on the other hand was the victim of sustained and institutionalised neglect and was not looking for affirmation on the Anvil but escape. This was his speech should anyone hear, should he actually say it. When he settled into the snow-hole, akin rather than identical to the one occupied by Espirit and Esta, he was not proving anything that wasn't already known.

The early climbers saved Tuvol's life. Whatever they thought of him for wandering stupidly up treacherous slopes they never mentioned it, neither did they mention to anyone, media especially, how Tuvol swore and insulted them when they found him. There were no thank yous, just curses, just venom spitting and swearing that would have blushed anyone in the cold.

At some point in his delirium, as his mind warmed up from its hypothermic state, Tuvol recalled why he was on the mountain and it was a more brutal re-awareness than might be expected. By surviving he had likely made things worse rather than better and when, rather than if, his identity became known he would be dragged through the streets for his ungrateful actions. He would be the suicide complainer who no one listened to. How could he care if doctors dismissed him for devaluing life; or how nurses roughly inserted IVs and other essentials that would be better served keeping those who wanted to live alive. Frozen then thawed he was hardly the best person to fight for anything. The death wish of his adolescence was being upgraded to a pathetic adulthood, the lackey son, the disappointing offspring arriving like a bad penny being rolled into hospital where only good people died.

After a long, dreamless sleep Tuvol awoke when it was still dark, the only light coming from the glow of machines, which flashed, syncopating to some sense of rhythm in his body. A soft voice close by reassured him; other voices further away seemed urgent, shouting for something. This was not a silent place. In the darkness it was possible to hear the whirr of the elevator and a distant phone call, number or codes being read off a list, the voice lifeless, moribund. Then there was Old Hope in the next room, his voice gurgling, reaching for sounds and blends to make words which only growled in his throat. It must have been frustrating for the great communicator, the silver tongued fox, to be rendered so inarticulate.

The young woman sitting beside Tuvol's bed nodded.

With encouragement he described his father, the present tense slipping awkwardly into the past. When Tuvol fell silent, his voice tiring easily, Espirit's mumblings took over as his loose vowels and slip-sliding consonants slurred their presence into the room. And then, as all coherence failed him, he howled, the sound coming from deep inside him, possibly primal but certainly desperate. Espirit was a man used to being listened to and understood.

The woman nodded again and moved closer to the side of the bed. As she leaned over him, Tuvol could smell her skin, the scent of the mountain, of rustling fabrics and something else.

She introduced herself as Dominique with a more formal handshake not long after her life-saving kiss. Tuvol had met no one he could offload his fetid burden onto; the compound was not exactly brimming with friends or soul-mates, just fostered families trying to regroup while Tuvol was trying to unwind. His inert privilege was way down the pecking order of need. Dominique didn't seem to care about that. She didn't try to see it from his point of view, she tried to make him see it from his father's point of view.

'From what you've said, your anger is damaging you more than it is him.'

Tuvol wondered if he was the first man she had saved.

Of course she wasn't the only one in the group that found him, there were three others and they all had a part to play but it was Dominique that had sparked something. The two men with beards and the older woman with weathered skin hadn't been the ones to lay him gently on the ground from his crumpled, fetal curl and push their lips against his. This Tuvol remembered like it was still happening; it was startling not just because it literally breathed life into him but because it served as the most intimate of introductions.

On the mountain, Tuvol saw the sky at first, still slightly shrouded by the morning mist. It looked out of focus, hazed by low cloud forming at the summit of the Anvil. When Dominique leant back from her initial resuscitation, Tuvol was quickly alert to her touch, her lips reaching his again, lingering long enough for him to smell a brief scent of her sweat that formed a light coating across her cheeks. He didn't hear what she said to the other climbers but their faces were all very serious as they rushed to loosen water bottles, unwrap energy bars and spread out emergency blankets. He had gone up the mountain to escape a well-meaning world and had been saved by the good will of strangers.

Although Dominique did not single-handedly save Tuvol, it was she who stayed with him after the other rescuers had gone back to their holiday, their part-time rescuing over for that day at least. It was Dominique who liaised with the administrators of the hospital and Dominique who made sure he was given nearly the best room. The best room in the intensive care suite, of course, had already gone.

Tuvol was sure he rambled. He was either talking or he was vomiting into cardboard funnels. The doctors had asked, 'Did you take something?'

'I was in a snow-hole.'

'Yes.'

'I wanted to sleep.'

'Okay. Did you take any pills?'

'No. I wanted to be where my father had been.'

'Your father is here, in the hospital. He is a very sick man now. He needs you. Why were you on the mountain?'

'I needed to be where he had been. Where I started.'

The doctors ran out of room on his chart.

When they left, Dominique was allowed to stay and she sat with tea she had brought in a flask. He sipped his. It tasted sweet, like a liqueur chocolate with cinnamon or cardamon.

'It's a kind of Chai. The people I work with drink a lot of it. It's good in the heat. Comforting. Energising, you know.'

Tuvol twitched with questions. 'Who are you?'

He closed his eyes but still listened as she pulled her chair closer to the bed.

'I grew up landlocked in a city arrondissement, a faded glory apartment which my parents retreated to after stints abroad. I am the product of how things should be. My grandmother looked after me, wished I was a boy I think and wished that her son and his wife had taken jobs nearer home. "Why do you work so far away when there are jobs here?" was her tune but no one wanted to listen. My parents worked hard for an NGO you will have heard of and now I am the same. You see, they worked in places few people wanted to go unless they had something to forget or something to give.'

The nurse came in to the room to check the monitors.

'Perfect for you by the sound of it!'

The nurse, adding to the squash of information on the chart, glanced at Dominique then looked again as she left, her eyes drawn to her unruly hair, her unironed clothes and perhaps her proximity to Tuvol.

'Do I look that suspicious?' she laughed. 'Anyway, parents? I can see them stumbling through the door at some ungodly hour, just about managing to throw down their luggage, lift me up and take me back to bed. You could smell their travel, you know, like a cocktail of sweat and alcohol and other people, other places, filling my room. I loved that room, blue ocean walls and a night ceiling – so I could see the stars every night.'

Tuvol spoke hoarsely. 'My father chose the pictures for my room; early line drawings of Homes for Peace structures.'

'I guess that's the Boy's Own version. I loved it when they came back, it was almost worth them being away. All the reassurances, the over-dosing of attention and the tropical nik-naks and them, just them, was the best thing, leaning either side of me, kisses goodnight, sugar and spice. Yeah. It was intoxicating, overwhelming.'

There was a pause and Dominique looked out the window, a slight sigh sounding in the hissing room.

She broke the moment with a quick laugh.

'The people I work with would have a good laugh at that. Dominique the professional getting homely with homilies for family life. But I'm on holiday, you know, and it's good to think about things, remember things without the starch of work.'

Dominique moved her chair close to the bed so that Tuvol could no longer hear the room, just her voice, its soft breath pressing in to him. She didn't let up. 'I can't stand these overhead lights.' She dimmed the fluorescence in the room until Tuvol wondered if he was still there.

'My history is simple. I am where I have been. I am where I want to be. It's not about travelling but being in a place. If you stay somewhere and I mean work, play, rest, love, you end up having most things; the good and the bad, the unexpected and the predictable. You get it all if you hang around long enough.'

Somewhere to go

When Tuvol could walk he visited Espirit and wished he hadn't. Esta had gone home he was told. No doubt, Tuvol thought, she was tired of waiting for one of them to get better, for one of them to die. Of course it was the right thing to do even though he had already seen him tubed and sedated, a pale shadow of his previously robust self. The doctors, nurses, even Dominique, all nodded their approval. There was a conspiracy of good will.

'A little walk would fit in with your physio routine,' Dominique chimed in, adding, 'besides, you are not going to lie there as your father dies, are you?'

Tuvol shrugged.

'Whatever happened, don't make it worse.'

This was the suddenness of events, the avalanche of chance as Dominique put it.

She was reaching the end of her holiday and her colleagues were preparing to leave. There was a bizarre awkwardness to it all. Tuvol was too numbed to make a move and she was on a timetable, scheduled R&R which was due to end before he was going to be allowed to move from his hospital bed. Still she visited twice a day right up until the evening of her departure and the more she visited, the stronger he got and the more they talked. They both got caught up in the rush; a surge of personal history, of mutual revelation. It was neither a blind date nor an arranged combination but it had elements of both as fate pushed Tuvol beyond the reasons for self-harm and caused Dominique to wave goodbye to her colleagues at the airport. After she left them, she headed straight back to the hospital, flowers in hands, a big smile wrapped across her face.

'They're not surprised.'

'What? You've done this sort of thing before?'

'Sure. Rescued failed suicides buried in snow-holes? No, I can say this is a first.'

Dominique sat on the bed and began to tie an elaborate knot in the bed sheet.

'They're not surprised because they know me or maybe they just know anything can happen. One moment you are driving along a dusty road and the next a spray of bullets shatters the windshield or you are stopped at a checkpoint and hauled out of the car by your fine hair. One moment, Tuvol, you can be sipping some Kasheen while a petty civil war sparks around you and the next you are pressed to a bamboo floor, collapsed in a heap with a rugged reporter, both of you exploding with fear and lust, thrashing in the splintering salvo. That could be me.'

'Was it?'

'What happens in the jungle stays in the jungle.'

'Catchy!'

'No one *talks* about such things in the field. To my co-workers, I am pretty much the cold fish; the dedicated pro obfuscating desire with care for others; the manufactured safety net that has little to do with anyone else. In the world I'm in for most of the year this isn't that unusual, most of us have this kind of armour; some call it a flak jacket, others call it part of the job and a few others see it as camouflage. If you're too busy helping other people no one is going to accuse you of being en-suite lonely.'

Tuvol had never talked so much in his life. He didn't even have to think; words just flowed about the past while the present close by was dying.

'Have you heard my father's voice yet?'

'No, I've only looked in a couple of times and he's been sedated.'

'It's going now but in its prime it thundered, bellowed, sang like an opera singer and then would melt, sweeten to be sugary; he'd become the softest whisperer to young children. Then moments later we would get back in the car, drive away from the public function and he would get personal, harden his voice to tell me I wasn't living up to his expectations.'

Dominique smiled. 'It can be hard living up to someone else's expectations.'

'I used to think there was nothing worse than living.'

Dominique laughed. 'See, you can talk sweet when you want to.'

'Thanks. I just found it confusing when so much good was being said about my father and yet what I got was different, the curtain got pulled and the act changed.'

'You mean he wasn't full of bon homie with his nearest and dearest?'

'Homes for Peace was his nearest and dearest.'

'A lot of busy people can't separate working and home life; it's not an unique issue. I saw my parents once in a whatever moon and look at me now.'

'What did your parents do when they came back home?'

'I told you. They fussed and loved, and crammed their parenthood into precious days.'

'Espirit came back and locked himself behind his study door.'

'You should have broken in, kicked the door down or hidden out and waited for him to return.'

'I didn't want to know.'

'Oh, c'mon!'

'I didn't. I just expected it to be same as everywhere else.'

Dominique shook her head. 'The cat killed the curiosity. Think I'm beginning to understand you.'

Taking a deep breath Tuvol moved awkwardly along the corridor. He slinked, his back to the wall, as nurses passed him, no doubt wondering which ward he had escaped from. A porter, emptying some terrible looking cardboard container, winked at him and gave him the thumbs up. Like him, Tuvol had no idea what he was being encouraged to do.

Dominique didn't believe in faffing about with such things.

'What's the problem? So you have issues with your father? Get in line. Most people do. Why fill up on stuff that's going to eat away at you? Why be a slave to regret, Tuvol?'

He stopped at the door, glimpsing just a white bony hand lying still on the bed, a tube attached umbilically to a deep purple vein. It was enough. For the second time in just a few weeks Tuvol walked away from his father as he lay wired to a hospital bed.

'Take me out the back way.'

'What?'

Dominique had stepped out of Tuvol's room to get a cup of coffee from the machine. He loved the look, it pricked desire, how her eyebrows arched and her mouth opened slightly. This was the first time in the brief time they had known each other that she hadn't known what was going to happen.

'I need to get out of here right now.'

'It went that well with your father?'

'It didn't go at all. I didn't see him and I am not going to see him.'

'So, he is dead now?'

'No, but that's an interesting way to ask; he's still got the machines, he's still got his damned spirit no doubt.'

'I mean he's dead to you.'

Tuvol said nothing. Just stared out the floor.

'Okay.'

Dominique was not a ditherer.

'No doubt there's paperwork but let admin catch you up and I'll phone Esta for you.'

'What will you say?'

'You've taken leave of your senses. You are no longer the person, the son she thought she had. *He's not necessarily gone but he is certainly lost... Sometimes taking your troubles with you can be a good thing...* That sort of thing. And to top it off I could tell her I believe that if you take core stuff to a cold place it gets frozen; take it to the tropics and it melts away.'

Tuvol gave her a quizzical look then searched for the car park exit.

'I know, maybe that's too fluid for you, you'll catch the drift later but listen, this isn't just for you, this is for Esta. Why not give her something while you, at long last, give yourself something. And you're lucky. Not everybody has the chance to plan their exit.'

'What exactly does Esta get from her only son running away having virtually spat in his father's grave?'

'Nicely put – from suicide by snow-hole to gallows exit humour, you have a penchant for the melodramatic. That's nice, I like that. Anybody can be realistic.'

'Esta?'

'Esta will understand when I tell her. You are leaving to find yourself. Just as Espirit stepped out into the world with a philanthropic spirit so are you leaving to help those who have not had the security that Esta provided. Although it is a difficult time to leave, it is also the only time to leave.'

'But I haven't said I'm going anywhere…'

Dominique sshed him and then installed him in the passenger seat of her hire car.

'If it gets difficult then I can always use the "if you love your son, you must set him free." But I don't think that will be necessary from what you've told me. I think she'll go for the cutting loose to help others type scenario.'

Tuvol shrugged. 'I'm not sure she cares enough to want reasons anyway.'

Holding on to the steering wheel for no good reason, sweating, cold and feverish, Tuvol asked her, 'But how exactly am I helping anyone else in all of this?'

'Yeah, I know, it's all very you, you, you. Don't worry. There's time enough for all that. We need to get the hospital air out of our lungs. Since you nearly killed yourself and I am still on holiday from a war zone, let's live a little.'

Hotel

Dominique listened to Tuvol as they curled up on her hotel bed – Tuvol didn't want to go back to his room in his parents' house. It would have felt strange, or at least stranger than clandestinely meeting a foreigner in a hotel room. There were degrees of expatriation no doubt but he felt, until the first kiss, the following touch, and the rising desire, like an awkward teenager with a twitching lust that felt painful when pressed. Suppressed. And the more he heard of Dominique's story from a city upbringing to an insurgent jungle the more he felt thrust into the spotlight and laid bare under the glare of expected performance.

Tuvol wasn't so much rusty as atrophied. Not that he was virgin. There had been drunken encounters, of desire loosened by damp, desperate escapes into the woods of the village, rustling leaves, stifling sounds and embarrassed, stiff movements. He had never been lithe, too tall to be elegant, too gawky for most people's taste but when you are young, when there was drink to be stolen and a dark place to be found nearby it didn't really matter. But in these fresh and even innocent moments, Espirit loomed. Not that he was actually there, hiding behind a Sycamore, sickened by his one and only losing what morals he had. But he was still *there*, disapproving. This from the man who fucked in a snow-hole.

But Tuvol was there because Espirit allowed him to be. The Home for Peace girls already knew who he was and tended to stay clear of him, protected carefully by the foster mothers. But girls from Bente were more likely to be impressed if they knew who he was or rather who he was the son of. As pathetic as it may sound, as hypocritical as it was, Tuvol was proud to proclaim Espirit as his father. He took the kudos and had hormones and blunt desire as his alibi. Of course such personal corruption didn't go unpunished and when he was kissing the village lass Tuvol would see his father lurking, dousing ardour with his goodness. These were rare, lust-propelled excursions into village life and the bitter taste of the hangover stayed longer than the memory of desire briefly fulfilled.

Dominique nodded listening to what she already knew, a man's need to bleed out embedded truths. She mopped up easily with room service and more champagne.

'It's okay, No, really it is. You don't have to apologise for anything, especially not being the perfect sexual being. Show me that and you will be showing me a façade, a deluded camouflage. The strong men I've known are usually brittle; emotional courage is easily tested and measurably breaks into pieces. So, sure, I'd rather be with a man that can talk, who can listen and not just be horny one moment and sleeping the next. The best thing you can be is not be a cliché.'

They were still in Bente or at least close to it, a characterless motel for ski drones in one of the many resorts that ringed the old town. Tuvol wasn't looking out the window. Dominique had come out of the forest, wild.

'No doubt, you got the odd cold shoulder from nursing staff? You tried to take your life. How did you think that was going to go down in a place where they try to save people? Same for the people I have lived and worked with for most of my adult life. Suicide isn't even in their vocabulary.'

Tuvol was inspired by Dominique's directness. It was a physical thing. It thrilled him, made him gaseous and erect; made him excited and terribly, archly nervous at the same time.

'So you want to save me from myself? What could I possibly have to offer?'

Dominique piled a dozen cubes into a high ball glass and let the gin pour over them, her eyes drifting out the window as the clear liquid flowed.

'What you have here is so different, a world apart in temperature and in temperament; a place where charity is easily won and where separation between those that have and those that have nothing is clearly marked; an expected demarcation. What you have here too is peace and a land saturated in affluence. Of course relatively, of course there are hardships for some, but a few, not a whole village, an array of communities, a race of people. But the few you know. They come distressed and disposed of through your gates; they come with infants squealing sometimes with nothing more to their name than what they have in their hands and pockets. Your world becomes suddenly closer to mine.'

All this, this strange pillow talk, this vehement but softly spoken pitch while they lay naked in the hotel room, the cable TV showing an old black and white film while they could hear the chink and rattle of a trolley in the corridor, the occasional knock for their room to be cleaned left ignored, laughter stifled by fluffy pillows.

'Aren't most of the people you work with from places like this?'

'A lot of them yes but most are much younger than you or I. They are starting out after their International Development degrees and are looking for experience in the field, any field as long as it's wet, hot and consists of a CV-level of difficulty.'

Dominique laughed a hollow laugh.

'Christ, I can't criticise them, these interns, toiling away in the jungle for a good cause but so many of them fall by the wayside. If the heat and mosquitoes don't get them then the basic living conditions will; then the abject suffering of the communities will impact so viciously on some that they have to be extracted back home, the PTSD symptoms shaking them all the way. Like my dad wrote, "good intentions surrender to the horror that inevitably unfolds. What is left is commitment.'"

She stopped for a moment, another glance out the window as though some answer was there, clinging to the same precipice Tuvol had buried himself under.

Of course they could laugh. It was difficult for truth to get serious when they were drunk and naked and desired. 'What is said here may well be blurred in retrospect, exact words lost in the fug of memory, but,' Dominique clinked glasses with Tuvol, 'let words mean something just for as long as they are heard.'

Another night surrounded their hotel room without curtains being drawn or the room being made up; without the overflow of room service being cleared from the carpet and the snigger that they were down now to pocket tissues and soggy towels in the bathroom. They were camping in the wilderness and didn't want to leave. They were trying to forestall the inevitable intrusion of the everyday. The moment when Dominique had to move on to her organisation's headquarters for debrief and to train up the unskilled and the inexperienced.

'I've been putting off telling you.'

Of course when she said this Tuvol imagined all manner of skeletons tumbling out of closets.

'I've failed the test? What's my prize?'

'Come and see what we do; see in action a Clinic which helps people internally displaced by war. You have never been to the tropics so you could consider it a holiday from ice; a chance to get a sense of what it is I do.'

Tuvol held her gaze, looking as deeply as he could into her eyes.

'It's not,' Dominique emphasised, 'just for them. You complained enough about the privations of privilege, the challenge now is to do something about it. It's not gung-ho but it has risks. They are measured, calculable and above all worth it. If you are too scared to move then something sooner or later will run you over anyway.'

That was all it took. Tuvol had already known he needed to get away, from Bente, from Homes for Peace, Esta and Espirit. He had wanted to leave it all but hadn't known how, apart from the whiteout of the snow-hole. There was no dilemma, no weighing of options.

Dominique and he clinked high balls and toasted his decision. 'Here's to the heat!' She laughed burrowing under the togged up duvet.

'Here's to a life worth living,' Tuvol said and raised his glass to the snow-capped Anvil he could see through the hotel window.

Ruess
From the video journal entitled *The Inexhaustible Vitality of Despair*
Field Notes #1

Dear Diary. Dear diary, fuck you. Dear Diary, I am a nobody. Dear Diary, this is my war. How do you start something like this? How do you start, when all around you... you'll be a dead soldier my son. How do you start and record what you see and what you hear; what you know and what you feel. How do you start? Start me up. Ain't no sunshine. Spatter liberally with telly-visual actions, musical keys and keep them guessing with oral cues, like trails of fire in the dark forest, so bright one moment and the next, and the next. Yeah, make sure you trail off, get elliptical make them work for their horror, not handed on a plate like some travel piece that says be careful or some liberal piece that says let's be caring. Save me from that. But there are some in this business, not here, god, there's precious anybody here but you go to the well-worn routes of charity and global concern and you can see it, hear about it. You can meet an awful lot of idiots in this business and just because someone means well and has signed up for some legitimate NGO doesn't mean anything. I've heard charitable names been used as colloquial terms for shit loads of sex and violence – you've just been *oxfammed* is synonymous with a double rape of a refugee whose life couldn't get much worse or *pet rescued* where some poor kid is saved from some mob or a burning village only to be passed on by his saviours to the highest bidder.

But I'm not there right now. I'll swing the camera around and let you have a look. A deep stare into the night, where the green has gone black and if I shut the fuck up, *please shut the fuck up,* you can hear the wall of sound, a full spectrum of chirps and warbles; creaks and howls that can freeze the blood if you don't know what they are and freeze the blood when you do. But of course it's always the silent ones when you are in a place like this, especially in the wet season when you are leeched, bitten and covered in beasts glad of the chance to commune with your flesh. We are always welcomed by nature here. We are compost.

Tuvol in the Tropics

Tuvol landed in a hot and humid city with Dominique's words in his head, looping like inflight entertainment, 'This tropical trip will take you from your cold world and heat you up; raise the temperature of your existence and melt some unwanted memories.'

Espirit hated cities. 'They are the dumping ground for the ruined and the breeding ground of the hopeless. All I can see is people staring at things in shop windows that they cannot afford while keeping their eyes away from a human rotting slowly in the gutter.'

So it seemed just right for Tuvol that the frenetic metropolis would ease the shock of the new with the fraternity of the communal rush. It was shocking to be sure but it was also exhilarating. He was not Espirit and he had hummed this mantra in time with the plane's engines as he read all he could about where he would be. The page-turning hadn't prepared him properly – how could it? – but with awe and enjoyment he found himself wrapped in the heat, a chest-tightening dampness that intoxicated. He looked at the tangle of people and vehicles through the clouds of street cooking and laughed at full volume.

Dominique had made careful arrangements for Tuvol. It would be a soft landing, he would not have to sleep where so many sleep, the fly-over encampments, the back street lean-to's and the ever extending zone of temporary housing with still no running water, no electricity. Tuvol would bypass this and be sucked into the luxury of air-con and a comfortable bed. This would ease the long haul but Dominique knew the rest was up to him. This was about not just a sense of jet-lag but cultural-lag where, as she said, 'your developed-world sense of self-worth will be initially caressed by the smiles and obsequious deference but will soon be challenged by the subtle yet creeping differences.' She would allow Tuvol by himself to be in places that eased or rather sealed the gap between the worlds; heat and cold; rich and poor.

'Please don't protect me from extremes.' If shown the deep end Tuvol knew he would want to jump.

On his first day, ignoring the many offers of taxis and guides, Tuvol walked purposefully out of the hotel and made his self-conscious entry into a different world. He didn't have a Pith helmet or a colonial attitude but his height and white skin quickly caused a ripple of stares, as people stopped mid-chat, even mid-mouthful to stare up at the pulpy foreigner striding into the street as though everywhere was as air-con'd as the hotel. Within minutes he was soaked with sweat, his new shirt sticking to his flesh.

The stride soon had to be downgraded to an amble and even then to a cautious step as he made his way towards the Dominique-recommended cafe. At the roadside an old woman rippling with skin creases was laughing at him and bid him over to her food stall. Her business was typical of others all along the road; glass trolleys heaving with claws and bright chillies, barbecued meat and luminous sauces glowing in plastic water bottles. There were queues at some while others had no one. This particular woman who seemed to be tall enough only to bisect his body, held out a steaming bowl of something. Tuvol peered in the two large aluminum pots and could not identify the dish. The pink bowl of white noodles was the only thing he could recognise. Tuvol smiled back at the tiny woman but hurried on. He was actually hungry but he was not ready for what Dominique called, 'the sense of immersion that comes only when you dip more than a toe into other people's lives.'

The city avenues stretched on as far as Tuvol could see, the blur of concrete merging with the soft focus of pollution; buildings shimmering, pixellated by the exhausts of queuing traffic. When Tuvol reached yet another busy intersection he was uncertain which way to go. It was clear Dominique had left some information off her map and it was vague about scale and distance. No doubt she didn't believe in anything being too easy. Espirit always told Tuvol that he had no sense of direction. 'You will see nothing looking at the floor; you will be blind to everything if you don't open your eyes. You must look up and out for opportunities so that you see them before they pass you by.'

Before they had got on the plane, Dominique had been supplying Tuvol with a steady flow of advice, its tone without the impatience his father would show as he passed on knowledge like a token tip to a waiter. Circumstance and no doubt intimacy helped; allowed him to listen when the gut instinct was to dismiss without consideration. He knew Dominique would have had a good laugh at him standing deciding what to do at a crossroads. In every sense of the word. Such a moment was a luxury in her eyes; it lacked the necessary urgency of real decision and had as much credibility as a life decision made with the help of a therapist; a sleep gained by the gulp of a pill.

'If you were in the city for any length of time, I would have given you directions to some of the expat areas and you'd begin to see how people have adapted and it's not pretty. I'm not talking acclimatising. More like de-sensitising. The men on their first tropical posting feel so superior because of height and girth, like kings endowed with riches and a big Western cock. They swagger and their exotic trophy wives drip smiles that sparkle with died-for diamonds. Those a little longer of tooth, who come with their lives, their wives intact are quickly assaulted by temptation and malaise. Saturday morning outings become opportunities for husbands to feel the sinew of a local rather than the flab from home while wives indulge in coffee mornings that creep into alcoholism. And yes, by all means, appreciate the local colour and nod politely when you are smothered by attention you neither asked for nor deserved. You will be a sweaty Farang wherever you go. You have to get used to that and soon. The best advice is to absorb everything, it's all relevant. Pick up language you don't understand and try out words you don't know how to say. Let people see your face and allow them to hear your voice. Above all, stay true to what are hopefully good and core values to you. None of it will work if you pretend to be something you are not but then maybe you already know that?'

Dominique's words would have been ringing still in Tuvol's head if he could hear them above the noise of the traffic, the swarm of mopeds, cars and buses converging on the intersection. He stood, probably for a longer moment than he intended, as unlikely loads on cyclos vied for road space with 4x4s ploughing through the throng, superior above the cyclists, pedestrians and moped drivers, like modern day chariots, their air-con'd passengers carried in relative safety to their destinations. But from what he saw, the true pecking order – if order was the right word – was not money but size and so the 4x4 would have to make way for the bright green bus carrying sweat-soaked workers and such buses in turn would have to give way to lorries churning tons of concrete, scattering all before them.

As they sat close and huddled on the plane, Dominique had told him of villagers that lived on tenterhooks while listening out for soldiers who would almost certainly rape, kill, mutilate, burn; she told him of queues for paltry supplies, essentials that are no longer in the land or have been taken away, polluted in streams and rivers by chemicals and decaying bodies upstream. He got a crash course in Dominique's 10 years of service to charities and NGOs and it seemed like not a moment had been wasted on fripperies, on worry or naval gazing. 'Crack On!' could have been her motto, her clarion call. After Tuvol's near-death experience she seemed determined that it would become his. This trip was hardly a holiday, it was an invitation revealing itself to be something more. Few people arrived here and left the same. 'You'll love and hate it but it's a world away from where you have been.' Tuvol was intrigued, wary and very hot.

Dominique had suggested the cafe because it was close by and Tuvol, on arriving, marveled at its location, looking up from the ground floor level of the 50 storey building that pushed aggressively full of gleam and steel into the low cloud and disappeared. As soon as he settled into the plush upholstery he noticed a gaggle of children who waved at him through the glass, who mouthed exaggerated *hellos* with broken-tooth smiles. 'You'll be fine there,' Dominique had told him. 'It's luxurious, a vacuum packed world, insulated against the heat and smog and noise of the city. It's a place to seal yourself in and think. In your case think about what you are going to see and hear.'

She'd provided him with a photograph of Ruess who she described as 'a photo and video journalist of 20 years' experience in the region.' The photograph had been taken in the field with a suitable backdrop of dense mangrove and was falling apart, its corners mildewed, its gloss fading. It was a studied portrait, this rugged face with deeply lined skin, an intense, corrosive stare that scratched against the lens; it revealed him as untamed as the jungle all around. It was, Tuvol knew, impressive, alluring.

Dominique was upfront in her assessment of the impression Ruess gave to people he met.

'Sure, the man presented himself as a bit of a rough diamond and there can be a lot of posturing from these journo types but Ruess was as near the genuine article as I have come across. He'd been around a long time, mostly freelance, not aligned with anyone and certainly no poodle for any agenda other than his own. He was not the kind to embed with anyone.'

'Was?'

The cafe had filled up fast with well-heeled locals and expats. Everyone seemed content to ignore the scruffy children who pushed themselves against the windows, their eyes following the waiters straining with trays piled high with food. It was hard for Tuvol to look at them, hard to look away and feel at ease. Every so often a guard would shoo them away, his baton half poised to strike them, and they would run and hide behind the concrete supports holding up a new flyover.

'We don't know where he is. His translator escaped an army attack and got his last tape to us. This has happened before but it's been a couple of months now.'

Dominique had been vehement in her advice. Tuvol didn't notice the zeal then but recalled it later.

'Smell the jungle, Tuv. Damp. Decay. Death. Beauty. It's all there.'

Tuvol thought Dominique had been laying it on thick but he still self-consciously sniffed the musty satchel as he opened it and there was, in truth, a sense of heat and fetid air.

'Nothing is written down in his documentaries; there is no script or storyboard – he can't afford to have any of these things on him. To be caught… well you just don't get caught. The thing to remember as you watch is that he is not being deliberately obtuse, rather he is encouraging you the viewer to follow his train of thought. You can think of it as an invitation. I think of it as intervention; cutting edge charity as one magazine described the last film. The one about village life on the run.'

Ruess
Field Notes #2

I am a video witness. So called. Self-denied. Dominique has declared me foremost but I am not sure what that means. I can hear her words above this bloody noise, 'no one else is doing what you are doing,

Ruess, we have to document what is going on here.' It's not about me – Dominique likes the idea of being rugged and into the wild. I've met a hundred like her. Lost yet found in the jungle exuberant, travel writer moments of being somewhere new, challenging themselves to duels; them against nature, our suicide friends. I've seen them fall like fruit, splat into the mud; I have seen them shiver malarial until their whole body is endlessly vibrating. It's not about them either. If they are soldiers, which they are not, they have already lost their battle and the war is still going on. They are Florences, attending those injured by war. And, yeah, I'm a fucking nightingale in shining armour, Dominique, I am foremost.

I liked our pillow talk or our hammock huddle, at least we could talk and I was not taking refuge in somebody's body where the voice could barely be understood. I have poor language skills, but I am supposed to speak for communities on the run; I have poor communication skills and yet here is my diary. Here is the diary I promised you Dominique, a gift from the forest, in remembrance shall we say of our last kiss. No. I'm not a romantic. Not here. Silva Rerum.

But it doesn't matter now. All that is distant and past. You are seeing this. It too is past.

What matters when you have nothing but the clothes you stand up in, when the only smells in the air are those of your home burning, your family incinerating inside, stewed in their own juices? What matters where the only sounds are those of the fleeing getting taken out one by one, their bodies crashing into trees or sucked into mud and then just the soldiers hacking the forest with their pangas just a few steps behind you?

That is foremost.

Verlaine

'This is a forest of things, Nha We, a forest of living, breathing things that you might not see, you might not touch but they are here nonetheless. You can hear the Uchin bird before you see it, its wings brushing the trees as it flies to its nest but you can't hear the insects under your feet or the Celap as it pushes its nose into the air to smell your scent. But both are here, both are close to you.'

The brothers, crouched in the rain-soaked bushes, sheltering under a small blue plastik stretched from one branch to another, listened to Verlaine's calm, resonant voice.

'This is a forest of things, Le Twe, it has life in darkness and in day; when we are asleep, the forest wakes its own; when we are asleep our dreams are awake to the sounds and movement of the forest. A tiger may leap into your mind but it will land softly inside you; a snake may slither by but it will wink at you and be on its way. When you are asleep there is nothing to fear; you are part of the forest and the forest is a part of you.'

Unlike the children Verlaine whispered his reassurance to, Leer shook his head, refusing to understand the improbable calm of the moment nor the violence of just hours before. How could there be one and the other? He slapped his palms together, loud enough for Lynch to see the frustration in his eyes, loud enough for the skin sound to be a noise from the forest for would-be listeners without sight. As long as he didn't scream. Lynch could see the fear on his brother's face, how scared he had been was still stuck in his expression, like the mud and blood that hadn't been washed off by the rain. He took his brother's head and pulled his forehead to his, keeping a firm grip on the sides of his temples. They had each other; even in the storm of bullets they had each other. Such was their empathy. There were times of course when they were out of sync, their personalities split from one moment to another but not when it mattered. They did not abandon each other.

As Verlaine comforted the sobbing and the distraught with stories the brothers had heard as they lay close to sleep in younger, better times, he beamed through the dark at his sons. While other children had nearly died of fright, his spirited, silenced boys did not. This was what Verlaine wanted; it was what he expected. His unexpected sons, his *miracle* sons it must be said, had grown up just enough.

His grip on the branch tightened so much his knuckles whitened. Je Lin.

Je Lin would have been surprised to hear him talk of miracles or tell tales from their parents' generation. They never agreed about such things. He had held his hand over her mouth sometimes, bound her arms and tied her hands when she just wouldn't stop. And now he was thinking of miracles! Sometimes he would jump up and down and scream into the bamboo walls when she would not stop. She'd laugh at him.

'You are upset but you cannot bear to be seen like this. You hide your self.'

'Ridiculous! When will your spirits give us a child? People look at us and see nothing there.'

He punched and broke the bamboo. Je Lin.

This wasn't a story he told the children and certainly not Lynch and Leer.

He had been checking traps in the fast flowing river some way from the village when Ye Pan Maw, midwife to so many of the village children, came rushing, out of breath, sweat flicking up into the air. She came not just to the water's edge but into the flow. She could barely stand. She could not speak.

'What is it? Je Lin? The babies?'

Verlaine froze in the current. Ye Pan Maw would not answer with her voice instead started to tremble in the heat, tears running down her face.

Verlaine grabbed her arm and waded through the red silted water. When she began to stumble on hidden rocks, he dragged her out of the water without a word. He'd gone to the furthest traps that day and had stayed a while watching the river pick up speed as it wound round the bend towards Jenla, the waterfalls. Sometimes he would go close to the still water before it broke and fell. It was a game he played with himself, closing his eyes he imagined how easily he would be swept over and dunked deathly in the cold mountain water. He had never seen anything like it anywhere else. The city had no such falls just many people lying on the ground. When he returned from the city it was the second place he had visited. The first had been Je Lin.

He held Ye Pan Maw's hand as they raced along the forest path, Verlaine jumping where Ye Pan Maw tripped and twisted. She was heavy and not made for running but no one cared about that. They all trusted her to bring another soul into the world. Verlaine was euphoric, spiritualised that finally he would be a father. He would be contributing to the village that he had left, had wanted to leave for so long, desperate to not be smothered by Je Lin's madness. But whatever the problems with Je Lin, now they could and should be dealt with.'

Ye Pan Maw found her voice. 'Here.' She showed him his own home. He didn't look at it but instead glanced around at many of the other villagers who had stopped what they were doing to stare at their rushed arrival. Even children seemed to pause in their playing.

In his mind he had already held his two children, close to his heart or lifting them above his head as he had done with every other child in the village. While adults were wary of his height and brooding mood, the children loved to be carried like birds, arms stretched wide to fly. He even thought that birth would bring peace to Je Lin. He wondered if she would become what he saw in other women and that they would be like other couples in the village. Burdened by everyday hardships perhaps but still living with joy, still in love. This was what he had been thinking of as he tended the traps in the river.

The villagers outside of his home fell back as they approached. It reminded him of the village joke, that clever, calculating Verlaine had built his home in the gloom.

'Your bungalow will be too dark!'

This was what everybody said when he built it close to the Shinla trees that stretched up towards the sun, blocking its every move.

'I am closer to the forest this way.'

But as he walked into his home with Ye Pan Maw he could see nothing. The scent of his bamboo bungalow normally pungent with Je Lin's incense was repugnant, like something sweet gone bad in the heat. The sound of his bamboo home used to Je Lin's humming incantations or the wind's quarrel with the trees was now silent. Their footfall into the room was the loudest thing. When a strand of bamboo creaked then snapped, they both shuddered; when two women stepped out through the incense smoke like shadows with their heads bowed, their step cowed, they faltered to a halt.

Verlaine held his arms out in the shaded room and felt nothing. There was nothing to touch.

'I can't see. Is that Je Lin? What has happened here? Where are the babies?'

He gagged on the moment, its pause bizarrely pregnant and still no one would say anything. He put his hand to his mouth as a sick feeling rushed through his body.

'Please. What has happened?'

When the two women were close to him he saw their faces, elder women of the village, their eyes not meeting his.

'It's wonderful. It really is.'

Their tone was not celebratory.

Ye Pan Maw quickly moved past Verlaine and took a basket from the women's arms and they moved back into the haze as silently as they could. Verlaine heard then saw his sons for the first time wrapped in colour, squirming then still then wriggling then yawning. Everything alive. There was not a cry but a gurgle, an infant expectoration of sound and fluid. He looked in the basket and let tears fall from his face. They were beautiful. They were beautiful of course, from what he could see but they had been wrapped up as though they could easily fall apart. He noticed Ye Pan Maw looking at him, standing very close to him sharing the moment with him as she had done countless times with others. Verlaine reached down to lift them into his arms, to be closer, but Ye Pan Maw backed away with the basket in her hands.

'It was difficult, they must rest, they must gain strength.'

She began to move away but Verlaine stopped, holding her arm firmly. He did not share his wife's belief in the supernatural but he trusted his instincts.

'Je Lin?'

'I'm sorry. Something happened. It was difficult.'

Verlaine heard his sons gurgle, a bubbling combination of air and spit and he could not take it in. They were alive, what could be wrong. It wasn't a moment for clarity. He imagined Je Lin would have a difficult birth; there was little in her life that had been easy. He fished near the falls because he needed to be as far away as possible.

It was a strange thing to think at that moment but his sons were alive, premature perhaps but not too young to live.

'Je Lin?' he asked again and Ye Pan Maw moved to the back of bungalow and did not stop Verlaine walking through the murk to find the table. He could see a shrouded body.

Verlaine remembered the boys' conception, a desperate, febrile passion with the mood soured by a sense of relief rather than love. They both knew this was their last chance. There were no artificial means. Guilt rose like bile in his throat.

'It's too dark! Is this Je Lin? This is my wife?'

'Yes.'

Verlaine buckled close to the table and he was too big for Ye Pan Maw to hold him. The women came out of the shadows and tried to take the basket from Ye Pan Maw.

Verlaine reared up, his temper rising, shock fuelling his fury.

'No!'

The women stopped, suddenly frozen by his tone.

'I want them here. My children, here. Not out of sight, here. With me, with their mother.'

They came back closer with the basket as Verlaine rose to Je Lin's bedside. A shroud had been placed over her but it could not hide the blood stains, nor a drip which landed quietly on the worn bamboo. There was a hush in the room as though something was expected or someone was expected to leave.

Part of him believed Je Lin would rise up, ghoulishly, like a children's game played to scare and tease, laughing when she spoke: 'I was right all along, Verlaine, there are many things more powerful than you or me.'

Verlaine watched her float up from the table, sticking her tongue out at him, thrusting her hips and her bloody sex at him as she tried to land on his shoulders.

'You were always better at flinching than touching, Verlaine.'

'No.'

The women had barely moved since his last shout and they looked at Ye Pan Maw to see if it was them that was causing this anger. She shook her head and tried gently to move Verlaine away from the shrouded figure of his wife.

Her touch came at the wrong moment and he turned from the thrusting ghostly form of Je Lin to her, and put his large hands round her neck. Her scream was quickly choked and so strong was his grip he lifted her easily off the ground. Ye Pan Maw pleaded with her eyes while the two women rushed back into the shadows. At the height, at the fevered pitch of his angry growl, Verlaine suddenly stopped not out of fear that he might kill Ye Pan Maw but for something he saw in her eyes. Not just fear, nor simply pain. This was the something else. She was scared of something she was keeping hidden.

He let her go and she fell heavily on to the floor, coughing. Verlaine lifted the shroud quickly from Je Lin's body, too quick for him to prepare himself; in too much of a hurry to prepare for its full impact. The lower part of her body was bruised and bloodied, her hands curled in some last grip. She lay slightly on her side, her back heavily arched as though her last movement had been a violent spasm that had then been frozen. Breathing heavily, his hair bristling with fear, his imagination intoxicated by a spectred Je Lin still in the room, he turned her head and his stomach turned. Many thought her unattractive but Verlaine had liked if not loved her wild features, her unusually full lips, her scattering eyes.

'You married for children, Verlaine, you didn't marry me.'

She was right of course and when he gave up trying, he rushed to the city for a new life.

There was no life nor wildness in the face he saw now.

But he didn't understand. If pain or spasm or her heart had caused her death then why was her face so swollen, so contorted? He rolled her gently onto her back and with tears filling his eyes but falling unnoticed he looked more closely at her mouth. It seemed full and yet why would it be? Had she choked, in childbirth?

Ye Pan Maw had recovered enough to stagger to her feet and grab an arm.

'Please, Verlaine, it is too upsetting. We must take her away and prepare her for ritual. This is not good for you.'

Without a word, he pushed her away and used both his hands to open Je Lin's mouth. With some effort he prised it open but could not understand what he saw and while Ye Pan Maw pleaded with him, tugging ineffectively on his arm, he stayed for several moments staring open mouthed. His skin tingled as rushes of cold sweat spread across his body.

'Bring…' he started to say to the two women but then thought better of it and strode over to them, snatching the basket out of their grasp.

'No…' Ye Pan Maw's voice was weak and she no longer tried to get up off the floor. She bowed her head and allowed sobs to shudder her body.

Verlaine lifted both infants out of their basket and shed them of their blankets, the naked, tiny forms a gentle shock to the dark room.

There was light enough to see the wonder of their features; the soft tone of their skin and the shock of their birth hair. He had seen newborn babies before and in every respect they were the same. Beautiful of course. But not their mouths. Their mouths had been torn, every side stretched so that the skin had broken and muscle exposed. It was the same for both and although it looked like someone had cleared away all the blood, the wounds were still very much open and seeping. These quiet boys were quiet no longer and unsurprisingly their voices grew from gurgle to throttled scream. It was, to Verlaine, a moment of relief, the sound of such young life, clear and present, a baby sound coming loud if not clear. It was this moment too that showed him what he already knew, when their mouths were painfully stretched, it was clear that where their tongues had been were only the tiniest of stumps. Rather than try to stop them screaming he let them carry on, holding them out first to the women who cried in the shadows, then to the prostrate Ye Pan Maw and finally he held them over Je Lin's body. He said nothing. He let his boys do all the talking.

Ruess
Field Notes #3

This is the sound of rain. Can you hear it? It's all I can hear. It's all anybody can hear at the moment. The village is quiet because of the rain. It's been raining for two hours now and the light has gone from the day, such as it was. We went from gloom to darkness like the drop of stone; from green to darkness, such a journey, eh? Who would have thought it? I would. Everyone here would, sheltering in their huts talking to each other over the rattle of the downpour onto the corrugated iron. It is the season and the rain arrived like clockwork, tick, tick and we all rushed for cover.

This is not their village, these people. I can't or rather won't say their name. It is risky for me but more so for them. I have somewhere to escape to after all. I am not from here. These people have nowhere else to go. They are from here. This sodden jungle is their home but not this sodden jungle, this infertile slope of land that would take a farmer's toil for hours to get some root to stick, some crop to possibly grow. We are not far from their home but it is far enough for them to have only what they could carry or what they could scavenge along the way.

This is more than the sound of rain. Can you hear it? I am an outsider and I have tried to stay that way. This isn't documentary, this is story-telling and there is a difference dear Dominique, dear viewer. I'm not sticking a microphone into anyone's face; I am not an anthropologist marred by academic dispassion or at ease with quantifying suffering, comparing dislocation. I stay on the outside looking in. But still they have opened their arms to me as a stranger who would have been welcomed by warm sweet tea and sour soup in better times but can still be met with a smile and a bow. I am not charity like so many foreigners here but not here. This is too far north or too far south or just too far *in* for them to come; those who give their time and sometimes their lives to help others. Brave souls, stupid souls, proselytising souls, death-wished souls, they are all here but not here, further back, on the edge where the concrete is; gathered in Mae Rot.

This is tear jerk. I know, sorry. No. I'm not sorry. There's not enough time to apologise.

Oh. Hold on.

Ree Paw

Ree Paw, instead of looking at the book in front of him, looked out the window over the campus of the University. He had been here for one month and he was still not sure what it was he was supposed to be learning. He was here for History and yet all he seemed to get was the present. There were no old textbooks like the ones his father had, detailing their ethnic lineage or ancient tribal battles or grand lore that described a rich and vivid past; a family history first recorded in words and song by his ancestors. There was nothing of that here. Instead there were thin, cheaply bound photocopied books printed on paper that you could see through. It amazed Ree Paw that he could hold not one, not three but five sheets of paper and still be able to see into the lecture theatre half full of students half asleep. These photocopied books did not attempt to rewrite history, they simply neglected to include it.

When Verlaine remembered the view from his room in Pinya Hall he shuddered at the months he had spent trying to study, trying to be something only the government wanted him to be. He represented a voluntary study-force gathered from the country and bussed to the city who would make up numbers for the front-line of a complicated application for international aid. Yes, he was told that the whole world was contributing to his further education and the education of many other ethnics brought together under one roof; umbrella'd uncomfortably with each other.

Verlaine remembered jumping on the bus at dawn in Mae Rot after walking through the night. Everyone had been asleep, Je Lin only just so but her snores rattled the bamboo as they always did. So it was nearly a quiet exit from a stultifying life. When the bus – kick-started and prayed for – trundled out of Mae Rot's bus station picking up speed through the sleepy streets before swerving on to the main road for the capital, most of the passengers resumed their doze but Verlaine kept looking out of the back window as though expecting someone to come running after him. 'Come back, we need you...'

Behind Verlaine were the once polished floors of the University where they all studied what was termed history, what was perceived as manipulated geography, every subject changed in some way by the government agency that had taken over the running of the University. Once this had been an internationally known and respected university, with students flocking from around the world to attend in an exotic location. It wasn't like that now. Since the government had taken over everything, they had scythed through the faculty for those with a record of dissent and left the students with a skeleton crew of acolytes doling out threadbare degrees that no one would recognise anymore.

Not that it mattered. No one could leave the country anyway unless it was approved.

Of course, this would be news to many students corralled into the program but Ree Paw through links to an anti-government group had been briefed about the situation. It was only after a while in the company of Verlaine, as they holed up in their rooms, forced to respect a curfew that forbade them to step outside the campus grounds after dark, that Ree Paw shared his inflammatory views that this wasn't education but consolidation; disinformation in a once proud academia that had caved into pressure from officious men in white shirts who were never far from an armed bodyguard. Even if some of the professors had written books to the contrary or presented original findings to international committees of learning, there was an unseemly rush to recant, an adjustment to what was acceptable to know and permissible to learn. Ree Paw had stood up in a lecture and asked for clarification of a clouded subject and was asked to sit down while the men in white shirts gathered and took note.

Behind every trembling presentation was a lecturer under pressure of being fired. Or worse. Indeed, not far from Verlaine's lecture hall were the remains of the student building that had been dynamited by the Tat in an offensive just a couple of years before. The government needed expertise to exploit the natural wealth of the country and this could not simply be got by hard, enforced labour; there had to be knowledge of how to discover, of how to make things work. Such knowledge was patrolled by an armed guard, the freedom that knowledge could give was kept in protective custody.

In front of Verlaine, looking beyond the neat gardens and over the gated and high fenced boundary that marked the grounds of the old University and the new slum that had been built, Ree Paw couldn't tear himself away from the window with its sad view.

'It's nearly two deep in some places. All the time, there is someone trying to find space to sell their coconuts or cigarettes but there is hardly any room now.'

'They are the lucky ones,' Verlaine said, sadly, showing Ree Paw the scrum of beggars closer to the campus gate; here there was maybe one item held out, a grubby bottle of shampoo showing some foreign woman with brilliant yellow hair or a packet of cheap razors, or simply the gaps in their leprotic hands where fingers were expected to be. Some children further down, below the low murmur of pitiful cries and under the outstretched limbs, cupped their hands and shut their eyes. When the students had gone for the day these people slowly made their way back into the back street dormitories or slept at the side of the road.

Ree Paw could not look any longer, it was easier to turn his eyes back into the fluorescent room, the strip light glare less painful to bear. Either way, he felt overwhelmed and both he and Verlaine sought solace in their lives back home.

'In the hills, we are poor, but we want for few things; the forest can feed us, protect us and hide us. Those people are dying in front of strangers, wasting away beside a competitor who will quickly take up their space. You will lie where you fall, no one will pick you up.

Verlaine nodded.

'In the hills, we know who is beside us, behind us. We can believe what we see in front of our eyes; we understand what is around us; the trees, the flowers, the shriek of Cochoa, the rattle of the Cicada. There is song to it all, uninterrupted. But here? Do you know what is here?'

Verlaine bowed then shook his head.

They faced each other sitting on their hard beds with their single rough blankets spread over the creaking metal frames. The strip light whitened their dark faces and sunk their eyes.

'I have never been in prison until now.'

As if to confirm Verlaine's curt assessment, an alarm went off somewhere, briefly piercing the night before it was abruptly stopped then the backfire from a motorbike, then the harsh gathering of phlegm from a security guard's smoky throat, and of course the hum of the generator. Night in the muted city came back once again and, with grim resolve, Ree Paw switched off the light.

'Darkness is better.'

On their last night before their ghostly and risky elopement, they flouted the lock-down hours of study in their rooms and walked the once august corridors of Pinya Hall. The corridor had once been lined with rosewood bookcases filled with books behind sliding, glass doors. Someone had forgotten to remove a photograph from the entrance hall which depicted a different world; of colonial ostentation and privilege where a different set of educators held forth with their opinion about how the world should be seen, determining what should be used to teach the history of the host country to wealthy foreigners and refined locals. There was a different elite now of course but nothing new had been added. There was simply dust.

Ree Paw ran his finger through the thickly coated grime, making patterns as his mind drifted back to where he was returning. 'In my village, I am the teacher. I do not have degrees as these professors do here; I do not have a computer or electronic aids but I know what I am saying and I know that the children sitting there are listening to my words not eating them whole then shitting them out undigested. The words we have heard are dirty, their knowledge is soiled and they would have us believe that it is the only knowledge to know and understand. It is insulting and yet we are threatened if we do not comply; we are told to understand that everything is better now. But what was the point in being here? There is nothing to learn if nothing has gone wrong; there is nothing to be improved if everything is perfect.'

When it was time to leave, to sneak out early morning, bribing the guards who sleepily acknowledged that they were going for coffee at one of the stalls adjacent to the University campus, Ree Paw did not and probably could not display too much of a good-bye or even a gesture of final affection. Such a parting would have attracted unwanted attention and both of them needed to slip away into the breaking day as just two commuters trudging into the daylight of the waking city. There were whispered words, sotto voce promises and a link retained in parting glances.

Soon, the day's lecturer would stand and be faced with two less people in his lecture, noticing that more than half of his students had disappeared since the beginning. He would note the names of the absent, pick up the thin photocopied book and read on from where he had left off.

Ruess
Field Notes #4

That was Muthraw. A timely intervention but not exactly who I was talking about. He was a farmer. Still would be if he had land to farm, to grow cabbages or rice or something, even though it would take longer to sow seed, to till soil, to pick growth with only one arm. It would take longer because of residual metal still lodged in his side that causes him to wince each and every time he bends down. He's a farmer for God's sake. Farmers bend down. It's what they do when there are no machines to do it for them. Muthraw is a farmer without land or tool; without arm but with pain. Each and every time he bends down. I can only imagine. But that was him, soaked to the skin just from his scamper from his shelter to mine; a slip in the dark, a slide in the mud and he was here. We are neighbours in the darkness and somehow he has cooked some rice; savoured rice, precious rice brought on his back from their escape, their great escape. There wasn't much to take with them or much time to take it but rice instinctively was on his back first. Through the dark, this meal came, a skinny brown arm, a broken tooth smile.

Personal space is something you share with somebody else here. To be in solitude is to be vulnerable. Not safety in numbers but comradeship that is friendship and kin all rolled into one. I can't remember my family now. Dead maybe, gone certainly but let's keep on the jungle path. Have a look. If I get this plastik out the way, you can see other fires burning, mottled splashes of light surviving somehow in this relentless rain that seems to be getting heavier. Our words had to be stage whispered to be heard above the tumult. Incredible. You think cities are noisy; come to this green cacophony; this place, this dank green gunge has got sounds enough with its cries and whirrs; its screams and coconut thumps; the rustle of unseen animals foraging in the undergrowth. It's not peaceful but I love its noise.

Here's something you need to know as you look-out on this tropical scene: someone, some in-the-field, on-the-ball NGOer counted three thousand killed or maimed by APL or UXO's; death and injury by abbreviation; lives and limbs cut short.

Sorry, but don't get me started. No. Do get me started. Somebody get started counting, yes to count yes, to stop, to repair, to stump care. A whole generation who have never lifted a weapon or fired a gun are limping like war wounded, the victims of walking in their own land, of walking with two feet in an area-denial zone. Land that was once theirs, cropped with food; now sown with ordnance. I have got started. I have it on film from the pain of bleeding women freshly amputated to a field of explosives that has a skull and cross bones sign stuck like a gravestone into the mud. Anger of course rises but I am video-witness, I am foremost. My role is not to tear-up but make others tear up. And pay up. Oh, even do something.

There is help. There are doctors and there are Kevlar'd experts who chart fields like archaeologists on a dig, plotting out what has been checked; the jungle in certain places is steaming with experts in the field who can switch from one mission to another. And, there is Dominique.

That wasn't a sigh, it was just the rain.

Verlaine's Return

Verlaine was different when he came back from the city. He wouldn't say the city had changed him but rather he had changed in the city. There was a difference. Through late night talks with Ree Paw he had been educated beyond himself, in a history other than his own. He had become energised, politicised to save his kin from the government who had only their own interests at heart if there was heart at all. His life in the city, though cooped up, had been eye-opening – he had seen life and living as he had never seen it. This, he had exclaimed to Ree Paw soon after he arrived as they hung out of the window catching what breeze they could, was a new frontier to him, this was where knowledge could be won.

Ree Paw shook his head with a smile.

'No, this is where knowledge has been lost, my friend. This is not the new frontier. It is in the forest, it is in your village, it is in your home.'

In the city he had learnt much about other people, other places and other governments. He had filled himself with information that remained undigested; a clog of other people's beliefs and a blockage of other people's administration. He learnt not only about how city people lived but how other people understood how he lived. In the urban setting he felt feral, if not unwashed then unscented, as though he was still coated in the kicked-up earth of his village. *Your skin is so dark*. Even in the liberal atmosphere of the University which had for years been cited as a hotbed for everything, there were distinctions and demarcations; from group to group; from skin to skin and of course language. Verlaine heard words he didn't know but understood their meaning and he heard words he understood but didn't want to know. Despite the learning opportunities, he felt assaulted by the environment and was glad to leave with everything unfinished. Verlaine passed by others who had nearly killed themselves to get to the city, their bodies torn and their clothes ragged. He understood why they had come but he knew why he was leaving.

It wasn't just political.

When the bus dropped him at Mae Rot he rushed through the night evading checkpoints by taking a risky forest route through land that could be booby-trapped by rebel or government soldier alike. His heart wasn't filled with the politics of the new but by desires of old. There had been no communication between him and Je Lin and he was not expecting any. Anything could have happened while he was away and he was determined to act as though nothing had. Desire should be kept simple.

Verlaine crept through his own home, a thief in his own territory. It was as he left it; a quiet village, the slow rumble of snores underpinning the sizzle of the forest night. He was not sure how his desire would be greeted but it was what fueled his hike through the forest and with every step he rekindled or perhaps reinvented what they had. He pushed to the back of his mind that their marriage had been an eldered affair, encouraged then executed by common consent that they were better off together than alone. It never seemed that way to Verlaine but he went along with it. For the children he wanted, that everyone needed. But when it didn't happen he had been glad to leave, disenchanted with love, disaffected by expectation and now he was returning, a rejuvenated soul bristling with anger and lust. When he arrived in the village he was exhausted, torn by thorns and bloodied by mosquitos but he felt strong enough.

She was asleep when he walked gently up the steps to their bungalow. Even in the dark he could tell it looked different, uncared for with broken bamboo and litter strewn across the floor. It was not a surprise. Je Lin had never cared for the daily chores, rushing through them so nothing was finished. It didn't matter. Verlaine wanted his body to be filled with desire not domesticity.

'It's me, Verlaine.'

She didn't react immediately but then sat upright quickly, her head turning from one side to the other so viciously Verlaine thought she would hurt herself.

'It's okay, Je Lin, it's me, Verlaine.'

She fixed her eyes on him and Verlaine could see even in the dark they were wide with fright.

This was not what he had in mind. He had made a mistake. He should have waited until morning and let the village greet him. He wanted to surprise not shock.

Je Lin opened her mouth wide and Verlaine knew what was coming.

He put his hand over her mouth and pulled the rest of her wiry body close to him. When she went crazy because of the spirits, because of what was inside her head, because of everything that Verlaine had never understood, when she stood in the middle of the home and feuded with spirits unseen to him but dancing provocatively in front of her; when they enticed her to speak to shadows in dark corners, her head twisting round to watch Verlaine watching her, this was when Verlaine reached out and drew her to him, easily nestling her in his arms. At least this was how it was for what seemed like a long time before Verlaine could no longer bear his skin being torn and could no longer stomach his own revulsion.

This moment was like so much of his time with her, locked in the wrong kind of embrace. There was restraint where there should have been freedom.

But the shock of his arrival was subsiding and he could feel her scrawny muscles relax as her nails withdrew from his skin. Her breathing slowed to a sigh but no words. This was his chance. He knew how that sounded but he also knew how it felt. His desire had been building up for a long time and the city had not discharged it. Many of the students saw prostitutes and then got very drunk. When there was money, this was thought a hedonistic celebration but Verlaine thought it toxic. He wouldn't have cared if he hadn't seen the men stagger back in with their desire numbed and their sense of passion intoxicated, a dribbling mess of guilt and diluted need. It was an unpleasant cocktail.

'Let me be your husband again.'

This was what he had rehearsed. Before he left for the city there were times even then when there had been desire, an electric need that fizzed around his body which he thought, he had hoped, Je Lin would notice. But even when she was with him she wasn't. He whispered his desire and she heard voices.

'I need you…'

'Did you hear that?'

She was chased round their home and out into the village by the need to do so many things that she seemed to have no choice about. Verlaine understood the faith-fuelled compulsion but wanted nothing to do with it. This was of his parents' generation. No one believed this anymore but few would decry it out of lingering superstition.

'Lie with me, here.'

'No, I can't. I must do this.'

The spirits in their home needed attending; she addressed or placated anything, any objects that had been inhabited by a spirit. If something needed deciding then spirits too must be involved. It seemed to Verlaine that he was not really part of this marriage and that Je Lin was more prepared to co-exist with the supernatural than be coerced into the natural. It made Verlaine vibrate with anger but he dampened it down and sweated it out in the hard work of farming, fishing and maintaining the village against the ravages of weather – in the wet season especially as the bungalows and rice stores barely survived the raging rain, he was caught up in such things with no time to think but of course there always comes a time, a moment when there is no movement, no sound.

'I need you. I'm sorry. But I do. It's been so long...'

Did he have to beg?

There were many nights when he hid his hurt and doused his desire; he listened to another couple make love, their soft groans merging with the night's sound, the fireworks of tones and explosions. The rhythmic creak of bamboo shredded what was left of nothing. In the corner of the room Je Lin was unnecessarily active, her rituals spilling over obsessively into night. She sang to herself and twitched.

The half-asleep Je Lin sunk back into bed, Verlaine supporting her back. She murmured something and he felt her body soften under his grip and he took these signs, as no doubt most men would, as a signal that he was doing the right thing. He undressed himself and lifted her soft cotton nightdress over her head. He could smell her musky skin and her sweat, which he brushed with his lips. His desire was strong and overwhelming. It had been so long. He noticed how hard her body was, how unresponsive she was to his fingertips, to his tongue, but he would not, could not stop now. Perhaps it was him, he was too eager, too clumsy. He could hear her murmuring something and Verlaine put his ear to her lips.

'I can feel him watching me, waiting for me.'

'Sssh, please.'

Just this moment was all he asked. Even if he would not be a father then this moment at least.

He manipulated Je Lin's body as she continued to mumble things that made no sense to him. She mumbled about soldiers and violence, slurred about the danger she felt and her voice grew agitated and he smothered her with his body, his sex heavy, his breath grasping for air. Her words were broken up into a moan. When he thrust he caught her exhalations in his mouth blowing them back out into the soft night air. With every moment his care for what she might feel left him and he soon abandoned her to herself as he thrust his hips, arched his back and cursed loudly into the night.

Je Lin turned her head to the side and saw the young soldier standing there naked, dripping with them both, erect and proud of himself. There was no spirit in him. His stare accused her, demeaned her and then he left without a backward glance, calmly pulling on his uniform as he walked off. It was hard not to think of him even as Verlaine burrowed into her. The pain he had caused was still there but this, this timing was right at least and she clasped Verlaine's back lightly without passion and she looked up into the night air, her breath whistling a tune she had been sung as a baby.

The Forest of Things

Lynch and Leer tried to count villagers that passed them, their backs burdened with belongings hastily gathered. They used their own fingers and then each others, trading digits for digits, confusing themselves until they gave up. The number of survivors wasn't important, only depressing. They stopped counting and instead stood like an honour guard, their bodies stiffening into a slight bow. They gently touched the hunched backs, swaddled in layers of clothes and each person looked up and nodded, a silent exchange. There was nothing to be said. They were the survivors of what had become just the latest of village massacres, of ethnic pruning, the government forces assuming that everyone was guilty, each sodden soul was a rebel. When the last one passed by Lynch let out a long sigh that set his brother nodding; they gripped each other's hands until the blood drained from their fingers.

Without being asked, Lynch wrote Salva's name in the mud. Leer nodded and put his palm to his mouth, always a sign of sadness unique to him. Lynch drew Salva, hands pressed together in prayer, his burning head looking up to the sky. It was not easy to draw flames in mud but Lynch had skill, deftly using small twigs to give the twists and turns of flames. In turn Leer signed out the name of Salawin and Leer punched the corner of his eyes with his sign of sad remembrance. And so they went on, recalling the names of children they played with, adults who laughed with them, admonished them, led them along safe paths to the river to bathe and watch the Kolwa fish fly out of the river, their skins glistening in the sun. Lynch created a muddy, shifting gallery of those he had last seen. This was what they were counting. This was what counted.

Others like Jel Unw, cursing the mosquitos that were clouding the air, nodded recognition at the names and drawings.

'Jaffe was weak where he should have been strong. He got crazy, brothers, heat and blood. Heat and blood. Everyone got that but not everyone used it like he did. He went the wrong way. The pigs that used to run around under Verlaine's house, they got it and Jpaw's family that we saw slaughtered in front of our eyes had heat and blood, now gone cold and wet, washed with mud, sunk into holes that soon will be wet season graves. Yeah. Heat and blood is nothing by itself. Was it Jaffe's heat and blood that fired bullets into girls he had kissed? I saw him. Jaffe lost his soul. Forgot who he was to save who he wanted to be.'

Leer nodded silently to the old woman who passed by without family then stared downhill and wondered if anyone had been forgotten.

'Either way, brothers. Jaffe's gone, lost to us and to himself. Our village has passed us now; our cousins and kin are stopping where they can find ground and sleeping in the safety of dark. Forget Jaffe. It's like Verlaine says, 'Fate will deal with him. It already has.' '

Lynch and Leer sank into the mud and closed their eyes to the falling night.

'This is the Forest of Things, Rel Weh; this is where we must stop for a while. We have been walking for so long we can no longer feel ourselves move. We slip but we do not fall; we trip but we do not need our hands to save us. The forest will see to that. Even in the dark there are many things to catch us. Sleep here, Rel Weh and you others too. We will keep watch; someone will always be keeping watch. No, don't keep one eye open. Sleep will simply pass you by. Trust those that watch over you.'

Verlaine found every child on the sprawled outline of villagers and told each and every one the same thing, managed to find the strength to soothe the jangling nerves of the children and the numb shock of the adults. It was only the children that were talking. Some had been whisked from sleep by frantic parents, their eyes still closed to the horrors that were raining down on the village; others, older ones, were quick enough to leap into the forest and run without looking back. No one was angry that they hadn't stayed and tried to help. What was there to be done in face of the Tat's vicious guns and fire? It was better for them to be alive in the jungle than dead in the village. Their strength was needed to help those who had barely escaped with their lives.

Verlaine didn't close his eyes as quickly as the exhausted villagers. He wanted to make sure the sentry would do his job and keep watch for the next few hours. They still had to be vigilant. The Tat army knew they would have fled into the hills and no one wanted to travel into the hills unless they had to in the rainy season. But if the villagers had managed it then so could government soldiers, on commission to wipe out those who sympathised with rebels. He could hear the night breath of the villagers merging with the forest song; and quieter than that, soft whimpering, cries smothered by sweating skin. The quiet was both a relief and a form of torture.

After Je Lin had died he couldn't sleep for the peace at night and in the day it was so quiet, each creak of bamboo or scuttling rat was enough to make him see her ghost descending.

This was his pattern now, this was Verlaine. People said that he kept his peace inside him, side by side with his anger. After Je Lin was buried he took his sons into his bungalow and shut the door. He cared for the infants himself without asking for any help although early on there was milk left for the boys and food for him. He was looked after discreetly. He didn't exactly imprison himself but certainly he isolated himself. His tall figure could often be seen on the veranda with the two boys in either arm and the villagers could see that despite the tragic death of his wife and his eccentric behaviour now, he was being a good father. And he had stayed.

A few days after the boys birth, villagers saw the midwife Ye Pan Maw visit him. Verlaine opened the rickety bamboo door and Ye Pan Maw remained inside for only a short time but when she emerged she was, as villagers often remarked, clearly shaken, trembling with something. It surprised few that she left the village. People thought that she must have made a fatal mistake during the birth that Verlaine could not forgive. When Verlaine heard this he was satisfied that it was close enough to the truth and reaffirmed to bury it all deep in the muddy ground.

When the boys were old enough they made fun of his moments of peace. They would make fun of him sitting on the veranda and take it in turns to poke twigs through the rope hammock or sing badly in his ears when they saw his eyes droop into sleep. Verlaine easily got lost in memory of the city or of Je Lin and her crazy incantations, her biting tongue. Her paranoid beliefs had long since gone from the house and whether she was now a spirit somehow in some object or in some old fool drunk on Kasheen cursing the forest for being green, Verlaine did not know and refused to care. Bury it deep was his motto. He did not get sentimental. The boys were better without a mother like Je Lin. The boys needed discipline and determination; their strength, their unique connection. He saw them as tall and strong even when they were not old enough to walk.

But then, when they were young, before the army came anywhere near, they were always full of games and tricks that the whole village had to endure as they mostly did with smiles and hands held to the sky. 'Boys will be…' but Verlaine knew it was more than just play; while something had been taken away from them, something else had been given to them. They could conjure up a world of their own around them, control it, make it dance or leap or lie low. Their hands and arms weaved and twisted through the hot air like living vines, writhing snakes. Whatever Verlaine believed or did not believe didn't matter, his boys had a strength that had nothing to do with muscle; there was something other than childhood about them.

Lynch and Leer pressed their ears to the small pink radio and nested under a thin plastik. The radio survived from the time a tradesman from Mae Rot has passed through the village. Verlaine had laughed when he saw what they proudly held out to him; he imagined they must have used their charm, their natural skill on the otherwise canny trader to part with something of such value. There was no money for such things and when the journalist introduced himself he gave them a bag full of batteries before going back into the forest.

'You wave your hands and the world is at your feet.'

They put the radio between their heads. This was a new location for their listening. Usually it was in the comfort and safety of their home with Verlaine snoring in the next room, sometimes it was by the river taking turns to hold it above them or balancing it on a rock, to get some voice or song through the crackle loud enough to be heard above the river. Now there were only twisting lianas branching over them, only the rotting leaves cushioning them and the jungle shriek had replaced sounds of reassurance.

In the dark, Lynch could see Leer's face enough to tell that he was lifting the corner of his mouth. Lynch nodded. It had to be something that would make them smile.

On some nights they had shivered when they heard a distant voice in a language they could not understand say words they had no way of knowing; in the quickest of moments, it could mean anything they wanted it to. A low voice together with a high-pitched one became a spirit chasing through the night forest; a singsong voice became a mad woman who leaned over their beds with a panga in her hands. They knew that they didn't have to understand the words. Sometimes during a bad storm when it felt as though Verlaine's house was going to be ripped from the soil and taken into the air, the very static that emerged from the radio, wrapped in plastic against the damp, became the howls of lost souls caught up in the storm, uprooted from their uneasy sleep.

They had rushed to show people. They played their strange and eerie sounds, sometimes music, sometimes disconnected tones that rushed and whirred and droned so that that they would sink in sync lower to the ground. And this was Lynch and Leer in movement; this was the boys at their best, Verlaine proudly noted as he watched them with the radio. Here was expression with someone else's sound. With music they gyrated, with words they ducked then entangled themselves in each other; knotting themselves like a tonal language that twisted their tongues, accentuated stunted sounds as they tried to imitate the international quirks of pronunciation.

So, Lynch and Leer became hosts to nights, live. They took the radio to the meeting place and nearly the whole village would gather as close as they could, the volume distorted for everyone to have a chance of hearing. It was disorientating at first as Lynch and Leer played with the stations some of which could only be heard faintly but as they both got to know what could be heard and what could easily be made sense of they knew what to let others hear. Of course music was always popular and people would add their own percussion, hitting sticks against aluminium pans, but spoken words hammed up for a radio audience would cause uproar and Lynch and Leer would explode to the sounds of such drama, the verbal ricochets of tetchy dialogue sending them reeling, cart wheeling into the night.

When the foreign journalist had come with his camera and a translator from Mae Rot, Verlaine let him take all the film he wanted, ask about what he needed to know. In the city Ree Paw had told him: 'People need to know what is happening and we can't tell them if no one comes to see or hear.'

Verlaine remembered seeing in the city a tour group of sweating tourists weighed down by cameras and water bottles who snapped happily at monks and gold monasteries but were moved on when they zoomed in on people's squalor or lean-to lives.

'These tourists are not interested in us. They are here on holiday. They sleep at hotels built by children. They go sightseeing at monasteries stained with blood and they never see us. We are dust, Verlaine, kicked up by the wind so no one can see.'

If only they could see his boys.

Without thought to their own safety they had picked up adults from the mud or reunited a distraught parent with a bawling baby. They neither fled nor ran; they were braver than men twice their age. Truly, as the village was whispering in the damp green forest, these two were gifted, close to the spirits if not spirits themselves. Bullets and knives had rushed at them and had been dissolved and blunted; soldiers charged at them, only to find themselves falling onto the ground. What they saw was no longer there; what they thought could no longer be believed.

The stories grew as the night wore on; in dreams and in hushed tones the boys were talked about as the rain began to fall again.

Lawe

Leer stopped for a moment, standing still in the mud. His feet sank deeper as he stood on the path that meandered through the bamboo and tarpaulin shelters the villagers had managed to build. While he listened, Lynch wiped small twigs and smears of mud from his brother's bare back. Leer laughed at himself when he saw Lawe; his first thought had been to run and hide as though he had done something wrong. They had all run and hid. They had done nothing wrong.

But it had often been that way when they first went to Lawe's school. They skirted it, watching the thin man with glasses half on half off his ears. They watched other village children drift in and Lawe greet them with a smile. 'You come to school you get a stool! You don't need to sit in mud to learn. I will read you a story from my favourite book.'

Lawe knew it was his only book, tattered and torn but with the words all there.

The boys edged closer, just about to step forward hand in hand to join the class, then they about turned with some of their mother's impulse and ran for the river, jumping as high as they could, laughing then bombing into the water.

Lawe had seen them of course. Who did not know them? But he would not chase after them and drag them to his school. All the children were here because they wanted to be. Soon enough though, Verlaine came back from his field and chased and chastised: 'If you grow up at all you will grow up as fools.'

Lawe didn't care who the boys were or where they came from. Many in the village were more than a little wary of the boys even as children. They were the twinned sons of Verlaine. It was hard to scold them. Lawe was different; young, energetic and educated in the city like Verlaine, although he completed his course and then declined a city position in favour of sponsorship from a foreign NGO. Like Verlaine he had hated the city and couldn't wait to return to where he had been born.

He knew how to teach but more importantly he knew how to reach children – the reluctant ones, the bored ones, the distracted ones and, in the brothers' case, the ones who could not speak. He had a movement, a technique for each one of them, settling them down, stirring them up. Even in his biggest class he orchestrated them all, each one learning something from what he had to say.

He held up his bag, an old sports bag that looked like nothing but Lawe spun a story about how the bag had been found on the highest peak in the Papen mountains which rose distant behind them. No one had known how long it had lain there, half stuck in the snow, gnawed at by bears and or even snow leopards. It wasn't Lawe who had found it but someone else who had tried to sell it in the market. No one wanted such a useless old bag and the man had eventually just tossed it into a pile of rubbish on the street.

'But what was in the bag?' one of the children asked, likely either Sha We or Nha We as they were always asking questions.

'The man in the mountain had looked but seen nothing; the people in the market he tried to sell it to had looked and seen nothing – even the rats in the rubbish at the side of the road did not see anything in it.'

'So there was nothing in it?'

Lawe shook the bag and a thin, black book fell out.

'A book! What's in it, why didn't they see it?'

'I don't know. The bag is black, maybe they didn't look hard enough. Maybe the book was hiding.'

'Hiding?'

Lawe held the book up. Both covers of the large, thin book were as black as night with not a word on them. It was strange they all agreed. The books they had seen had been delivered by missionaries, their covers always colourful always full of the sun and even the ones from Mae Rot, dog eared, were never like this. There was not even a title!

'What's it about?'

By this time the children were eager to know, keen to listen and all eyes were on him. It was a simple thing but it helped all. Not a trick but a tool. And that was only just the start. When he showed them the inside of the book, the first two pages were white or close to white, there was a translucent grey tone too once the eyes got used to the contrast.

'What is it?' The children squinted their heads left and right, trying to make sense of what they were seeing.

'Ice.'

'Ice?'

'Ice.'

'Like the ice on the Papen hills?'

'Yes, except this has been polished smooth, rubbed and buffed by hundreds of feet sliding across the ice over and over again.'

The children stared in awe at the sight trying to comprehend such a thing. Lawe smiled.

'You're looking, that's good, but you are not seeing. You are like the man up in the hills who found the bag; you are like the people in the market who looked but did not see. Look carefully at these pages, is there nothing there but ice?'

It was Leer who noticed the face first. His sharp eyes were always on the look-out for something, trouble some people said but others just thought his wits were quick. He stood and shaped a head in the air in front of him. Lawe nodded.

'Do you see the face? Here.'

Lawe's finger found a small face hidden in greyish white, its skin the colour of cold, the whites of the ice blurred with water, camouflaged. Only the tiny black pupils seemed to be focussing. But when everyone found the face and then caught the stare gasps of shock and ripples of possibility spread through the children, amazement raising their voices from whisper into shout into shrieks. Leer remained still and reached out to put a fingertip on the strange, opaque face of the man lying still under the ice.

When the brothers had first joined his lessons, Lawe had taken time to look in their mouths and see the damage done for himself. He understood quickly that sounds and words were not going to come easily if at all but he got them to sound out what they could. He let them know it was okay they didn't speak like the others. He recognised that they preferred silence to mangled words and he helped them communicate with their bodies, every part of their body being used to signify something. Later, trust earned, they stayed behind after lessons and spent an hour without talk, the only sound between them giggles and the movement of objects.

Building up their signing vocabulary, Lawe took them through a silent lexicon of movement for survival, clustered fingers for everyday life, combinations of gestures and expressions so that they could indicate need and choice to those who wanted to know and above all they could learn how to communicate their emotions.

'Just because you are silent doesn't mean you have nothing to say. If you are distressed you need to be able to say why and with eyes and hands and movement you will. There is little that needs to be told that can only be said with words.'

The brothers' recall of this was strong. Lawe understood not their silence but their need to make some noise. He nodded where others shook their heads. That was the difference.

This was different.

When Lawe found them in the forest, he slumped exhausted under their plastik and tried to speak but his voice cracked and sank; a few words drowned out by the rain.

It seemed all around in the dark forest there were whispers of survival, sighs of fate intervening and the hushed, sad realisations of the isolation of their survival. It was not easy for Lawe to describe his escape from death when his wife was captured by it. He knew about this. In reading, in theory and now in truth. In such circumstances, when a world has collapsed there is no real sense of survival. Just a limbo, he told the brothers, where the spirits dangle you, holding you high by your armpits as they decide what will happen to you. This is what he believed.

'We had been holding hands. Shien was so frightened she couldn't stop shaking and so I took her hand, held it tight to still us both. Our home was on fire, flames all around us and with such fierce heat, touching and burning the soles of our feet as we jumped out of the window. We jumped and landed together, our hands still joined. I remember our hands more than anything else because that's where the soldier who saw us aimed and fired. Not at our heads or our hearts but at our hands. He missed mine but shot a hole through Shien's, a gaping, bloody hole where her palm had once been.'

Lawe's quiet sobbing was offered into the darkness and his tears folded into the night rain. The boys said nothing. They wished they had been better students. They both remembered themselves in Lawe's classroom, the forest floor they sat on under the awning of blue tarpaulin. The worst thing they did at the beginning, at least the worst thing in their eyes, in their memory now as their teacher cried, was to barge into the map of the world when they were rough-housing, showing off their strength, which they often did in retaliation when other children muffled their voices and mimicked the brother's vowels. They crashed into it when Leer lifted up his heavier brother and the map ripped in half, a vertical line, a sudden earthquake ripping through the world. There was symbolism of course and it was not lost on Lawe but when they tumbled onto the ground wrapped in the mildewed map he barely contained his anger. Other teachers would have beaten the boys, chased after them with sticks but Lawe refused to do that. He knew better than that. He barred them from his class for a few days, let them hang back and look enviously as he carried on with the education of the other children.

Jel Unw didn't go to Lawe's school.

'I know already what I need to know.'

Salva went to the lessons but before the body fell and broke his arm – broke his spirit – he was mouthy, quick of wit where Leer would be quick to snarl, Lynch quick to draw in the mud. Whenever Salva opened his mouth Lawe was not sure what would come out. For a teacher he was a challenge; as a young person he was a saviour. His brill and soul was the antidote to the fatalism of the elders. Lawe would ask his students, at the end of a lesson, if they wanted to sing a song, a well-known rebel song, and Salva would love this – it gave him the chance to rise above everyone else with his soulful tone. Lawe would smile.

'If I just taught them how to read and write I wouldn't be doing my job.'

Salva had been like the brothers, a twinkle and a rage in his young eyes, a lip to his mouth that shocked most but not the brothers, to them he was a friend in every sense of the word, a brother in soul, a spirit in their midst. There was barely a moment since their evacuation that the brothers had not held him close or had him around, his laughing breath fogging up their eyes.

In the forest that night as stories like Lawe's were told to all who couldn't sleep – stories of just being alive, of just missing being dead – there was always a mention for the brothers Lynch and Leer. Not the circumstances of their silence, their rope tricks nor their parts as actors on show, but the new emergent Lynch and Leer. Many who had been given one God to believe in by visiting missionaries still reassured themselves with imported superstition. The boys were spirits, so talk went, at least they had the spirits with them, in their favour and no harm nor bullet no flaming torch could hurt them. Such was the state of shock it was difficult and for most unnecessary to pin anything down on certainties. Lynch and Leer were in their midst and they owed a limb or a life to them.

The Lesson

Before the Tat had attacked the village, there had been more than thirty children in Lawe's class and he struggled to find enough pen and paper for them to write down the exercises he wrote out on the blackboard every morning. They were all different ages but they all needed to read and write and he took pride in guiding the youngest into first sounds, the oldest into first writing. Education was his defiance. It was quite simply his line in the earth. Knowledge would prevail over ignorance and it couldn't start too young. Nor too old.

With tears he rang the bell he had held on to when the Tat came and he watched the surprise, the smiles of both adults and children as they responded to the sound. No one would have expected this to be a normal school day – how could it be when they had all slept under plastiks, the lucky ones in hammocks, the others simply on the ground, bitten and eaten by the night – but the bell pricked up the ears of children desperate for something familiar.

Lawe had scrambled together a makeshift school in their makeshift village, a home on the run, slip sliding in the mud. There were only eight children in front of him and there was nothing in their hands, and for two of them at least, nothing in their eyes. Their bodies were there but nothing else. He rammed the chalkboard into the ground like a flag of defiance. He let his tears run freely.

This was no ordinary school day and Lawe expected nothing. Minds were already busy. His students were replaying and reliving in silent, rigid horror. Maybe they would count, maybe they would repeat words or just sing if any of them could find their voices. On a stump of a tree not even bothering to shelter under the low canopy of banana leaves, a six year old the brothers knew as Le Twe Aw swayed back and forth on her skinny haunches, the only sound the gentle squelch as tiny heels splashed into the red mud.

Jel Unw called out to her, 'Le Twe, Le Twe, you'll be okay. We will look after you. No one will harm you.'

Lawe was used to telling off the brothers and the tall, loud-mouthed Jel Unw when he bothered to come. Today he was glad of their presence.

Lawe himself was immersed in memory, a steady pour of flashbacks or you should have done this or thats. He believed his wife was with him still but there had been no sleep and he should have cancelled this class but he was better off here. They all were. How could they all retreat at once?

He hadn't just been thinking of the children's education when he escaped into the jungle with the chalkboard – the brothers had wanted to carry it on their shoulders when they found him cowering underneath it, but he had refused. When his wife's life had been taken by bullet and fire he picked up the board and ran, shielding himself, fleeing in blind fright. This was not an educational freedom. Had he survived to live for nothing except to watch himself rot with grief and anger?

His hand was trembling as he wrote and he used the other to steady it.

The brothers remembered Le Twe's father chasing them away one day after they had teased his chickens until their squawk filled the village. Le Twe, who had been sitting on the steps to the hut, laughed, hiding her wide smile behind the palms of her hands. She hadn't been rocking then, Lynch observed, kneeling down to Le Twe's height, pressing his hands on to hers. No one had seen what had happened to her parents but they were not in the camp and no one had seen them flee the village. There was no need to ask the girl.

While Lynch shut his eyes and tried not to let the girl see his tears or feel his sadness, Leer grew more tense, the pulse of his blood quickening in his temples. He watched Lawe and his six students struggle with the short pieces of coloured chalk that kept falling into the mud. Leer couldn't keep in the roar that rushed up his throat like bile; an acid burn, the sickening taste of humans smoked.

When Lynch put his arms around his brother it wasn't just to hold him in comfort. It was to hold him in place. He had seen it before, of course, this temper, this explosion, which could be both destructive and self-harming. This was with or without words. As a child it didn't matter as much, temper then was just a tantrum with small hands and feet pummelling a world which smirked, a quick rush of wind and he was flat in the mud for all to laugh at. But a few years later when strength was stirring in his limbs, the kicks could hurt. And now with the boundless energy of a near teenager no one wanted to be near him when his temper unleashed. It wasn't just blows that people were wary of but his cruelty. As a young boy he skewered frogs and then threw them as croaking and squealing spears aimed at who ever had earned his anger; he had grabbed geckos and torn their limbs off, smearing their insides against the skin of his tormentor. But it wasn't just animals this temper found, he picked on those who were younger and less able to fend him off. He twisted the skin of cousins until they screamed in pain or pulled the hair of boy or girl until it came out in clumps in his hand. His was a temper that needed to be corralled and kept tight until his calm, as it always did, returned.

People looked at the almost serene presence of Verlaine and wondered where the boy got it from – at least until they remembered the sight of the midwife hurriedly leaving the village, a look of terror on her face.

Lynch wasn't sure he could hold his brother. Previous tempers had sprung from village life, the everyday contact with people he knew and not from the after effects of a violent attack by the army. He buried his head in his brother's back and pleaded with him to stay calm. Sign language, touch language, his eyes boring into his brother's mind.

Jel Unw understood and moved in to help.

'For the sake of everyone, please, Leer. Stay with me and Le Twe. Help me help her, you know, like we said we would. Please Leer, stay calm.'

Verlaine had heard the roar and was rushing down the slope where he had been scouting the next place for them to move, for he knew they couldn't stay more than one night in their camp. He heard the roar and knew it was time, knew there was no time left. The Tat forces would not have retreated back to their camp; Verlaine's village may not have been first on their route and it was unlikely it was the last. The Tat Generals believed that there were rebels in every village in the jungle. They would find what they were looking for even if it wasn't there.

The youngest child in Lawe's diminished class was at the board as Leer's wail reached a new decibel. The little girl hesitated but Lawe encouraged her to ignore the screech and draw her picture while he kept a close watch on this unpredictable youth. He had seen bullets ripping through bamboo partitions and yet not touch the flesh of Leer or his brother. The spirits had been watching over both the brothers and no one would easily forget that. No one wanted to. Such survival was something to believe in when homes and crops were burned like tinder sticks.

Back in the old village, Lawe always asked the children to draw something at the beginning of each lesson for he knew children used their eyes better than a lot of adults. They were keen to see, not dulled to know. They had drawn animals they had seen in the mangroves, maybe spotting a civet and transforming it into a tiger that only a few of the elders had actually seen. Sometimes they drew each other jumping into the river by the village that threatened to carry them away in the wet season; these daily drawings were a source of discussion and laughter for even the poorest artists could manage a stick figure or an other-worldly animal. For Lawe it was all part of their education.

The children lining up now were silent as they watched the first girl draw a picture of her home on fire with soldiers dancing around it while people, maybe her, maybe her family ran away with their hair on fire, strands wriggling up into the sky like fire flies. When she was finished, a boy drew a swarm of mosquitoes the size of crows descending on a village, their giant elongated spikes dripping with blood and while he waited Juyn Ka sat in the mud cross-legged, shaking his head free of the flies buzzing around him.

Lawe didn't ask what Juyn Ka was drawing when his turn came. This was not a time for questions. There was no violence in his earth picture, the edges of which melted and mutated as fast as he could draw them; there was no blood or guns or fire, there was just a family, two adults, two children, standing outside their hut. Nothing had happened to them but their smiles were quickly turned downwards by the pouring rain.

Verlaine whispered into Leer's ear as he watched Lawe's class.

'We have to protect them. *You* have to protect them. You and your brother. When I leave, it will be up to you. Find a better place, go further up the slopes, there is some fertile ground. Stay there until I come back.'

Lynch joined them and Verlaine drew them both to him like he used to when sat outside their hut watching the fire, his long arms around their hunched shoulders. He had prepared this, said it over to himself in the night. He invoked Je Lin with bitter spirit.

'The villagers have seen what you can do; they know that because of the spirits in the trees that bent to take the soldiers' bullets; the ground that made holes to swallow them; the bullets themselves finding only sky; our brothers and sisters, cousins and grandparents believe that you can save them. So do I but you have to be more than you have been; you are not boys pissing yourselves anymore playing hide and seek, little kids just wanting to be loved. With what we have seen do you think you can be that anymore? There is no time. This is the time. If we are attacked again we will not suffer as we have. If we are attacked again, you, me and all the villagers will be ready. I will bring help but you must bring courage to yourself and everyone else. You must be vigourous and brave.'

The boys stared open mouthed after Verlaine, who turned swiftly, tying the bag of his last valuables to trade with to his waist. They held up their hands in unison, their palms upwards, their eyes wide.

Without looking back, Verlaine replied softly, 'It's all about you now boys. It's about who you are, how you came to be. *Ma Kan Kyin Seit.* Your silence is our strength.'

The boys looked at Verlaine as he headed back down the hill

towards their old village. When he was beyond reach they linked eyes then voices and started to hum, crouching their high tones in the depths of their throats.

Lawe's blackboard-scape showed, with its colourful drawings of jungle and blood, bodies and coconuts, not just how much life had changed but how much life was still there. But it was different now, everything was different now and no less for Lawe who drifted off into his personal grief. What happened to other villages had happened to them. What they'd had. What they had left. The playground of their childhood was now charred and strewn with still smoking embers and their way forward slid before them, a river of mud. Lawe did not touch the blackboard. This was not something to rub off. He left it as it was for all to see.

The Clinic

Not for the first time and not for the last, Tuvol wondered what he was doing here. He had no blood or gore stories to offer; there were no terrible tales of suffering he could call on to match all of this. Tuvol was the son of a man who scooped urchins from the sewer and placed them in a home; Tuvol was the son of a woman who had known only duty and service to the cause of a greater good. Tuvol was offspring. There was no substance to his history.

On the journey away from the city everyone seemed either to be on the road or living beside it. Tuvol could not see the land beyond but when they stopped for iced coffee thickened with sweet, condensed milk he got a sense of where he was and how it seemed to work. At first sight of course it was chaos, he knew to expect that miscomprehension; it's the tropical expectation, the exotic claim that for the foreign, western visitor order will be different and organisation will seem non-existent. 'But,' Dominique advised him, 'stay still for a moment and preconceptions if not replaced at least will get more complicated.'

The basics were there to see beside the roaring, horn-honking road; old lorries and shaky mopeds thronged around fuel stops where petrol and oil were kept in plastic coke bottles and an attendant, covered in oil, would grab the grubby notes with one hand while waving a tube with the other. The food stalls were lit up like miniature fairground rides, a fluorescent strip highlighting scrawny legs of chicken and piles of rice noodles that seemed to squirm in the glare. Behind some steaming pot, a swarthy woman would multi-task, stirring with one hand, squirting chilli sauce with the other while somehow barking instructions to a young girl who glided between the three tables, each with six plastic stools with barely enough room to keep even such slight men on them. But it all balanced and the men drank from brown beer bottles while they ate with relish, gesticulating wildly and laughing loudly as volume rose from each table.

It wasn't hard to feel cumbersome once out of the air-conditioned car. Tuvol was too tall. People stared open-mouthed; children would tug on their parents arms to make them notice him and one van, full of Durian fruit and presumably their pickers, stopped and then reversed so that everyone had the chance to have a good look at the tall foreigner, sweating up and glowing red.

There was nothing but curiosity in their stares and this was on Dominique's acclimatisation checklist she only half-jokingly presented to him at the airport.

'Of course, its better to find out most things for yourself. You are not simply going on a tropical vacation but actually going to be living and breathing humid air, visiting people who will have seen foreigners before – our organisation has always employed a mixture of foreign workers and local hires – but being around people who will be surprised to see someone as tall and as white as you!'

'I'm not expecting to feel comfortable.'

'Good. There are stares and there are stares. In one place you can look at someone and they think you want to attack them so just a quick glance can be an aggressive challenge and yet in another all manner of questions are asked in a stare. Stares and smiles that's part of it, part of being somewhere different is getting to know what they mean. Fortunately, everything is not usually what it seems.'

Dominique's checklist could have been lifted out of any guide to the tropics – what to take, what not to take, medications, inoculations, cultural expectations – and Tuvol guessed it was better to wait for experience to catch up with information. As the journey progressed from the gleaming city into the glowering country; from a crisp dawn start on tarmac'd road to the coming dusk on an increasingly potholed track, he had plenty of time to drag himself into where he was rather than who he was; Tuvol had sickened himself with his own pre-occupation and travelling halfway across the world had only intensified the claustrophobia. The stopover in the city had got him used to *something*, being elsewhere perhaps, but it had also allowed him to spend too much time with himself and so it was the right time to watch what Dominique called the Ruess Tapes.

She had left him to his own devices.

'I have things to do. When any of us are in the city we tend to stock up on medicines of course but books too and pencils, treats for the kids, tools for the adults. As much as possible from a wish list that's as long as the jungle is hot.'

It wasn't just cafés or restaurants Tuvol stayed in. He tried culture and went to museums and galleries. He bought postcards although he wasn't sure who he would send them to. It felt strange to be in tourist mode. He didn't even have a camera. Tuvol was as unprepared and ill-equipped for this holiday as he was for his walk in the mountains. He was just here. He was just there. When he had his fill he was glad to retreat to the café he had first visited, where the waiters recognised and exaggerated their long look up and down, laughing as they rubbed their necks with mock pain. Tuvol took a deep breath, ordered his coffee iced now and settled down to watch the films.

The tapes, half a dozen of them running from Ruess's first steps into the jungle to the point where a group of the villagers were in hiding, were intimate, confessional and above all fragile. His narration was eclectic but never less than intense and the outside world disappeared when Tuvol watched Ruess's craggy, sweat stained face close to the camera whisper descriptions of the jungle and the relentless rain that poured onto the tarpaulin. It was hard to believe that very soon Tuvol himself would be led into this vivid green.

In the car more than an hour out of the city Dominique and Tuvol had still barely said a word. Their relationship was different. Their connection, however Dominique had described it in the ski hotel in Bente, had changed. Each time Dominique caught up with him in a café, she had kissed him on the cheeks when he reached for her lips. His desire had travelled with him long haul but he remained alone in his hotel draining the mini-bar, surprised to find himself wide awake in the middle of the night thinking of her. Tuvol had thought that they would hole up at the hotel and become closer, in sense, in smell, in feeling. It hadn't been anything like that. While he paced the soft carpet of the hotel, the volume turned up on some incomprehensible news, all he had was the note that she had pushed under his door. 'Try these places. You may like them. Watch the tapes. Get used to being here.'

Dominique was back at work. Tuvol was on holiday. Their roles had changed and he was being silly, a loved-up teen not knowing what to do with his desire except make it serious, life-affirming and character defining. Come on, he told himself as he found his concentration wandering, as he found his gaze going from the screen to the throb of life partitioned by smearless glass. COME ON. Tuvol could not be what he was in Bente, a lackey to charity; the offspring of goodness. If he could not be more than that he was a skivvy like Esta; he was a papa's un-boy, emasculated until proven otherwise.

As they sat in the car, Dominique asked him about the tapes, glancing up from her laptop. Her tone was supportive but matter of fact as though she already knew his response and was simply waiting for him to confirm its effect. Tuvol noticed her expression, glared by her laptop screen; it seemed hard, brittle even, but he didn't trust his own interpretation; he didn't consider himself a good judge of character.

In the cool of the car he had an opportunity to express himself which he thought was the point – Dominique wouldn't want to know some emotional retard; a silent spin-off from the main event. He had to have more than a soul born in ice. There were so many issues brought up, already, by Ruess, by just being here – a bewildering array of human condition mixed with a verve to live and simple pleasures. It was all here. A bio-pic from the jungle. So Tuvol managed to say, suddenly choked by his own self-restraint.

'Did you have a relationship with Ruess?'

Dominique didn't even look up from her laptop.

'What?'

'Did you have a relationship with Ruess?'

'Is that the point?'

'I don't know, I'm just asking.'

It clicked with Tuvol that it was the wrong path to take. He knew nothing about the jungle.

'For Christ's sake. What the fuck does that matter? Was that fucking *Emmanuelle, Horny in the Jungle* I gave you by mistake?'

Tuvol shrunk back into his seat.

'While you were vacuumed in the hotel and cafés I thought it would give you some moments to take in what is out here, what is just a couple of hours away from here, if we can ford the river okay. What you had in the city was just a climatic bridge between your cold world and this humid heaven and hell. You had the chance to get a sense of what we do through the literature I gave you, to take a look at some serious footage of what its like for a lot of people where we are going and you get all jealous and wonder if I got hot and sweaty for reasons other than weather. Jesus.'

Dominique flipped her laptop back open and stared intently at the sleeping screen. He could see the driver's eyes in the mirror and for a moment held their gaze before he switched them back to the road. Maybe he had witnessed such things before, it was difficult to tell. But Tuvol understood the hush in the car all too well. He was used to it; a dark cloud condensing with intention.

Ruess
Field Notes # 5

Hello. Everyone is moving on. This will be dark footage and I don't mean more blood. There's no light yet and I feel like I've just fallen asleep. Sorry. Even a rugged reporter's got to sleep. Yeah. This is their way with or without a home. You make the most of the day by getting up in the dark. There's not much to pack for them or for me. I have my essentials, they have everything that's left. You gotta be careful what you pack… No, I'm not going to say *in the field* like a rookie logistician, a fledgling *No Go*. I hate that expression – are we trying to make out we are in a clean and comfortable meadowed world? There is nothing tame here, not for these people who seem doomed to be eternally displaced.

Anyway, this is not the video-witnessing that Dominique likes. She's said it many times: 'Ruess, I love your voice, your voice is what makes these films so moving, so involving but sometimes maybe you should swing the camera away from you and point it at everyone else.'

Good point. Dominique likes to think she keeps me on the straight and narrow like she's fretting I might turn into some kind of media whore who will bend the rules to suit some personal narrative; who will re-shoot scenes to get nature right, hiring actors when locals can't remember their lines. Like a lot of her kind, she's wary of reconstruction when really its destruction that matters at the moment. Communicate that. I've shot dozens of films here and in other jungles and there's nothing that's not been manipulated by the moment, by what's gone before and what's going to come next as soon as the camera is switched off. I'm not manufacturing news but recording it for more than any sense of posterity. Film it, watch it and do something for fuck's sake about it.

But sure, here's what the view offers today. Hold on... there you go. Much like it was yesterday, 100 or so people; men, women and children getting balanced in the mud with what they have on their backs – pots and pans, rice bags, blankets, plastiks – it's a pathetic inventory that doesn't even cover their basic needs but what I understand is that everyone is clinging for dear life onto something they love. And there you have it, that's the teacher lugging his blackboard and his bag of what... chalk... coloured chalk. Wow that's dedication, that's more than nine to five. Education is crucial here and the literacy rate remains high despite the threat of death. There are no statistics just a desperate belief that knowledge will give them a way out of this, a chance of... okay, its too early for that but you catch the drift. You don't see people living and dying by a blackboard very often.

I've got to go, Soh Mai is coming to help. None of this would have been possible without him. Yeah, that's the start of my acceptance speech and that's the end.

In the Heat

'You see things here that make everything back home seem unimportant.'

Tuvol nodded but didn't really listen.

'But then that's the tropical trap. People donate to distant countries while poverty snares their neighbours. I guess it's easier to help people you can't see.'

Sweat was pouring down Tuvol's face as he knelt beside the intern interpreter who was talking to a man, maybe 30 years old, a farmer, a father of two children, a widower for nearly two years, who had lost both his arms. His stumps were now waving at Tuvol as he talked via the eager yet already jaundiced interpreter, desperate to tell his story. Tri Wan looked at Tuvol all the time even though he knew he couldn't understand his words. Dominique touched his arm and they bowed and moved on as best they could through the throng of children wearing t-shirts from a bygone promotion.

'He told the interpreter that he has nothing to do now but wait for someone to bring him food. He used to grow vegetables and now he has to beg for food. He's a recent step-on. He'll adapt, make do. Most do, somehow. We give them as much support as we can before they have to return to what might not be there.'

'Step-on?'

'An unexploded ordinance victim or more specifically a land mine victim who has walked into a mined area. Did you read the list I gave you?'

'There was a lot to take in and I didn't know there would be a test.'

'Maybe you were overwhelmed by Ruess.'

'What do you mean, overwhelmed?'

'Does it matter? Look where we are!'

'I know where we are, I looked at the map. I wasn't overwhelmed by Ruess, I was curious for God's sake.'

Dominique sighed then smiled faintly. There was a breath of release in her tone. She stepped sideways when Tuvol thought she would have stepped forward, to be closer to him and further away from the intern who seemed to have keen ears for any language. His mind was being simmered by the heat and he was having difficulty reading the signs of the unsaid. Dominique spoke quietly.

'Sssh. These people may not understand our words but they can see body language and our interpreter could translate a lovers' tiff at 20 metres.'

'This is a lovers' tiff?'

'No! Jesus. Let's try and keep this simple. Do you want to be here?'

'Yes.'

'So this isn't a mistake, a ridiculous whim to you?'

'I don't think so but I've only just arrived.'

'Ever decisive. Do you want to understand who these people are, why they are here and why the foreigners that help here are willing to risk death and disease?'

'Yes.'

'Then let's agree there is no hidden agenda. Our emotions are a luxury. When you've spent some time here you can see why most foreigners never leave.'

From the moment Tuvol watched Ruess on screen, ad-libbing with his translator as they waited out a rainstorm, to the moment he heard his bassy yet excitable voice do its best to not whisper into the microphone, Tuvol knew that he wished he was him. It was a pathetic response and not one he dared voice to anyone, least of all Dominique, but it was nonetheless hard to watch the short films with their sudden breaks and scratchy sound without being comparative. He appeared to have everything Tuvol didn't. He was living and breathing in the moment not dying and sighing, aching with some redundant past. His voice, lilting sometimes as he joked with the translator, gave him an air of not so much arrogance but a knowing confidence; he knew what he was doing was dangerous but worthwhile and it was simply what he did. He was needed.

The Clinic was a collection of huts surrounding one concrete building. It was a compound of sorts with a bamboo fence perimeter but this was to mark location rather than act as deterrent. At every part of the fence was another kind of accommodation, more makeshift, fragile and only partly covered by tarpaulin where a whole range of forest floor life – pigs, chickens, small children and weary adults – were sleeping or staring back into the deep jungle. They had driven down a rough red clay road that was inaccessible for at least half the year and, so Tuvol was told, this was one of the best times to visit. Less mosquitoes although he was already scratching at bumps where they had found exposed skin. Dominique was quick to part company with Tuvol after they arrived.

'I need some jungle air; I'm tired of being iced up in that car.' She looked at Tuvol suddenly aware that ice may be a trigger word. 'Sorry but you know what I mean. Breathe in the forest air, Tuvol, you have arrived. The city was a perfumed toilet. This is the real thing. Jasmine, jungle and decay. I'll be back but I gotta say my hellos. Take a look around. This is your home for the next... dot dot dot.'

Tuvol had already attracted a gathering of small children who tugged at his trousers as they tried to leap up in front of him, making themselves as tall as him. In Bente when some visiting benefactor would pay a visit to see what their tax-evading donation had bought them, it would be his job to show them around if Espirit was away. He imagined he was fairly ungracious, not exactly the perfect guide and he remembered dignateries looking at him, their thin smiles barely hiding their surprise that such an ungainly young man could be representative of such a perfect charity. Pretty soon, he was sure, his narcotic disenchantment would show and there would no longer be a fine line between his welcome and his contempt.

In the forest the children gawped, the adults giggled and nudged each other, some with full arms and others with only stumps that were lifted to point at Tuvol. Tuvol was hardly a pioneering white man thrashing his way through the undergrowth and these people were not a rare tribe unexposed to different skin but a new arrival, a new foreigner, was a diversion from aches and horrors. For Tuvol, this was a moment to savour, a moment to think nothing of himself. Everyone would have been proud. He was not self-centred; he was in disarray.

As Dominique greeted her colleagues and settled down on the porch in front of the Clinic, Tuvol was pushed like some well-meaning celebrity into a sudden throng, the middle of a guddle of children and volunteers. People marvelled at his height and laughed at how pink his skin was in the heat. For Tuvol it was the touch that was so far removed from his experience; where touch was anger or dismissal, a gesture to get out or to stay back. Tuvol felt limp with passivity as though a white flag waved above him without any effort at all.

The noise subsided when one voice spoke up in near accentless English.

'I'm not dead yet, though I have seen many people die.' The man shouted up from the ground where he lay with his right leg intact and his left a bandaged stump. 'Did I get your attention?' He chuckled and his dark brown skin stretched tautly across sharp cheekbones while his eyes screwed up against the sun piercing through the trees. 'My Name is Lew Kwin. I lived in the city. I was a journalist. Still am. But I have nothing to report anymore.'

'Why?' Tuvol stumbled into conversation.

'The news is already known and nobody wants to hear it anyway. In the city when the trouble started, we were amongst the first they came for. That's what happens, I know. We journalists were among the first to go. Our profession implicated us. Our people can read – literacy was once a tool for good – until the regime made journalists write lies. Or die. But not me. I would not. I will not.'

Tuvol stared open mouthed at the man below him and he felt awkward about his height, his origin, his ignorance.

Lew Kwin took in his stare with a nod.

'I know. I know. It is okay to be surprised. I dream in English now. It was my job to interpret an outside world that has now gone, for a readership who themselves have disappeared, so I will, if you don't mind, talk with you a little longer. But could you help me move into the shade?'

It wasn't hard for Tuvol to move him. Even with two whole legs he would have been light. When he leaned against him Tuvol could not hide the shudder of repulsion, the disturbing sensation of skin rubbing against bone as though the muscles of his arms had just melted away. Propped up against the trunk of the tree, Lew Kwin shut his eyes for a moment.

'Would you like some water?'

He nodded.

When he opened his eyes, he took the bottle in his hand and unexpectedly laughed, a giggle really as though he was a child watching a cartoon, glad that he had got the joke.

'That's the same brand I was drinking before they raided the office. You couldn't drink the water in the city although people did if they had no money. We bought water from a big company who employed many people, who brought our own water to us, cleaned and safe. When we finished the water bottles there would be a huddle of people waiting to take them away and sell them to make money to live.'

Dominique had told Tuvol in the car that the best way to understand what it was her NGO did was to spend some time at the camp and listen to people's stories.

'Everyone has something to say. Everyone has been through something to get to the Clinic. Nobody wants to be here but they are all made welcome. Nobody is turned away.'

Lew Kwin handed the bottle back to Tuvol and shook his head, his laughter subsiding, sliding into the earth he kicked with his gnarled toes.

'I was lucky. I was out when they came for the journalists. I was out meeting one of the few sources we had left in the government who had the courage to meet and evade the following footsteps of military intelligence. On the street, in cafes, in the post office watching what you post, these men and women with their starched clothing and new shoes were everywhere in the city. This informer was close to one of the aides to the minister of state and we talked for maybe an hour in a café whose owner was careful to keep a watch out for anyone that might want to listen in. There were plenty of people like him who were willing to silently oppose, to watch the watchers and hope than some day we could all look where we wanted.

'My government contact was very nervous when I met him and he looked over his shoulder as he talked. He told me that it wasn't safe for either of us anymore; he would have to stop meeting me and I would have to stop working for the newspaper. "Pack up now and move; don't go back to work; don't say goodbye, this isn't the time for goodbyes." There was no reason not to believe him, everything that he had told me had always been accurate but still, you must understand this, to leave one's friends and colleagues you have worked with for years is not an easy thing especially if there is danger. You have a saying for this, don't you?'

'At the drop of a hat?'

'Yes, in war everything is at the drop of a hat; sudden evacuation; sudden sound of a shot being fired; sudden ending of a life. I understand and I understand that is what happened to my friends and colleagues, the drop of them is not my fault. Not my fault.'

Tuvol wasn't sure what he meant and he was uncertain how to comfort as Lew Kwin's voice faded into his body, a deep breath taking back words about to be spoken. The strain was grooved in Lew Kwin's sallow skin. He froze as memory took hold. What was left of his body remained unmoving, his voice stretching out over the words, the syllables drawled and sometimes slurred, the words slicked with bitter spit.

'I didn't go back and I wish I had. My mind tells me that is stupid but it's different for the heart – isn't it always? It was fate that I survived. But I would have all my limbs and be whole rather than what you see before you now. Survived yet crushed; alive yet dead.'

He smiled again, suddenly, almost shockingly as though this was the lightest of conversations.

'Can you imagine such a wish? I am an educated man, with two degrees. I can speak your language, I can dream in your language and be a reporter in two more but I can make no sense of such a wish. To be where my colleagues were? No one would wish that.'

'Where were they?'

'They were taken away by the police, all of them from the typists to the editor, everyone, and then handed over to the Tat. One eyewitness said they saw a high-ranking officer there, not sure what rank but he had bright shining stars, as the witness described, on his epaulets. Can you understand that? Our country is now a general with bright shining stars. A sad fate to be sure. I look at the sky and see only shadows.'

Tuvol said nothing. He knew it wasn't the right thing to do but he had no words in his head.

'There must have been someone around that day with more of a sense of drama than the usual police had. If you found yourself in the wrong in their eyes, you would be tortured then imprisoned or tortured then executed. This is the way the world over. I know that. But this day, this day someone decided that it should be different for my friends and colleagues; maybe the person advising the government had a grudge against the newspaper. Maybe he had been criticised or overlooked; maybe he was trying to win favour or maybe he was trying to save face.

'Maybe someone gave him a bad review. There can be so many reasons for an unjust act. And yet often just one outcome. This time. They took my friends and colleagues and put them into the back of a police van. Instead of rushing them through the traffic to the high security police head quarters, they took them to the airport. It was once a busy place full of tourists coming to see our wonderful country but now, who wants to come?'

Tuvol noticed a few other people sitting close by. He wasn't sure they understood Lew Kwin's English but it didn't seem to matter. He looked curiously at their faces expecting to see confusion or lack of understanding but instead they appeared grimly attentive as though intonation was enough to convey the story; maybe they had seen the ending.

'I saw it even though I wasn't there. They took my friends and colleagues to the airport and put them on a helicopter while the high ranking officials stayed on the ground to watch and to film like it was, what would you say, an air show, like entertainment that people wanted to watch. And people did want to watch; they must because I wasn't the only one to see. It was everywhere on the internet, the grim, grainy film of my friends and colleagues jumping one by one out of the helicopter. I hear that people in the West do this for fun, for excitement like a sport or a fairground ride? Not this time. The film I saw had them fall like stones, their arms outstretched maybe hoping that something would break their fall. One by one, they were pushed out of the helicopter, free to fall to become broken bodies. There is no sound on the film except the sound of applause from the officers with stars that do not shine.'

Not for the first time since watching the Ruess tapes, Tuvol felt as though he was holding a microphone, that he was the appointed listener to life stories even though he was not family or friend. For this, he was the curious outsider, the foreigner who needed to hear.

The Clinic seemed strangely out of place, its whitewashed walls gleaming in the twilight. Concrete gave the building a sense of permanence that nothing else had – the bamboo lean-to's; the injured and the dying; the volunteer workers and the guards with their tatty uniforms – all could not and would not call this place home but it was haven, it was the only chance of medical help for a long way in any direction.

Tuvol continued to wander through the camp being greeted all the time, by *Hellos!* from children who joined the conga behind him and by nods and waves from the adults who were used to aid workers in their midst. This was their country, their land which they used to farm or hunt, before government forces had turned fields into minefields.

Tuvol wasn't sure he could take in much more and yet felt an incipient guilt for his reactions, his contained emotions. He smiled back at the children and used his Bente training to present himself as he knew he should – benign, caring, listening – but inside he was crawling with fear, disgust, loathing. And he could not get away from his physical presence – he felt bulky, oozing fat and opulence amidst these rake thin people; he was lumpen from bites and grazes and his feet seemed to swell as his face reddened. And he was tired of the heat, the penetrating humidity, the hot soak that had made his two handkerchiefs useless rags now. He was losing patience with his own inability to cope with the amputations and the dying, and the jungle was an oppressive backdrop to it all; a whole army was just behind the trees, their arms wrapped around creepers, their guns aimed at an already downed enemy.

'Maybe it's the heat…' He began to say and then found himself betrayed by his legs, which buckled beneath him. It was ridiculous. He wanted to reassure those around him that he was amazed by the place, such wonderful people living with endurance who had been through so much and yet come out smiling. He did not want to be weak, to give in to either the elements or the horror. It was too late. When he stumbled to a sitting position, sweat oozing from every possible pore, his head just fell, all strength going from his neck, from his limbs. Struggling to reach him Lew Kwin put a reassuring arm around him.

'Missing your snow-hole, Tuvol?'

Tuvol was inside the concrete clinic. Lying on one of the beds, a thin mattress barely cushioning the hard wood underneath him, he felt immediately foolish, as though he had lost what face he possessed and so in the eyes of people amputated and isolated, he was a weak Westerner unused to heat or horror. But it wasn't just that, it wasn't only the humidity and the smell of antiseptic. It wasn't just everything that was new; it was everything that was old. He had not travelled light. He woke up, expecting his own death.

'Blood and heat, Tuv, it's got most of us. Don't worry about it.'

Tuvol let Dominique put a friendly and physically supportive arm around him as they slowly shuffled out of the twelve-bed ward. There were a lot of people in a relatively small space – orderlies, nurses and, he assumed, a doctor bent over a patient who was contorted with pain. Tuvol cast glances at everyone he thought was looking at him. How many people were laughing at him for his collapse, smirking behind the palms of their hands? He felt pretty groggy but even so he could see that no one was paying him any attention. The subdued, undulating sound of pain was enough to occupy everyone.

'I feel like a fool.'

Dominique helped him into an office adjacent to the ward. A typical field office with few luxuries except for a slow-turning ceiling fan that caressed rather than moved the air. The room itself was packed with the paraphernalia of intervention: a bamboo shelf of medical textbooks, dictionaries and a battered metal table for an equally hard-worn computer with NGO stickers plastered all over the monitor. Tuvol saw a Save The Whale sticker and managed a smile. When he sat down in the small plastic chair he could barely squeeze into, he smiled again. It was all ridiculous. A cockroach scuttled across the grey concrete; a thin cat stretched lazily out on another plastic chair while a radio was playing folk tunes, distorted by poor reception.

'Welcome to my field office. Back in the city, the technology is shinier and faster but I like this a whole lot more. It's real. The computer needs a kick to start and there is no sense of routine. When I'm in the field anything can happen. My last rotation before I took leave lasted six months. It's not meant to be as long as that but the Tat launched one of their most vicious offensives yet and for the first time they did not stop for the wet season when the weather makes movement much harder. They just used more villagers as porters forcing them to ford the river that swept so many away and they used helicopters – new ones that someone thought was a good idea to sell them – to search and strafe those who they would call Rebel soldiers but really were just villagers, IDPs who had no where else to go. It was bad, the worst I've seen and I couldn't leave. I was so tired and volunteer after volunteer was caving in and begging to go – how could I stop them? They were just kids most of them, trying to do good in a gap year. I didn't want to break them, I didn't want the experience to damage them. We need them to come back. We need them to intern here. Simply to stay involved. Even some of the seasoned medics who've seen war zones the world over were getting edgy. And when supplies get short it tests everyone to their limit.'

'And then I arrive and faint like a rookie.'

'It doesn't matter. Everybody reacts somehow. But anyway, I like your style.'

'What?'

'Doing your walkabout thing, talking to Lew Kwin. That's the way to do it. He's a good man. He was a respected journalist in the city. His writing highly thought of. Now he's here, like so many, on the run.'

'It's awful. People hobbling instead of walking. I'd rather be dead than lose a leg.'

'No you wouldn't. You say that as if it was a wish, a chosen luxury. Many of these people have others who rely on them. As difficult as it is, the attitude quickly becomes how far can I go with one leg; how much can I farm with one arm? When land mine or UXO victims arrive at the Clinic, the ones we can save are fevered and terrified but within days they are eager to return, to take part and help the others in their uprooted community. This isn't a feel good story. There is nothing that feels good about any of this but there is no time for convalescence, even less for sorrow. Everybody has a role to play. It is the essence of survival.

'We are not missionaries, Tuv, we haven't come hear to spread the word of the Lord even though plenty have. That's a rule. No politics and essential ethnic blindness. We needed to let these people know when we first came here that we were not just going to fling some medicines at them, leave them enough water purification tablets for a few days and then bugger off back to the city feeling a whole lot better and still find room in the budget for a slap up meal in the hotel restaurant.'

On the walls of her office, Dominique had photos of all the volunteers, their photographs turning sepia and curling at the edges from the humidity which hung cloying and thick around them. Dominique had even brought in a few filing cabinets with labels long since worn off and a stack of files overflowed on to the floor. Everywhere there was a sense of things being too busy, of a bureaucracy teetering on the edge of breakdown.

'I know its not much to look at it but it all seems to work somehow and these walls,' Dominique knocked the walls with her knuckles, 'mean something; the concrete of this clinic says it all. It might look and smell damp and maybe it wouldn't be out of place in some urban wasteland, but concrete means we are here to stay.'

Later, in the dark with rice wine in hand, Tuvol and Dominique sat side by side with volunteer medics and student adventurers at a battered bamboo table in the canteen. This was the closest they had been since arriving at the Clinic but there was little sign of intimacy and little sign from Dominique that she expected it. It flitted into Tuvol's mind, most likely because of the rice wine, that there could be more but it was soon lost in talk of land mines and injury; of people displaced and of righteous cause found. Everyone knew why they were here, their stories were testament to that.

Tuvol didn't venture his own forward even though he could feel others' expectation. He wasn't sure it was what these young enthusiasts wanted to hear. *Yeah, I'm here because I tried to kill myself...* He scratched a bite absently, shutting his eyes as one of Espirit's clarion calls to the faithful trundled through his mind, its loop dismal, relentless.

Dominique whispered into his ear.

'Come on, Tuv, concentrate. You have to listen to all this. Why is your head anywhere else but here? Aren't you tired of your own world?'

Tuvol nodded but said nothing and let Dominique return her attention to the conversation as his stare veered from the glistening faces to the darkness beyond the canteen wall. He could see small fires burning where the families of Clinic patients had set up camp waiting for return of a loved one. And that was the smell; jungle dampness mixed with rice, burning wood and pungent fish sauce. On either side of the clinic were the two wards for pre and post surgery, but the groans sounded the same from both. No spikes of agony, just rumbling tones of suffering. Everybody else clinked glasses and quipped with ease but it was hard for Tuvol to toast life when death was so close.

Then Khin

Tuvol and Dominique did not sleep together. The setting did not make it easy and there were few moments of privacy but it wasn't just location. The experience was gradually sapping Tuvol of his desire for sex, which had been so vividly awakened by Dominique. In the heat of the jungle, in the midst of pain, desire seemed selfish and his mind cramped with imagery and sound; strange smells and the feeling of soft earth under his feet.

It was hard to sleep. Perhaps jet-lag still played its role in his wide-awake state despite a few glasses of jaw-clenching rice wine. 'Go easy with that stuff,' Dominique had warned him as she downed a glass with the flick of a wrist. 'There's been many a volunteer who has staggered into walls after a few glasses of this hooch.'

Tuvol walked around the encampment. He noticed a few guards armed with rusty looking rifles crouched near the entrance to the Clinic, their skinny bodies barely fitting the fatigues. When one lit a cigarette, the flame flickered briefly across all their faces. They looked young. They nodded as he past. Nothing was said, but it was hardly silent. Tuvol had learned that much. The night forest was never silent; a wall of generated noise that sometimes undulated but never stopped. He could not see what was causing this unseen orchestration but he had been told of cicadas and crickets; lizards, geckos and Fewler night birds who sounded off like car alarms on a city street.

He probably made too much noise. He was probably drunker than he thought. It was certainly possible he was about to make a fool of himself again in a place where nobody knew him and where no one spoke his language. Near the out-patients section of the Clinic someone called his name. He was startled at first and looked quickly around him, peering ridiculously into the dark as though he would be able to tell one shadow from another. He could see huddles of people faintly lit by dying fires and when his eyes adjusted more he could see stooped figures going about family business – comforting restless children, eating bowls of rice, staring at the dark space in front of them.

He heard the voice again and thought it must be Lew Kwin. He was after all the only person he had spoken to at any length and maybe he was coming back to tell him more. He hoped so. But the voice didn't belong to Lew Kwin. Another man stepped out of the shadows as silent as still air. Tuvol was getting used to the stealth; he knew it wasn't covert, just light footed. This was not a place where meetings had to be dated and arranged, timed and allocated. Calendar was in season and light; in the rain that fell, the sun that burned. There was a rolling, fateful rhythm to events here.

The man's breath was of raw meat and it came in shallow gasps, pulling then spitting the air out of his lungs. His face, darkened by the night, only reached Tuvol's chest and they both had to adjust their gaze. Tuvol felt as though he was in the presence of a child. He was still adjusting to all of this, from expectation to surprise; to what he thought he knew to what he wished he knew.

The man said nothing but searched him with his wild eyes. There was rice wine in him, Tuvol thought, but before he took a step back he remembered there was rice wine in himself. There was both curiosity with an adventurous slur and a trip-wired sensitivity. Around him the night forest shrieked and howled, a colliding, tonal confusion that was more than background; it was humidity itself, an aural sweat that covered pores and encased the spirit.

The man was trembling in the heat. Even in the night light it was possible to make out his vibrating, willowy frame. His thin arms, stretched out by his sides as though restrained, were taut, his hands curled into tight fists. His shudder was malarial, Tuvol guessed, since he had been warned by Dominique to take his preventative medicine. It was rife in the area and the people on the run with nowhere to go often had little or no protection.

'Can I help you?'

Tuvol thought he sounded like a shop assistant but what else could he say? He felt awkward, unsure of what to do but instinctively he knew not to move on. There was nothing between this man and him; his odour, his fear, his illness were as close as the jungle air and it wrapped around Tuvol slowly but tightly. And when the man reached out and touched Tuvol's arms he was glad he did not recoil. Here it would have been a rejection and a terrible one at that. Dominique's words were still there: 'It's not that there is no concept of personal space, it's just that you must expect to share it with someone else.'

'Are you all right?'

Tuvol smiled. He could smell what he had drunk himself. The man stumbled and they both sank to the earth. Tuvol thought the man had laughed. He hadn't. He cried for a moment, was silent for a moment longer and then patted Tuvol's arm.

'You friend of Miss Dominique?'

'Yes.'

The man nodded as though this was all he wanted to know.

'Why you come here?'

'I wanted to see the Clinic. I wanted to see if I could help.'

He nodded again. Tuvol's eyes were growing used to the mirk and now the man looked younger than he had first thought, the lines in his face had been exaggerated by dirt, his wild hair made ashen by dust. This was not someone who had seen much shelter.

'That's why I came here. To see if anyone can. To see if anyone has seen her.'

'Seen who?'

'My daughter, I lose my daughter.'

Tears slowly tracked down the grooves on his face.

'I'm sorry to hear that. What is your name?'

'Then Khin.'

'My name is Tuvol. What happened to you, to your daughter?'

'We did not get away from the soldiers, we should have got ready quicker but we think they not come so far into the forest, so deep into the forest. We think we were safe. Verlaine try to make us go but people did not know what to take. People did not want to leave their things for the soldiers. But it took too long... too long'

'Who's Verlaine?'

'He is, he was... I'm sorry my English is not good. I learn it from my father who work for the British. I use it with the traders when there was something to trade. It's always the past I get mixed up with the present. Yeah.'

Then Khin's eyes then drifted off so dramatically that Tuvol thought he was going to pass out. He leant over and held the man's hand. It was not instinctive but he knew it was the right thing to do.

'It's okay. Go on.'

'The soldiers come to our village and destroy everything. The people who listen to Verlaine and his boys got away, they are the ones that are hid by the forest, it save them from bullets and flame. Bullets and flame, yeah. These soldier, they are not like us. They are from the city and they have no care for our village, no care for us. They burn the houses and the rice stores; they take our plastiks and broke our pots. They don't want us to come back. We have to leave with nowhere to go.

My daughter ask me to just leave – "Go please go," she say – when she heard the first shots but I have to help my wife. Her leg is hurting her from a fall and she could not walk fast. I say, "Leh Un, my daughter, just go, follow the other, run and we will be right behind you." Except we are not. We are not right behind. I'm sorry. This present, this past, is so difficult. But it is true. We are still caught up in our home, we get the last few things when the soldiers came.'

The tears trickled down Then Khin's face but he made no attempt to wipe them. His stare was into the night away from them both but his hand gradually returned Tuvol's grip.

'They set fire to our house. I can hear them laughing when they did it, they use words I didn't understand. But I understand the flames, the smell of the smoke and their voices, their voices are like children playing or maybe animals. The way they shout and cry as they fight. We try to get to the back of our home where there is a window, was a window… just above where Leh Un slept. I think she is still there since there is a blanket lying there but she have left it in her hurry. I am so happy that it was not her still there waiting for us. But then I saw the flames come into the window like snake, you know, hot snake that miss me but caught my wife. They touched her and I fell back on to the floor. I don't know how that happened but I bang my head and it takes a moment just a moment and when I look up my wife is kneeling in flames by the window. She not say anything but her mouth is open but there are no words, no shout or cry. Her beautiful shirt is on fire and falling to the floor; the fire has caught her clothes, her beautiful shirt she make with her own hands with colour and fine cotton. I loved it. I love her. The way she looked and the way she smelt. But not then, the smell then is still in my nose. I can feel the heat on skin. I can smell how she burn. It's terrible. Was terrible. Still, she did not say anything. There was nothing to cover the flames with. Leh Un's blanket is on fire too and there is no water, nothing that can stop the fire covering her body. Her eyes are still open even and the flames take away her skin and I cannot stop it, I cannot stop myself. Though she make no sound I can still hear her cry, I go into the fire and hold her. Like we did when we slept or when we wake. I do not feel the fire and my face is with her, my arms are round her and I hope that maybe the fire will come to me, I hope the flames will leave her body and come to mine and I will run out and throw myself at those soldiers, make them burn like they make my wife burn, let them feel the pain that she hold so silent. But our touch does not last. Is our last. I know the flames will not leave her and she lifts up her arms full of flame and pushes me with such strength that I fall. I watch as her eyes close and the face I have known since we were both children disappear into fire.'

When Tuvol looked at Then Khin more closely he saw that the lines of dirt were not dirt at all but charred and scarred skin; half his face barely covered by anything that could be called skin. His right ear had shrivelled into nothing and when he raised his skeletal arms he saw the raw, third degree burns that left shreds of skin on his arms and shoulders. It seemed incredible that he was still alive. There were no words that Tuvol could find. Instead he took this man, as light and fragile as a child, and held him gently.

Ruess
Field Notes # 6

We've stopped for a moment, thank God. It's difficult to see anything in this rain and I've got to keep the equipment as dry as possible even though it was sold to me as ideal for tropical use. There's little ideal about this for anyone here. None of these people, you know dear viewer, should be going fucking anywhere excuse my language. Bleep that out if you need to, editors. Not in this rain, not at this time. These paths could slide away at any moment and what's left of a once proud village would be drowned in mud. There are simple patterns here that have been interrupted; ways of being for centuries that have been ruined. The government wants to eradicate troublesome ethnics and build roads and energy conduits. The talk in shitty Mae Rot is once the ethnics are gone they will dig up the mountains and every bit of gleaming ore will be theirs.

Jesus. I can't pan this camera wide enough to record what needs to be seen.

Hope you can hear this above the rain. The boys are running past, back down the line, the refugee crocodile, the conga that no one wants to dance. Sure, reign it in. I know. Stay away from wordplay. Let's stick to the point as Dominique would prefer me to but then all this *is* the point. Wow! These boys don't run, they fly lighter than light. No mud gonna get in their way. So they say of course. So they say. But all these people, hooded against the rain limping with rotten legs, bowed with bleeding heads, all used to live a different life. I saw it when I first arrived. Okay? No. Stop.

It Changes Now

The days sped up. What had been a leisurely, observational pace quickened to a hands-on interaction; the busier Tuvol became the less he saw of Dominique who was either hidden behind people and paperwork or off with a quick wave, jumping into an open topped four wheel drive. Maybe this was what it was like. He was completely naive, absurdly inexperienced in such matters. He had never worked or lived with someone he'd had sex with. His fumbles in the dark in the grounds of Homes for Peace were so fleeting, so anonymous and pressed against the wall that he easily forgot most details, remembering only soft, warm kisses and thrusting hip movements. And yet, at the same time, he wanted to say I love you. To drunken teenagers, to a one-week girlfriend, to a woman that saved him from suicide on a mountain. He rushed to say these words and was spurned by laughter or incredulity.

Dominique liked to sum him up; wind up his fragile ego.

'You know your trouble, Tuvol, is that you don't know whether you want to live or die.'

When he didn't know how to answer that, she added, 'But at least you are here, Tuv, I'll give you that. You made a big decision under difficult circumstances and you've ended up in the right place.'

Within a few weeks at the Clinic he had become just another foreigner there to help. Dominique spoke to him about how difficult circumstances can create a sense of intimacy, a sense of community that is fragile.

'We have to remember that even though we are saving lives we are still, in many ways, guests if not on their land, certainly in their social structure. We have to act accordingly. So, that means a few rules that I write into peoples contract – engineers, medics, gap year fuzzies – all the same for them. No fraternization. It's written in legalese obviously in their contracts but anyone arriving gets the more to-the-point spiel: Don't fuck the refugees. Yes, they're cute, innocent and pretty virginal but it doesn't mean they want some white man to succor and overpower them. We have to be careful here, amongst all this good. It's a breeding ground for the less than.

'You didn't give me that spiel.'

'I didn't think I needed to. You don't seem the type.'

'I guess that's a compliment.'

'I guess it is.'

Tuvol got into routine quickly, becoming familiar with the workings of the camp as he sat near the entrance with Lew Kwin and his stories of life and work in the capital. When Tuvol moved on he would usually find Then Khin as close to the edge of the camp as it was possible, sitting silently by the guards. While nearly everybody's pitched home was turned inwards facing the concrete clinic building, Then Khin sat under his plastik, sheltering from the rain, his eyes focused on the forest. Tuvol would sit with him and often nothing was said. Tuvol didn't try to start conversations; he found the silence, if not comforting then certainly familiar.

In contrast, at lunchtimes, Tuvol saw just how many people were involved in the Clinic. If there was a hierarchy it wasn't socially important; an expat doctor sat with local nurses who would usually have some orphan sitting beside them, quietly eating rice, big eyes staring out over the scores of people half shouting at each other, arms and hands in the air while the laughter was infectious. Lunchtimes became Tuvol's favourite time of the day. Not for the food but for the good will that seemed to swell when they were all gathered under the concrete roof. There was nowhere like it for miles, all around. A clearing in the jungle.

This was how it was when Tuvol got the news. In the crowded room the news found him; a rushing zoom, a filmic snake twisting through the exuberant diners until it stopped suddenly in the face of a rugged messenger dripping with sweat; his checked shirt sticking to his bony frame, his angular face searching, swivelling as he scanned the crowded room. One hand was raised so that someone who knew him would see him even if they couldn't hear him. He waited, one hand aloft the other gripping a clear plastic wallet.

When Dominique saw the messenger, she put a spoon full of rice back in her bowl untouched and walked briskly over to him, ignoring greetings or comments from colleagues. It didn't seem like anyone else apart from her had noticed the dripping man who held out the wallet. Without a word to the messenger she tore at the seal and read. Tuvol was sitting with the young and enthusiastic volunteers only half listening, his mind filled with Then Khin's silent exile. He thought he might start to take lunch with him sometimes. They could eat rice together, say nothing and just look out at the green.

When Tuvol saw Dominique, he thought it was odd that she was already staring at him; it was stranger still that she held his gaze while raising the letter in her hand for him to see.

Esta

Your father has died, today, March 17th. All arrangements made. No need to come home. Esta.

Dominique

She believed it was important for the image to be there even though she felt a little self-conscious about it; that it might reveal her as a sentimentalist rather than an efficient logistician. It was one stop short of something furry on her desk and thus Dominique would be shown stereotypical; a woman prettying up her environment. It was funny really but it wasn't. The photo wasn't there to comfort but to provoke.

Her parents stared back at her, their faces crumpled by wear and tear from their travels and the penetrating humidity of the jungle; the skin on their tanned faces leathery then and now. They were in the heat as they nearly always were. It wasn't that they preferred it, it's just where there was the greatest need. They were doctors nearly permanently employed by the Organisation, flying out for missions as short as three weeks to as long as three years. They started off as fresh-faced junior doctors, looking for something other than being interned as a resident in some urban hospital, treating grazes and cuts from drunken fights. They both graduated with the same, laudable aim: to treat those who had no other means of treatment; to work in remote areas of the developing world.

Dominique had read all about them in the study they kept permanently stacked with papers and books; dossiers and files, books they had co-authored or contributed to with titles like *In It For the Long Run* and *Wearing Their Hearts on Our Sleeve*. They had been well-known in their field and when at home in the old apartment, visitors called round on a regular basis. They were as leathery as her parents, as brimming with stories of treatment problems and solutions and the never ending tales of suffering – tales for which her parents had gently ushered Dominique out when she was younger although she would listen at the door anyway. Sometimes after a particularly harrowing description of a convoy attacked by an unseen enemy, shells ripping through the cars carrying expat aid workers and local hires with bodies left mangled, entangled with the ripped metal, they would fall silent, each not so much sighing as breathing in. Taking a deep breath as though the air around them had just been sucked thin.

Later Dominique understood why these get-togethers were a mainstay of their return. Who else but doctors and aid workers would listen to such a horrific litany? And who else had her mother and father to talk to as they tried to extract themselves, physically and visually from a different world? Dominique's grandmother, her father's mother, refused to join in when these visitors arrived.

'I'm not listening to all of that. Why couldn't you have settled here, started a practice together or worked at the *l'hopital de medicine tropical*?'

But Dominique's father would smile, gently usher her away and open a bottle of red wine that was ready with glasses on the table.

Dominique was born into a way of life she quickly learned about from her parents' stories, from their writings and from other medics who stuffed them with praise. Everyone she met was quick to exemplify them as *the* interventionist expatriates as opposed to the neo-colonial expatriates who proselytised English and workshopped governance. From listening at the door to the noisy reunions of clinking glasses and horror stories, Dominique already knew. She was the quintessential chip off the old block and only her grandmother tutted her disapproval when she went off to study international development.

The Organisation was so littered with loners seeking enhancement and divorcees escaping disenchantment that it welcomed the daughter of a happily married couple so dedicated to the cause. She fell easily into the pace of her first assignment in the stifling air of an isolated province of an arid country. As an assistant logistician she had mostly menial tasks to deal with, and no responsibility was too quickly given to her. She knew she could not only do this job but also that of her superiors and better. She had that gene, that superiority complex that automatically gave her the gall and the confidence to believe that she knew what was best.

She kept it to herself, which was more than her colleagues did. Their fieldwork extended beyond the compound and into the town, a pitiful collection of shacks and bomb-damaged concrete buildings that hadn't even seen better days. Bars and clubs were created out of building debris; where a near derelict bank had once been, it was soon kitted out with ridiculous paraphernalia, icons and kitsch motifs from home countries inspired by clichés and rampant sentimentality. Dominique despised their lack of commitment. They had made the dust bowl town a red light area, a go-go market of saved people being made slaves. Under the flag of peace jeep-fulls came. This was a place for men with an erection they didn't want to be alone with.

She had heard her parents talk about the lifestyle; how an apparently peaceful day could suddenly and irrevocably be changed by a sweep of politics or a swelling of fundamental differences and hatreds; economically influenced, racially motivated. All of it. Dominique knew from her parents there were many fundamental reasons why conflict occurred and one definable outcome; suffering. In the dust bowl town the front line got a lot closer and the many male medics and engineers quickly sobered up and pulled on their trousers as the first torn flesh arrived.

Dominique was by no means numbed to the mutilations and death throes that occurred in the field hospital; she could not fail to be moved by the innocent ripped of their flesh, the young terminated with neck twists, the old euthanised with machetes. It was of course strange but she found herself unsqueamish, not even nauseated by sights most could barely imagine. While other newbies fainted and rushed outside to vomit, she would still be asking a few questions and making sure the doctors and nurses had what they needed to hand.

She wasn't trying to impress nor exude a rock hard exterior. Perhaps inducted by her parents florid descriptions, perhaps naturally calm with a strong stomach, either way she took on board the praise the experienced heaped on her and didn't see any reason to question her natural ability to endure other people's suffering.

When she was asked, as the bereaved often are, what she would say if she had the chance to say it, she had nothing to say. Dominique knew all there was to know about her parents. There was no mystery except for the fact there was no mystery.

'Laundry,' as her mother put it, 'should always be air dried. Secrets, torments and lies fester and thrive in dark corners and your father and I have seen a lot of such places. Dominique, *ma cherie*, it does not matter where you are in this job, it is who you are and we can help you with that. Those are your questions to ask.'

They understood too that such distanced parenting had potential problems and what could not be addressed with cuddly toys and kisses when she was young was later allowed to be reasoned and explained. If Dominique was angry with them they made sure they painted a target.

None of this made their death easier for Dominique. How could it?

'Hello?'

It was to be their first assignment together, a rare, two generation commitment in the field; this was certainly unusual in the peripatetic, transient world of the NGO and everyone was looking forward to the posting. Finally Dominique could see her parents at work; their words would be seen in action and she was looking forward to learning more from them. As treacly as that sounds, and several of her colleagues commented on this, it remained true.

'Hello!'

They were on their way. So was she. They were coming from the north, she from the south. The road was rough with civilian potholes and bomb craters in the south. Their journey was longer, riskier, while Dominique's just had miles and miles of bumpy track. It didn't matter. Tarmac wouldn't have saved anyone. A hundred times she would have traded places to be jolted in a different way. To see a different dust kicked up into the air.

'How the hell are you, no in fact *where* are you?'

Dominique's father laughed, that ridiculous high-pitched hyena that was his trademark and no doubt much imitated.

'We passed our third burnt out APC so I guess we are well on our way. What about you?'

'I've been in this car for hours. I've already lost count.'

'What does it look like out the window?'

'Beautiful. Endless.'

'Just as it should be. Describe it.'

– On behalf of the Organisation we would like you to say a few words; sentiments that could only come from you. We will use these in our press release. I know it's sudden but people will want to know.

The friendly voice at the city end of the line was encouraging but hard to listen to as she stood where they were all meant to be, local children buzzing excitedly around her feet.

– One moment while I press a few buttons then you will be on record.

But the phone was too alive. All Dominique could think of was death.

'There's a road block ahead.'

Dominique's mother sounded bored and Dominique knew she would hate this part. A long road journey with numerous roadblocks.

Her father wrestled the phone back. 'Ignore her. She gets grumpy with these road journeys. Tell me, what are you seeing?'

Dominique looked back up the road, dust clouds from vehicles in the distance shimmered in the heat, their sense of arrival and expectation a mirage.

– As the Press Officer I am here to make sure you are given your privacy at this difficult time but as a colleague who met your parents on a number of occasions, can I say that they did a remarkable job promoting their work. More than I could, they represented the...

– Thanks.

Dominique put the phone down quickly. She couldn't bear to hear others coming to terms with her loss. She threw the phone down into the earth and, alone now with the inquisitive children long gone, she sat at the edge of the dust track outside the camp they had all been sent to. Thoughtfully someone had placed a slow burning torch of twisted, compacted Burling branches and she watched the small flames flicker out towards the darkness of the road.

'Looks like we will be stopping at this roadblock. We've sailed through the last two but this looks different and the driver's on the nervous side of caution. Mind you, he's been like that since the airport. It's his first time and I've been telling him to relax, we're not in a hurry, just get us there in one piece.'

In pieces. She stared at the torch, dropping fiery branches into the dust.

They tried again. She cursed their communication.

– I'm here to help cushion the blow.

Dominique kicked the sand up into the air.

– I'm not sure I can say anything. Sorry.

– Take your time. We have all the time you need. It would really help for others to understand what a tragedy this is.

Dominique crunched the dust in her mouth she'd kicked up with her feet. She wrote frantically in her notebook trying to scrawl out the words that described who they were. As soon as they were written, she read into the phone, her voice tight and breathless.

– They were literate, careful providers of life-saving skills. They went beyond the medical and rallied around the ethical.

– That's great. Anything else?

– They told me someone gave them an ivory letter opener as a present at the end of a posting and they smiled, bowed deeply and took it with both hands. They knew how to say thank you even though they were vegetarian and despised the trade in elephant body parts.

– That's interesting. Thanks.

– They told me, 'To thine own self be true.'

– Uh huh.

– I can hear my father's voice when I was young and waiting for them to come back…the smell of red wine on his breath… his heavy sigh as he hugged me to him. He whispered good night in a different language every time. When he ran out he just made it up.

– Miss Dominique?

Dominique answered, her body and voice vibrating.

– Yes?

– Thank you for your help at this difficult time.

The PR officer terminated the call.

Dominique felt she had helped someone.

'Honey, the driver's stopped and is having words with the checkpoint soldiers. You can picture this, can't you? Young soldiers, a rudimentary roadblock of oil drums and barbed wire. There's a half a dozen of them although only two seem that interested in dealing with us. There's a lot of talk going on and one soldier, young enough to be smaller than the height of his own gun, keeps looking in, dead eyes, Dominique. Those terrible dead eyes. No doubt a conscript, drugged up to believe in nothing, the *foie de gras* of soldiering. Force fed and trained at gun point for a better life.'

'Are you okay? How's mum?'

'Honey, the driver has got out the car and is offering the soldiers cigarettes. Currency of course and hopefully he knows how to bargain. I'm trying to hide the phone as one of the other soldiers, one of the other children better to say, is scouting around the car. I'm going to put you on speaker so don't be alarmed if the quality isn't good. This is a chance for us to be on location together already. This is live!'

Dominique could hear a loud harrumph and smiled. This was a sound she recognised. Her father's vibrant colour was always shaded by her mother's worry; just as her concern was always cared for by his confidence.

'God, they are just boys and one, Jesus, looks about ten – do they recruit that young here? – Someone's given him something, amphetamine probably but the poor kid is vibrating and I mean vibrating, I can hear his teeth from inside the car. The others are laughing at him. Awful. What chance has he got?'

Dominique glanced away from the road and looked back at the encampment. Fires sparked into the darkness, flames as brief as fireflies, illuminating the rows of tents hastily erected on relatively neutral ground. Everything was up and running but the outgoing co-ordinator had told her that they were desperate for medics. 'It's great you are all coming. I've wanted to work with your parents for a long time and this will be a good posting for you too, some real challenges. I'm glad they took my call, I didn't want to leave it to chance.' It was now Dominique's job to recruit new medical personnel.

'Honey, the driver's still talking to the soldier and your mother's getting impatient.'

'I'm not...'

Dominique smiled. She could easily see the repartee, a pantomime of mock hurt and brickbats; her parents had this down – a quick fire line was followed by the squeeze of a hand, knowing looks like children ganging up on adults.

Her head hung heavy in the night, her eyes wavering from the dark horizon. She knew she should phone her grandmother. She would be pacing the townhouse crawling with grief, a phone in her hand but no reply. Dominique was adding insult to injury by not replying, not thinking of her feelings. She was only thinking of her own. That and the ghostly dust whipped up from the road by a sudden breeze.

'Sheesh, it doesn't seem to be going well. The driver's hands are either up in the air or pointing at us. Negotiations shouldn't take this long.'

'Don't...'

'I'm not.'

'Don't even think about it.'

'I tell you I'm not going anywhere. Your mother thinks I'm going to get out like some hot headed rookie and steam on in there with righteous anger and/or a wad of cash. "I'm a doctor, let me through" doesn't always go down well. You have to be careful who you say you are.'

'There's no other way?'

'No. This is the only road from the...'

Dominique jumped when she heard a gun shot. She looked around her, a quick 360 of dust and then she stopped. It was here. It was there.

'Dad!'

'Honey, it's okay. The crazy, vibrating kid has fired his gun into the ground. He doesn't know what he's doing. He's not trigger happy. He's not happy at all, you know, eyes open but seeing nothing.'

Dominique was trying to picture the scene but she kept seeing something terrible, of rapid fire and buckling bodies. A tease from the future, her imagination tickling her unease.

Then there was rapid fire.

'It's okay, it's okay...'

'It's not!'

'Sorry, I just need to talk to your mother.'

Dominique pressed the phone close to her ear but she could not hear distinct words; she heard breath and muffled whispers; the intonation of reassurance.

Then a single shot.

'Oh God!'

'Dad?'

'Oh God!'

'What's happening?'

'They've shot the driver. In the head. One of… One of the soldiers just fired point blank. Jesus. Listen you must phone HQ tell them what's happening. We could be hostaged here. It's nearly happened before.'

Dominique could not contain the panic that poured out of her.

'Dad, please get out of there. Somehow. Get out of there.'

'Honey, it's okay…'

Dominique listened to her own voice as though it had been recorded, live for a rolling news broadcast. It just went on and on. She saw footage of burned out cars and cratered market places; piles of plastic shoes and bloody car seats. Her visual memory reminded her of other people's horror. Suddenly, it was prime time for her. It was live before they were dead. She hung on the phone like she hung on the horizon 24 hours later, her stare dissolving the distance, a shimmering nothing between her and anything else.

'What's happening?'

'Okay, we have to be calm here. The soldiers are coming over. Maybe they are going to help the boy, the vibrating boy. Oh God, the poor driver. He was so new to it all. No. They are ignoring the boy, laughing at him. He needs to be sedated. He's going to pop. It's okay dear, my love. We will be fine. Nothing will harm us. They know we are doctors. They will likely ask us to help them. They are bound to have wounded. Please. Don't cry, we must smile and greet them. Remember. This is what we must do. We are not weak. We are strong. We can help them. We can help them.'

Dominique heard the car door and knew what her father was doing. He ignored protocol and stepped out the car. Dominique could see him, lifting himself out of car, maybe slightly stiff in the hips from the long journey but quick to smile nonetheless, that broad beam of his, an arm outstretched and a friendly greeting with lilting intonation. He was an expert at meet and greet, his charm offensive a useful détente in difficult situations. She heard his hello in their language and then one shot, a long scream from the car that must have been picked up by the mobile still in the car and then another closer to the phone.

Dominique could see what happened. With the phone still on she heard the shouts of the soldiers, the pounding feet of the vibrating boy. She could hear the drag of bodies, the rush to eliminate what happened. The car's engine started and the mobile was suddenly switched off. She was disconnected but was still there. 24 hours later they should all have been together. She had imagined they would be opening a bottle of wine from home and toasting the night sky, glad to be together, ready to do what they could. They were there to help people and now no one could help them.

Lew Kwin and Tuvol

Lew Kwin moved awkwardly on his legs. He preferred to call them legs even in their truncated form and even though most amputees described them as stumps no matter where the cut off point had been. The doctors and nurses encouraged such description because it was a way of acknowledging the change, the shocking truth, the humiliating dependence. It helped get over the night terrors too, the looping spool of a violent act and being woken by the twitches of a leg long since gone. In the doctor's way of seeing, spurred on by motivational training, patients reclaimed a sense of mobility by using the word stump; they could still get around, they could still be active in their community.

His home near the perimeter of the Clinic was a far cry from Lew Kwin's 'community', his grand but crumbling lodgings in the old part of the city; a forsaken embassy of colonial stone now being slowly strangled with ivy and long since evacuated. Sooner or later, it was said and hoped, those that had left in a hurry would come back, would again have some kind of diplomatic presence in the city. They had taken nearly everything of value and what had been left was soon stripped and redistributed – the window shutters had been snapped from their hinges and the tiles from the swimming pool had been taken off, a few broken shards still lying in the stagnant pools. Their pattern was from a different era.

When Lew Kwin had first arrived there was a sense of community about the house; two people to a room and sharing just one bathroom. It reassured Lew Kwin that this was something worthwhile even though his parents had worried about both his profession and his point of view. Another reason to like the house was just that; it was full of opinions, as loud and clear as they wanted to be. No one, at least in the early days, was worried about voicing an opinion that even whispered on the street could get you hauled off to prison for re-education or for disappearance. Breakfast and dinner could be heated with words; simmering arguments about the best way forward spilling out into the room filled with cooking smells. Amidst the cigarette smoke the men, and it was just men, waved their hands in the air dismissing, mostly with good nature, another's opinion. Lew Kwin joined in of course but sometimes he just liked to sip his iced lotus-leaf tea and watch the others, enjoying the friction of ideas.

It didn't last. Lew Kwin hadn't been working at the newspaper long when the house started to empty and the same table was suddenly quieter, the journalists noticeably less forthright with their ideas, more circumspect with their opinions. Conversations that would have lasted for hours a month before were now shorter, more circuitous in nature and certainly less animated. It exasperated Lew Kwin that no one would talk in the same way and one man, older than the rest, would shake his head sensing Lew Kwin's frustration and put his finger to his lips. Lew Kwin replied sharply by zipping his own lips and throwing his hands into the air. Such was the silence of their dialogue now.

There had been a disappearance. A young journalist, who had written increasingly provocative articles about corruption and the government's complicity in internally awarded contracts, had gone to work one morning and not come back. He shared a room with another man who worked for the same paper who moved out the next day. Then the police had called round and brusquely combed through the house for everyone's papers and one man who had lost his identity card was led away. He wasn't seen again either and very quickly the house became half-occupied with people partitioned between their own life and the stale bedclothes and belongings of people who had not come back; their tea half drunk from chipped porcelain, their foreign books still lying face down waiting to be finished.

Just before Lew Kwin left the city, he had sat with the older man at the dinner table. Their food had barely been touched and the gloom was only partly lifted by the oil lamp shining dull yellow in the kitchen. The power had not been on for some time and the air in the house hung heavy with the smell of damp concrete; the mustiness was now the scent of the house and its garden, once blooming with bourganvillier and frangipani, had grown thick with knotweed and the threat of snakes.

'Should I be quiet now, sir, do these stinking walls have ears?'

Lew Kwin's tone was provocative and disrespectful.

'You are angry.'

His fingernails were digging into the table, his legs crossing tight on his lap. His eyes would not leave the old man.

'Of course I am angry. There is nothing left here. Everyone has gone, just when this city needs them most.'

'People are scared, Lew Kwin, they go back to their families, they go back to countryside and grow things. The city is not safe any more.'

'Grow things? We should be growing words! Cultivating the ideas that every single man spoke of just a short time ago. We should be nurturing the seeds of change!'

'Those are revolutionary words, but there will be no revolution.'

'So defeatist, so dry. What do you know, old man? You write of theatre which no one goes to; you write of drama where there is none, just tired actors mimicking life, who do not believe what they are saying.'

'You can insult me, of course. There is, you hope, no one to hear it now. But your disrespect is nothing compared to what awaits us. We are entering a time when we can only dream of change. This is not hope, it isn't even approaching hope and it certainly isn't revolution. No one wants to die quickly; we shall contemplate our slow deaths instead.'

'You depress me, you disappoint me. How can you say that? There are people not far from here, in fact in every part of this city, in small groups, in huddles in cafes who need and still believe that things can change; they have no weapons but they do have hope; they have the courage that seems to have deserted you.'

'Their hope will fade when the army comes; their courage will desert them when they see their loved ones' throats slit, one by one.'

'I will continue to write what I want, that will be both my hope and my courage.'

'There will be no one to read your brave words because there will be no newspaper to carry them. Your freedom of expression will be torn up in front of you and your opinions will survive only until you start to starve. The best you can hope for is to report righteously from abroad. I know all of this. I have already been you.'

Lew Kwin was the last one in the house. He echoed himself in his room; footfalls, sighs and the occasional scream in the dark as night took his thoughts and skewered them, roasted them, until he was dripping with sweat. He had been basted with ideas, dangerous ideas that no one wanted to hear anymore, at least not that anyone could admit. No one was returning his calls and men in white shirts were peering through the windows at night to see who was in, who was left. In the dark he threw his belongings into a battered suitcase. He foraged in the other rooms for anything that might be of use – books, stationery, momentos of lives hurriedly evacuated. He had too much to carry and procured another case so that he was heavily weighed down as he waited for the bus to the countryside. He couldn't leave empty-handed just as he couldn't survive empty-headed; every last book was worth it even if it broke his back. He had watched the theatre critic leave just a few days before and he had spat out of the window. The old man did not even look back, just kept on going through the broken, wrought iron gates. Lew Kwin despised the man's cowardice just as he now hated himself. But he knew if he did not leave then sooner or later he would he arrested and he might yet find himself in the sky falling, like a stone, to the dusty ground.

Lew Kwin had held Tuvol like a baby every night, his hands pressed to the sides of his head as his own mother had done when he was shivering with fever. There was not much room in this displaced home or rather, as Lew Kwin preferred to think of it, his makeshift shelter. This was not home, this blue plastik barely big enough to angle sufficiently to let the rain pour into the mud and it would never have been enough to keep his belongings dry; the relics from a former life would have been made rotten now if it wasn't for the lip lock box Dominique had given. It wasn't much to look at but it sealed away the past waiting for drier, better times.

The people here were kind and generous and everyone helped everyone; they had all suffered one way or another at the hands of the regime but they were all in survival mode; living from hand to mouth, from one suppurating injury to another. They were not waiting around to die but neither were they living; this Clinic, saviour of so many lives, was limbo, a suspension of thought was required to live here. To think would be to remember how hopeless the situation seemed. *Was* for many but only *seemed* for Lew Kwin. He was the poster boy for Hope, Dominique had declared.

Dominique had found Lew Kwin quickly after his arrival. His step-on status did not single him out, nor did his articulate, fluent English, although this was unusual amongst the literate but ethnically lingual tribespeople. It was the speed of his recovery, the strength of his resolve, the immediacy of his hope and his natural empathy that saw him, despite his wounds, drag himself to other people with mine-damaged bodies. When there were visitors to the camp, funders and fundraisers alike, local officials and NGOers, they were all introduced to Lew Kwin. He could articulate his experience without neutrality, and his opinions carried the weight of his experience just like his arms carried the weight of his body. He was that strong, and if officials had doubts about the legitimacy of the Clinic or the Organisation wondered if this outreach was a stretch too far then they only had to listen to Lew Kwin.

He wasn't surprised that Tuvol had said next to nothing for nearly a week. It was possible he was shocked, although from what Dominique had told him his father's death was not unexpected. Tuvol was not beside himself with grief, he was inside himself.

Dominique had come to the shelter every day since Tuvol had stumbled along the slippery, muddy path from the Clinic to Lew Kwin's shelter, the telegram Dominique had given him hanging limply from his wet fingers. With deference to Lew Kwin, she asked Tuvol gently if he would prefer to rest in the Clinic, which would offer better shelter from the rain and slightly more privacy. Tuvol would simply say 'No thank you' as though he was turning down the offer of a cup of tea. When Dominique withdrew she would ask if there was anything Lew Kwin needed and he would always say no. Not out of pride but out of respect for Dominique's own rule that all IDPs should be treated the same, no matter who they were or whether they had bereaved foreigners camped out under their plastik.

Tuvol had not cried at first, his face remained neutral; his puffy red skin tightening as it stretched to contain what must have been under the surface. When Lew Kwin read the telegram, he understood. This was what grief did to people. It made them unique for only they could grieve for the person they had known; in death, it became a special relationship not to be experienced by anyone else. Lew Kwin had seen quite a few dead bodies in his life – in the street, on beds, one strung up on a tree, another floating, bloated in the city river – but he had seen many more people affected by death. Whole families crying en masse; single fathers staring still at the spot where only the blood was left, drying; and always, there were wives mourning husbands who had been disappeared or taken. Of course dead bodies were terrible, gut-wrenching. but the weight of other people's grief became a more difficult burden. Not just a glimpse of horror but the story of it; word for word; tear for tear.

Tuvol's silence was broken during one of the first storms of the rainy season.

It started like the rain. Those of the land knew when the rain was coming – by the light, the smell, the hours of the day, all were signs of the nearing downpour and so it was with grief; and a man's grief at that, where tears were punched rather than coaxed out.

Tuvol sat up and looked around him. He was no longer portly but thin. His face still puffy with mosquito bites had a gaunt quality, his skin was waxy, his eyes watery and red rimmed. The crying had begun, Lew Kwin could see that.

'I cry like a baby.' Tuvol choked on his laugh, spluttering into the stinking towel Lew Kwin had used to wipe away his endless sweat.

'A big baby, Mr Tuvol.'

'I am an orphan now.'

'Your mother...?'

'Is alive.'

'Then, I don't see...'

'I know. It's a figure of speech.'

Tuvol did little more than sit up but Lew Kwin looked at him intently. He appeared different. Lew Kwin saw him as a man in grief and distress, certainly, but also no longer standing out as a visitor floating like pink and white jelly on a sea of mud.

That was typical of Lew Kwin's style. He liked to be florid. He had met English-speaking journalists in the city who had thought him native when they read his work but his style came not from a command of the English language but from a need to counter the minimal, cold language of the regime. Their language was functional and only held passion when cruelty was involved but then words like torture or execution had no lyrical quality. This was the language of damage; a sustained attack on its own people by a regime content to be known by abbreviation alone.

'You have the look of the jungle about you, Mr Tuvol.'

'Just Tuvol, Lew Kwin, just Tuvol. And thanks, I'm sure I've looked better but I'm not sure I've felt better.' Tuvol's voice was quiet. 'I'm sorry. What does it mean to you, to have a grown man who you barely know crying in your arms?'

'You were upset. Understandably. You think men don't cry? It's the start of healing. Staying quiet does nothing except make the worst kind of silence. I have no problem that you cried.'

'I wasn't crying for my father.'

'No?'

'I was crying for me.'

'Why?'

'Because I have been dead for so long. Do you understand what I mean? This must sound crazy I know.'

'There are people, I have seen them with my own eyes – not here, people are so innocent, simple here – in the city, I have seen them. They are dead in the head, is that how you say it? Their bodies are moving around but their minds have stopped. There is air but no breath. Unfortunately I have seen that these people often have much power; they are driven around in expensive cars; they dine in expensive restaurants feeding their bodies but nothing for their head. They speak without feeling; they talk without meaning. Some of them are killers who don't even know they have murdered themselves.'

'I nearly killed myself once – this was how I met Dominique.'

'This I do not understand Tuvol. Suicide seems strange to me when there are many here who would hold on to life given the chance.'

'I know, I know. This is why I was crying. I have lived more than thirty-five years and there is not one year of it I believe was worth living for. Maybe the odd week; a day here and there but nothing more than that. It's pathetic. It's a slag heap of missed opportunities.'

'I don't understand what you mean, Mr Tuvol.'

Lew Kwin re-established some distance between them and Tuvol knew that he had gone too far. He had vomited his thoughts and expected Lew Kwin to know the pattern the mess made. He realised that the value of Lew Kwin was his natural empathy, his ability to comfort without prejudice. But Tuvol's mind was in decadent cascade and his words, having been dammed for some time, needed to flood.

Tuvol made sure he hugged Lew Kwin before he left. He went without tears and without words. It was just as it should be. Lew Kwin had held him without question and now Tuvol did the same. Apart from Dominique there had not been another human being he had touched with such sincerity.

When Dominique saw him stepping carefully through the groups of people who lifted their arms up to steady him when he lost his footing, she got up so quickly from her desk the chair clattered to the ground. Her assistant nodded her head and smiled. This was what should be happening. It was hard to keep secrets in such a tight-knit group and secrets had a way of oozing out sometimes, helped by spirits late into the night. Everybody knew it wasn't just a stranger who had been in their midst for nearly a month; it was someone special to Dominique crumpled in the hammock at the edge of the camp.

Ruess
Field Notes # 7

The village close to the border still carries out farming practices that have been used for generations. The land is fairly gentle and the soil nutrient rich so that crops of rice and vegetables have been steady. The villagers lead a simple life undisturbed by news that government forces have begun a military operation directed at villages such as these which they believe to harbour and support rebel soldiers...

That's Ruess: *The Early Years*. Don't listen to him, to that pondering, plodding journo. Sounds like one of these anthros you get out here from time to time, on the coat-tails of some NGO, desperately trying to get some field (there's that word again) research into their PhD, to authenticate what they pontificate; to embed their hypothesis in some jungle vegetation with the benefit of a fat research grant. Thanks but no thanks. Only thing worse than the anthros are the celebs, not seen them here yet, thank fuck, too dangerous, too low a profile for them to have reached a care threshold as they pass a taxed one. But I have seen it elsewhere, when some bleeding heart watches some bleeding heart, then stages an intervention for us all to be impressed by their motivation, by the production of values.

Most villagers are armed with nothing more than the Panga, a traditional scythe…

Really? He sounds like he's switched to the wildlife channel but give the guy some credit, he was giving background and atmosphere to a situation most people know nothing about. It's important to know that these people haven't always been on the run. They *have* run lighter than light, working hard on their crops but nestling around fires as darkness falls, the men having a few sips of whatever, some pretty raw Kasheen I believe, the women cooking up rice and vegetables and maybe fish or meat. Whatever. There would be laughter, some tales, some singing and the boys, man, these boys would do their thing. Lynch and Leer invited me to join them once because of the camera but I said no, I wanted to stay back, wanted to just record not participate. It was hard then, but it's harder now. I am not detached. Even when I did stay at the edge of the village I could see their acrobatic silhouettes against the flames.

'I'm going to show you to the world,' is what I said and Soh Mai translated. They yelped and cartwheeled away. What the world would make of them I don't know.

Oh, have to move again. Can't stay put. Just getting going too, eh? Nice flow. Slick but have to go. Sign of the times. Sound of the moment is our step in knee-high mud. But one moment – he won't want me to do this, but let's do an ad lib that Dominique will approve of – a little cut-away to my translator and good friend who's been with me since we started this little trek. He's too shy; he says; 'I don't want to be on film. I will translate and negotiate but please do not put me on camera.' Sure. Say cheese.

Lynch, Leer and friends in the forest

If they were too young, no one said so. So many men were dead or gone with only a few elders left slipping in the mud. The villagers staring out from under plastiks looked at them and hoped. These mute entertainers were suddenly serious actors in a theatre of encroaching war. They had grown if not in body then in the eyes of the villagers.

Jel Unw, an assembly of taut muscle and jangly nerves, didn't watch them in the same way. Neither did Nha We, a young skin of a thing who, together with the puffy cheeked Sha We, teased the brothers by running into the forest and trying to shout like men, throwing sticks at branches to make them move and threaten. The boys smiled through this. These two younger ones hadn't forgotten but they couldn't remain frozen by fear; their bodies had to move. And Jel Unw. He was different. He was a born fighter, a battler, a combative sinewed teenager who understood all too well and was wound tight with thoughts of revenge. He stood on a tree stump and hit his chest hard.

'We will stand this ground. Where others have stepped softly, we will stamp, like they stamped on us. Yeah, that is for sure.'

The brothers reached out for Nha We and Sha We as Jel Unw, who had taken off his threadbare shirt, cut violently at dead roots under the Shinla tree and fanfared his opinions. Before the army had come the brothers would tease him back with their charm, their palms pressed to their ears. Jel Unw liked to be heard. They pretended not to listen.

'Your father will find no one in Mae Rot who wants to help. That's where everyone hides not where they fight and now that everyone's under attack, why should they come and help us? We're too far into the forest, too high up in the hills. We don't need them, we have you.'

The brothers lowered their heads, their gaze to the ground.

With a flourish, Jel Unw held the rusty blade up to the sky and then bowed, swiftly striking the earth with his weapon, a spray of deadwood and mud filling the air. Sha We and Nha We applauded the display. Lynch and Leer looked into the forest and nowhere else.

Ruess
Field Notes # 8

This is background. *Not on camera, please, not on camera.* Okay but here's the context anyway. When Soh Mai agreed to come along and I swung from the god-awful noise of the Mae Rot market he turned his face away and refused to look back until the camera was pointing somewhere else. I apologised for my enthusiasm and told him that I understood that most people would not want to be filmed for personal security reasons and possible backlash against family and confidants. At that stage I had no idea who, if anyone, would see the footage but its good practice to protect sources of course and I explained that all locals shown on film would have their identities protected, their faces pixellated, voices changed.

'No, Mr Ruess, not for these reasons. I have nothing but contempt for this government. This is not my home anymore. I live across the border now and help those who have nothing. This is not about me. Don't make it about me. This is about people like this.'

You have to admire that standpoint but you can get an idea why Soh Mai and Dominique got on like a hut on fire when they met. Jesus, I could hardly get a word in edgeways when those too started jarring; talking up places they'd both been to, people they'd both met or worked with. It sounded like an NGO who's who; hardened expats and colourful locals; the highlights of some festival celebration, the low-lights of some carnage they had both picked their way through. It was heart-warming but pretty dull if you weren't there.

Like I say, I admire it but I don't agree with it. I need my ego boosted on a daily basis and here's some personal colour that can be my bio, live and cultured. My parents were media whores who slept around and needed their fix of seeing themselves through someone else's eyes. I was brought up on that, suckled by the stare of strangers, the glare of the television screen. My parents weren't worried about exposure to TV or film, they worried I wasn't getting enough. 'Are you sure you don't want to stay up and watch this. It'll do you good. You can sleep anytime...'

Okay, that's not true. This is.

I can show you these people, let you hear them trudging through the mud, their voices subdued, the children too exhausted to cry, the sound of branches being scythed and I can stay off camera, the disembodied narrator on their jungle lives as though they were shy creatures whose lives could only be caught on film from a distance by a whispering observer. Fuck that, viewer; edit that shit. I want people to see me in the same place as the people I'm filming; taking the same risks – as far as I can anyway. If people see me as well as hear me there is more chance that they will identify with me, listen to me and maybe take some notice. It's not about ego. It's not about whispering. It's about believing in what you do. What does Dominique call it? 'Taking ownership.' Whatever. Burn the diplomacy, make it real.

Verlaine in Mae Rot

Verlaine hated Mae Rot. Especially at night when its edge became menacing but even arriving in daylight he got caught up in the market flow, the noise of human shriek and motorbike engine setting him on edge the moment he first swerved to avoid being run over. You would get used to it and Verlaine had endured it on many occasions when he and Je Lin came to the market to sell their fruit and vegetables. These trips were their courtship and it made Verlaine laugh to think of it like that. Others stood in the dew of the damp forest and kissed a first kiss, the vibrant, living touch of expectation. It wasn't like that for Verlaine. He was the man who had not married. Women had tried but were rebuffed with a cool calm, dispatched without desire. It was unusual but no one blamed him for it. Most concluded it meant more time for them, for the village but it was different for Je Lin. Verlaine was of the green, preferred the company of himself, the embracing forest and not the embalming bars of Mae Rot. Je Lin was, to most, simply crazy.

'They are made for each other,' was the whispered laugh.

'Here,' Je Lin would say, 'they'll think us less strange if you drink.'

She poured Kasheen down his throat until he could no longer think, until the gawdy lights brightened and the leering men came into focus as they traced fingers on young skin, loosening their tongues on moist lips or curling their fists at anyone who would interfere. Most times he passed out on the floor to join others who could go no further and his last glance would be to Je Lin, carousing loudly as he should have been in the eyes of the traders and their women, a raucous menagerie Je Lin was entirely comfortable with.

This would have all been too much, a binge too far, if there were not moments back in the village when she sat on the steps to his home, leaned over her legs and let her long black hair fall between her thighs, her head then rising up with her laugh. She caught him looking and he did not want to hide his stare and in private he let himself buckle into passion. His tremble was of fear masked by desire.

In the village of old and even in their temporary camp there was a sense of calm, of nature being allowed to breathe despite the anxious state of them all. But in the town, a lone Verlaine twitched and tensed with every step, ignoring people who knew him while looking for people who didn't. It was said that amidst the clandestine, corner-hugging plain clothes police, the military intelligence officers supping tea with their ears to the ground, the jaded rebel soldiers hiding AWOL, amidst all of this crowded parade of men and guns, there were the gung-ho foreign mercenaries who would fight against the regime's soldiers not out of survival but out of choice. Verlaine had been told by Ree Paw, back in the city dormitory, that he had met several foreigners like this.

'They slip over the border by crossing the river. Nobody knows why they are here and no one can pay them much. They say it is a good fight and they are good at fighting. No one really trusts them either but they come with new guns and stories of blood everywhere. Some feel safer when they arrive and others when they leave. It depends what you need.'

Mae Rot was filled with debris. At one time it had been a busy but peaceful trading post for all manner of goods, some of value but most of necessity. Over the years the mountains had been mined of precious stones and rare elements and when the rainy season came all manner of person was washed into the town, a mud slide of avarice and desperation.

While waiting in tea shops and bars for the right people to come along, Verlaine had plenty of time to watch the world go by. He wasn't alone in this. When someone wasn't working, the next best thing was to watch someone else work. He squatted on a small stool and watched the wind whip up countless plastic bags, and when they landed they threw up dust and spat out bones of long dead chickens. He wanted to stay away from the Kasheen, knowing it would be better to be sober, to know where he was and why he was here. But others were less focused on what they wanted. Others simply had no focus at all; for the refugees, the escapees from the army who had nowhere to go but Mae Rot, the world shimmered and convulsed, got angry, got rueful, got sad and often in that order as the Kasheen took hold. In the hours he sat on the stool Verlaine was witness to the drunken sadness of villagers boiled from rage to a simmering revenge to the cold storage of defeat. Many of the men with bold survival plans ended up in the alley without shelter, unconscious, only to be licked awake by dogs.

Verlaine could hear anecdotes, fragments of stories, but if he leaned in too close the talk changed to the weather and the price of cabbage; a man sitting alone could easily have been military intelligence. There were no foreigners in the bar, just ragged locals and he paid up and moved on.

His cousin, Eun Sang, told him, 'The foreigners with the guns have already gone, a few rebels met them and they've gone. The foreigners with medicine are still there, in the forest.'

His cousin, never someone he liked, laughed without humour.

'There's a few men left in town, men with guns but most likely no ammunition; a mix of rebels and deserting soldiers without ambition. They got a taste for Kasheen now most likely.'

'Where are they?' Verlaine asked, thinking his cousin quick to judge.

'Try a bar near the market, you'll probably see them there.'

'Thanks.'

His cousin shouted after him, spitting an arc of betel nut on to the muddy road. 'There's no one left here who can help you. You're better off in the forest.'

Walking from one bar to another in the market it was easy to see that a crop of young men had been harvested from the town and so young children shouldered burdens too heavy for them; in twos or threes they carried rice sacks to mothers and sisters at stalls. An older generation used to nodding off when they could were pressed into action, serving when they would rather be sleeping. The gem and currency traders still barked at waiters in teahouses but there were fewer of these disreputable men. The traders' paths through the mountains had become fraught with danger from Tat and Rebel alike and even when they weren't there, their mines were.

Mae Rot reminded Verlaine of Je Lin, its wildness was tempered only by necessity and when that was put aside anything could happen. The town had everything a lot of people didn't want. Men came to defuse their libido, spurt their anger and dissipate their lust. Not for hundreds of miles could you gamble or drink or have sex as much as you could in this town. Walk an early morning in the town and it was like any other town, a wholesome mix of essential commerce; walk a late night and this town with few police interested in anything apart from themselves became a tense affair. The lack of grid electricity meant there were many thrusting, cursing shadows to be avoided and even when the throb of a generator broke light onto otherwise candled bars there was little to be illuminated that needed to be seen.

Verlaine was less than open minded about it all. He lost Je Lin once on a market day visit. One moment they were bargaining over Durians and the next she was gone, a flash of belly skin. Men winked at him and women shook their head. Je Lin, like him, had not spent all of her life in the village; like him she had left in search of something else. He had gone to the city and found compromised education; she had gone to Mae Rot and found... she never said. In their time together it remained unspoken.

And now he understood his cousin was right. There was no one to find. There was no one to help. They were gone. Around the bar he could hear snippets of stories, shards of horror embedded in words. He was not the only one to have been through what had happened. It was a familiar tale told by drunken men who tried to shrug off the memories, drown them all with Kasheen. The bar was awash with it, its strength making men weak as they staggered then fell into each other. There was no anger, there was no sense of brawl at least not to this bar, at this time. When the rush of unprotected emotion rose up it was like an explosion, and truth injured them all.

Verlaine was no different and he threw his iced tea onto the floor and ordered Kasheen. He stopped being the observer in the corner and joined others awash or adrift or both. Verlaine had no idea the name of the bar but knew he was near the market – its pungent smell could still be made out through the fumes of alcohol and tobacco –

and Verlaine easily joined the noise. Some knew of him, some wanted to know and others just hugged him without a word being said.

As the alcohol raced through his body, pulsing his blood, rippling his brain as only Kasheen can do, he lost control of his voice. One moment it was rising with the rest of them into a howl of disapproval and lament, and the next he slumped into his small plastic chair and melted into silence. But he was not sleepy drunk – his mind was burning with thoughts, there was just no voice. Others around him stood on tables and swore oaths and vengeance and laughed at the silent Verlaine who looked out of the window or rather through air framed by bamboo, and watched the night sky waiting for something or someone to fall.

Verlaine knew then that they were on their own. There was no one to help them. They had to help themselves.

Tuvol and Dominique

'So this is how it feels to be alive?'

'That's a loaded question.'

Dominique watched the man sitting uncomfortably on the edge of the small plastic chair and felt her own emotions churning as his hands played with threads from his torn shirt. Their intimacy seemed more distant now, a world away, the quick lick of a holiday romance and yet here he was, sweating, confused. Grieving. She felt empathy for this awkward, cumbersome man. To Dominique, Tuvol seemed at that moment damaged beyond bereavement and suicide ice-holes.

There was no blame attached to how he was handling the death of his father. She had no successful model for dealing with bereavement. Here, in the forest, how they saw it at the Clinic, it was always painful and mostly drawn out. Here, although death was expected, its cruelty was accentuated by the circumstances it provided for those left behind. This of course amounted to little or nothing; a woman standing in the forest holding a swaddled baby, a younger child tugging at her hand, everybody wanting to go to a home that was no longer there.

'Lew Kwin must think I am deranged by grief; ranting to him, going on and on about me and how bad it is.'

Dominique shook her head.

'I wouldn't worry, he's a good listener and has an amazing amount of compassion.'

'I've been going round in circles. I should be there, I should be here. I should be in the hospital. My mind is melting.'

'It's going to be difficult for some time but if you need answers maybe this isn't the place for them.'

Tuvol looked up and stopped swinging on the plastic chair which didn't look like it could take much more of his bulk.

'Or maybe it is. Maybe I shall just stay here, make a home for myself in the forest. A home for *my* peace, you know.'

'That's easier said than done.'

'What the fuck isn't?'

Tuvol pushed himself back into the tight-fitting seat and shifted his gaze to the nurses milling around in the Clinic.

'Sorry.'

'You sound like me.'

'I sure as hell don't sound like myself.'

Dominique smiled. Somehow this reminded her of their time spent in Bente.

'There must be many things I can do here. I've been here a month nearly and I see how things work, how you help people and how they help themselves. I've picked up a few words here and there and I know what a mine looks like and I know what it does.'

'Are you applying for a job?'

'Are you interviewing?'

'What would you be doing here?'

'I have many talents…'

'No, I mean what would *you* be doing here?'

'What do you mean?'

Dominique weighed up her next sentence and tried it out a couple of times in her head. She didn't like brutal words that were lathered with niceties and she didn't like to provoke to get a reaction. But she knew this was an important moment and it was essential she was honest. And provocative.

'Could you be any more on the run, Tuvol?'

'What do you mean?'

'Get a backpack and get moving. Go and see something of a more beautiful world; there's a lot of much prettier, much more interesting and much safer places than this.'

'You trying to get rid of me?'

'You've already tried to do that, remember?'

'You are trying to scare me off, so I don't become a jungle bum or a burden on your burden. You think I should go back to the mountains from whence I came?'

'The last thing you need is for me to answer your questions. There's plenty for me to ask though. What's going to happen to Homes for Peace? To Esta?'

'Do you have rice wine?'

'You sure you need it?'

'You sure I don't?'

Dominique dusted off a bottle on the shelf next to the patients' files. 'You sound like Ruess when he used to come in from the field.'

'Ah, now that's compliment; to be compared to him…'

Dominique shook her head as he slugged from the bottle. 'Your grief hasn't impaired your sarcasm.'

'Thank you.'

'It's not a compliment. Ruess would come back from the field, hand over his tapes saying "do something righteous with these" and then reach for the bottle, to toast the jungle he had just arrived from.'

'Chip off the old block then.'

'Not quite.'

Tuvol was silent for a while as the alcohol trickled a hot stream into his body, a race of fluid as his skin suddenly exploded with perspiration.

'From where I'm sitting I can see myself on the Anvil.'

'How's the view?'

'Cold. Numbed. Pointless. But very pretty.'

'Sounds about right.'

'I don't think the doctors at the hospital understood me. Some nurse said I should walk around the cancer ward to get a proper perspective on life. "Look at you," she said, "You are the son of the town's most famous resident who founded a world-renowned charity organisation. Look at what you stand to inherit. Why would you want to freeze yourself to death?" I told her I was already dead.'

'Tuvol…'

'You know what this rice wine does?'

'God yes, but tell me your unique take.'

Tuvol waved the bottle at Dominique, his eyesight already shuddering a little. 'Makes the truth easier to swallow.'

'Really? And what is the truth?

'That sounds therapeutic and I don't want therapy.'

'I mean what is it you really want to say?'

Tuvol rolled the bottle around in his palm squinting out in the ward. A few patients were groaning, one snored while two nurses whispered in the corner. All such quiet sounds.

'You're free to say what you want to, what you need to hear, to me.'

Tuvol nodded bringing his gaze back into the room.

'I know, I know, I appreciate that. It's all me, me, me again isn't it? Sorry. Life defined by one pronoun. How sad.'

Dominique snatched the bottle from Tuvol's flaying hand. 'Fuck's sake. What's sad is doing nothing to either help yourself or help someone else. Haul yourself into the present, please. You're not on safari looking at the wild from the safety of a 4x4. This is life and death and usually not for you or me.'

Tuvol reached out for the rice wine but only half-heartedly and then slumped back in his plastic chair, the hinges buckling once again.

'When I talk about Ruess, I'm not on some kick to make you jealous. We are all beyond that now aren't we? He is a professional; with more than a decade's worth of front-line, in the field, up to his neck in mud, sand and blood; he is not green he is grizzled, you know what I'm saying here. He is not an idealist – in fact last time I saw him drinking the same rice wine, he was a fucked-up cynic still clinging to a sense of right and wrong with humour, the last salve, the last state of mind to have before you crack and nothing matters, least of all yourself. And that, Tuvol, is what worries me.'

'What do you mean?'

'Normally we would have seen him by now but there have been casualties from the area he was in – not just land mines but rebels with gunshot wounds and women with bullets in their back, the sign of a Tat offensive. Ruess wouldn't necessarily get out the way. The terrible things that happen are the situations he needs to witness.'

'You know the quote he uses at the beginning of his documentaries?' Dominique asked.

'You mean *Evidence. Blood-dripping, child-crying, women-begging evidence. Strong enough not to be ignored.*'

'Exactly.'

When Tuvol looked into the jungle he thought he saw the shadow of a child, all skin and bone, crossing the path to one of the many home fires burning. When he looked more closely, it was an adult, diminutive and in silhouette, barely a sound from their footfall, their movement filled with silence.

Dominique flicked the insects out of her green tea and sighed as quietly as she could. While she knew this was necessary and no doubt useful for Tuvol, it was tiring and in the way. The rice wine talk had reminded her of Ruess. It brought him closer than he had been for a while. Last time he had been around she had felt erratic, filled with debris, seething, longing, crying in a junkyard of circumstance. The head nurse reminded her that the heat got to everyone eventually, local and foreigner. 'I'll stay in front of the fan as much as possible,' Dominique joked with her.

'I'm not talking about temperature, Miss Dominique.'

'I know.'

Ruess used to say, "You see the wound, Dominique, you see it and do your best to mend it. I see the wound getting made, the bullet tear through skin and cartilage and bone and blood and do my best to forget about it."

That always used to annoy Dominique and she knew that was the intention.

'So what the fuck am I, Ruess? Florence Nightingale? Is that how I am to be presented? A bit-of-good-in-all-of-us type of woman? Last time you came back and downed the rice wine I was a Joan of Arc hybrid, sacrificing myself for the state of humankind. I would look good on fire I believe you said.'

Ruess slurred his laugh, 'Yeah, you're hot, all right…'

Dominique knew that these were provocations but this was their relationship.

Before Ruess there had been a few casual affairs in other times and places but nothing that lasted or was of the heart. She had been too keen to get moving and so Ruess was the perfect suitor. They both accepted the personal deprivations of the field and bound them up realistically with the fluidity of contact, the regular disappearances and, in Ruess's case, the very real chance that he might not come back.

Like the sober one at a party, Dominique was on the look-out for words and truth loosened by alcohol. She didn't have to wait long. Tuvol rolled the bottle away and watched it come to rest against the filing cabinet.

'I've never seen anything like it. You'll know that. I'd read the history you told me to read, gathered up the politics, but it doesn't prepare you does it? It's necessary background but Ruess's tapes are in your face, of the moment. I can only begin to understand what those villagers are going through. I think, because you see what they had in the first few tapes to what they have left in the last couple, it makes it worse. They have virtually nothing left.'

Dominique nodded. She drank the last of the green tea and waited for more.

'The *Nowhere to Hide* film… documentary… episode… I don't know quite what to call it. I watched it when Lew Kwin had fallen asleep and I held the screen to my eyes so the glow wouldn't wake him. Saw jungle in the jungle. Strange. But…'

'What?'

'Even though you can't hear what Ruess is saying because of rain I just knew…

'Knew what?'

'You know the part that made me cry?'

'The end?'

'How did you guess?'

'Tuvol…'

Dominique could see Tuvol's pulse in the snake vein at the side of his head.

'It changed me, Dominique, at least it changed the way I was thinking.'

'And you've found yourself here?'

'You sound like you're going to be cynical…'

'Excuse me but I've heard it before. Volunteers rushing in and limping out; brave souls weakened quickly by fever and burying babies.

They've read motivational books with motivational stories about making a difference, about creating sustained hope for communities in danger. I'm not being cynical about you, your aspiration. Good for you. I'm just tired of phoning HQ and asking them to take another unsuitably placed person out. They seem to quickly forget that at least they can leave.'

'So it's okay to say I've found myself here?'

'Sure. You're not the typical volunteer. We already knew this.'

There was silence between them. This was the most they had talked since lying naked beside each other in the ski hotel in Bente. Eventually, Tuvol broke the quiet. He was hot again, the alcohol flushing him even though the heat was ebbing from the day as the Clinic workers drifted off to the canteen and then home. Dominique made sure they were well fed if not well paid. In every culture she had worked in, filling someone's belly was a hearts and minds winner.

Wiping the sweat from his face with a sodden cloth he looked directly at Dominique. Having resisted the temptation to ask if there was more Kasheen, he swallowed his slur as best he could.

'You probably won't think I'll say this in the morning. You'll think I am being sentimental because I am bereaved but I have given this a lot of thought.'

Dominique interrupted him, gently.

'You hear those groans. Yeah, those. I know who that is. Haven't spoken to him but I know his groans. A double stump; one land mine but it was packed and it just tore most of his legs to shreds. The Doc just looked at the red soggy mess and reached for his saw. Every time he does that I wish we had better anesthesia. What we have helps but there's a world of difference between numbing yourself from memory and blocking out searing, red-hot pain. I really want to be able to advance beyond emergency field medicine but with the numbers we have passing through especially with the Tat now so close only the lucky few get sedated while the rest scream into the dusk then groan through the night.'

'Is this aversion therapy?'

'No, it's life at the Clinic. Ask not what we can do for you but what you can do for us.'

'I wish I could help you here. I understand that, I could be a third rate medic and get in the way, or faint at the sight of a little blood; I could be admin but that's all in hand isn't it?'

'Maybe you could go find Ruess?' Dominique was only half joking. 'He's out there somewhere. There's a good chance he was killed in an attack. He wouldn't be the first foreigner to die in this one-sided affair and it would be a fraction against the number of hill people, rebel soldiers and urban refugees who have perished. But he would be sorely missed. I've met people a whole world away from here who've seen his advocacy, the front line witnessing that lets people see what is really happening. How else would they know? There's no mainstream news media with an anchor here. Too coiffured for such a sweaty location.'

'From what I've seen, he seems like a survivor. Maybe he escaped to Mae Rot or into the forest?'

Dominique nodded.

'I hope so. But if he has escaped I wish he had escaped here.'

Ruess
Field Notes # 9

I'm going back on what I said in the last entry. Sorry, but at least I'm honest about it; I'm telling you what I'm up to, all in a good cause. The only hidden agenda is the one I have for all to see; creep through jungle, crossing the border illegally and follow the path these displaced villagers have been forced to walk. If I am lucky I get to smuggle out the film. This revolution may not be televised but it will be tribunalised; evidence gathered and documented by me and a few others could go a long way. It'll be a top ten hit, a must-see with 5 stars. It should be. If there was any sense to all of this, it would be.

I want you to let me shut the fuck up and just watch the boys in action.

You see what I mean. They were kids when I first saw them, all silliness and squeak. I don't have the footage here, its all safe and sound somewhere I hope, and I may sound like my maiden aunt but they are like miniature young men now; high-pitched men, growing little bumps of muscle and some height sure but not tall, not yet, maybe not ever. Height wouldn't do you much good here. There's nothing to see but jungle and the taller you stand the more of a target you make, but you get the gist. Scraggly little boys they are no longer.

Their animation as you can see has taken on a different form, a graver need. They may have grown up a bit but it's amazing to see the villagers kow tow to these sticky boys. I mean these people love kids of course but it's adults, the older the better, they usually respect. Yet here they are keeping everyone moving, hugging the stragglers, picking up little kids, waving encouragement and somehow without words raising spirits and energy. It's not really a surprise. I wish there could still be some awe about it. But these marshalling skills, these little NCOs have been *advanced by circumstance* as the NGOers put it; brutalised by war as the tabloids might put it if one fucking journo actually made the effort to get their quista somewhere nearer than his internet connection back in the city.

I've seen it before. Filmed it all before. If you are a regular viewer – and Dominique assures me that you are plentiful – you will have been glued to your seat when I reported on children conscripted by force into the Tat army and sent to the front-line where they were pushed forward to act as human shields or be little mine-sweepers, go lightly my son. There's loads of eye-witness accounts of life in these youth army camps, one of the main NGOs has taken statements and recorded interviews with boys who managed to get away, escaping usually once they were sent out into the jungle. Some didn't even make it out the camp. Soh Mai told me about a drunk brigade commander who shot two boys while they slept because they did not obey his order to wake up.

Hold on, Soh Mai's whispering in my ear trying to be off camera, of course. Okay. Sure. We've got time. They are taking a rest. Thank fuck. Listen to this. Hold on a minute. Am turning off then on again once I've found the tape, think I still have it.

Tuvol

'Am I wearing you out yet?'

'Why do you say that?'

'Well, there's a lot of important things you have to do here; lives to save, a clinic to run with a skeleton workforce and then you have this grieving foreigner under your feet.'

'Don't worry, the important things are getting done and you're not under my feet, you're in my hammock.'

'I appreciate you letting me stay.'

'Doesn't mean I don't think you should go back. I keep thinking, what about Esta, what about your mum? Always it's Espirit this, Espirit that… Barely a mention?'

'She said not to come.'

'Read beyond the words, Tuvol.'

'What would I do?'

'Christ, you know, help her come to terms with her grief, make her cups of tea, let her know that she can rely on you to take care of her.'

'She can't.'

'Can't what?'

'She can't rely on me to take care of her, Dominique, I barely know how to take care of myself. She'll do just fine. She was encouraged to be self-reliant; everyone in the community was expected to help themselves first, and others second. If I go back now, we will just sit awkwardly opposite each other knowing that we should say something but struggling to say anything at all.'

'So, you should stay here?'

'Why not? A new start.'

'But it's an old beginning. Tried and batik'd, a tropical cliché. You are already not here. Go back. Make peace, maybe even make a future. These people aren't your people.'

Tuvol threw what he had in his hands – a sweaty handkerchief – into the air in what looked to Dominique like a prepared moment of frustration.

'I have seen and heard things I never imagined. I have heard and spoken with some courageous and inspiring people.'

'You've met an ideal. Good for you. You passed a few tests – you came, you cared, you didn't leave. This was of course good. But to be truly useful here you need to have medical skills or a briefcase full of cash or medicines. Good intentions have never been enough here.'

'Nor were they where I'm from. Homes for Peace was not just some emotional whim, a sentimental luxury on Espirit's part. It provided support for young families and mothers who had no where else to turn.'

Dominique took hold of Tuvol's hand – roughly at first so to ease the emotional charge – but then gently, her fingers stroking his, from knuckle to knuckle. Tuvol's eyes went from fright to watchful in a second.

'You see, you know already. I don't think I have heard you defend Espirit before. That's a start, isn't it? Don't get distracted by the exotic. It's a trap; the jungle-is-always-greener kind of thing.'

'It's not the jungle I'm distracted by.'

Dominique smiled and broke off her touch with Tuvol, who persisted.

'I would stay if you asked me to.'

Dominique looked away, past the nurses and volunteer medics scrubbing the floor of the ward, somehow managing to keep a clinical atmosphere intact.

'I don't know how long any of us can stay here. Our security advice is to be on standby to evacuate all non-local staff. The situation now is two levels before actually evacuating. Most of the time we have been told to be on alert but to carry on with our duties with due care, but the government soldiers have already made incursions across the border. The message is that we have been tolerated up until now but the latest government manoeuvres suggest that they don't care about anything we do. If their goal is to eradicate the villages that support or supply the rebels then we are in the way. Why would they want a clinic operating to repair what they want broken?'

The vulnerability of the Clinic had not occurred to Tuvol. He had assumed as fragile and basic as the Clinic was it was at least safe from attack.

'Tuvol, if things get bad, I can't guarantee you will be choppered out of here and taken to safety. My experience of this sort of thing is that it usually comes down to the wire and it's a sure thing that none of us want to pull out unless we really, really have to.'

Tuvol looked around the clinic grounds, Lew Kwin and a few others slowly making their way by, throwing out greetings as they passed clumps of people, shrouded in rice clouds.

'But it isn't just us, right?'

'No. The questions must always be, if we left what would happen to the patients and to the local staff? The patients would rot where they were and the local staff – everyone from the nurses to the porters to the cooks – could be killed or arrested and tortured for information about rebel activity. Local staff would not be seen as aid workers; they would be collaborators.'

Tuvol looked as far into the forest as he could, as though wondering whether the shimmering heat was hiding soldiers camouflaged in green, eyes still, teeth clenched. Without turning back he asked, 'If I went back would you come with me?'

Dominique laughed and stood up, picking up a stack of papers the fan had blown onto the floor.

'I've already had a vacation in the snow, thanks.'

'That's not what I meant.'

'I know it's not what you meant. I am needed here more than ever, and I want to be here. It's what I do. It's as simple as that. Don't complicate it.'

'With desire?'

'With impractical suggestions that are irrelevant to the matter at hand.'

'Which is?'

'Come on. You want to go back but need a way to go back that doesn't seem like you are trickling back home. I have a job to do here and you have grieving to do there. We are at different points in our life.'

Dominique looked down at the pile of papers on her desk.

Tuvol stood up and pushed his hands into his pockets. 'Conversation over?'

Without looking up, Dominique nodded.

'Yes. There's so much to do. See you at dinner.'

But Tuvol's long strides had already taken him out of earshot.

Mae Rot

The silver-haired woman had been sitting there for a long time.

As much as a town could be a crossroads, teeming with people stretched from where they came from to where they were trying to be, this was it. Mae Rot was the knot that tied human sinew together, to produce a collection of people as diverse as they were colourful or dangerous, or filled with sad grace like the old woman beside the road selling a single pomelo, her bare feet slipping out of orange plastic shoes two sizes too big for her. She would look up and see the rush of pick-ups filled with workers from a factory, their clothes stained with oil, cigarettes dangling from their mouths. The children cycling by would wave at her as they went to and from the school that lay off the tarmaced road. The old woman would wave back and smile a gap-toothed smile but then the smile would disappear as an army truck or police van sped by, throwing dust into the air and into her eyes. She would spit out a red stream of betel nut and brush the dirt from the smooth skin of the pomelo and look hard at the cloud disappearing along the road.

Eventually, a foreigner, an NGOer, stopped his bicycle and nodded a hello at her. He didn't know her language but she replied in it anyway. She had seen him before and wondered how his white skin stayed so white in the sun and his clothes so clean in the dirt. She marvelled at his clothes which were without crease, not colourful just beige, but they had been made nicely – she knew because she used to make clothes in a small rented shop in the centre of town. Her business had gone, the landlord imprisoned for something and slowly and sadly she made her way to live by the side of the main road. The foreigner pressed the pomelo, juggled it between his large hands as though trying to decide if it was ripe. It was but she just smiled at him. He asked how much and she held up her fingers. He nodded, juggled it again and then reached into his pocket and pulled out his money. The note was more than she asked but he smiled and while she noticed how perfect his teeth were, he put the pomelo in the bike's basket and rode off.

Lee Paw Hin, which in her language meant Awakening Beauty, gathered up the shawl she used to protect her from the sun, slid her feet into the too big shoes and stood up, shakily, her back curved from all those years making and mending clothes. She turned her back on the road and walked the long walk through homes without walls to a shelter made of tarpaulin, corrugated iron and the odd bit of wood used to support the roof. The battered aluminium pot was already on the stove. Her two sons would be home soon. Her husband was outside working on a broken bike.

When the ragged group stepped with blinking eyes out of the forest, they were linked together, arm in arm, wrapped like Senshita vines but instead of green hooks, their fingers were caked in mud and blood. Sha We's grip to Jel Unw was the strongest because she was the weakest, the pain in her legs making her walk with a limp rhythm, a violent spasm accompanied by a low whimper. Jel Unw eyed the road and carefully pulled everyone to him, keeping the link between them by placing the boys' hands with the younger ones.

'Mae Rot is not far.'

Lynch and Leer barely reacted. They had grown quieter and quieter with each passing day. They hadn't been the only flotsam to float downstream away from the violence. Like torn branches snagged by a rocky outcrop, She We and Nha We clung with tender grip until Lynch and Leer drifted into sight, their reunion muted by pain and shock. With heavy breath they slumped onto the river bank and watched as debris flowed past. Jel Unw saw them twitch and cry, saw them hold each other in silence, their hands remaining linked even when their eyes went to the forest floor. And now they looked at the dust on the ground as though they had lost something! It annoyed Jel Unw. It wasn't where they should be looking. It annoyed Jel Unw who had survived by keeping his eyes open for a gap in the fighting and running to the river with all his sinewy strength. It wasn't where they should be looking.

'If we get to Mae Rot then we can find help. Help for us, help for Sha We and Nha We.'

Leer pushed the wooden gun further up his shoulder, pulling his sweat-covered shirt across his chest. Lynch looked back into the jungle then turned quickly towards Jel Unw making a V sign on his chest. Leer shook his head and spat what saliva he had in his dry mouth. Jel Unw shrugged.

'If he's there I am sure we will find him but, you know…'

Jel Unw had never been known for his subtlety. Lawe had struggled with him more than any other child in the village. He had already grown up by the time Lawe tried to reach him. He was too late. Not for learning, of course, but for nurturing. Lawe used to say to him, 'Let your thoughts guide your actions and not the other way round.'

'…you never know.'

Jel Unw knew this was better unsaid but what did it matter anyway. It wasn't his father. His died on the spot, split apart by a grenade. He thought of the smoldering bodies back in the forest, of the brothers trembling, pissing themselves with fear but still holding their little wooden guns while Verlaine stood behind them. Jel Unw heard his voice and thought the brothers had let their radio loose, the tone of the words was all wrong in any kind of language.

'Now is the time to howl like wolves!'

Lynch and Leer had been only once to Mae Rot, clinging to Verlaine as though afraid they would be caught by the current. The narrow streets they encountered now were the same collision of voice and noise, smells and sights. They held hands and Leer still kept his gun slung over his shoulder, covering it awkwardly with his ragged shirt.

In the market no one paid them any attention. Bodies were pressed against each other, breath from unknown mouths mixing smoke with the smell of decay from the animal body parts littering the stalls. So they would not lose each other they walked in a tight knit column weaving through the throng of women holding and gutting fish. Nha We and Sha We pressed their palms into their ears while Jel Unw kept looking around hoping to see someone he knew. When they stopped for a moment to decide on direction other children holding strings of white lotus flowers or trays of disposable lighters and chewing gum eyed them. They did not belong here. They had the pace of the forest about them.

Verlaine had told them that Mae Rot had once been a village not much bigger than their own but when the government had taken over the country and the Tat had started to take land, the village had become a town filled with displaced people looking for something – a home, security, money, work. It had got even bigger when the foreigners came to help, making rows of shelters, bringing doctors, teachers who lived in new concrete, all the while the shacks and shops of the market getting squeezed into a smaller and smaller place. The life was being suffocated out of the people as their walls closed in.

Jel Unw led them through the market then into quieter streets with their mix of wooden huts and shacks. This seemed an altogether older place; they saw writing they did not recognise over doors and windows; red lanterns with gold leaf paint swinging loosely in the air. These streets were nearly deserted, their inhabitants locked away behind doors with heavy padlocks and high walls with razor wire on top. When someone did pass them by, Jel Unw told them all to hold out their hands and to look into the eyes of the people.

'They will see who we are and what we need. No one will pass you by.'

Of course they did. Some walked by without a glance, others looked then looked away, other children shouted at them, identified them with the forest, darkening their skin with their comments. A few spat at them.

'Stay here. I will know where you are.'

Lynch and Leer looked at him. There was no expression. It seemed to Jel Unw that more than their tongues had been taken away.

Sha We and Nha We held their feverish bodies close to each other.

'I will be back, don't worry. I will find help.'

Leer looked away shrugging his shoulders.

Lynch V'd his chest.

'I know. I will look for Verlaine too. It's better for me to look by myself. I can move more quickly.'

Lynch began to cry and let the V slide up to cover his tears.

Leer turned back and held his brother's hand.

They watched Jel Unw walk up the street, peering down small paths to either side. The town was filled with such paths, dusty in the dry season and streams of mud in the wet. They led to smaller homes built of concrete, blackened and creeping with rising damp. They were mostly shacks however, squeezed into spaces where rubbish was thrown, bamboo poles holding up the plastiks that were angled to drain the rainwater into buckets at each corner.

The four of them huddled by the roadside waiting for someone to stop, to intervene. Darkness made them more invisible as they sunk down on to the road without cover or light or food. So quiet were they, a few times they were cursed for scaring someone who only at the last moment saw their huddled forms, whites of eyes catching the brief glare of a bicycle light in the unlit street. No one stopped. Everyone had somewhere to go and the shadows of those rushing away grew faint by their own light until only the pitch black remained.

In the dark, as the others slept slumped against each other, fitfully reacting to the roar of an occasional moped racing along the street, Leer un-shouldered his gun and laid it on his lap, the smooth wood warm against his skin. He found a small area close to the trigger that had splintered slightly and began to work at it with a flat stone. Lynch stirred beside him, his arms stretching out across his brother's legs. Leer lifted the gun and aimed it down the dark street. There was no one there. Nothing to aim at. He wished there was.

Ruess
Field Notes # 10

We have to move again. Some rest but Verlaine and the boys don't like to stay still too long.

I wasn't there.

Soh Mai is tugging at me as I speak – I know, I know.

I wasn't there, I'm telling you the regular viewer, the one that has paid their subscription to endless bad news. Sorry but you missed the worst. I was absent. A terrible neglect; the worst offence for a witness.

IDPs

Lynch thought it was Verlaine. He saw only shadow and long arms reaching down towards him. He could smell the night air of the forest, hear its screech, the throaty staccato of geckos and his brother snoring beside him. They could both make the sound of a pig and many a waking morning was spent imitating the other's noises from the night before. It brought a smile to Lynch's cracked, dehydrated lips. In sleep he had been resting in the bed Verlaine had made for them, his arms spread out into the dark, all the space he wanted despite his brother shuffling beside him. When he woke up to see a man stretching out his hand, his arms fell with fright into the gutter, a foul smell splashing from the mud on to his skin. Leer woke up with a start and saw the man's other hand had his gun and he snatched it back, leaping to his feet. The man, not old but roughly shaven, his skin battered by weather, one eye glaciered by disease, staggered back slightly as Leer then Lynch howled into his face, a terrible and unexpected sound that sent the man running down the street.

Sha We had woken suddenly too and had started to cry with shock or realisation or pain. Probably all of them. Nha We was quick to comfort her and held her hand as Lynch and Leer stared after the fast disappearing thief.

'It's okay, it's okay, Jel Unw will be here soon then he will take us to… a home, someone's home. A friend. We can…'

Nha We got caught by some kind of memory, the inevitable snare; such were the biting traps that all of them kept stopping mid-word or action; mid-step with a long pause for terrible thoughts. These were not flashbacks but ignitions of the present, a far more flammable substance than the past.

Lynch scraped the street from his skin and made the V sign to Leer. He had already begun to abbreviate the reminder; such was hope and its fading trajectory.

Leer shook his head and turned away. He was tired of the question. It made him feel sick.

Lynch asked about Jel Unw, raising his palm above his head and flexed his strong biceps to indicate Jel Unw's height and strength.

His brother shook his head. He had a bad feeling in his stomach. More than just sickness. More than just hunger.

Lynch got Nha We and Sha We up, dusting the mud and dust from their clothes. A cyclist pedalled by slowly then speeded up when Leer held out his hand. Leer sounded their next move to Lynch and walked his fingers through the air.

'Jel Unw?' Nha We asked looking in the direction he had gone the night before.

The brothers shrugged their shoulders. They had no food, no water left, no money. Nha We was young but old enough to know they could not stay where they were.

When Leer looked back he aimed his gun at the cardboard boxes they had arranged under them. There was nothing to kill that wasn't already dead but it was a way of saying something. He imagined the bullets ripping into the boxes, singeing then burning the flattened cartons. These were the bullets Verlaine wanted to see; the ones he wanted everyone to believe in.

After he stopped shooting, Leer could still hear gunfire.

Nha We whined and Sha We cried as they walked along the empty street.

'I'm hungry.'

'So am I.'

Lynch drew a map in the dust and showed Leer the way back to market.

A few people exercised by the roadside, some rotating like windmills others walking back and forward a short distance, turning robotically on their heels when a certain number of steps had been achieved. As they walked, more people appeared; tired-looking mothers with infants, fathers stoic and stern as they pushed their mobile stalls, bubbling pots making rudimentary kitchens that cooked up endless bowls of noodle soup served hot with knuckles of meat and heaps of weeds and herbs.

Leer kept looking for Jel Unw, Lynch for Verlaine and the young ones just looked at the ground.

Somehow they had taken a wrong turning and were back on the main road again, the sudden roar of a lorry laden with logs shook them and then shrouded them in road dust. They couldn't see for a while but no one moved. Inevitably the dust would clear and they would still be where they were.

'Stand there long enough and you'll be a cloud.'

Lee Paw Hin shouted over the sound of another lorry going by. Her laugh was deep and when they saw her she was beckoning them with her hand.

'Come here! What are you doing out here?'

No parents wanted their children near this road and those without parents stayed around the market. There was nothing here except lorries, dust and old Lee Paw Hin's fruit stall. She had just arrived and she had a good selection of pomelo, oranges, dragon fruit, longtans and some of the small bananas the foreigners liked. They would stop specially and buy up what she had.

She looked at the children in front of her and tch'd. Lynch had a good idea what they must look like – they had washed in the river when it was near the path but that had been some time ago and the mud of the forest, the dirt of the town had layered them. They had woken up wet with dew and now dust was their second skin.

It wasn't such a surprising sight. The market area was swollen with such children separated from parents, clinging to each other, reduced to survival in town, all of them disappearing from view when the army came.

'You've come from the forest.'

Lynch dusted himself down, then Leer, then Nha We and Sha We as though they were on parade.

Lee Paw Hin laughed again.

'It'll take more than that to get this dust off. I know. I don't remember how long I've sat here for but long enough to not even see the dust anymore. It's red because of the earth being dug up for the mine. Don't know what they're looking for but whatever it is they find a lot. These lorries come by every few minutes, every day, every week. Oh, you get used to it alright.'

She spread out an old rug she had rolled up for a pillow, to sleep under her lean-to when it was lunchtime. As busy a town as it was, Mae Rot still slumped into an exhausted crumple at midday.

'Here, sit down.'

Lee Paw Hin looked at the two youngest, noticing Sha We's leg wound.

'Bananas. That's what you need. And here's some water for you. Careful though. Slowly. It's not good to fill yourself too quickly.'

She scrutinised the brothers, looking at their cuts and scratches, watching their eyes that refused to stay still. She noticed how much they looked at each other, noticed that there was nothing said, just nods and glances and she noticed their flinch when an old truck backfired. All of them seemed to be shaking.

'You all from the same family?'

'No.' Nha We smiled at her. 'Thank you for this fruit.'

'Ah, you can talk.'

'My sister is ill.'

Lee Paw Hin nodded. 'I can see.'

'She has a fever. '

Lynch stroked her feverish skin. Nha We continued. 'It's her legs, they were hurt when we were attacked.'

'Looks like it has gone to her head.'

'She needs help.'

'What are your names?'

'Yes. I'm Nha We, this is my sister Sha We. These are the brothers Lynch and Leer. They are famous.'

Lynch glared at Nha We. 'Sssh.'

Lee Paw Hin looked at the boys again. 'Really. Famous for what?'

'Ssh.'

Leer this time glared at Nha We.

'Nothing.'

His sister was looking at them all.

'They helped us. They helped everybody.'

'Well, that's good. Not enough people helping other people these days.'

It was truer than these children knew, Lee Paw Hin thought. She'd heard her husband's friends talk of villagers invading their town, of the dark-skinned farmers getting drunk in the market and fighting with locals over money and women. And more. She hated the talk, everyone was so quick to forget their neighbours, to draw lines between them which no one could cross. She hated these desperate divisions even more than she hated the soldiers who sped by in their trucks, whistling at her, throwing cigarette butts at her, hoping to burn her or set her rug alight. And even when they stopped they would pick the best fruit and refuse to pay, getting back on their truck and throwing the peeled skin back to her stall.

She hated the talk because she had come out of the forest herself when she was younger even than these children and her father and mother had somehow brought her up, fed and clothed her even though they died young and left her with nothing more than they had. She never complained; she felt lucky and slapped her husband a few times when he got leery and offensive towards anyone less fortunate. 'You are just afraid of being in their place,' she told him. If someone asks for help then you should give but even if they don't you should offer. This is what she believed.

'So what makes you special, brothers?' She smiled at Lynch and Leer who did not know what to do. 'Come here.'

She beckoned Lynch with her hand. He let go of his brother's hand reluctantly. 'It's okay.'

She gently pulled Lynch's head towards her. Leer twitched and stepped forward, his hands going to his wooden gun.

Lee Paw Hin noticed and smiled.

'It's okay. I want to see if…'

She prised open Lynch's mouth who began to cry softly either with pain or fright or memory. 'The spirits took away your tongues?'

Lynch shrugged and Leer looked away.

'They were born like that,' Nha We said

'No one knows why,' Sha We said.

Lee Paw Hin nodded. 'This can happen when people don't want the truth to be told.'

She cleared a space on the ground.

'You can draw?' she asked Leer who shook his head and pointed to his brother.

'So, Lynch? Draw me what happened to you.'

While he drew, Lee Paw Hin served a local woman who gave the children a wide berth and a dirty look. She made sure she threw her change back at her.

'I see. I understand.'

She looked away from the drawings and up and down the road.

'It's not safe here for any of you but for you two especially. The army won't care that someone took your tongues, it doesn't matter to them that you can't speak only that you can listen. If they see you they will take you. You have age enough to carry more than a wooden gun. I have seen it.'

Lynch was not there suddenly. He felt the thump of the man landing in their village. Then another thump, another body and this time it was Jel Unw. He couldn't stop it. Lynch squeezed his eyes tight shut.

'Here, rest under here for a while and I will see what I can do.'

Under the musky blanket Leer held the sleeping Sha We and Lynch tried to get Nha We to eat some fruit. He was so thin, skin translucent and pale on his small frame but he would not eat. It made him sick. Lynch shook his head and wondered how this could be. When they were younger Verlaine would always laugh at them.

'You eat like there was more than one of you. You eat for your brother and he eats for you. Will there be enough food in this village for you?'

He wrote his father's name in the dust. Thought for a moment and then added Jel Unw.

They sat up from sleep, past the midday sun, a confused, stretching line of skin and bone.

Lynch was looking up at the sky wondering if he could hear a plane; Leer was looking down the long road thinking he could see Jel Unw running with a gun; Nha We sobbed quietly still in sleep with a dream that clung on and Sha We was feverish, holding her leg which was dark and swollen.

Lee Paw Hin tch'd as she gave them water.

'You are all too thin.'

It was true they had all lost weight they could not afford to lose and Lynch was closer to Leer now, his ribs sticking out, his face angular, his cheeks deflated.

'Come here.'

She gathered them to her, the brothers standing tall as she perched on her plastic stool. She smiled at them.

'I wish I could help you. You brothers are just like my two sons when they were your age. And little Sha We could have been me when I was growing up here, same hair and smile when you can see it, eh?'

Lee Paw Hin touched Sha We's face. Turning to the brothers, she spoke quietly but seriously.

'Your sister is very sick. She needs help and I have nothing to help her with. I have no medicine, no money to give and this blanket is no kind of shelter for children. I would say that sooner or later something bad would happen but then it already has. You must go to the Clinic run by the foreigners. It is in the forest and it is a long way. It is, I am sorry to say, also dangerous. The army is there and when they are not they leave bombs in the ground for all to step on. It doesn't matter how young or light you are; step on it and it will be your last step.'

The brothers' eyes widened.

Lee Paw Hin continued, 'You can use this. It will help carry the young ones and save your strength for each other.'

The woman creakily raised herself from the stool and led them towards them an old market trolley with a wide flat base and three wheels.

Leer smiled quickly, immediately seeing its use.

'I use it for my fruit but I can make do without it for a few days – those lazy sons of mine can help for a change – and when you reach the Clinic just tell someone… Just write down my name or draw me where I am and someone will be able to bring it back. They know me, the foreigners. Lee Paw Hin. Best fruit, best prices, that's what I say, that's the truth!'

She laughed loudly and then noticed that she had two customers.

'See! I will draw you a map, Lynch, and then you must keep this notebook and pencil.'

Lynch opened his palms and looked at her.

One of customers looked at him curiously, a young woman holding a child wrapped tightly against the sun, its eyes glistening with cataracts.

'You draw so beautifully but the mud is no place to draw. You make something and then it disappears because the wind or rain or someone's foot rubs it off. There is too much of that. You draw something in here that you want and it will stay.'

Ruess
Field Notes # 11

This is how it was. This is flashback. This is penance and hell. Is the camera on? Okay. Everybody, from the skinny kids who kicked at my heels the whole time I was there, pinching me to see if I was real and then running away squawking with laughter to the gap-tooth old women of the village who sat with their grandchildren on their knees somehow cooking and cleaning all at the same time, made me feel welcome. Not everyone wants a camera shoved in their faces and I've learned not to hold it like a weapon, ready, just in case, to shoot. For me, the camera is the last thing to come out in these situations. Voice and eye contact is crucial and although jungle villages operate pretty similarly there is nothing to be jaded about and everything to be enthralled by. Don't forget, viewer, I know whose side I'm on. I pity those who don't.

Soh Mai's as precious as the chunk of jade he keeps round his neck for good luck. Dominique's used him at the Clinic as an interpreter and go-between and I've kinda poached him. Here's some background on someone who wants to stay in it. Dominique can't pay him too much and he's got a wife and kids who are pretty breadline, so I pay him more and he goes freelance with me but every few weeks making the long journey back to Mae Rot. Without Soh Mai easing the way I would never have been able to stay in the village.

The forest of things. Silva Rerum. I understand that. Have I mentioned that? Waking up in the village, hearing the stirrings of the adults, the clatter of pots, the growing chatter, the scattering of children tumbling out of the huts, the smell of wood smoke, the dew heavy in the air. Man, you cut it all with a knife and slice up some atmosphere. There was no need to put on the camera straight away. It was enough to soak up a way of life and get a sense of their relationships with each other, which are always more complicated than first appears. It takes time to listen. It takes time to learn enough to ask the right questions.

This isn't just background. It's more than. This is a village that is no longer and this old footage has taken on a different meaning. It has sights and sounds that have been burned to the ground and only memory can bring them back; memory and this digital flicker. This is the sequence. It has to be told now because I wasn't there, so cut me some... never mind.

Soh Mai went back to see his family in Mae Rot and I went with him. I love-hate the place, its self-styled Wild West status of smuggling, muling and the whole caboodle of illicit stuff that goes on when there are borders. I should whisper this in case some gangster climbs down from the tree and machetes my head. I mean come on! It's exciting, depressing and intimidating but mostly there is just a lot of poverty and people who would rather be somewhere else. I've got footage and maybe I'll do a rough guide, show you the sights. *Here in the forest, youthful, adventure reporter Ruess Le Beau follows the lives of native peoples as they go about their daily...*

Maybe not.

Where the hell was I? This is going audio. There is nothing to see except me. In recall, in regret.

Soh Mai curled up with his family and I checked into a hotel, charged my batteries both soul and lithium, took a needed shower and slept on a bed of fleas. In the morning I looked around for stuff for the kids in the village. On our way back, Soh Mai took advice from some rebel soldiers who had stopped at a village that had been renamed the Village of the Widows since all the men had either been killed or were being used by the Tat to bring supplies to a new road they were carving into the jungle north of Mae Rot, kindly funded by friendly foreigners. None of this was very far from our path back and Soh Mai cautioned about our return. 'It could be dangerous for you, for both of us.' The rebel soldiers agreed with him and offered to accompany us.

I have seen before and after but not during. That is the failure, dear viewer, of my witnessing. I cannot emphasise this more. I should have been there. On the forest path not far from the village we could smell the cinders in the air, and see them as we drew closer. The soldiers were twitchy and went ahead, scouting for signs that the Tat were nearby. We hung back, both of us as silent as the forest for all its buzzing and cawing had stopped and it was as if all of us, human and plant, were waiting, baited, trapped by the silence of expectation. Soh Mai wouldn't look at me and I couldn't look at him; anticipation tempts fate and neither of us wanted to betray hope with dread that the worse must have happened.

The cinders that fell, the thin flakes, were not of foliage but of charred skin, the brittle, blackened fall of the burned.

Ever wondered what horrors befall a village of innocent, unarmed people when attacked by a zealous, drugged army of boy soldiers and hardened psychopaths?

I can't remember how long we waited but long enough for the light to change from dim to dusk and when eventually the rebel soldiers came back there was just enough light to see how ashen their young faces had become; their eyes were fixed in a horrified stare not on us but on things already seen, still being witnessed, a repeating reel of the death of a village.

There was nothing of the soldier about those boys then, just an overwhelming, defeated sadness.

In the Forest Again

It was a long, hot walk. The brothers pushed the younger ones on the trolley, a bumpy ride but it was easier for them all and the brothers took it in turn to push them as old trucks passed them by, their drivers looking down at them but not stopping. They kept an eye out for army vehicles but saw none. They were walking so slowly that other walkers passed them usually with something to say. Leer kicked the dusty ground when yet another man reeking of Kasheen shook his wild-hair head and could not stop a laugh that erupted when he took in the sight of the forlorn group. 'What's this? Are you puppets, lost without their string?'

Each time they passed with their laughter and swearing, Leer took his wooden gun from his shoulder and fired into the back of a head. He had already seen how a bullet looked when it came out of a head and this was no different. He did not wait to watch the body fall but still he could see the bullet, its hot, gory trail punching through the air then falling to the ground. They didn't laugh anymore as he breathed in the smoke from his gun.

Lee Paw Hin had told the brothers, 'The spirits may have taken your tongues but you are still here and these two need you; without you they will not survive.'

When someone fell in the village someone would be there to clean the wound, brush away the dirt, to reassure, to help them to their feet. There was knowledge that the forest could heal with leaf and sap. The boys had known only care and this was first disrupted by the violence of the army and now by the indifference of Mae Rot. Leer howled as only he could and a few passers-by smirked as though this was just another ploy to get money.

Lynch knew better and hugged his brother as much as he could. Sweat ran from one's arm to the other's shoulder.

Sha We sat on the trolley trembling as though wired to a motor and the wounds on her legs bled new blood through the crusts of blackened scabs.

The sun had already sunk below the tree line when they reached the path that led in to the forest. Lynch checked Lee Paw Hin's map again and smiled as they entered the twilight, the dark green wrapped around them leaving the yellow dusk of the road behind them. This was not where they were from but they understood where they were. It was too far from the Clinic so they found a place to rest and drink from the bottle of water Lee Paw Hin had given them along with the last of her bananas.

They had hugged her when they left and she had smiled through tears.

'When the trolley comes back I will be happy.'

The brothers knew what she meant. When something goes the worse part is waiting for it to return.

Both Nha We and Sha We slept better than they had for a while. Lynch drew sketches of them, of the village, line drawings of their home, of Verlaine standing on the porch, of Leer jumping up, trying to catch a branch to swing from while Salva sat on the steps and watched. Even though there were plenty of pages in the notebook, he wasted nothing; he drew a forlorn Nha We on the steps with Sha We squeezed in beside Verlaine's legs, he drew himself side by side with his brother, their heads turning different ways, back and forward, then and now. The scenes shimmered beside each other and Lynch did not stop at the figures but drew the background of both village and forest, making alive the trees and vines that surrounded them.

In Leer's silence there were no pictures, just violent sparks of cries and shouts and gunfire. The grip on his gun never loosened even when, eventually, sleep slumped them against each other, their heads not touching the ground.

The explosion happened at dawn. The bright flash of light against Lynch and Leer's closed eyes could not have been the sun in the dark of the forest. There was only a brief moment of confusion as they came from sleep to waking; only a brief glance to a startled Sha We and an absent Nha We. Even in the half light of dawn it was not difficult to see the small plume of smoke coming from 10 or 15 metres away, where the slight clearing they had found ended and the thick forest began. They both got up and sniffed the air, its cordite scent mixed with something else. A ruptured dawn.

'Nha We?'

This was how they were. This is what they had become. They knew to expect what they shouldn't have experienced; they saw what they shouldn't have imagined. In the forest you had to be careful where you walked, the ground held no safety anymore, and the earth was not what it seemed. It used to be bites and stings they had to be careful of. There were no longer crops to be damaged but bodies to be ripped apart. The brothers, stepping carefully as far as the path would take them and not a step further, saw what Nha We had done. Whether with eyes open or shut, he had walked off the path and through the bamboo. They could not see him on the ground. Whatever had exploded had thrown him away. But not everything. Looking up they saw his small hands still gripping a branch. His arms had gone with the rest of him but steady drops of blood dripped on to the ground.

Tuvol

Lew Kwin was crouched on the ground, his body leaning forward and his pencil pressing onto the paper, thin and lined like children use at school. It was all there was but it didn't matter; as if the quality of paper mattered. Some of the bravest words he had ever read were printed on translucent newspaper but not now. He rarely saw newspapers now and when he did there were no names he recognised and no stories that had any truth. The government could say what they wanted. Lew Kwin had used their news to light fires, but his skin crawled at the sight of the paper burning, words curling then bleeding their black ink into the mud. Sickened, he vowed not to burn words but write them.

'Mr Tuvol, Mr Tuvol!'

'Just Tuvol, Lew Kwin, just simple Tuvol.'

'Ah,' Lew Kwin smiled, 'but it's never just simple for you foreigners. It's usually just complicated.'

Tuvol laughed and sat down at Lew Kwin's tarpaulin'd home. 'But not me. Enough of me. How are you?'

'I have started to write again.'

'That's great. What are you writing?'

'What I can only write about. This place. What is happening here, why it is happening.'

'I can imagine you have a lot to say. You've been here nearly as long as the Clinic.'

'I am burning with things to say. The words are on fire when they leave my pencil!'

'Who will read what you have written?'

Lew Kwin sighed and poured the iced tea for them both from his plastic jug. 'This is the problem. In the city at the newspaper we had machines and we had paper then people to distribute. There is nothing in this jungle except mosquitos and pain. And mud. I have come back in time by coming here.'

'So what will you do? Maybe you could photocopy, from Dominique?'

Lew Kwin shook his head sadly. 'The machine has rotted in this jungle. It hasn't worked for a long time. No, Mr Tuvol, I must write out my words over and over again; I have plenty of exercise books and I have plenty of time, do I not? I am not going anywhere. I have nowhere to go.'

'That's a lot of writing.'

Lew Kwin laughed. 'Maybe my hand will fall off like my legs! Everyone should read about what people do here, how they help, how they hurt. I love writing. It's what I do.'

Tuvol found Then Khin in the same place he had left him. His burns had been treated and his damaged skin looked stretched and silvery, pores and contours eradicated by the fire so much that if he smiled when Tuvol arrived it wasn't with his mouth. Tuvol held his gaze, trying to gauge how he was feeling.

Recovery.

'You still here? That is good. The doctors help me and say I live.'

Tuvol noticed that there was no intonation of joy or relief in his voice.

'I'm glad you are better.'

'But I look bad, yeah? I scare the children. To be burned like this is bad luck – it is how you say with no fortune. I have an ugly face.'

'They did not burn your spirit, Then Khin. You still have that.'

Then Khin nodded and closed his singed eyelids for a moment.

Tuvol had found the right words to say at the right moment and to the right person. He could have punched the air, high fived a tree. It may seem strange even egotistical for Tuvol to celebrate that but Espirit's eloquence had made Tuvol feel like a verbal klutz. Tuvol was known to limp through conversations and his father would often hijack his sentences, finishing them off brusquely. But not with Dominique, not here in the forest and not with Lew Kwin and Then Khin.

Tuvol wandered around the perimeter of the compound nodding at the nods of recognition from the families camped under their plastiks and making sure he replied to each high pitch HELLO from the kids. Nothing, of course, had changed while he'd been locked in grief. He understood this. The change in circumstance was new only to him.

Anyone could see that Tuvol had arrived at a crossroads. He was aware that he had stalled when others would rev. And now he wanted to kickstart the machine.

Ruess
Field Notes # 12

Look at them! It has to be seen to be believed that these are the same boys who lazed around their father's hut; idling, joking and talking back to anyone and everyone. Soh Mai has heard people say the boys have been possessed by spirits; that this new found energy is that of dead soldiers still wanting to fight; a powerful force channelled from beyond by their mother herself. They cannot fight, so Soh Mai hears, because they have not let the blood of their enemy. Let? Is that the verb? Seems such strange permission when it often results in death.

As twins they are fraternal, being neither identical nor even alike in body or in character apart from their inability or unwillingness to speak. I'm not sure about that either – there's more wild rumours, Soh Mai tells me, about their silence, like their voice was taken by a spirit and used to fan some hot deities; a wild beast snatched their tongues from their cradle and ran into the forest speaking in… Sorry, I get on my facetious horse and get carried away. Soh Mai darkened and said a few thought their mother had bitten off their tongues at birth.

I don't know much about any of that but faith in anything seems pretty crunched at the moment. It's like they say, those who kneel and pray are the first to get killed in the stampede. But what do I know? The boys look like boys but with an edge that something or someone has given them, that's for sure.

Dominique

She did not notice them at first. She was on the phone to the Organisation's security consultant, an ex-something who Dominique never really wanted to speak to. In her experience these well-paid security consultants were always ex-something – marine, commando, human being – all the solid macho words and worlds which they had now left due to either paunch or fear to become an expert in somebody else's war. Wayne, as he was probably called, updated her daily on security concerns for her part of the country and this was progressively less good as the security level teetered on the get-the-hell-out level, as Wayne so diplomatically put it.

'It's as bad as I have seen. There seems to be a major push on and the border is porous. It doesn't matter so much which side you are on but your proximity to it.'

'Okay.'

There was nothing else to say. This was not news. It was being delivered with more urgency than usual but it was, as the kids liked to say, same same.

She held the phone for a moment in mid-air as she watched new arrivals – always a sad scene tempered by relief that they had actually made it – but this time, the nurses rushed to help a young girl who had collapsed in front of the Clinic doors as she was released from the grasp of two older boys. There was obviously a lot of relief in their arrival and they hugged each other and held on, locked, until nurses gently prised them apart to check for injuries.

'Where are they from?'

Dominique stood at the door and asked Mul Wa, an experienced nurse from Mae Rot who had given up her job in a private hospital to devote time and expertise to the care of IDPs.

'I don't know, they won't answer.'

A nurse had guided the boys to the plastic stools in what amounted to a waiting room.

Mul Wa shook her head and opened her palms to the sky.

'It is getting so bad now that only the children come.'

Dominique nodded.

'They are lucky to have reached us. No injuries?'

'Not a scratch.'

She smiled every time she heard Mul Wa use that expression. When the nurse went over to sit beside the boys, Dominique hung back. Those were always Ruess's words when he came back from

173

the jungle and she insisted that Mul Wa take a look at him. Ruess for all his dedication was notorious for neglecting his own health and Dominique wouldn't stand for it.

Dominique had to either accept his disappearance as confirmation of his death or hang on waiting to hear news. The waiting to hear was routine when it came to Ruess but it was not clinical. They had been intimate; she had felt him from all angles, his sweat mixing with her own, and it had counted for something; when he drifted back into the forest her emotions were still flexed with desire. She was not ready to mourn him yet.

Dominique stepped out of her office to introduce herself to the boys, as she liked to do with all the patients. She was struck not by their size, for they were both small, nor by how thin they were, for bone and muscle could be seen through skin but these boys' eyes were still sharp with intensity, still wide and clear despite being on the run. When she shook their hands, they held her stare longer than they limply gripped her. Aggressive, wary, vulnerable all in an unblinking thrall and the effect was mesmerising. They were synchronised. When they turned to look around at the compound they did so in unison and when they heard Sha We call out from inside the Clinic their heads jerked towards the sound.

Dominique reassured them and a nurse translated for her.

'We will look after your sister. She is very sick but we will try.'

Lynch nodded. Leer stared back out of the small room, which had been sparsely furnished with red plastic chairs and a red plastic table.

Dominique fetched some biscuits from her office that she kept for the children when they came, while they waited often for hours to know if a mother or father had survived. The boys nodded and smiled and ate the biscuits quickly, licking the sugary crumbs off their fingers with loud smacks. One of the nurses asked them where they had come from but Lynch turned away and Leer pointed towards the jungle, in the direction they had come from. She asked them if there had been anyone else with them. They looked at each other and both shook their heads looking at the nurse directly, holding her stare until she looked away then at Dominique, who could feel the strange string attached to all their looks, their meaning tangled in the woven air.

'I will see how your sister is.'

Dominique left them with the remaining biscuits and asked the nurse to keep an eye on them. Silence was not unusual especially with children but they were at least communicating and not frozen by their experiences. Mul Wa looked back at the boys who were pretending to fight over the last biscuit. They behaved as any children would do but Mul Wa rolled her eyes a little and tapped her head.

'They are damaged in the head.'

It was neither a kind nor a medical definition. Mul Wa could be right but Dominique knew it was too early to tell.

Lynch and Leer

It was a strange moment for such a game. Verlaine would watch them clapping their right to left, left to right, two hands to two hands in some kind of rhythm and get dizzy watching the speed of it. The tempo would change down sometimes so that their hands moved as though through glue but still with rhythm then with a yelp it would gear up and suddenly they were like a blur, trails of fingers, imprints of palms in the thick humid air.

It was a playground game that all the children played but none like the brothers. For them it was conversation, hand-to-hand competition that was their vocal sparring, the challenge and delight of conversation.

The village setting had been changed to the dried earth of the Clinic grounds and nurses stopped mid-suture to watch the brothers.

'Surely they must be exhausted,' Dominique commented.

'This energy, Miss Dominique,' Mul Wa spoke softly even though the boys could not have heard above their hand claps, 'comes from their spirit not from their body.'

For Lynch and Leer, each slap of their skin took an image away, a boo to the ghosts.

There was nothing else to communicate. The last of their energy had carried the whimpering Sha We until medics at the Clinic saw them at the gate and rushed to help. The nurses' soothing words were the first they had heard since leaving Lee Paw Hin, and while Lynch was relieved to pass the unconscious Sha We to a medic, Leer stood with the last of Jel Unw's cheroots hanging in his mouth and suspiciously took in the compound, taking in too the white skinned foreigner smiling at him, keeping his gun pressed to his side under his shirt. He would still need it.

Lynch smiled at the medics until Leer punched his arm, his way of getting his brother to face him.

Leer shifted his eyes left and right and then pointed back to the jungle path they had just come from. Lynch shook his head, pointing to the ground, first holding clasped palms between them then hugging his brother, holding as he would hold a branch that lay across a swollen and turbulent river.

Dominique

'So how do I say this?' Mul Wa shrugged wearily.

'Like all the other times?'

'This is not like all the other times.'

Dominique nodded.

Mul Wa gently touched the shrouded body, blood stains already blossoming on the white cotton.

'There is more of everything. Sadness, anger, it like Mr Ruess said, it the "What the hell factor."'

Dominique had to smile at that. Ruess had offered to give a lecture to all the Clinic staff about his experiences in the field and as soon as he started she realised she should have known better. In a 30 minute presentation he managed to scare the expats to the point of resignation and the local workers to the point of revolution. Of course he didn't *mean* to upset his audience but foreigners with little experience need to be handled carefully and eye witness accounts need to be diluted when there are relatives in the audience. It was the language of tact that Ruess didn't speak.

It was usual that Dominique didn't need Mul Wa for the immediate delivery of bad news. There was a language barrier between the expat doctors and nurses, not an intelligence barrier, and relatives watched keenly every moment of the process from triage to treatment, from calm attention to frantic last movements. Words were often not the first communication. It had already been done with the body, a defeated stance, the sad expression in the eyes. The cliché for all expats was that you could never get used to moments like these when the truth was that you could. The heart was either hardened to protect itself or the mind got oblique, taking a detour from direct emotion and biding its time with worldly statistics or spiritual metaphors. Ruess was a master of this. He dripped with tears and sweat when he reported an atrocity to the outside world but Dominique had seen him brush the dried gristle of unknown body parts from his boots as he reached for his drink, his conversation hard and fast on the suffering of the people who had spattered his clothes.

When Dominique walked into the waiting room the boys were already looking at her, their hands joined, their eyes locked on her steps towards them. She tried to keep her expression neutral but with Mul Wa beside her, it was difficult to achieve. Lynch turned his head away from Dominique and looked at his brother, facing the palms of his hands downwards and moving them outwards as though he was flattening something. Leer watched the hands, looked up first at Lynch then at Dominique and finally at Mul Wa. No one had said a word and the loudest noise in the room at that moment was the sound of those still alive, moaning in recovery, the whirring overhead fans and the more distant games being played by children.

Leer broke the near silence with his howl. Lynch did not or could not stop him, his head sinking into his hands and his shoulders caving in. He went from half man to young child in an instant, over-burden suddenly pummeling his thin body closer to the ground. He fell off the chair as though punched hard and as both Dominique and Mul Wa went to his aid, Leer kicked his little red plastic chair high into the air and ran out of the waiting room.

Ruess
Field Notes # 13

Did someone say magic?

"They just stood there. They had a shield around them. The spirits made them a shield and no bullet could touch them… their tongues turned black… they had the strength of ten men… they protected not just themselves but many of us… we are so tired of running and these brothers have told us to stop running… Verlaine will bring help and the boys…"

Okay, let's pause that. You thought you'd tuned into the show, 'Let's

See How The Cookie Crumbles.' Maybe you have and I'm all that's left of who I was but sure thing I've never experienced anything like it. Usually in the jungle, in the thick, skin gouging scrub it can be difficult to get people to talk about what has happened and I try not to be that idiot journo who asks the defoliated kid, the napalm-tanned, shock-ridden jelly they are interviewing, *how are you feeling right now…?* You give me people and they will talk; ask the right questions that offer some sense of empathy, implicit in the wording or just some honest to goodness sympathy, all of that has some value if you want to hear people's stories of what they have been through, of how they survived. The villagers who have already seen me in their midst have got used to me and thanks to Soh Mai have understood why I was with them.

Sorry if I sound tired but there's not been much sleep. When we finally caught up with the villagers they didn't rush to tell me of the horror and violence that had ripped through their village on a rain-drenched dawn. They wanted to say how the brothers had walked through the village gathering people as they went; urging them to safety, protecting them as they rushed into the jungle, bullets ricocheting off burning huts and the trunks of the ancient Yurla trees.

It was unbelievable. There was a queue. That's these people for you. I was expecting them to be furious with me, for absconding at their time of need; for bringing them bad fortune by leaving the village to go to Mae Rot with Soh Mai. It was his expectation too, "The villagers may not be happy to see us, Mr Ruess, they may think that we must have known something bad was going to happen, and that by thinking that and leaving we caused it to happen. Not all will think that, the older ones for sure but not everyone. I don't know how they will feel. I don't know I feel."

But it wasn't like that. We set up camp and they turned the camera on themselves. Here's more.

"They weaved through the smoke, their bodies like snakes… Some soldiers had machetes and the blades would bounce off their shoulders…"

Soh Mai was breathless with both their energy and the rush to translate.

The brothers were not at the centre of this crowd of enthusiastic survivors. I remember them sitting a little away. When I could I took the camera to them since they wouldn't come to me. They wouldn't talk to me. For the first time, they shook their heads and turned away from the lens. These were the same brothers who had been natural performers, for the villagers and for the camera, never flinching when I flicked on record.

One of the boys, the rough-tough one called Jel Unw, sitting beside the brothers got up and said quietly to Soh Mai, 'Mr Ruess cannot talk to the brothers at the moment. They need to rest. They need to gather their strength in case the army finds us again. Now is not the time for talking.'

It may look quiet now but under the ashes there is a fire.

Stand Off

Tuvol was jolted out of his bereaved state by the sight of a furious young boy running towards him.

Lew Kwin was looking at his writing. He didn't like it and he was embarrassed that he had got so excited and talked about it to not just Tuvol but to Dominique and anyone who would listen. It needed work. He shivered when the scream came from the other side of the compound.

Dominique did not catch Lynch before he hit the bamboo floor but she did, along with Mul Wa, manage to scoop him up so that his body writhed in her lap and his head in Mul Wa's. Dominique had seen what shock and grief and all the horror could do to children. There would be arm swinging, leg kicking anger. There would be crying. There would be extended silence. One moment light and the next dark. Moods could swing in such children with unseen stimulus. The nurses would squeeze these children with endless hugs until their bodies had no air left in them but there was nothing for their minds; short of narcotically entombing them, they were left to process the delayed horror of memory.

'You're okay, everything is all right, you are safe and sound. No one will hurt you.'

She tried not to think of Wayne's dire predictions.

Lynch was squirming so much it was hard for the two women to keep control of him. As he struggled they felt the nudge of his sharp bones dig into them but there was that strength that can be gathered in times of distress and Dominique knew she would have to hold on for a while with all of her own strength until fatigue set in. Meanwhile other staff came to see what the commotion was and they were just in time to see Leer cascade back along the path, his arms wind-milling as though he was determined to destroy everything in his path.

A patient recovering from eye surgery but with one eye working perfectly well, watched from outside the waiting room, her bandaged head shaking slowly.

'These are the boys, Miss Dominique.'

Dominique found it hard to turn round without losing her grip on the wrestling Lynch. She did not want him loose like his brother; who knew what damage they could do to themselves or others.

'What about them?'

'They are the ones. They are the ones who have the spirits in them. From a village in the forest. They fight the army with their hands. They fight them with air. It's them Miss Dominique. Trouble will follow Miss Dominique.'

Lynch was certainly a handful, Dominique conceded, but this was a tantrum not a possession. Given time he would exhaust himself.

'She's right,' another patient said, a reed thin woman with a sleeping baby slung across her chest. 'These are the boys who have no words. Their tongues were taken from them at birth.'

She heard Leer's howl again and she shivered.

Leer slowed down as he neared the compound exit. His wooden gun was in his hands now and when he looked sideways he could see people shrinking back under their plastiks while ahead of him the two guards at the compound gate came out from under their tattered umbrella. When they reached for their old rifles – discards from old Tat weaponry and most likely bought in Mae Rot – Leer stopped mid-step and shouldered his weapon, spinning 360 degrees before aiming forward, his eyes squinting shut.

This was how Verlaine had wanted him to be. He would have been proud if he were here, if he had been there, in the forest; if he had stuck round for long enough to see the bullets fly from a carved wooden gun. This wood was special so everybody had said, they praised its texture, its weight and its strength and though Leer's crude carving was far from good craftsmanship everybody standing around at the camp said it looked great, like the real thing.

'It *is* the real thing,' Verlaine had told them. 'It is more real than our pangas, our bamboo spears. This gun has bullets that can pass through ten bodies; bullets that cannot miss.'

Leer felt the paint on his face as though it was still there, caked and dried from the moment Verlaine had daubed it on. It hadn't been just them, he had gathered all the children together and used Lawe's school paints to graffiti their skin with red and black stripes. Verlaine watched and nodded approval as the paint transformed them. Others were not so sure and quietly questioned this encouragement. They were just children, after all.

Verlaine was dismissive of any dissent. 'Run then,' he told them, 'run into the forest.'

He told the villagers that the soldiers will never have seen such a sight, that they will be disorientated by fight back, by their bodies being suddenly filled with bullets they had neither seen nor heard.

'We have been driven from our village and if they treat us as rebels then we shall rebel.'

Leer recalled the smell of Lawe's paint and as he striped mud from the compound ground on to his face; he could still smell the burn from colours that were not supposed to be on skin.

'The red is for our anger, the black is for their hearts.'

Verlaine had assembled his modern primitives, their faded and torn Coca-Cola T-shirts and fifth-hand swimming shorts and paraded them as though for the foreigner's camera, an excited group on a mound in the forest on the eve of battle. The paint excited all of the children while the wooden guns in Lynch and Leer's arms made them feel proud and strong; willing, as Verlaine urged them to stand firm.

The adults sat down and laid their pangas and bamboo spears on the ground. They watched the children thriving on this camouflaged energy and were fearful not of them but for them. They sat and watched their fate develop.

The ill and the well all watched Leer's movements as he striped and crossed himself, from his face down his neck to bony chest. The thick mud around his eyes deepened their colour, sunk their hazel ovals deeper into his skull.

He looked around the compound and saw no one he knew. Everybody was somewhere else. He was the only one here.

The guards weren't sure what to do or who this boy was or why he was behaving violently, but they had been trained by old-hand rebels and held on to their guns, keeping their aim on the agitated movements of the boy. The guns were old enough for the safety catch release to sound like a shot.

A loud, breathless voice punched into the quietened compound.

'Please. No. Don't shoot. He's frightened. Just scared.'

The guards didn't react.

Tuvol was surprised to hear his voice sounding calm as though he was trained in mediating. One moment he was in the forest caught up in himself and the next he was thrust into the present, the glare of danger challenging him not to cower.

After quickly flicking his head left then right he held the eyes of the runaway boy and smiled, remaining still but gradually softening both his mouth and his stance. He used only gesture. He thought the boy would not understand his words. He slowly reduced his height, no quick movements just a slow screwing into the ground. He knew how ridiculously tall he was to these people and he had got used to being on his knees. He opened his hands, palm upwards. It seemed the most open gesture to make.

He looked directly at the thin, mud-caked boy, vibrating with energy, taut with anger or fear or both. He smiled as though apologising but it was still broad and warm.

Leer didn't smile back. He turned his aim from the guards to Tuvol.

Tuvol did not move but waited. He could feel the heat of the day on his head and face but he would not move.

Nothing was said.

Leer's sweat became cold on his skin. Was this the army? There was no uniform. The army was here again? They had followed them to this place and Sha We? Poor Sha We. Here was another face to be strung up in front of him bobbing with the branches in the wind, hanging like bloody fruit on the Hurpla tree. This was all he could see. Static expressions caught between life and death. And Verlaine.

Verlaine shouted in his ear, 'You don't need a gun, *you* are the weapon.'

Sha We shuddered in his ear, 'Soldiers like this killed me.'

Nha We placed a bloody hand around his mouth, letting his finger hold the stub of Leer's tongue.

Leer screamed. A shrill cry that resonated through a compound used to terrible sounds.

He tried to keep his aim on Tuvol but his gun was shaking now.

Verlaine levelled his face with the boy's aim.

'You have special gifts, those in the village believe that, I believe it and your dead mother knew it. You stood in our village and the bullets missed you, they raced by you and round and straight back into the soldiers.'

Leer screwed his eyes tight shut and shoved his father aside.

'The bullets missed us, the pangas missed us, everything missed us but not everyone else. Not Salawin, not Salva, not Sha We. Why did they have to die?'

Tuvol heard the boy scream again but not a scream. A splutter of garbled sounds rushed out of his mouth as it contorted, squeezing words that couldn't be understood. Tuvol knew then he was not going to pull the trigger. His enemy was not in front of him.

'You have to believe, Leer. Your brother does. He understands that you are very special.'

Lynch looked at the ground and said nothing. His heart was in the soil, in the roots of the forest. He could not bear to look up.

Verlaine kissed him and his brother and stepped back.

'No one is going to hurt you.' Tuvol's voice whispered the words.

Leer swiveled around quickly.

Dominique stood only metres away holding on to a mildly sedated Lynch. She silently implored Tuvol to understand what she was doing.

'He needs you.'

As soon as he saw the boy turn Tuvol rushed forward and grabbed him, not aggressively but carefully, taking the gun out of his hands and throwing it to the ground.

Wooden. Tuvol let go out of surprise and Leer leapt forward to gather his brother into his arms.

Dominique raised her hands away so that they could embrace unencumbered. Tuvol slumped onto the ground and laughed.

'Wooden?'

Dominique nodded.

They both watched the boys cry into each other's faces.

Ruess
Field Notes # 14

Sssh. I have to be quiet. Soh Mai is still asleep next to me and I don't want to wake him up. Verlaine has come back, you see him? He must have walked through night. It's just before dawn and Verlaine has come back. He's alone. Shit. A lot of people were expecting him to bring help. Where's the cavalry, man? I'm just going to move slightly, get out from under this stinking plastik or maybe it's me that's gone earthy; encrusted like some tree hugger I used to take photographs of in an endangered woodland… hold on… that's it… sssh.

If I am found here I will be seen as a sympathiser, a supporter. I will not exactly be welcomed. The embassy won't even know I've gone and I'll float off down the Shaween, blotched and bloated.

'Verlaine has come back?'

'Sorry, I know it's early.'

'This is the forest, everyone gets up early.'

'He is alone.'

'Yes.'

'Then this is all there is, Mr Ruess.'

'A few villagers armed with machetes and half a dozen soldiers against a hardened Tat brigade?'

'The brothers will help. They have special powers.'

'You believe that?'

'They believe that. That is what's important.'

'You should go back to Mae Rot. Be with your family.'

'No. Not this time. I stay if you stay.'

Lynch

'You'll be okay, you'll be all right, don't worry, we will help you.'

Lynch nodded and shook his head. Keeping his mouth shut, his twisted sounds silent. His shoulder curled in towards his chest as he opened his palms, concentrating on the drawing in his notebook. He used his body to give answers to questions.

'It's the shock,' a nurse said as she handed him to someone else.

Lynch could see his brother lying on one of the beds in the ward.

His legs were twitching.

He drew him flying upwards but then turned the paper and drew him falling through puffed up clouds.

Lynch remembered how Verlaine used to grab and hold Leer when he was like this, like the storm he could be, racing through the trees tearing plants from the soil, breaking vines with his angry grip. Verlaine would hug him and whisper stories of magical night animals that flew through the sky in the dark and blessed those who saw them with happiness. When Leer quietened and stopped fighting Verlaine's hold, they both listened to the crickets and night sounds; this was medication; a firm grip, a whispered story and the forest song. Leer would push Verlaine for more, wanting to hear everything he could, shutting his eyes and embracing tales of survival and courage.

Verlaine would nod. 'Good stories remind us of who we really are.'

When Lynch tried to draw Verlaine smiling down at him from their home he could get the long legs, could draw the thick, strong arms but when it came to his face he couldn't do it. Of course ears, nose, mouth, and the thick hair – he could draw the body parts but their arrangement was wrong. When he drew Verlaine's features he didn't recognise the dead eyes looking back at him.

'He's different to his brother. You think they're twins, right?'

'Sure. Fraternal twins. This one is probably the oldest.'

Lynch could see the foreigners holding his brother as he kicked against their grip. He was quiet one moment and then the next it took two of them to hold him down while a third got near with a syringe.

'He'll hurt himself if we don't.'

'Agreed.'

But Leer was always like that, Lynch thought, and he never hurt himself. This was Leer. In the village when everything was right he was wrong. Getting into trouble, causing trouble. This was what he did. Sometimes it was funny, sometimes people got angry with him and hit and kicked him. Lynch didn't like that and tried to get Leer away but then Leer would get angry with him and in the end there were no words that anyone wanted to say.

Leer slumped into the foreigners' arms.

'Your brother will be fine, we just need him to calm down.'

The foreigners' words were translated for him but he already understood the reassurance. They were safe now. Safe from what?

Dominique

The brothers were proving a distraction and Dominique was only half-heartedly reminding people of the many daily chores that needed to be done. She herself covered for a few of the local staff who were to be found either at Leer's bedside or with Lynch in the canteen as the cooks plied the boy with food. Some of the other local staff pushed other orphaned children along the bench, sliding them towards some kind of affinity, from one orphan to another, and everyone then sat in silence waiting for words.

None came. Lynch made sure he sat where he could see his brother lying on the bed. When he ate from his bowl he chewed every mouthful with his gaze on Leer. Even as other children looked in his ears to see what was blocking them, he waved at them like flies buzzing around his head. In the ward he followed the plastic tube going into his brother's arm from the machine and wondered when he would wake up. And he slept in a hammock that one of the nurses slung up at the side of the bed, both of them sleeping under the one small mosquito net, both of them, as one of the doctors observed, breathing in unison, breath for breath.

Lew Kwin had something to write about and Dominique saw him hovering around the ward where all the patients, pre and post op, were kept. It wasn't just Lew Kwin but several of the older patients, men and women, who had been cured but had nowhere to go and who stayed, desperately trying to make themselves useful. It was sometimes those with little to give whose donation mattered.

She had tried that line on Ruess and it hadn't gone down well.

'I know you mean well, Dom, but fuck me that's trite. I'm not one of your funders looking for a slogan to put on a poster. I'm better than that shit. I am your lover who emerges from the jungle to ravage and who then disappears again.'

Dominique laughed at that.

'You are describing the opportunist, wham-bam attitude that prevails in these parts. The only difference is that I don't have the same colour skin as the crushed beauties whose slim figures are squashed by horny white men.'

Ruess laughed at that. This was their spark that Dominique recalled every day he was gone.

'Yeah, I've not heard much complaining. The jungle can't come soon enough when I've been around for a while, eh?'

Ruess liked to miss the point. Dominique encouraged him to. It was their running joke. She looked to the forest and knew he would come back, a sweaty cliché for her to embrace.

Still, it was true, the Clinic could not function without the local workers and yet Dominique was aware that there was risk involved, not the least of which was the current security assessment by the increasingly pessimistic Wayne. Years before it would have been an international incident for the regime's army to cross the border. Now it was different. There were wars in other places that were more explosive than endemic and the TV executives had had their fill of jungle. This was why, Dominique knew, Ruess had to be alive. Yes anyone could point and click a camera, regurgitate with feeling for sub-prime news but Ruess had verve and stamina.

Tuvol seemed to her as caught up in the brothers as everyone else. She hadn't said anything but she had been impressed by his calm handling of Leer. He hadn't panicked, he didn't judge. Two prime qualities for an NGOer.

In the makeshift village of temporary homes that surrounded the Clinic, Tuvol watched over the boys as they were moved out of the ward. Already, new patients were arriving from another attack on a village and he saw them limp into the compound, some of them shredded by bullets, charred by fire. Tuvol could feel the tears in his eyes and his thoughts were to make sure the boys did not see these new arrivals; they had been through enough already. He thought this necessary but the boys continued to chew the gum he had given them, their jaws in rhythm. The wild one with the wooden gun clung on to it, holding it close to his bare chest. Tuvol clumsily stood up in front of them, trying to block their view, raising his arms like a lone steward in front of stampede.

The boys weren't looking. Leer spat his gum into a coconut shell ashtray, dislodging a few cigarette butts, and took another stick offered by Tuvol without looking up. Lynch gnawed at the skin around his fingernails.

Nobody said anything. They were quiet company. The boys looked at the ground, the forest and then Tuvol in that order, over and and over again. They heard the arrivals but they did not react. Leer spat out his chewing gum into the coconut shell again. He held out his hand for another and smiled at Tuvol.

Ruess
Field Notes # 15

Soh Mai ?
   'Mr Ruess, Mr Ruess!'
   'What's up Sohy?'
   'I've been to see the brothers.'
   'Jel Unw let you?'
   'It's okay when it's just me.'
   'So, what did you see?'
   'Everybody is there and the boys are making guns.'
   'Eh?'
   'They are making guns.'
   'How can you make guns in the middle of the forest. Is this more hocus pocus?'
   'They are making… what is is the word… carving, they are carving guns, Lynch and Leer, from wood. The wood of the Elsham tree. That is why everyone is there. Sha We and Nha We found a young tree just up the slope and they knew what it looked like because their father used to show them one near the village. The wood of this tree is very strong, Mr Ruess, but more than that it is believed spirits can make it live so that a tool made out of this wood can have special qualities. A bowl made from such wood will never be empty of food, a cup will never be dry. It is a fortunate wood to find. Everybody knows that. Such wood is rare now. Plenty of people have cut it down and sold it in Mae Rot. Plenty of people want to buy such a thing. But no one has been here before. It is so lucky.'
   'And the boys are making guns from this wood?'
   'Yes. It is lucky. Fatal.'
   'Fateful.'
   'Yes. Exactly.'

'And these guns will fire what? Magic bullets?'

'Of course.'

'You sound like you believe it, Soh Mai.'

'It is very fortunate indeed to find such a tree here. Highly unusual.'

'This is a forest. What the fuck do you expect?'

'What is wrong Mr Ruess?'

'It's just hard, Soh Mai. I feel bad I wasn't at the village when it was attacked, getting film that no one will have seen but it doesn't mean I want it to happen again. I saw the aftermath. I never want to see it again. No evidence is worth that. It's hard to say, but sure whatever you believe is fine by me.'

'I don't understand the problem. If you imagine something bad will happen it will. More important to see something good coming out of this forest. Like a lot of you foreigners, Mr Ruess, you are a slave to your imagination not a master of it.'

'I know, I know. But these are boys watched by adults making a weapon made out of wood when maybe a hundred soldiers are bearing down on us with metal and lead.'

'It is the way of things.'

Okay. Hold on. Sorry Dominique maybe you don't want a live discussion but would you not do the same? If you had a protocol would you not break it, would you not tell everybody to get the hell out of here and leave the wooden guns behind. JESUS! We should get the hell out of here. You can feel it can't you, Soh Mai, It's in the fucking air tonight!… god…wa…was… at. Mortar?

Viewers, Dominique, I am pretty sure a mortar round. Detonated quite far up the slope but the ground shook.

'We must go now, Mr Ruess!'

Dominique

The Organisation's security consultant, Wayne as he wasn't called, was rarely off the phone – the expensive satellite phone wasn't often used but now she had been told to keep it with her at all times. She didn't want to listen out for it, to hear that her security was now compromised or decomposed or whatever the jargon was. The Army was near, illegal incursions had been made across recognised boundaries as the Tat pushed to eradicate any last pockets of rebel soldiers and their villager supporters.

Wayne didn't say if there was international condemnation, nor whether there was any aid expected as medical and essential supplies ran out, but Dominique didn't need to ask that question. Despite the contact with her superiors in an urban world hundreds of miles away, they were alone in the jungle.

This wasn't what concerned Dominique. This after all was part of the job, no risk assessment could tell her more than she already knew. This was a dangerous place. People back home who lived cutting edge urban lives updated by intricate gadgetry wondered how she could live with the threat of violence when her own parents had met such a violent end. Of course these people didn't know her now. What they knew of her was past. She wrote to tell them grandly that she wasn't living for the moment she was living in it. What had once been important no longer carried weight.

Ruess would have rolled his eyes at that one. She would have loved to have been told off right that moment, admonished but held by a half-cut Ruess swilling his rice wine like a local, reeking of the forest.

This was not just about her. If the emergency evacuation plan was enacted what would happen to the local workers, the nurses, the IDPs camped around the Clinic, Lew Kwin with his notepad, the new brothers with their heavy silence? None of them were accounted for in the plan which carried the trembling expats to safety in an air-con 4x4. What was she supposed to do? Wave at them all through the back window and get on with her life? What life would there be after that? She had no death wish but her survival would be diminished by the thought of those she had worked with being left to the cruel horror of the Tat.

Wayne was on the phone again as she walked through the Clinic saying hello to the children who helloed her, briefly stopping to smile and reassure recovering patients who did not understand her words but could interpret her smile. She turned him to mute. This was of course irresponsible since she was acting on behalf of the other expats – two doctors, two volunteer engineers and two nurses – but no one was going anywhere until the latest arrivals had received the medical treatment they required. She doubted anyone would panic just yet and she was sure all the people here were not the type to bolt at the first sign of trouble. Still, as she sat on the porch wondering how many people were now in the Clinic compound, she checked her belt for the 4x4 keys dangling there.

Tuvol

Tuvol watched the silence of the brothers' communication for days and realised, as only a few had done before, that there was more sound and movement and expression between them than your typical conversation. He hardly moved from his spot. He secured his hammock and even arranged with Dominique for food and drink to be brought out, instead of going to the canteen.

'You're making something of them, Tuv?'

'I feel as though I know them already.'

'They're forest children; village kids who have known mostly the jungle. Like a lot of these people here they have been pushed out into territory they wouldn't consider home.' Dominique paused and said without hiding her exhaustion, 'What can you have in common with that?'

'You are being disingenuous.'

'Am I?'

'Of course. You know all kinds of connections can be made despite appearances.'

They both looked at the boys who were sitting close to each other, shaking off the flies, grooming each other's hair, drinking long gulps from the bottled water Tuvol had put in front of them. Leer had been unsedated for a few days now and gradually the doctors and nurses kept less of an eye on him.

Dominique smiled.

'Okay. Say you're right, you can make such a connection, reach out through a whole jungle of differences, then what? You think the ground you are about to tread isn't well worn. Colonialists, missionaries, NGOers, renegade adopting agencies, they've all made a difference haven't they?'

'Sarcastic, eh? I just said I thought I had made a connection with them, that's all.'

'Oh come on, Tuvol, don't get defensive. Say what you mean. Where's the spunk I've seen?' Dominique laughed loud enough for the two boys to look at them quizzically. Tuvol smiled back at them.

'I've seen these children, their like before, that's all. Circumstances and location are different but it's the same.'

'Really? The kids in Bente were orphans right? Unwanted or uncared for or simply unknown? These two are victims of war, internally displaced children most likely from a secure and happy home. It's not the same thing.'

'The children in Bente were victims of a different kind of trauma. The point is, Dominique, they can be helped.'

'I know, I know. You think I don't know what you see. You see the chance to help; to intervene at a young enough age to make a difference. The thousands of IDPs who are over the hill, too wrinkled to rejuvenate, can take their chances with the army and poverty but let's save the children. If you are on a mission Tuvol you should join one. Jesus Christ. Everybody needs helps here. Lew Kwin ain't necessarily cute and huggable but it doesn't mean he couldn't use a step up, the chance of a safer life.'

'I have no experience of that; there are others better qualified to help them but something has to start somewhere, Dominique. What did the Organisation think before they sent you here? Somebody else will help them? Oh, we won't bother sending anyone there, there are too many people to help.'

'That's not the point.'

'What *is* the point?'

'There's a few but try this: there's more to helping someone than crying with them, holding their hand and saying you understand.'

'I know that. I've seen that. Remember who the fuck I am!'

'Who you are? You are sounding more like your father every day.'

Tuvol's sudden, exasperated AARGH was enough to cause a few birds to fly out of the trees, the triage nurse to jump and for Lynch and Leer to stare intently.

Dominique stood up quickly, alarmed.

'Tuvol, don't…'

'I know. I know. No one needs to hear me. There's enough suffering here without me adding to it. Someone told me such things were better out than in.'

'Sure, but a little warning, eh?'

The sound of the broad, red-tipped wings of the Perpetaw flocking overhead filled the moment.

'You going home, Tuvol?'

Esta

The wind ripped through the trees, rattling branches, causing a flurry of twigs to fall to the ground. The pneumatic air's wild and shifting blow made it a tormented, bad tempered creature, bucking madly, grazing rooftops and loosening tiles. It wasn't long before the first snow fell. Once there had been celebrations for such an event but now there was a collective shrug of adult shoulders and a bolting of the doors as the cellophane was rolled out and stuck to the windows – Fuege's idea of insulation was less than successful. Once there had been a knowing joy at welcoming the cold, aware of its power but not afraid still to live – like the teenagers diving into the icy lake with only pink skin to protect them or the foster mothers sponsored to knit the longest scarf. It was different now. The cold was a nuisance, a seasonal endurance test that caused outdoor life to be curtailed and indoor activities to splutter into life. People jostled with their pets at the misted up windows as they looked out into the white.

Esta nodded at the thoughts, a tumble of memories, but did not linger too long. It was of course pretty, inspiring even to see the gradual smothering of snow and watch the patterns fall like sequenced dancing, like sequins glinting… but its attractiveness had already been appreciated. It didn't need more.

She shut the door on the impending whiteout knowing that it would only get worse and the world would quickly get smaller. It wasn't just about visibility of course, the world had been getting smaller for a while. When she shut the heavy door, bolting it once then twice, she left unlocked the last bolt, the heaviest, which Espirit had thought would give extra security. Even he found it to difficult to move. She shrugged as she looked at it. What did security matter now? There was nothing she could be protected from that hadn't already reached her.

When she walked the musty corridor – hat racks, coat stands, hooks laden with Espirit's considerable wardrobe – she was reminded again how she had been advised to clear things out by her unwanted but entitled care worker. Esta cleared her throat of phlegm and spat into the bin, flipping open the lid with her foot.

'I'm not saying it is wrong, Miss Esta,' the young woman said. She was foreign to Bente but well aware of the status of the widow she was assigned to help. 'I never say that, these things can remind you of love, can they not. But sometimes it can be too much, yes?'

Esta wondered what Carmisle would say if she mentioned casually that she was going to burn every last item of clothing that had belonged to Espirit and make a pyre that would block out the sun.

There was a single knock at the door.

'Go away.'

The kitchen was tidy – it always was. Used to be there was rarely a moment when there was an unwashed plate or pan lying around. A stain on anything. Even when Espirit had entertained heads of this or CEOs of that, she had stayed up extra late to make sure everything was the way it should be.

Everything should look as though it had never happened.

It was different now. If she wanted to she could run her finger across any surface and it would gather grease and dust and while there were no dishes in the sink there was an unwashed feel to the kitchen as though everything had been wiped with a stale cloth.

'Go away!'

She said it more urgently this time and got back up and rushed to the door. She didn't pull it open in order to startle whoever was trying to startle her. This time she opened it slowly and tentatively peered out.

There was nothing there of course. She could see it all so clearly.

There had been no family to question her decision, to persuade her that an attractive young woman such as herself, with slim hips and deeply set eyes, did not have to marry the first man who took an interest in her. No one advised her that she should give herself time to grow, see something of life, to get to know more of the world. These were concepts considered a luxury by her friends at the orphanage, all a similar age to her, all on the cusp of reaching the age when they could no longer stay at the grim building in the centre of Bente. They had to move on, either to mundane jobs or, if they were lucky, to be plucked from the cold room where powerful men were allowed to view. This was how her friends saw it. She was lucky to have the eyes of a stranger on her; a man who could literally take her away there and then to a new life. Her friends packed their bags to get ready to move into municipal housing – grey boxes on the outskirts of the town where their status would be lowly and certainly vulnerable. There was no question they were envious of Esta as a large, plump man took her by the hand and led her out to a waiting car.

She had been so overwhelmed by her new life that she didn't realise how much it resembled her old one.

She closed the door as the snow flurried inside.

She hated the compound house – the dripping taps, the clunks of the boiler in winter, the snapping of wires in the summer; the house wasn't alive as some houses could be – it was a chronic patient who groaned and moaned day and night. It was too big where she was used to the close proximity of others in the dormitory and so she tended to stay in the kitchen surrounded by the tools of service and provision, idling hours away listening to the radio, singing to songs, humming to tunes and staring out the kitchen window at the Anvil which loomed over the town, casting shifting shadows in the summer and darkening the town to gothic gloom in the winter.

Carmisle asked the questions she didn't want to answer. She liked that. She hated that.

'Have you been into Mr Espirit's office?'

Esta knew the girl would have little idea as to the dynamics of their household although it was possible she had some awareness of the situation. Carmisle had come armed with a bereavement qualification but could find no place for it, so instead found herself helping with the household chores. It wasn't what she had expected. She had imagined that everyone would be sad to no longer have the founder of Homes for Peace, would be devastated to have lost a husband – but his wife sat in silence, his son was nowhere to be seen and she found herself grouting old tiles.

'No.'

'Don't you need to?'

'Of course there are matters to be settled – you missed a bit there – but there is no hurry. The will is with the solicitor and everyone knows where they stand.'

'What will happen to the charity. Will it stop?'

'It won't 'stop' as you put it. The board will run it just as they always have wanted to. It will be a smooth transition. They will be in charge.'

'And you?'

Esta smiled and nearly rebuffed the question as she so easily could have but it wasn't aggressive, just inquisitive. It was certainly relevant. The board had collectively sent her a telegram that had spelt her name wrong and had struggled to amount to three sentences. *Dear Esther.* Their condolences were formal and a long way from being heartfelt. Esta had no place in the business of Homes for Peace and she understood that she would be sidelined; perhaps kept as the widow of the founder; an accompaniment to the figurehead.

She'd better get a new hat.

Esta's laughed slipped out of her like a wounded moan.

'But Miss Esta, what of your son? Tuvol, isn't it? Surely he will come back when he hears about the death of his father?'

Esta knew this was probably a little outwith the parameters of Carmisle's training. Incoming help could be heard as well as seen but they were not encouraged to be so questioning. Esta liked her. There was something about Carmisle's naiveté which was refreshing, unguarded. Besides, nobody had the asked the question until now:

'Where is your son?'

Esta did not rebuff nor counter with half-truths or platitudes. A smile, silently leaked, was enough. When she was told both of Espirit's death and Tuvol's disappearance she barely reacted and certainly didn't speak. She allowed herself to be ushered to a waiting car by a Homes for Peace flunky before cameras could find her. But the question remained. Where was Tuvol?

Tuvol

Tuvol had been dreaming that Ruess came running up to him at the Clinic, sweating sap from the forest, his skin camouflaged with mud and blood; he grabbed him by the throat and yelled, 'Abduction or adoption?' Then he'd woken up on the plane, felt the vibration of the engines change as it shuddered through some turbulence.

He was vibrating still.

Esta

'Go away!'

For the tenth time that day, Esta shouted at the door.

'Esta?'

'Go away!'

But this time she distinctly heard words. She crept to the door, her shrinking body light as it was stiff.

'It's me.'

Esta opened the door slightly, enough for outside light to cut into the gloom of the hallway. She saw the outline of Tuvol but not his face.

'Oh.'

It was not an exclamation as such, more mild surprise.

When she opened the door wider and looked down expecting to see luggage, she saw two small children with dark olive skin and oval eyes that stared at her from under bright woolly hats.

'God.'

For those who briefly met her, for those who shook her hand or pecked her cheek, Esta was a curiosity, a dour counterpoint to Espirit's vigour who took no part in the daring, *darling* repartee that characterised so many fundraisers.

'It was love at first sight!' This was his standard quip usually accompanied by a conspiratorial wink as though she was in on the joke. She wasn't laughing. When Espirit saw her for the first time he appraised her, felt her flanks as though she was a mare and this was a market, which of course it was. There was plenty of time for her to consider that. To revisit their first meeting and wonder why she was chosen when others were left behind. It did occur to her that this was not a match made by fate, an incredible intervention so that two kindreds could meet. When he moved her face from side to side it was more about good teeth than true love.

The air-kissers who did not know her had expected her to dissolve or disintegrate into widowhood, the pause where men have been. Far from it. The kitchen was transformed from a place of preparation to a place of living. She turned on her radio and danced to tunes from countries she had never heard of, drums with gongs and soaring strings. Then, afterwards, sweating in the cold, she lay in the dark on

197

the tiled floor and listened to plays – on words, with drama, of ideas, and there was resonance; an inspiration to the words that somehow lingered.

'You should come in, it's freezing cold out here.'

'I know. It feels good after the heat we have been in.'

Esta looked at the two children as they shivered past her. Boys, she guessed. They were insulated with puffed-up jackets, thick trousers and woollen hats but Esta could feel their shudder as they passed. She stood in the doorway for a moment ignoring her own instruction and watched as her son ushered the two boys into the living room gently placing his hands on their shoulders, bending to talk softly and reassuringly.

He looked thinner.

Esta had never imagined Tuvol with children. Perhaps that in itself was strange, that she did not look forward to the possible role of grandmother. There was no experience for her to draw on for it and she was not inclined to believe the milestone it provided others with.

Tuvol was still a boy who's whiny squeak then sulky baritone had been as much a tone in the house as the creak of the roof and drip of taps. Tuvol reproductive? No. How could a child give life to another child?

Not quite believing what was happening, Esta closed the front door and followed the visitors but instead of striding into her own living room she peered round the open door. There had been no warning of anything.

Of course she had to do something. This was stranger and more awkward than any of the surprises Espirit used to spring on her. As a teenage girl she used to imagine there would be moments when she was swept off her feet rather than worked off them by chores. She held on to such tender thoughts even when the girls at the orphanage warned her that a man's needs predicated spontaneous moments of ardour, of rippling lust. 'You have to be ready. You don't want to disappoint.' Esta shuddered at the thought. She had been around benefactors for most of her adult life. She was tired of taking being disguised as giving.

Typically Espirit would call harassed but excited to say ten visitors were coming and could she prepare something for them all? There was nothing she could do but say yes and she learned to prepare in advance for the unexpected. Such skills however had been mothballed and she had not expected to see Tuvol again. She knew if there were people around wanting to hear her thoughts they would be appalled at that; a mother giving up on her son? It didn't matter, it was what she believed. Usually when people leave they don't come back. Why would they?

'I'll make tea.'

Tuvol smiled and showed the two boys to an armchair which they both squeezed onto, still wrapped in their thermal jackets. They rustled as silence grew. Their feet didn't touch the floor.

At the airport there had been fuss over Leer's wooden gun. He did not understand that when it went in the suitcase disappearing down the conveyor belt that he would get it back. Not everything you had was always in your hands, within eyeshot. Tuvol drew a picture sequence that opened Leer's eyes wide but eventually he nodded. His brother was less concerned about what was inside the airport than what was on the other side of the glass. He was excited by the prospect of being in a plane he had only previously seen like a toy against the blue sky.

Esta cast a backward glance. She had a plan. There were things in the freezer, things in tins. There was always something in case of emergencies. There were still left-overs.

At the airport the paperwork had taken some time. The boys had swung their legs on the plastic moulded chairs while Tuvol laid out forms in front of sceptical officers whose eyes widened appreciatively when they looked into who he was the son of.

In the living room the boys' legs swung quickly in time as they bumped them hard into the velvet covers. Tuvol carefully unwrapped them but they held on to their wooly hats placing them on their laps.

Esta had never seen children quite like them.

'Looks to me like these two should have a leash on them,' she said bluntly.

One looked feral, razor sharp as though every bone was fighting to emerge from his skin while the other looked damaged, nodding forward slightly in his chair, his shoulders rounded, curled in on himself, his eyes boring into the carpet. The sharp looking one, whose fingers were wrapped around what looked like a wooden gun, its features worn and flattened as though it had been squeezed too hard, looked around the room and only briefly caught Esta's incredulous glare. She had seen the look in his eyes. It was familiar.

Tuvol stayed standing once he had put the tray of cups on the table, the stains on the glass top only slightly covered up by a circle of faded cream linen. This was no longer a room that Esta looked after. Like the rest of the house, it had been given over to dust and damp. The two boys stared at the tray and Esta unwaveringly stared at the boys.

'Well, then,' Tuvol said awkwardly, as though about to give a presentation to the unconvinced.

'Esta, this is Lynch and this is Leer. They've come to stay with us for a while.'

Esta said nothing in reply just kept on looking at the boys who both turned their stares to her.

'And, boys, this is Esta, my mother.'

The silence was louder than all the drips and creaks, clanks and groans of the house. Tuvol's head swiveled between the boys and his mother. Finally, he reached for the tray and poured the tea, the liquid sounding like the rush of a waterfall in canyon.

'It's good to be home,' he offered brightly.

No one understood what he meant.

Lynch and Leer

Leer had never been in a car like it before. He had been on a couple of rickety trucks on the muddy road that led down from the hills towards Mae Rot but those rides were bumpy, full of dust and shout, the horn of the driver blaring constantly as he tried to clear the road in front of him. When the door shut in the Clinic's four wheel drive, the world changed with one quick sucking sound. One moment there was the jungle and the next there wasn't; one moment there was prickly, humid heat and the next there was a cold he had rarely felt. It was like someone with cold breath was sitting right beside you. He imagined that if a dead body could breath this would be its air.

Tuvol strapped them both in, tight to the back seat so that their torsos remained still but their legs flew up into the air with each pothole. It made Leer laugh. It was exciting to be moving in a car with a full stomach, with a mind racing. He had always loved the state of doing something from playing to fighting; from holding a toy to holding his gun. It felt real, it made his thoughts seem like something, made his dreams do something.

His excitement wasn't shared by Lynch who was sobbing beside him on the leather seats. When Leer put his arm around his brother it was shrugged off. He took the notebook and pen never far from his brother's grip, and drew them both in the car – crude drawings as he didn't have his brother's skill and he hoped that it would make him laugh – but Lynch grabbed the pen and drew what nearly every page of the notebook had. The tall figure of their father, then a line-up of those who were not present. Lynch jabbed his finger into the paper until their bodies blurred.

Leer could see Tuvol watching in the rear view mirror but he looked away when Leer tried to hold his eyes. Like all foreigners this tall man, this Tuvol did not like to be looked at. People said the brothers had sharp eyes because they couldn't speak properly but Leer saw what he saw. Looking can make people flinch. He had tried to get his brother to look out of the car windows as they left and although it was barely dawn dozens of faces peered through the cloying mist trailed by the retreating night. Those awake at the Clinic were keen to see this departure, to be witness.

They got away.

They got taken away.

The twins were not aware of the distinction nor the compound-wide discussions. It was enough for Lynch to raise his head and emerge from his blanket shroud, the emblem of the Organisation coincidentally close to his heart. Still snuffling, his eyes puffy and red, Lynch watched the people gathered. A few were smiling, a few waved, but mostly they stood as impassive as such dramatic circumstances would allow. The arrival and departure of the four wheel drive car was always something to look at and this awkward, slippery exit was something that most wanted to see.

'Keep your eyes forward boys, that's where we are going now.'

They watched Tuvol nodding to the Organisation's driver and he translated Tuvol's sentence into the brother's language. It didn't matter, they still looked back, sideways, even at the floor, its carpeted feel strange and ticklish for their feet. They could see the tall foreigner smiling at them, felt it even, and they half glanced at his sign language, which approximated their own but was not the same. Someone waving for help was not the same as someone waving goodbye. He kept on smiling as he drew on the back of a map with a thick blue felt pen. The brothers could see it was a plane. Written on the fuselage was:

Air Tuvol!

The boys did not understand.

As his brother waved and pulled faces at other children, Lynch saw ghosts – it was not a farewell gathering outside the car but a reunion of those who could not be there. Verlaine holding hands with a mother known only through description. And Salva. The golden child blessed with good fortune whose luck had evaporated in the heat of battle as his body swung with his parents, a rope through his neck. When they exchanged looks, his bloody glare dissolved the tint of the windows more used to shielding the sun and poverty from its occupants. Without the empathy of his brother, so caught up as he could be in the excitement of the moment, he was alone to face their family and friends as they silently stared.

This was not a moment to forget.

He would remember for both of them.

Lynch put his arm round his brother and said nothing.

Tuvol

The wood burning stove in the living room had not been used for some time and the air around them refused to be warmed. Tuvol stamped his feet while the boys put their puffed jackets back on, wedging the woollen hats tight on their heads so only their eyes could be seen.

Esta shook her head at the scene and let her cup clatter onto the saucer. She asked Tuvol to join her in the kitchen.

'What are you doing, Tuvol?'

Esta's tiny eyes were widened with anger and she gripped on to the kitchen table with both hands.

On the long haul flight over, Tuvol was riddled with doubt. Everything had been for them, as it should be, and there had been no time to think beyond the immediate but once they had slumped together so small on airline seats, Tuvol found his body short of air.

'What are you doing, Tuvol?'

This time it was Esta questioning his reasoning if not his motives.

There was much to be said but the simple answer was:

'They need a home.'

Esta let go of the kitchen table where so many meals had been prepared with barely thanks or acknowledgement given.

'Home? Why are you here? You think this is your home? You left remember, your father was dying and you left without even a goodbye, just some nonsense from a complete stranger. Who was she? Was the circus in town? It meant nothing. How can you expect me to welcome you back?'

As Tuvol had watched the boys sleep on the plane, curled as ever together, their legs twitching, faces illuminated by the map that showed them moving further and further away from their home, he had imagined there would be a certain frostiness on his return to Bente. Open arms of welcome, hugs and kisses had never been in the meet and greet of the family; a dry peck on a cheek had once happened but it was an emotional skirmish, never repeated. But the venom of Esta's words, their aggressive tone was a shock. What had been polite was no longer; what had been hidden was now on the surface.

Tuvol had thought, with the insulated verve of the reborn, he was the only one that was new.

'In your telegram, you asked me not to come back for the funeral.'

Esta laughed, full of volume without any sense of heart and humour.

'If you had truly cared you would have ignored that, crumpled it up and made sure you were on the first flight home. Did it matter at all, did it mean anything to you in your sunny paradise? How brown you are Tuvol. I thought you would burn.'

If Esta had been looking for triggers then this was certainly one.

'You think these boys come from paradise? You think I was lying on a beach somewhere getting tanned? Maybe a letter wasn't enough but the news remains the same. I grieved for Espirit. In a strange place it all came home to me and it wasn't easy, it wasn't simple.'

'So you grieved with strangers?'

'So you went to a funeral with official strangers?'

Esta recoiled and looked away. The sounds of the house tracked the moment as they had done on countless occasions.

In a necessarily softer tone, Tuvol asked, 'How was the funeral?'

'Everybody came.'

Tuvol pictured, as he was meant to, himself, holed and hidden; damp like a snail evicted from its shell, there at the depth of his despair on a blue plastik, entrenched in the humid jungle with Lew Kwin watching over him. But then he also pictured himself in black by a graveside surrounded by charitable acolytes, the Homes for Peace groupies that fell over themselves with their own largesse and hoped to link themselves in whatever way possible to Espirit's pedigree. Esta of course would have been closest to the grave but the second spot, in his absence, would have been crowded with visible mourners, calculated grief.

'Your father was honoured by representatives of governments he had been closely involved with. The cortege was long and the minister gave good account of your father's life.'

'Espirit wasn't religious.'

'*Your father* wanted the moment properly commemorated. Atheists, I am told, do very mundane and incomplete funerals. They fudge on the important issues.'

'He told you what he wanted to happen, that must have been an unusually personal conversation.'

'Stop it.'

'Stop what?'

'Your comments are provocative, hostile and, like your father, dripping with guilt.'

Tuvol was taken aback by her words. 'I'm just surprised that he talked to you about such things. I didn't hear.'

'Not everything was within your earshot. You share his arrogance; if you didn't know about it, it didn't happen. Really? And I just read cookbooks of course. Anyway, Tuvol, he talked quite eloquently to his lawyer about all his death and post-death requirements and I saw no need to interfere.'

'Were there many people upset?'

'You mean were there people crying at the graveside?'

'Yes.'

'Yes.'

There was a pause as they assembled their strategic awareness,

'I cried. Is that what you need to know? How long? How hard? It would have been difficult not to have been upset.'

'I just want to picture the scene.'

'You could have seen it if you were there.'

Tuvol took a long look at the smiling boys in the living room, framed by the serving hatch. He wondered what they were laughing at before realising it was themselves, playing, lost in their own game.

Esta moved to wipe a kitchen surface.

'Was it so very different where you were?'

'I was in a tropical forest helping people, helping myself.' Tuvol had rehearsed that. 'I tried to find who I was.'

Esta snorted.

'I thought you'd found that woman, what was her name?'

'Dominique. And she found me actually but that's not what I mean...'

Esta slammed both her hands down on the surface she had just wiped.

'I know exactly what you mean. I read your letter even though it was full of with platitudes – as if I hadn't had a lifetime of that! I understood where you went, boy, I just don't understand why you came back. And with children! Don't we have enough of them already in this godforsaken place?'

Tuvol moved between Esta and the serving hatch, blocking out the brothers' view.

'Please. Don't raise your voice. They've had so much noise already in their lives.'

'And I've had so much quiet in mine I've gone quite deaf.'

Tuvol's mouth dropped open a little. He wondered if perhaps Espirit's death had unhinged her, had taken away the scaffolding of a fragile life and now her mind was disintegrating. If he had been here then maybe he could have stopped that but then he had been here all that time, childhood, adolescence, nondescript adult years and had not intervened. What could he possibly say?

Why had he come back? Not for him. For the boys. For something more than him.

Esta let out a long, tired sigh and sat on her chair, its seat bevelled by her routine. 'You were saying, you found yourself...'

'Yes. I know how that sounds. Maybe it's the wrong expression but I do understand the value of things more; I appreciate what life means more.'

Esta's tone in reply was bitterly cold. 'You appreciate what life means by leaving your father to die? What you have learned means nothing. You are still the same selfish and insecure boy you always were.'

When Tuvol went into the living room the boys had got out of the damp armchairs and had their faces pressed to the windows, their hands spread on the cold glass and they were giggling with each other, their bubbling conversation animated by the swirling snow that rushed towards them then retreated away. It sounded to Tuvol like they were on a rollercoaster.

Dominique and Tuvol

So this was Tuvol? Not the pale shadow? Not the ungainly man stretched by circumstances?

She watched him with the brothers and saw a surprising skill. He was good with children, at least these two children. Dominique had him marked as being too awkward, too stiff to be flexible with wit and body. She saw his big frame and could not see him stooping to hug or lifting up to carry aloft then swoop with playful danger. He had barely mentioned the children of Bente and had only given her brief biography as to his own childhood. None of it was recalled with any relish.

There was nothing dramatic about his interaction. He didn't play the clown as some adults would nor was he teachery, assuming an authority laced with condescension. He sat with them, cross-legged on an olive green ground-sheet with the Organisation's logo emblazoned on it. Talk would have been hard since there was no common language but there was still communication as they swapped hand signals, facial gesturing and single words whispered into each other's ears. A sudden intimacy for all of them, Dominique imagined. Tuvol had animation in his face that the boys found intriguing – his skin, his eye colour fascinated them and questions found a way to be asked just as he tried his best to answer. Tuvol's writing pad was filled with scrawls and sketches but there was sound too. Dominique listened to their full throated, high pitched laughter and watched as they drew their lives into Tuvol's notebook – houses, people, the forest. When the notebook got too small for them they drew the Clinic's buildings –Tuvol tall like a tree and the nurses with bright smiles – flicked firmly by a finger into the ground.

It was like this for days. Dominique was relieved. She had been wishing he would leave; professionally and personally her life was more complicated with him around. She was used to being absorbed in life and death, the energy used for that could not easily be redirected into the sluggish mire of relationship or even friendship. It was hard to care about feelings when blood was dripping onto the ground. When Wayne arrived, she left Tuvol and the boys to their soil tapestry.

Some of the foreigners respected Wayne and thought Ruess was gung-ho, too rugged for his own good or to do any real good, but Dominique knew better. Wayne was everything Ruess hated. Dominique wondered why he had come all this way. She soon found out why.

'You have your evacuation plan in place?'

'Yes. It's on standby as advised.'

'Change the alert level to active as from now.'

Dominique knew what this meant. She remembered her brief. All non-essentials to leave. It meant Tuvol too. That was his status; a representative from Homes for Peace.

The evacuation plan for the Clinic was not particularly hi-tech. In some parts of the world where the Organisation worked there was clear and present danger and significant numbers of personnel helicopters were available for airlift. It was never going to be like that in this forest.

Wayne flicked ash from his cigarette onto the Clinic's out-patient floor. He held the burning end in towards his palm as though his smoking had been done mostly on tough, cold fronts.

'This has been coming for a while, you know that, and God knows you will have seen the casualties. It's likely the wet season river will stop no one, rebel or government. The border will be suspended.'

Ruess would have poo-pooed him and swaggered off into the jungle with his righteousness blazing. Dominique knew that and understood too that acting as an individual could be reckless or even fatal in such a situation. She couldn't do that. Wayne was a ham but he knew what he was doing and he didn't want to see anyone hurt anymore than Dominique did.

'I can take the non-essentials with me when I leave. What about this Tuvol?'

'He's helping with new arrivals at the moment.'

'Okay, make him aware of our timeframe. I don't recommend that he stays as long as the essentials. It could get difficult.'

'I understand.'

'He a friend of yours?'

Dominique laughed, unnecessarily and nervously. 'Yes.'

'How's he finding it in the heat and jungle?'

'He quite taken with it.'

'Well, he'd best enjoy it while he can.'

Wayne checked in with the guards, kicked the tyres and slammed the doors on the two 4x4s for the two waves of evacuation.

Dominique already knew what the expat medical staff would say. The husband and wife, doctor and surgeon partnership would not leave prematurely and certainly not while there was still work to do. They weren't the type to bail out, neither were the two student nurses who had arrived with little experience but who had flourished where others had wilted. Nobody was about to drop stethoscopes and get out and with the local staff it was the same but more complicated.

They had nowhere to run to. Some lived in Mae Rot while others had come across the border and all were in danger from the Tat who did not like to see their enemy repaired. No one at the Clinic would be safe and this ultimately included the foreigners. While they might not be the first casualties they would eventually be killed. Dominique was well aware of this without any briefing. They were all a long way from home. Nobody would really care. Governments would voice protest at the murders – or unattributed deaths – in a far off place and while the consul might be sent sweating out of his quinine-soaked colonial digs there would be but a few inside pages which would follow then slowly drop the story. Her parents had been a paragraph and then *In Brief* and then nothing. Like the sun setting in the tropics; the story would be dropped like a stone and correspondents and diplomats would return to their bars, the fate of those in the forest left to the unknown which was always known.

While she watched Wayne do his routine checks, Mul Wa spoke to her knowing full well what his visit meant.

'What will happen to all these people we care for?'

Dominique noticed how she phrased what she said. It was not about her.

'It doesn't look good. We will stay as long as we can, Mul Wa.'

'We know. You have done so much for these people but this is not your war. If they bring their fire to us then it is time for you to leave. And your friend.'

Dominique looked over at Tuvol still sitting with the two brothers, the ground around them etched with their conversations, their lively tone accented by their gesturing arms.

'He will have to go before us. There is not enough room in the last jeep.'

'He will not want to go.'

Dominique nodded.

Mul Wa continued, her voice quiet. 'I mean he will not want to go alone.'

Dominique tightened her lips.

Mul Wa's voice grew quieter still. 'The boys are orphans most likely, no one is going to come here to ask for them.'

'As far as we know. We can't be certain of that.'

Mul Wa was. 'They would have come. It is too late for them. Who will take them, two hungry boys when there is not enough food? They damaged too.'

'Ssh, we don't know that, Mul Wa, and I don't like the word *damaged*. They are special.'

Mul Wa shook her head. 'They are dead.'

The Organisation was very clear on such matters. Dominique's parents had told her there had been several occasions when they had come very close to giving her a sister from a different place; as spontaneous as her parents often were, even they would hesitate when about to bundle some poor waif into a car.

'It was hard,' her mother explained as she held a photograph of them in front of some tropical clinic, surrounded by rag-tag, smiling children. 'This was a desperate place, barely an oasis of calm between two fronts and we were the last NGO to leave – the medics so often are. When people picked up their bundles and moved out there were a few strays, unclaimed children that civilisation had left behind.'

'What did you do?'

'There was nothing we could do. You can't always get what you want; you can't always give what you need.'

The handbook made it clear: 'The Organisation would not permit under any circumstances the adoption or fostering of children. It is understood that workers and volunteers often provide surrogate roles which may lead to emotional attachments being formed. However, it is a mark of the professionalism of all those working for the Organisation to disengage and assist the many rather than the selected few. While alleviating suffering of vulnerable people of all ages in the field is one of our primary goals, it is neither possible nor desirable to replace impossibility with false hope and misrepresentative roles.'

As her mother had said, with a sarcasm that burned her, 'You can't take the refugee out of the field and you can't take the field out of the refugee.'

'What?'

'I want to take the brothers with me.'

Dominique had already thought it through since the time Mul Wa had observed what she failed to see coming but she played for time, wanting to hear what Tuvol had to say, wanting to hear the reasons she already knew.

'The brothers? You mean the ones that came in with the sister who died.'

'Yes,' Tuvol said impatiently. 'The brothers who came in with the sister who died who went crazy after she died, one of them trying to shoot a guard with a toy gun and neither of them saying a word to anyone apart from themselves.'

'Oh them!'

'C'mon. You know who I'm talking about; the whole camp does.'

'Sure, I know who you mean. I meant to say to you…'

Tuvol looked up from his notes, the observations he had made of

Lynch and Leer since they had arrived at the camp; notes on their signals and words that Tuvol had tried to attach meaning to. When the shy Lynch brought out his notepad, half torn with damp pages somehow clinging to the spiral bind, he tried to put it away when he saw Tuvol looking.

'No, no, it's okay, look I have one too. See, it's okay. Here is mine.'

Lynch smiled when Tuvol held his own notebook up and then clapped his hands and laughed loudly when he showed him his thin trees bending alongside people nearly as tall and thin as bamboo. The drawings were funny of course but the communication was serious and Tuvol had never felt such elation. This is what it was like. Rather than being different he was making a difference. He had to smile as he rolled the words around in his head. Finally a slogan he could call his own. Everyone else had one.

'Did I tell you that?'

'Tell me what?

'I said we got word of an abortive attempt to take about 50 children of out of a country.'

'Here?'

'No.'

'What happened?'

'A small-time NGO with a missionary rep had gathered up the kids all under the age of ten and took them to their HQ for treatment by expat doctors.'

'Sound pretty typical.'

'No. Most of the children had been taken from their families because they were deemed to be seriously ill and in need of treatment, which not only could not be provided in the field, it could not be provided in the host country. As a result, an airlift was attempted when a Hercules landed on a small airstrip with no official permission and no documentation detailing what was to happen to the children.'

'What did happen?'

'The children were to have been taken and placed with adopting families. There was no money involved, this NGO was simply relocating these children. It was seen as an ethical redistribution.'

'How sick were they?'

'Of course that is the rub. They were not sick at all. Diseases were made up, convincing distraught families that there was no way they could be treated in situ and had to be taken away to be helped. They didn't know they were being taken out of the country for ever.'

'Abduction not adoption.'

'Exactly.'

'I see. What happened to the NGOers?'

'They were mostly jailed then pardoned after some intervention from their government. They got lucky. Some places would have had them shot. Or worse.'

'Thanks for telling me that.'

'I thought it might help.'

'Who?'

'You.'

'I see.'

Tuvol took Dominique's hand and led her out of her Clinic office to where the boys had covered the earth with drawings and scripts. This was the conversation Tuvol had been part of, this was their chatter now held precariously in the earth; fragile, like so much about them. One storm and their story would be washed away, one gust of wind and their words would be carried back into the jungle.

'I have an idea who these boys are, I have had a glimpse as to what they have been through. They have shared this with me.'

'It's impressive.'

'I have an idea where they have come from and they don't believe they can go back. What they had is gone and the future in this story is a full stop.'

'You can't know that.'

'I know how they symbolised the end of their story. There is nothing more after their arrival here.'

'That's not what I mean. There could be someone searching for them right now; someone they know desperate to find them and re-establish them with family and community.'

'They have no family left. Their community went up in flames.'

'How do you know?'

'It's in the story, it's there in the ground and it's in their eyes when they look at each other, when they look at me even.'

'You still don't know. You can never be sure. They are children. You are proposing an action that can have no certainty about it.'

'And if they are left here by your great evacuation plan, Dominique, will they survive, can you be sure of that?'

'No.'

'So by doing nothing it is more likely they won't survive than the definite help I can give.'

'Definite help, Tuvol? I wasn't sure you were capable of helping yourself.'

Tuvol nodded.

'I knew you would say something like that. Do you think I am the same man you first met?'

'Do you think people can change that quickly?'

'Maybe not change but, evolve, grow up, realise.'

'And what do you realize, Tuvol?'

'That my father is dead and I have to make peace with my home.'

'Cute. The slogans are in your genes but what does it mean?'

'There's a lot of things not right for me back there – things that were bad and things I made bad – but you yourself said that you can't run away from all that stuff, it always catches up.'

'It sounds like my point of view but what's this to do with the two boys. Are they part of this life plan?'

'Of course.'

'For them or for you?'

'Both.'

'Ah, children as cement, to hold things together. Hold you together.'

Tuvol shook his head vigorously.

'Not at all. I'm not airlifting them out just for kicks; they would be adopted by Homes for Peace not abducted. They would be given safe shelter, provided with food and accommodation and have a chance to lead a normal life.'

'Thousands of miles from the home they were born into.'

'A home which is no longer in use. This isn't a perfect solution but at least it is one.'

'Another slogan. You're hitting the spot.'

'Are you being facetious with all these questions?'

'Who are you to play God?'

'Playing God? I'm being human.'

Dominique smiled at Tuvol who didn't notice. She thought of her mother waving goodbye to children she could have saved; she thought of the doctors here tidying up as best they could the inevitable loose sutures of lives still in the balance. Happy endings hadn't been prominent in her family for generations, unless she counted her grandmother decaying in the arrondissement, the smell covered up with perfume. Dominique kept on smiling at Tuvol even though his head was buried in his notebook. Her heart had become accustomed to being hard, her tears had been trained to well but not fall. She was, she believed, that in control, and wiping tears from her face after a decision had been made only emphasised that it was the right one. She didn't cry over mistakes.

'Tuvol, I was always going to say yes. I just needed to hear what you felt.'

Tuvol looked up startled form his notebook, his red face flushed and confused.

'My God, I mean, that's great. Thank you.'

He stepped forward to embrace her but Dominique backed away.

'No. You don't quite understand. By yes I mean I am not going to stop you from care-lifting the boys from a conflict zone, which I could do if I wanted, okay? You are a guest of the Organisation and if you do this you will be flouting our rules and challenging the morality of quite a few that work here. I cannot and will not officially condone the taking of these two boys away from their homeland to a foreign fostering facility. However, a situation might arise that necessitates a certain sequence of actions and in the heat of the moment, Tuvol, I can't be everywhere.'

'I understand.'

'I hope so.'

'You are staying here?'

'I will be the last to leave. That's how it should be.'

Lynch and Leer in Tuvol's world

In Tuvol's bedroom the boys pressed themselves against the window. Lynch had stuck the palms of his hands to the window coated with condensation and was watching the streaks of cold water rush down the pane as though racing against each other to the sill. Leer's tongue was pressed against the cold glass licking up the streams while his eyes were wild with the outside.

They knew about snow. Lawe's lessons had been comprehensive and what they lacked for in direct experience was embellished with the flourish of his descriptions, his words an avalanche of images for his students. 'It will freeze you,' he told them, trying to scare the younger children with a broad and wicked smile. 'It comes slowly, flake by flake but if you sleep you will wake up under it. Your eyes open into white. Nothing. Just cold, white snow.' The children screamed with delight as they switched the night scene to a white one. All of them knew what it was like not to see anything in front of their eyes.

Leer tried to open one of Fuege's windows which was painted shut from the spring coat of a slapdash handyman. He nudged his brother who stared out into the distance, the snow thick enough for him to see only trees. But not his trees. There was no heat except the heat from the big jackets Tuvol had given them. It was not the same. Leer nudged him more viciously and together they pulled at the window until it burst open bringing in the storm.

They both shrieked and covered their faces as if the snow was something else, as if the soft melt of snowflakes was the sudden burn of flame, the scarring mist of phosphorous. A snowdrift formed at their arms which were locked together in bonded fear until they both understood. Shock turned to surprise, rolling into laughter. They watched the snow build up, ploughing it with their gloved hands and then they stretched out over the windowsill and opened their mouths and shut their eyes, turning their heads upwards, waiting for the flakes to land perfectly white for a moment on their skin until the heat from their bodies melted it away.

The Homes for Peace children were playing in the snow just as they always did. This was Bente's postcard, snow scenes from a bygone era. The one thing Fuege seemed to get right was to allow for snowfall – from its first gentle flakes trickling through icy air to flurries of thicker patterns and spirals above the children's hands who measured their success by how many flakes could be caught unspoiled, unmelted. The houses were built against the perfect setting and the architect claimed all he could for the driving snow that created arcs from the svelte drifts, strange wispy pile-ups in hidden corners of the compound. With Fuege's help the snow transformed the utilitarian simplicity of Homes for Peace into a voluptuous, complicated thing, all hips and curves, with no beginning and no end.

For Tuvol, standing without a coat and relishing the ice and snow, nothing appeared to have changed. Of course it had only been a matter of months but this was not how his time away was being measured. It would be like measuring grief in terms of how long someone had been dead. He wanted to shed his body of his clothes, rid himself of the stink of heat, the hum of humidity and just smell nothing.

Then there was the jet-lagged twist of dislocation; was he here or there or anywhere? This was the mediocre, ill-tempoed song playing in his head as he stepped outside to get a sense of where he was. The old Tuvol would have slumped, round shouldered the situation into a skin-picking huff but this one tried to take hold of what was important. Dominique had told him to grip his past, to shake it until all the loose change had fallen out. She had laughed at her own suggestion but it was sloppy advice as far as Tuvol was concerned. The past should be shaken until there was no life left in it.

Although Tuvol had identified himself as Homes for Peace, used its renowned name to forge a bureaucratic path, he was not Espirit. He had no plan that he could pay more than lip service to, or state with PR prose his intentions – *they will have a new life of nurtured challenges that encompass the best of their culture while removing them from imminent threat their location creates.* He looked at the boys and wondered if they would hate him for this.

Esta and Carmisle

Trays of cold food wouldn't do it. Esta knew that. She cursed Tuvol for the hundredth time. She hadn't thought she would have to worry about someone else eating for the rest of her life. She had hoped she was finished with preparation.

Instead of worrying what a visiting dignitary might want as an hors d'oeuvre she now had to think what two alien boys would want to eat. They had eaten the biscuits she had put out but that was no surprise; sweet things were international. There wasn't much else. Carmisle, the lively help for the old and dying, was due to bring in groceries. Esta tapped her fingers on the kitchen table as she waited for her.

'You look out the window a lot, Miss Esta, what do you see?'

Esta shook her head and flickered an insincere smile as Carmisle arrived. She urged herself to say that the garden was looking nice. How the gardeners must have worked hard since Espirit's death; she wanted to comment on the unrelenting cold weather, how iced up the inside of the windows were. All around her, she felt eyes watching, assessing her mental state as though she was as fragile as a Fuege house. She could not afford to be honest. She interlocked her fingers and pulled with all her strength.

'I think the garden is beautiful in the snow.'

'Yes.'

'Carmisle, I...' Esta felt the hesitation even before it hung between them.

'Yes, Miss Esta...?' Carmisle was attentive and she leaned slightly closer to Esta in case there was a need to whisper.

Esta could hear the wind rush into the eaves of the house, each gust creating a creaking sound as though her home was on the sea and it was being rolled by waves that just kept on coming.

'Have you met our two guests?' It wasn't what she was going to say but it fitted the moment.

'Guests?'

'In Tuvol's room. Have a look.'

Esta wished the wind would be done. *Blow all you will and spill us into the snow.* Everything. Espirit's study, Tuvol's room, her kitchen – a climatic push of air that would spring clean this home in the depth of winter; a pyre of memorabilia awaiting the douse of fuel, the spark of ignition. With ease, she saw herself dance around the fire, laughing as flames seared her skin, feeling warmth rather than heat and when Carmisle's hands tried to ungrip her own, she did not jerk it away; it was like an embrace as the fire licked around them.

'There are two boys in Mr Tuvol's room.'

'Yes.'

'Mr Tuvol came back?'

'Yes.'

'With these two boys?'

'Yes.'

'Goodness.'

Esta smirked at Carmisle's obsequious surprise. 'Yes. Of course. This family is occupied with good intentions. Any bad feelings were interned long ago. We only do good here.'

Carmisle did not react to Esta's tone. It was not her place. When she had looked around the door she was not expecting to see Lynch and Leer. She heard a sound and expected there to be mice or worse, the rats that had plagued all the homes the previous year. Carmisle had not met Tuvol but she had heard of him, listened to the whisperings of the foster mothers who had grown less guarded since Espirit's death. Few had anything good to say about Tuvol – he was a lay-about, he was an over-sized fool, he needed help, he needed *psychiatric* help – a whole range of opinion was given out about him. Esta had added little when Carmisle was assigned to her care. It was like entering a crematorium late when the next funeral was already being prepared. She would catch Esta in brief moments of stillness but that was it. There seemed to be no place for introspection.

The boys met her gaze with eyes that scanned her from head to foot.

Carmisle smiled back. It was her own smile. It was not her serviced expression, a well lined crease of the lips and cheeks that many found charming but which could be turned on and off at will except when it came to the children. Even when she was having to be strict she let her smile be part of the children she was with. It just leaked out.

'Hello.'

The two boys said nothing to her and they resumed their play. She thought perhaps they were overspill from the permanently full Homes for Peace and that somehow Esta had decided to take on more children.

In the kitchen, Esta nodded at Carmisle's reaction. 'They are Tuvol's children.' Esta said this without enthusiasm.

'How did he find... get... them. I'm sorry I cannot find the right word.'

Esta snorted. 'Neither can I.'

She sunk on to the day bed in the kitchen, its once fine material now faded and worn.

'They are to be part of Homes for Peace now?'

Esta snapped, irritated by the uselessness of the conversation.

'What do I care? Ask Espirit.'

Carmisle withdrew quietly.

Later, with her duties completed, she looked in on the boys.

They were back in their puffy jackets, sitting cross-legged facing each other, their hands held up, pressing each other's palms. When Carmisle peered more closely into the room she noticed their eyes were closed. But they were not still; their hands moved in unison, first left going down then right going up; they directed each other, mirrored each other and the effect was beguiling. If Carmisle hadn't caused the rotten door to creak she felt it could have gone on for a long time. When they heard the sound, their arms dropped lifeless on to their laps, their eyes shifting to look through Carmisle who slowly shut the door until she heard it click.

Tuvol and Esta

The snow storm had enveloped the compound to a degree that everyone had retreated inside – disappointed children now sulked behind steamed up windows and the handymen, relieved of their endless task of keeping the compound breathing for once, had time to smoke and chat round their wood-burning stove. Beyond the compound walls the snowfall had brought the whole of Bente to a quiet, dignified halt.

Before Tuvol opened the back door he could see through the glass partition that Esta was preparing her words; her face was churning loose skin from cheek to jowl, her limpid eyes carefully following his moves as he shook the snow from his boots.

'How was your walk?'

'Fine.'

She paused as though gauging how long the pleasantries should last. Not long. 'I am too old for this.'

Without thinking, without looking, Tuvol snapped back. 'They are too young for this.'

Esta smiled. 'You think you have your father's gift for repartee?'

'I don't know.'

'You don't.'

'Okay.'

Esta ushered Tuvol into the kitchen from the back door as the wind pushed against the glass.

'Come in, come in. This winter will be death of us; the end of these houses. Everything, everyone is on their last legs.' Esta peered out the window, as though she was a buyer looking in. 'How does it all look?'

'We're going to talk about the weather?'

'I meant the compound, the grounds.'

'The same. Worse. Better. It's difficult to say. It's all under snow.'

'The atmosphere?'

'Cold.'

'That would be the temperature.' Esta chuckled then coughed into a handkerchief.

'How are you, mum?'

Esta laughed. 'Mum? How long were you away? No one has ever called me mum in this house. We were all so close we were on first name terms.'

It was true that Espirit liked and memo'd the use of first names throughout the organisation even between the foster mothers and the orphans. He told the AGM, 'We need the familiarity of first names not the sterility of surnames, and it is a cornerstone of our philosophy that the son or daughter are unique and of themselves.'

Tuvol persevered and sat down at the large kitchen table, its wooden surface scarred with the hacks of kitchen knives, stained by years of food now etched into the grain of the wood. Even with a cursory glance, Tuvol could see it wasn't the same. 'Esta, then. How are you?'

'Is that a question or a can or worms I see before me? Let's see. I've lost my husband to an early death; my only son runs away and disappears in the tropics for months; I am left with the garbage of someone else's life as well as the responsibility and I am expected still to be dutiful in a leaking, cold, shithouse of a home just as my own health seems to be diminishing day by day. So, to answer your question more succinctly, not good. But it's great to see you.'

'Why are you being sarcastic?'

'Why are you bleating for sympathy?'

'I'm not.'

'You are. As always'

'No.'

Esta smiled. 'Ah least we have that, our back and forth; a conversation that any generation can know and which every family will be familiar with. Mother and son, how wonderful. Where's my rosette?'

Tuvol shook his head. 'I don't remember you being like this.'

'Like what?'

Esta sat down opposite him, lifting a pile of recipe books and a menu Rolodex for days when there were many visitors with varied dietary requirements. She had to be Halal one moment and Kosher the next; she was asked to reflect Bente's high protein cuisine with that of the visiting dignitaries no matter where they were from and she travelled the world as much as Espirit with her ingredients.

'Feed their peccadilloes, Esta,' Espirit enthused.

Esta imagined hundreds of mouths straining to be fed, her hands holding morsels above them, tantalisingly close.

'This... this drip drip sarcasm.'

'Maybe you weren't listening?'

Tuvol opened his palms wide just like the brothers when there was a question with many answers.

'You never said anything. To me, to anyone.'

'Is that right?'

'It's what I remember.'

'You weren't listening.'

Esta buried her head in her hands. She thought of Espirit or more accurately her life with Espirit for the hundredth time that day and rode the same ride; the inevitable roller-coaster that she was expected to get in and cling on to; tough out the journey either proud with courage or riddled with fear. All she felt she could do at any given moment was to keep her head in her hands until she was ready to put it somewhere else. Carmisle witnessed this Esta more than anyone; her head on recipe books, her dry, wrinkled skin furrowed with old dough.

'Do you want me to help you to come to terms with your father's death?'

Tuvol looked at her, noticing how wild her eyes seemed. Like the brothers. Everybody was burning. This was what it was like to feel?

'Well, I guess, yes, but I know it's difficult for you.'

Esta screamed into one of the books on the table, the shrillness only partially dampened by paper. 'Oh god, don't spare my feelings, don't act as though you care how I am.'

'But I do.'

'Enough to communicate with me for the last...? Enough to ask how I am, who I am – all the things you can ask an adult when you actually become one. You were so caught up in yourself that you didn't even know I was here. Right here! I have seen everything of you – how can you possibly expect to hide?'

Tuvol thought of Lynch and Leer's world. 'What do you mean?'

'Oh Tuvol. You go away for a few months and come back a changed person, judging me by opinions newly adopted. Like stray children from the jungle.'

'I'm just trying to make sense of things, you know.'

'Look at things with a fresh perspective?'

'Exactly.'

'Remember incidences from your childhood that bring up painful memories.'

'And good memories too.'

'Is there a balance?'

'No.'

'You should be angry with me. I should be angry with you. And we both should be angry with Espirit.'

'I don't understand.'

'That's because you haven't thought what it's like to be me. You don't know what it was like to be your father. That's what Carmisle said, a young woman she may be but with a sound head. She said children only begin to understand their parents when they die. If they are lucky there is still one left to ask but if both go before their time, before the son or daughter is ready then, well, they are left to mop up as best they can; upturning stones to find truth and reading letters to hear their parents' voice.'

Tuvol thought for a moment. 'Then I'm glad you are still alive.'

Lynch and Leer

Lynch watched the snow, head straining as the knot of his scarf, tied tightly by his brother, pressed into his neck. It felt like a strong grip each time he swallowed. Too tight. When Lynch complained, Leer brrr'd and hugged himself for warmth then brrr'd again, liking how it sounded in the air, how it clouded around him. Leer had taken another jacket, an old one of Tuvol's as it happened, and he was now drowned in frayed, musty fabric; the stale smell of damp clothing reminding him of home, the drip of sweat now the drip of melting ice.

Lynch kept looking, ignoring Leer's darting nudges to his ribs. Leer tumbled by himself for a while, falling into the snow, rising up through clumps of ice that remained attached to him, giving him a strange shape. His smile was broad. When he grew tired he sat with his brother under a tree at the edge of the compound and looked up to see what was more interesting than playing in the snow.

Their eyes met the point of an icicle some six feet long, the shaft of ice broadening out towards a branch thickened with snow. It hung there not in silence nor in stillness, slight movements of the branch caused creaks and splinters and when a longer crack was heard they gripped each other and wondered if it was snow or wood that had made the sound.

They had come this far and could move no further. They sat entranced in the falling snow and after a while the grey and brown shades of their clothing began to whiten, their bodies disappearing into the background.

When there was a gust of wind they gasped and smiled with the tease of possibility. Leer reached around in the snow and picked up a fallen branch. When he threw it at the icicle, Lynch dived to the side sending a flurry of snow into the air. Leer missed but Lynch dug deep into the snow and gripped a handful of gravel, throwing it at the icicle. He missed too and soon both were off balance on the ground buried temporarily in the snow and the ruptured giggle of confusion they were known for in the village sounded out in the quiet of the compound. For a moment they were both helpless. Leer continued to laugh, opening his arms up and holding them out into the flurries of snow. Lynch closed his eyes and saw white, cold but with a strange creaking heat, like the swing of a hammock; he saw legs first then torso then the rotten head of Verlaine, a snake weaving its way in and out of the eyeless sockets.

Lynch screamed and reached for snow to cover his face, the cold burn taking away the sudden flame.

Leer didn't notice the tone of his scream and Lynch felt no need to tell him. They had already shared everything.

They walked the last light out of the day, dusk deepening around the compound, as their steps got lost in snow-hollows, unexpected drifts hiding stones or tree stumps. There was no path to see anymore as the white claimed the last shadows of the afternoon, only the hardy pine trees retained their outline; tall sentinels remaining to watch over the night.

Leer let himself fall into a thick drift where the wind had pushed the snow against the silvery skin of a birch. The trees were still young and some branches faltered under the snows' weight and when Leer descended into the icy cushion another load fell on him. More laughter, more screams and groans. Leer spat the snow out of his mouth and Lynch fell too, not into snow but into mud in the torrid sweat of the forest.

He had tripped over a root and fallen without laughter but with pain as more mud came from somewhere and landed on his face. It was slapstick without humour, not like their performances which use to beguile the villagers. Those were loved, they were loved. But not a root, an arm, that lay stiff in the mud still clutching a stick that had been used for attack when it had not been enough for defence.

Lynch recoiled, slipping again in the mud that streamed around them, like the loosened bowels of the earth. The noise of fighting was all around him – rapid gun fire and terrible screams; the slicing of forest and thump of objects heavy and light, of collision and explosion; of standing and staying where they were when everything in him, of him said RUN. This was no place to stay but Verlaine, large and terrible, already bloodied reached down and took his hand while kicking away the still arm belonging to the dead body, hoisting him to a stunned vertical.

'Hold my hand!'

Verlaine shouted at him and bent over to pick up Leer who had been there a moment ago, before Lynch had fallen. Leer was hoisted up too and they looked without blinking into each other's eyes. It was not a look they had given each other before.

'Hold on to the guns! Do not drop them!'

Verlaine pressed their hands on to their wooden guns, releasing his own grip and stepping back. They were unsteady on their feet as the grip of mud rushed around their ankles and as they wobbled they had to grip each other more firmly. Verlaine's voice spoke into their ears, his voice deep but not calm, there was an edge to his instruction, a simmering fear in his tone. They could feel his fright, the stink of everybody's panic. It hung in the air. It polluted them.

'Stand firm, boys. Everyone is counting on you. We are all with you. Fire your guns, think of the bullets flying through the air and stopping in the soldier's body. They will not harm you. They will not harm us.'

Verlaine stepped back again and the boys looked out into dawn gloom that had been lit up with traces of gunfire. They held up their guns and they heard the encouragement of the few around them who cursed the soldiers as they swung their pangas. The boys stood where they were. Their mouths were open but not a sound came out.

Dominique and Ruess

Dear Tuvol, It's just me and doctors left now…

Dominique let the letter drop. The heat was intense and the envelope and pen slipped easily from her grasp, their slight clatter on to the bamboo floor a coda for the cicadas, but a mere pin drop against the forest's night noise. She closed her eyes as she reached for the small camcorder and didn't open them until the flicker of the jungle was electronically shimmering in front of her. She giggled, stopping the frame, as though caught doing something she shouldn't and for a moment she felt self-conscious. But she was alone in her office. The two doctors were sitting in the canteen playing cards, sewing up their day of life and death. This was Dominique's time. This was her footage.

'How do you like the camera on you?'
'The camera never lies.'

'*Oh, c'mon, any media student knows it lies through its teeth, through its fickle lens.*'

'*It's a given here, isn't it, for us both. Nothing is what it seems.*'

'*And nobody is who they say they are.*'

'*Who are you, Ruess? Tell us. This is a take away, a – what do they call it – a blooper reel…*'

'*I don't think your terminology is right. You want to film me making a mistake?*'

'*No! That's not what I meant. I mean just film you being you.*'

'*You mean fly-on-the-wall, mosquito-on-the-skin kind of thing?*'

'*Yes.*'

'*This is it. This is all there is. Besides what's anyone going to see when we both shoot from the hip?*'

Dominique tried to muffle her shriek of embarrassment in the canvas of the hammock but some of it still leaked into the night. She recalled her self-conscious pan to the left and right of Ruess, up and down his muscled but jungle scarred body. Her way of seeing was immediately voyeuristic and she blushed when she remembered the raw desire she had for this enigmatic, distant man. She played it cool to keep others guessing. But she knew. When they met after his long spells in the jungle they would entangle each other's arms, each other's sex while the unwinding of experiences, the necessary re-telling of events was pummeled by intercourse and blurred by alcohol.

The camera swung as Ruess squeezed into the hammock and they were glued by prickly heat, their sweat sticking skin to skin and their smothered laughter at the sound of their unstick. It was rare farce in the forest as every creak of the hammock was covered with coughs or a raised voice, the rhythm of their conversation see-sawing as much as their bodies.

Dominique understood the complexities of desire but after each Ruess return she was not sure she could go on being some kind of antidote to the horrors he had witnessed; a body to hold; a mind to assault with description and a sex to punish with aggression, the inevitable fallout from so much violence.

The Ruess on camera now was the same Ruess who had cried into her body, tears burning her skin. The same Ruess who had swaggered and staggered with drunken ego declaring that he was going to save everybody, including Dominique. She hadn't thought she needed saving but she smiled and went with it knowing full well that Ruess for all his masculine blow was usually felled quickly by the intoxicating mix of exhaustion and alcohol. Invariably his rants would be chased by sleep.

In the morning his coffee steamed into the mist, a brief moment of chill before the heat of the day closed in. Ruess didn't flinch from next day evaluation, the ritual of his return, the necessary regret, anger, relief, release. Many of the Organisation's employees chose the counselling contractually offered. Such psychiatric help sought to untangle the PTSD threads that could wind tighter and tighter as time in the field went on. Dominique had seen the long-term field workers tic their way through the day; recoiling in horror at everyday objects then doubled-over, laughing. Freelancers like Ruess were unlikely to receive such post-operative care. Such men bristled like cacti, their confidence rooted in delusion while relying on luck. Their key element was cracking on, nipping any propensity for self-reflection neatly and efficiently in the bud. It was in the blood.

As Ruess talked about who and what he had seen, his coffee still warm in the enamel mug Dominique was always sure to give – a lewd drawing of a naked woman on the side of the cup was something for them both to laugh at – his conversation easily turned to the next stage of the plan to interview as many people as he could affected by this slow-quick-slow war. To go deeper into the forest to find more isolated villages and IDPs. It was as though he came from one direction, spun a bottle of rice wine and went off in the direction it showed.

There was no friction between Ruess and Dominique about this and the coming and going occurred more than half a dozen times. Even by the second time she adopted a routine, standing at the edge of the jungle and waving goodbye. She cried silently the first time and by the sixth she walked to the perimeter of the compound with him and kissed him until he gently let go, lifting his backpack and walking off without looking round.

Tuvol

Tuvol looked at Esta with a mixture of pity and confusion. Her mind seemed to be deteriorating and her behaviour seemed to him, well, erratic. Where had all these words come from? He wondered whether she had spent so long in the house that she needed now to monologue, to chat with walls, to converse with utensils. Her skin seemed to have a greasy sheen to it and when she coughed she spat out the phlegm into the sink. When they stood together in the kitchen Tuvol could smell the fumes from a thousand meals clinging to the air.

'You should ask me questions,' Said Esta.

'Sorry?'

'Better than that.'

'I don't know what you mean.'

'Sharp as a tack as ever, eh? I'm getting old…'

'You're not that old.'

'I have been aged but I know what's important.'

'Okay, what's important?'

Esta tugged sulkily at her hair with a brush clogged with grey, matted strands. 'Information.'

'Information?'

'Details that are not known to you; history to be discovered, that sort of thing.'

'I don't know what you are talking about.'

Esta sighed and pulled irritably at her hair one last time. She threw the brush back into the wash bag she kept by the sink.

'I had no parents to ask, I had no history to find out about except the admission form that gave the barest facts.'

'So what do you want me to ask?'

'What was our wedding like?'

Tuvol sat down awkwardly, his long legs bumping into the table. This was a mother and son moment he had neither expected nor wanted.

'Ok. What was your wedding like?'

Tuvol had never seen a wedding photograph.

'Ridiculous. Inevitable. Lucky – by an orphan's standards, which as you can imagine are not that high. The priest slurred his way through the ceremony, drunk on communion wine, Sister Aseret smirked her compliance and talked in hushed tones with Espirit's leathery, powdered relatives. I signed on the dotted line. I was so lucky.'

She coughed several times, her chest heaving.

'Your father didn't carry me over a threshold; he guided me across a wobbly plank into our home, a moat of mud awaiting me if I should have fallen.'

Tuvol looked at the older Esta and couldn't see the younger. She had always been this old.

'We slept in this house, half-finished, a roof of night sky. There was little or no furniture, the only room that was complete was the study. Of course. When it came to sleep, Espirit gave me two blankets, one for the floor and one for a cover. "I have to work," he told me.

'This was your wedding… night?'

Esta laughed. 'How delicate you are. No need. Espirit wasn't. There was no… wedding night. Nor any other night for that matter until… well you know what until. You've heard the one about the taking of a young virgin in virgin snow? Of course you have, everybody has, but he always told his side of that story. Not mine. Never mine.'

Tuvol noticed Esta turn away and sit on the day bed in the kitchen, her head bowed and buried in a grey handkerchief. Tuvol recognised the motion; he saw in Esta grief working its way from the inside out; her skin a tough barrier but not strong enough to keep in the pain and its bitter trajectory.

She wasn't old but she had been aged.

'So, I could ask you another question then?'

Esta pushed her sodden handkerchief up her sleeve.

'That's generally what happens.'

'Were you happy then?'

She laughed, slammed the palms of her hands onto the table.

'Finally, a question that deserves an answer. Maybe you learned something in that jungle of yours after all.'

Tuvol puffed out his chest. 'Were you?'

'Of course. I was enamored, enthralled. I was whisked off my feet from an orphanage for Christ's sake. I was saved from a lifetime alone by a lifetime of loneliness.'

'I hate your sarcasm. You ask for a question then you ridicule it.'

Esta shook her head. 'Did Espirit make me happy? Did you make me happy?'

'No one can make you happy, it's up to you.'

'I was not made happy.' Her words drilled into the table.

'Esta… Mum…'

His voice was too quiet and Esta didn't hear. He cleared his throat and changed his mind. 'I was going to ask where Espirit is buried.'

Esta didn't appear to have heard.

'Your father looked at me in the orphanage, chose me from the waif parade because he thought I had a tongue in my head; he said he could see fire at work in my eyes.' She sighed then laughed, quietly. 'There was, once. He put it out. Doused it well and truly.' Esta's voice rose, its tone melodramatic, a sad crescendo. 'He should have said to you on his death bed – never have dreams, son. No one including yourself will ever let them come true.'

'What were his last words?'

'No.'

'You're not going to tell me?'

'*No* was his last word. His shortest speech ever.' She laughed again but Tuvol saw tears in her eyes.

'I'm fond of you,' he said to me. I remember him saying it in the car as we drove away from the orphanage. I heard it as romantic. I was lost and now I was… Dear God… my feet were not supposed to touch the ground. But I misheard, maybe it was because of the car's engine or my own revving thoughts but he didn't say that, how could he?'

'What did he say?'

'I own you. He changed gear and I stalled. It was as simple as that.'

Neither of them knew how to fill this latest silence, as visible to them as the drips of the Fuege roof. Then Esta pushed words past her choke.

'Your father is buried in the cemetery in Bente. You know the one. Carmisle says there are more living people in it than dead – teenagers apparently getting drunk, sacrilege she says, but the dead don't mind. I haven't been back and I don't tend the grave. I don't need to remember him because I haven't forgot him.'

Tuvol felt the cut of her words. 'Thank you. I'm sorry to ask.'

Esta stopped still for a moment. 'I'm glad you did.'

Her words hung in the air and Tuvol thought them sharp again until he noticed her thin, pruned lips turn into the slightest of smiles and he believed her. He left the kitchen for once without slamming the door.

Lynch, Leer and Esta

'You shouldn't go, Miss Esta, not in this weather. It is a terrible storm. In my country when the winds are strong, you shut yourself inside and hide and hope that everything will be there the next day.'

Carmisle was standing in front of the door and was close to barring her way.

'Why shouldn't I? They are not in their rooms; they are not in their own country for Christ's sake. We should know where they are.'

'But Mr Tuvol…'

Esta snorted.

'*Mr* Tuvol is a fool, the offspring of bad genes. He wouldn't know responsibility if he held someone dangling over a cliff…'

'It is too cold. You must not go out. At your age…'

'At my age I should be in widow prime but since I'm not I am going outside to find my two house guests. This is not the first time we have had snow. This town was built on it. Hah!'

Esta laughed and pushed Carmisle out of the way. Carmisle knew better than to argue but she at least managed to put a thick coat over Esta's shoulders as she hunched against the snow, opening the door just enough to squeeze out into the white.

Without looking, she knew where they would be.

'There you are! I thought you might be here. I know it well. This is a special place; a shelter from the storm.'

The boys stared at her, made statuesque by weather and fear. The spot was not that sheltered. It might have been once but part of the compound fence had been broken by vandals or wind and it had, like many things recently, gone unrepaired. The winter winds that had once been thwarted now rushed up the slope, weaving between the snow-laden trees and snapping like a bad temper at the boys as they stood still, overwhelmed. There was nothing to see in the whiteout except the white itself and this was not the colour of their home – the greens and browns, lightning and darkening as the day rose and fell, the colour of undergrowth, of the river in full spate, of the earth they kicked under bare feet. White was about bones washed up in the river, buffed by the current to a smooth finish; white was their teeth carefully looked after by Verlaine and then under pain of punishment by themselves. Nothing could have prepared the boys for the whiteness of the compound in the worst winter in Bente anyone could remember.

'It's terrible weather isn't it…'

Esta shouted this close to the boys but she followed it with a louder laugh. How ridiculous!

The boys' eyes widened.

Carmisle looked through the whiteout for figures and saw nothing. She pictured herself turning around and going back into the warmth, putting her feet up to wait for this crazy family to sort themselves out.

Shaking her head, she began to trace the deep steps made by Esta.

Esta had sunk suddenly to her knees as though the punishing wind had knocked her down, but she voluntarily pressed her face into the soft, fresh snow and turned it from side to side. Lynch and Leer stared at this old woman who did not look alive when they had seen her in the florescent kitchen, the white light making her look sickly, a skin toned for dying.

She rolled on to her back and spat snow out of her mouth; the brothers took a step back, startled by the sound amidst the muffled landscape. Then she laughed a laugh that came from her chest, not the acidic leak that was her reaction to most things. She felt she had been pickled in absurdity. A loveless marriage at someone else's convenience, stuck in a compound that had a wrought-iron sign now covered with frost which proudly stated: Homes for Peace; Compassionate Pragmatism. That made her laugh every time she saw it. What kind of sign said Pragmatism?

Esta sat upright and smiled at the boys who blinked at her from under hats and wraps.

'I love the snow!'

She shifted backwards and leaned with a loud sigh against one of the trees, the bark gnarled and scraped with initials of compound kids declaring love for each other and hatred of the town kids who bullied them.

'I don't even know if you have seen snow before. My geography is poor, my education my own. I've only understood what I have seen and what I have heard. But look at you, you've found the best place in the whole compound to play. You don't need to know what anything's called. How does it feel? It doesn't matter. You don't have to speak. There's been too many words already.'

Esta settled back against the tree and, using a flat piece of bark she pulled from the tree, she smoothed out the snow either side of her, digging a little and creating two levels of compacted snow. The wind was still strong but the old tree took most of it and she motioned to the brothers to join her, patting the snow seats with her hands. Even with their layers, the boys took up little room and when they sat down either side of Esta they hardly made a dent in the seats.

The wind momentarily changed direction and whipped into their faces. Esta shrieked and covered her face; the boys laughed and covered theirs. When she shifted her hands slightly from her face and looked either side of her, both Lynch and Leer had mimicked her and were looking at her through their fingers. They knew this game, they had played it when they were younger.

When the wind changed direction again, Esta laid her hands back on her lap and stared ahead of her. She shifted quickly from a playful frame of mind to her usual insular one. It's what her mind was used to and during the hours she had spent listening to Espirit in public places she had adopted this pose; she had been told by a delegate once that she looked demure and after inquiring what this meant, she decided to keep the position for all her public appearances. Espirit no doubt approved but he was sparing in his compliments; the pose was about rigidity rather than comfort and her straight back and stare had indicated compliance.

Esta shook her head now – snow falling in clumps – and did not want this decorum. There was no one left to care how she sat, what she said, what she did or did not know. Just two boys wondering what she would do next and it came to her, like a found object rather than a feeling. This was the right thing to do. She understood that. She reached out with both hands and tussled with the swish and squeeze of fabric until she found and gripped their slender fingers, letting her eyes hold their gaze as she did so. This was harder for them, she told herself. This was no time to freeze.

Carmisle arrived in time to unlock the embrace, which had been frozen and coated with new snowfall, prising the strange amalgamated grip apart and wishing she had a sledge so that everybody could be pulled back to the warmth. If Esta was unhinged before all this then she was flapping in the wind now – returning son and tropical orphans all too much for her fragile state.

They all staggered like drunks, their forms rounded by large clumps of snow, back from wilderness of the far corner of the compound to find Tuvol standing outside Esta's house.

Tuvol

The grave had been simpler than he had imagined it would be. Espirit would have left detailed instructions, would have outlined exactly how he was to carried, buried and remembered. But there was nothing to it. A functional slab of stone, a brief *Here Lies* inscription and a municipal flower provided by the undertaker. There were a few cards and notes pinned to the earth but already the ink had run, their sentiments blurred and illegible.

Tuvol looked for someone in the cemetery, somebody in charge who could explain. Only one man, sheepish as soon as he saw Tuvol, stopped long enough to tell.

'We had the instructions but Miss Esta cancelled them. Everything. The band, the speakers, the food. All cancelled. It was her wish. We had to respect the wishes of the widow.'

Tuvol looked at the grave for as long as he could stand. The cold. The act of remembrance. He could think of nothing to add. He picked up some frozen soil but had already walked away by the time it fell out of his hand.

Now he knelt down to look at Lynch and Leer, brushing the snow away from their faces.

'Where have you been?' Tuvol squeezed their hands to see if there is still blood in them. 'Why were you all out in this weather?'

Esta crumpled into a heap of snow someone had piled away from the path. 'Tuvol, you want to be a father to these boys?'

Tuvol looked at Esta trying to gauge her tone. He had become skittish about her expression, unsure what she was going to say next.

'I want to look after them, care for them as much as I can, with the help of this community, with you, with Carmisle even.'

Esta's tone remained the same, a kind of neutral enquiry. 'Where is their father?'

'No one knows. Lynch, who has real talent with drawing, showed me how their village was attacked and how they tried to defend it but it went wrong and their father disappeared.'

'Killed?'

'Most likely but they think disappeared. They think so many things have disappeared for them – their home, their friends even their school, gone in a puff of smoke.'

'And then you appeared?'

'Yes.'

Tuvol watched her carefully as she got up slowly and creakily. By the time he tried to help she was already up, shaking off his outstretched hand.

'I can understand, Tuvol. Giving someone a home is an honourable thing.'

Tuvol felt relief like warmth though his body. He realised that he needed to hear this.

Esta opened the back door just enough for them to squeeze through without letting in too much of the snow. The tone in her voice changed quickly, cutting through the moment.

'But it's what you do after that really counts.'

Dominique and Lew Kwin

Lew Kwin drew closer to the fire not because of the heat but because of the light. His eyes had been staring into darkness for too long and he was grateful for Dominique's invitation to join her. The flicker of flame and snap of wood on fire was reassuringly alive; a counterpoint to the still darkness around them.

'I'm an internally displaced person. I've heard your people talk about me. Not me I mean but *us*, the people here. We are the victims of an ageing war that comes in waves like the sea, yes? In the city there was a chance we could fight back; there were people who wanted to say NO, who believed they must stand with those who no longer could. I never thought Miss Dominique that I would be one that cannot stand. But it does not matter. I have my voice, I have my words. They cannot take that away from me.'

'Your family, Lew Kwin?'

'When they came for me and I wasn't there, they did what such forces always do. They went after my family. It is systematic.'

Lew Kwin rolled back, taking the weight away from what remained of his legs and he rocked for a moment, a unique movement given the centre of his balance.

'I am nothing here, in this compound as you call. I am sorry, I am not ungrateful, I know I would have died like so many people here without your help. I say thank you for them and for me. But me, what am I now? I am like Mr Tuvol, eh!'

Dominique quickly flashed an image of Tuvol from the file in her mind, outdated perhaps but he would always be the sweating, lanky foreigner constantly moving to swat mosquitoes and scratch the bites swelling up on his skin.

'I'm sorry, Lew Kwin, I am tired, I can't think. What do you mean?'

Lew Kwin brought himself closer to both Dominique and the fire, wet branches billowing smoke into the sky.

'Do you know of the saying *a sein* in my language?'

'I'm sorry, I don't. I've learnt too little in my time here.'

'You communicate in other ways, Miss Dominique. *A sein* means untimely death. When someone dies an untimely death, this man or woman, boy or girl, dies with a great attachment to life and sometimes an intense hatred toward those responsible for their death. I believe, like many in this country, that such a person becomes a spirit. Can you imagine how many such spirits there must be?'

'Here you mean, in the forest?'

Lew Kwin raised himself up onto his stumps and held his arms wide above his head.

'Not just here but in the city and in Mae Rot. The air is filled with spirits, furious at being killed before they had enough life.'

Dominique looked about her, at the fiery embers sparking in the night sky. She imagined a crowd of spirits congealed on the ceiling of the ward where so many had died, unsaved, stuck like bugs to fly paper.

Lew Kwin stopped, taking a moment to look at Dominique's face.

'But do not think I am afraid of these spirits with their howling and screeching. They are not ghosts, I am not, how do you say, hunted?'

'No, but yes. It's a good word.'

'I understand why they are angry. I share their anger and I used to join with their cries but someone would throw something and tell me to shut up.'

'Not everyone hears these spirits then?'

Lew Kwin sat back down, exhausted by his sudden burst of energy.

'Maybe they do, maybe they don't. Maybe they think it is some animal deep in the green. I don't know.'

The fire crackled between them. Dominique could hear the quiet murmur of the doctor's nightly card game, still sticking to their routine, drink in hand as though it was just another night at the club.

'Like Mr Tuvol.'

'Sorry?'

'Mr Tuvol could hear the spirits. I knew he could when I first met him. He was not from here but his eyes were open, his mind was open.'

Dominique laughed lightly.

'You think so? A lot of the time he was complaining, about the heat, the mosquitoes, the food…'

'He was not from here. Such is this place. If I went to his country maybe I would freeze or die of loneliness. I don't know. But he was in pain not from the heat or bites.'

Dominique looked steadily at Lew Kwin and tried to work out what was getting skewed in translation. The man had lost family and colleagues to terrible deaths; he had been deprived of movement and very nearly his life. If anyone had the need to define pain, it was him. Tuvol? Tuvol had institutionalised angst as far Dominique was concerned. He'd had one of those privileged but neglectful upbringings that secured the practicalities but cast the heart adrift. He'd hate her for thinking such a thing but Dominique did not rate the pain Tuvol felt, not on her Richter scale of human suffering. Tuvol had received too much not too little.

'Miss Dominique. I lost my father too but as soon as he died I knew who I had lost. He taught me more than my teachers; he made me read things I didn't understand because he knew I would some day; he argued with me to help me see what someone else might think but he also said sometimes just run or walk or jump up and down;

sometimes just move to make sure you are not the one standing still.'

'I understand, Lew Kwin. To share memories of a loved one is a special thing. Amidst all this dying and suffering it means a lot to hear what you have to say. My parents too are dead. I know people believe that those who have died are present in a spirit. For me, they are here in my heart and in my head.'

Lew Kwin nodded and threw snapped, thin branches on to the fire.

'But Tuvol. He is like a… this is not my metaphor… he is a ship without a… you know what I mean?'

Dominique smiled, strange how they could share such comparison. 'Anchor?'

'Yes, of course. That is what he does not have. Maybe you?'

Dominique laughed. 'Oh, Lew Kwin. No. My work is here. This is my anchor.'

'And your heart too is located in this mud?'

Dominique smiled again, uneasily camouflaging her feelings. This was not the time. There would never be a time in fact.

'What would they build for me Dom?'

Ruess had kicked the ground and spat out Kasheen, a yellow jet of spit and alcohol.

'What would you have them build?'

'They could build me a fucking ark so I can float out of this place and save everybody that needs to be saved, two by two, village by village.'

Dominique didn't try to hold him as he raged, his voice tapering into a plea. 'For once, just let me look down on something untouched, on lives unfucked.'

Lew Kwin and Dominique talked into the night, through it and all its jungle cries, its eerie calls. They excavated their past and laid it out for analysis, as forensic as the land mine experts who had long since left. This was dangerous territory. Not since Ruess had she opened up to such still raw memories, unhealed in the humid heat of the forest. Not since Tuvol had she remembered how much she liked to talk.

Long after the doctors had finished their restorative games, Lew Kwin and Dominique were still talking, still laughing. There was nothing important beyond their small patch of earth.

Suddenly No One Believed

Leer was trying not to cough up the dirt. It had lodged in his throat, small stones and dried tufts of forest, but he kept his hand over his mouth and slowly, without gagging, he swallowed the earth. It was hot, heavy and the stink of fighting was everywhere, hanging in the air, penetrating the many arms and legs above and around him. Despite his discomfort this was the best thing to have done. He was sure of it and sure that even though he could feel the weight of many bodies, he knew the grip of his own brother's hand.

In a moment, everything had changed. One moment Verlaine was there, rooted like the Shinla tree, the next he had disappeared, vanished. When they felt his absence and looked behind them, Lynch wailed and Leer swore. Where they had been told to stand firm by Verlaine, to hold off whatever might come there was a flood of people coming towards them, a tidal rush of panic and fear and the desperate need to escape. Pangas and sticks had been hurriedly dropped.

Suddenly no one believed.

There was no time to get out the way and nowhere to go anyway. Just time to interlock their fingers more tightly and then the rush of bodies was on them. No longer standing, and some instantly no longer living, the panicked villagers fell on top of them. Some of them exploded just as they reached the boys, their faces losing everything from skin to bone; others were forced into the air by an array of bullets, their backs torn open and their bodies crashing on to others who tried to duck but were tripped up by those who had been pumped skyward by a mortar that filled the air with earth.

By the time the dead and the dying were lying on top of them they already knew they had to keep quiet and very still. Sporadic shots and the sound of the forest breaking were all around them, as were the soldiers' voices with their distinctive city growl. There were shouts in the distance followed by the staccato of gunfire then a few cheers. They didn't have to imagine what was going on. They had already seen it. Under the sickening crush of groaning, leaking bodies the boys shivered in the heat at the sound of the executions.

Voices got closer and the soldiers closed in on what must have been a still writhing pile of arms and legs. They could hear the cut and scythe of pangas and they held their breath, not that it was easy to breathe in such a death scrum. Lynch felt his hand squeezed. He knew what it meant. Hold on. Leer felt the draught from a panga come close to his face and felt an arm fall past him, fist forward into the ground.

Where was Verlaine? Leer could feel tears of sadness and anger roll down his face and he knew he couldn't sob, he knew that tears were the last thing the situation needed but they were the first thing he felt when the panga scythe came close to him. Where was Verlaine? Lynch could not understand how he could be there one moment and not the next. He let his gun go slowly, let it be taken by some weak grip that curled fingers around the wood and gradually pulled it deeper into the pile. Leer's gun remained slung over his back, twisted vines keeping it close to his skin.

They didn't count the time. There was no way of knowing it but they listened for quiet, the raucous voices dying, the gun shots receding as the hunt no doubt went further afield for those who had managed to run. And some time after that when the sounds of the forest slid back, Lynch and Leer let go of each other's hands and erupted from the piles of bodies that had both saved them and nearly smothered them. Of course it was a risk but they couldn't wait any longer. The forest was never going to get as quiet as it was then and when they ungripped the last fingers of someone's last grip from their torn clothes, they ran as far as they could. They barely saw anything as they jumped over the bodies of the villagers, slaloming past dead childhood friends none of whom they had been able to protect. The powers Verlaine had believed in were useless and the only thing they had left was to jump, their eyes shut, their arms as wide as they could go, into the river, hoping the muddy water would wash them away.

Coming in from the cold

The boys noticed her brown skin and gave her a long lingering look as Carmisle wrapped them in blankets and pushed them close but not too close to the wood burning stove.

'You notice, eh? That's right. I don't look like Miss Esta or Mr Tuvol. Like you, I'm not from here.'

'They won't understand you. They don't speak our language,' Esta called out from the kitchen.

Carmisle opened the door of the wood burning stove and stoked the embers. She winked at the boys.

'It's not my language either.'

The boys kept on staring at the fire, at the flames they could see through the open door of the stove. When Carmisle went to close it, Lynch exclaimed, a sudden whelp of pain. Carmisle looked at him, at them both and the fire.

'Sure, *mi querido*. If it helps.'

Lynch held up his notebook and showed the page he was working on.

Carmisle nodded, looking at the line drawing of flames shooting out of the wood burning stove, except that his stove looked more like a head, the open door a mouth with grey flames curling out. Like a cartoon.

'You need some colour. I'll find some pens. Flames have to be bright, don't they?'

Lynch took back the notepad and continued to draw. His brother leaned on his wooden gun and said nothing.

Esta was suddenly in cooking mode, making soup, cocoa, biscuits and tea. Carmisle had not seen her so focused. 'Slow down, Miss Esta, those boys look like they have been hungry for a long time.'

When Tuvol walked in Carmisle was opening the pine-effect shutters, letting light into the room while Esta was handing out bowls of soup. Nobody said welcome home but it felt like a home, like he had walked into someone else's house, fostered with warmth and family spirit. Slumping into one of the formal chairs, he gawped at the scene and could find no words to add. With iced up vision he saw Esta chatting easily with Carmisle who made sure the boys, still wrapped in their puffed up jackets and woolen hats, were okay and eating enough soup.

Tuvol felt ill, fevered with heat and cold and he slipped down the chair unable to maintain his posture. The graveyard had followed him home. He had been determined to confront Esta. How could she not commemorate Espirit? She had desecrated his memory by giving him a paupers grave. He boiled, then simmered then went lukewarm.

He could see Esta and Carmisle stop mid-flow, watching him, cups paused at their lips. Tuvol tried to smile and say something but his throat tightened as though one of the Yarla snakes had slithered around his neck. He wanted to tell them that Espirit was sitting opposite him and was desperately trying to make himself heard, his arms raised up, his hands punching the air. Carmisle and Esta chatted about the boys and Tuvol's head went slowly into his hands, tears flowing, first hot like the forest's day and then black, as dark as the forest's night.

Esta nodded calmly to Carmisle who gently coaxed the brothers away from the food, cake crumbs falling from their mouths as she led them quietly past the dissolving Tuvol. Esta waited until they had gone and for a moment regarded Tuvol before rising stiffly to her feet. She touched him lightly on the shoulder as she went out, being careful not to slam the door.

Esta and Tuvol

'The first time I was up here I wasn't even born.'

Esta nodded but said nothing. The crunch of snow underfoot was the loudest thing at that moment.

'And the last time I was up here I was determined to die.'

'Uh huh.' Esta's voice disappeared into the thick coat she had worn for years, a gift from a donor that Espirit had passed on with a, 'Happy Birthday!' It was meant sarcastically.

Tuvol was surprised. This had been Esta's idea. Things had been going her way since the children had warmed up her kitchen again. She had begun to glow. The kids were the trigger, Lynch with his sweet smile, Leer with his sly grin, leaning on his gun. Tuvol was of course glad; this was the sense of home he had imagined for them. They had his bedroom while he wrecked his back on the cushions laid out on the living room floor. Esta had had her doubts.

'You are too tall for the floor!'

'There's nowhere else. I want the boys to have their own room. Shall I sleep on your kitchen table and cut my toe nails in the sink?'

'There is another room.'

'No.'

In the snow Esta shivered with cold and memory. 'How do you remember your father?'

Tuvol tried to remain neutral. 'I remember he had a strong

speaking voice.'

Esta spluttered, amazed that Tuvol could have said something so asinine. 'Oh, very strong, especially when he told the world that you were conceived on this mountain.'

They reached a small plateau and they both stopped to breathe in the thinning air. Down below, Bente was shrouded by low cloud, rooftops just about visible, the pine trees bending under the weight of snow. Like Esta at that moment. But there was still energy there. A dark, trembling energy that had her small, spindly legs kicking at the icy ground like a frustrated child.

'It's not far now,' said Esta.

'I know. I've been here before, remember?'

'Remember? All I do is remember.'

Tuvol's fingers dug into his palms. 'Then why are we here?'

'Don't shout. You'll bring the snow on top of us and then we would both be buried. Again.' Esta laughed then sighed as she stood.

'You don't know everything. And maybe you should. It could help you. It could hurt you. Either. Let's go on.'

Tuvol let the conversation slip away and he gripped on to silence as much as he did to the icy shale. He clenched his fists and bumped them into his legs. A movement for circulation, an understandable exercise to keep the blood flowing but then his blood was flowing just fine; his pulse was beating through the veins in his head and he made sure the thud of his fists could be felt through the layers of his warm clothing.

'This is it,' declared Esta.

Tuvol was surprised. He had thought it further but then the topography of the mountain had changed, the elements as well as his memory shifting paths and crevasses. But there was no doubting Esta's belief that this was the location.

Tuvol found it hard to bite his tongue in the cold. Every passionate and mundane moment with Dominique had encouraged him to say what he felt, to relinquish his reluctance and spit it out, and he knew that if his mind was racing and his body tensing then something must be said. He was tired of saying nothing.

'What are you expecting to see here?'

'Tuvol, it doesn't have to be here to be here. Years of drift and ice, storm and sun will have seen to that. This mountain will have changed since the last time you were up here, never mind me. But let's mind me just a moment. You may think you know this place but I know it better.'

'Is there an X that marks the spot?'

Esta turned round from admiring the view to face Tuvol. Tuvol saw the fury on her face that he had seen before. When he had strayed into the kitchen as a child, or later as an adult when her malaise could not be interrupted and the door to the kitchen would be slammed and slammed again.

'You think you are clever, better than me, the orphan lifted out of the gutter by the king of charity?'

'No, I don't think that.'

Esta laughed unexpectedly, her grim face suddenly sparked. She paused, looking around as though she had lost something. 'It was here.'

Tuvol looked back down the mountain and tried to guess where their house was now, hidden by the layers of snow clouds rolling in. He would rather be there in front of the wood-burning stove than here in the cold. They had trudged up the hill in search of Esta's past but there was a part of him soaring out into the cloud cover. He already felt his heels lift off the ground. The altitude was making them both a little crazy as his mother began to paw at the ice.

'It should be here, it should be here.'

Tuvol closed his eyes and swayed with the view. In the perfectly chilled air he felt like opening his arms, puffing out his chest, raising his voice to the mountain.

Esta wailed.

She had pushed her face into the burning snow and as she raised it up into the air Tuvol could see how red her skin had become. He worried that she might push her body into a stroke or heart attack but when the wail repeated itself, her eyes tight shut, he worried more that the mountain would come down on them. The previous year a group of climbers had died close to the peak when their premature cheer brought a precipice down on their heads.

Esta wailed again and he felt compelled to both hold her and shut her up, a simultaneous movement of care and necessity. She was becoming unhinged. The crevasse of snow beneath them shuddered. Tuvol let his exasperation out.

'Esta. Mother. It doesn't matter, not now. It happened. It was a good thing and I know now where it all started but Espirit is gone. Let's go down into the warmth and see the boys. They will be wondering where we are.'

Esta hit the snow with both fists as ice fell out of her mouth, tiny shards sticking to her blue lips.

'You don't know anything. Your father raped me. He gave me pain not love and if you want to know anything, if you are trying to discover yourself, you are the offspring of that.'

Tuvol stared at Esta's rippling face then looked up at the mountain's summit. He thought the snow must have avalanched without warning: he was suddenly frozen, entombed in ice.

'What?'

'I didn't want him to choose me at the orphanage and I hid behind one of the fat sisters who hit me and kept shoving me forward. There wasn't much choice left, just a deaf girl, a girl with a flat chest and me. Espirit liked breasts and he looked at them longer than he looked at my face. He was of course outspoken. His future wife needed to be able to listen to him and needed to have breasts.'

Esta looked down at her body wrapped in snow.

'He grabbed hold of me and pressed me hard into the ground. No one dug a snow-hole; he used me to compress fresh snow into ice. "You're my wife. This is my right." Word for word that is what he said. When he lay on top of me his weight took the air from my lungs but God, not from his.' Esta breathed out slowly. 'I can remember his laugh. Do you?'

Tuvol couldn't think.

'It was loud?'

'Loud? It was sickening. Like a retch. His lips were still greasy from his breakfast and his hands had the smell of the gutter about them. He had been waiting for this. Timing it, scheduling it so that it could all be fitted in. I thought we were going to look at the view from the mountain, our first walk together.'

'Oh God.'

'You don't want to know this?'

Tuvol put his hand on his ears and collapsed onto his knees facing away from Esta, looking at the cloud rolling across the steeples of Bente.

'Listen. If it wasn't for this you wouldn't be here.'

Esta punched her tiny fist into Tuvol's padded jacket. It was a useless punch, a kindergarten hook that was like a fan of air on the skin but the violence was not in its impact but in the act itself. It was pure anger with no expectation of atonement. He knew that if his mother had been able to reach she would have aimed for his face.

Tuvol pushed her away from him, hard enough for her to lose her balance and he began to run downhill, the loose stones kicking up into the air.

At Home in the Cold

Tuvol had never run as fast as that, certainly not down the Anvil with its slippery shale and precarious edges. The icy wind that had swept him from the mountain followed him into the house trapping swirling flakes like snow in an airless globe.

He stepped lightly up the stairs but it was a confident step. He was neither hiding nor sulking; holed up or hiding out. He didn't even notice the usual cracks of the rotten floorboards that would drive Esta and Espirit mad, as they tried to covertly move around their own home. The brothers were still there. Of course. This was their home. They were camping in what was left of his childhood but that would change. Soon the room would be their present not his past.

Downstairs the wind was taking advantage of the open door and a mini-drift had already begun as smooth layers of whipped up snow covered the coat-stand, filling empty pockets. Esta. Tuvol knew that at her pace, light would fade and the temperature would fall before she made it back to the house. The study door was straining at its hinges as gusts picked years of dirt from places where no one had bothered to clean. It was not like it used to be; the house was not the same. Esta was not in her kitchen, Espirit was not slammed in his study and he was not holed up in his room. They had all been replaced by events.

He sat down on the front door step. Squinting through the blast of snow, there was no sign of life in the compound, no charcoal burning nor rice being steamed or fish being fried. He looked behind him and everything that had been loose on the floor or hanging from the coat stand had been tumbled into the corner by the study, jamming the door with old coats and umbrellas. It was debris. It didn't matter. This house needed air.

He would give it a few minutes then make his way towards the footpath to the mountain. Even with slow walking Esta probably wasn't far behind. She was probably close to the car park by now. If she was, it was an easy walk from there to the compound. But Tuvol immediately reassessed that. Looking at the sky, feeling the burn of the wind on his skin, reeling from what had been said, seeing her crumple in the snow, he knew there was nothing easy about this.

What kind of son would just sit here? The kind of son who would walk away and not come back.

He stopped at the beginning of the path to the Anvil, slightly breathless and light headed, but he started running again when he saw a small figure slipping and sliding down the path from the mountain.

Dominique

When Dominique woke up from her dream she felt the heat of morning press into her chest and she gasped for air, shocked to be awake. She had dreamed of yesterday's only admission to the Clinic. A new record. There had always been more than that but the trickles of the last few weeks had dwindled to one burnt child. Her body was the only one left in the ward.

Dominique sat up in her hammock but then stopped to listen to sounds she no longer heard. It had never been so quiet. Gone were the familiar atmospherics of daily life – the squeaking of trolley wheels, the clank of pots and pans in the kitchen, the constant whirr of those lucky enough to have fans. And of course the shriek of children, their presence had always been welcome; they were both pulse and life-blood of the compound. But even this had stopped when patients and families alike bid their farewells, hugging the nurses, the doctors, lifting or trying to lift Dominique off her feet, squeezing her until there was no air left in her lungs. Without them there was only a sense of time gone, of disappearance, the past.

When the doctors had tended to the smoking girl, dressing wounds, talking comfortingly while her mother stood by nervously, they urged

Dominique to make a decision.

'She is the last one now. The old woman was taken away by her son to Mae Rot.'

'I know. I said goodbye but they were in a hurry. Everyone's in a hurry now aren't they. Seems like only yesterday we were trying to get people to move on so we could get some more space.'

'Fewer reasons to stay when the place you arrive in is more dangerous than the one you left.'

'True. More may arrive tomorrow though.'

'More may always arrive tomorrow. What did Wayne say? Does HQ have an idea how close the front line is?'

'Wayne laughed and said we were the front line now. He said they were likely to garrison in Mae Rot – gives the soldiers something to do with their money and their nights – and from there push to the border. We are likely to hear gunfire soon and there will be casualties.'

'There are always casualties.'

'I guess he means will we be here to treat them?'

'And will we? It's your call. Your parents are medics right?'

The question sounded strange to Dominique. Unnecessary. 'Were. They died.'

'Sorry. But you will know from them, that you will have to order us to evacuate. It's never easy to leave.'

'Wayne was pretty clear about it. The car will come back just once. It is up to us to make sure we are in it.'

Dominique had stopped listening but was glad when they stepped away and the smoking child was no longer smoking. Her mother cried when she carried her away, with relief, desperation, shock. The doctors nodded and cleaned and cleared for the last time. Dominique watched the mother and child stagger out of the compound to as uncertain a future as many who had left. And those who stayed? She noticed too the choreographed actions of the doctors as they prepared the theatre as though tomorrow would just be another day of sawing and suturing.

'Even if this was our last operation, it's important to leave it ready so that someone like us can step in and start again. If they have to.'

Dominique knew the tone even though they tried to hide it. The briskness of effective intervention could be intoxicating. The doctors, life-savers of so many, would go to the next posting and do good there.

Their professionalism was gleaming.

Dominique knew she felt a little jealous, a strange but passing envy tickling inside her as she looked around her chaotic office. The doctors were all about completion, job done. Great. They moved on but Dominique was ongoing. She was unfinished because what was important wasn't ever finished. It was a belief not a protocol. Her office was a shrine to the fact that things didn't have to be in order to work. So she left the doctors to their efficiency and went to stand outside the canteen. The smokers had been banished to this spot, their own separate tressel table, but although none of them were smokers it was where she and Lew Kwin, Tuvol and Ruess had all sat at some point. They preferred it ironically because it was in the fresh air and away from the canteen fug.

The difference in the compound was striking. Gone were the sights of women cooking around pots, families crouched around campfires, hungry children sticking close by. These spots had now been abandoned with little left behind apart from the scorched forest floor and the little plastic bags that seemed like currency everywhere she went.

Maybe this was the time to drink some Kasheen and get into the spirit of the moment, like Tuvol with his blotchy tempest, like Ruess with his voice slurring the weight off his shoulders. But it didn't seem right to her, to be senseless in such a sensuous place. She wanted to remember; not just the next day but the next week, month, year. She wanted to keep, collect her experiences. Unlike so many she had met she was not escaping anything. She had baggage with her sure; it was clearly labelled and she didn't want to leave anything behind.

She wasn't going anywhere.

Standing by the canteen, she found it hard to fend off creeping sentiments; sequences of scenes and sounds that would characterise her years at the Clinic. Wayne had told her: 'The enemy is close by, they might recce the compound first or head into Mae Rot and gather there. Either way the car will be with you within the hour. You know the procedure; be ready to go; no unnecessary delays; save the emotion for when you are safe.'

Save the emotion! Yet another fucking man happy to advise how to deal with any situation but unable to recognise his own sublimation of fear. Fire a gun at it; put it in a line up and fill it with holes. That will sort it out. Dominique squeezed the phone until she felt its charge leak down her arm.

She'd said, 'Thanks for the advice, Wayne, I'll tell the doctors,' and now they were already in the 4x4. The driver was twitchy, imagining the trip back. One of the doctors spoke through the car window.

'Are you ready?'

'I'm not coming.'

'What?'

'I'm staying here.'

'You're crazy! What for?'

Dominique knew they would ask her that question and if she had bothered to answer Wayne's last call she was sure he would have asked her that as well. Nothing but truth rang true. She scrambled a lie.

'I've been asked to stay. To be a representative.'

'Of what? To whom? This is insane.'

'I can always get to Mae Rot and evacuate from there. I'll be okay. I have Lew Kwin, he is still here.'

'Great, maybe you can organise an evacuation on his skateboard.'

Dominique allowed the doctor that because he had save so many lives but she cut the conversation. It wasn't as if she was looking for his approval. It didn't matter. She nodded to the driver who was only too happy to take her cue.

'Be sure to check in with Wayne when you get back.'

'But what will we tell him?'

'The heart is a lonely hunter.'

'What?'

The driver lurched the car forward.

'What did you say?'

The engine roared.

'Tell him there is still work to be done.'

The doctors said nothing more but kept on looking back as the 4x4 bumped and jived over the dirt track.

She kept on watching the car and its kicked-up dust until every last piece of mud had returned to earth.

Ruess had asked her once, with a slur but always with a smile, 'Hey

Dom, you think you'll ever leave the jungle and settle down in some cosy little arrondissement with soft furnishing and a hard life behind you?'

'Is this a proposal?'

'Hell no!'

'Didn't think so.'

'Well?'

'Some people think that by never leaving, by devoting all their time to the job, they are being dedicated, but what good is some cranky, burnt-out NGOer who hates the work but can't bear to leave it? That's not me though, you know, I *am* happy here. All I need is some cold, some mountain air once in a while; I know what is important and I know what I want.'

'And me?'

'You? You've long since gone bamboo. This mud is in your veins and that camera has fused to your head; it's your only way of seeing now.'

With filmic timing she heard a snap of wood in the forest, a rustle of leaves and branches. She nodded.

'It's my only way of seeing now.'

Her words matched Ruess's tone when spoken aloud. She laughed at herself. Sooner or later everyone talked to themselves out here.

'Miss Dominique!'

She saw Lew Kwin making his way up the path.

'I'm glad you stayed. The ship wouldn't be sinking if all the rats left.'

Dominique smiled and was grateful Lew Kwin hadn't asked why she was still there. She had supplies, a locker full of rations that could last them both for some time. She just needed to be here. This spot was good. With her back to the Clinic she had a clear view of the forest.

'Ah Miss Dominique, we have time now, all the time we need. It is so quiet is it not? I will show you what I have written.' Lew Kwin had strapped a bundle of notebooks to his back, thick dossiers, curling yellow at the edges. 'I will read these to you; my life in the city, this life here in the jungle and then you, it will be your turn.'

Dominique smiled.

'Ah Lew Kwin, my story is yet to happen.'

Lew Kwin shifted himself to be close beside her.

'I'm sure it will, Miss Dominique.'

Dominique looked out into the jungle. 'I'm sure it will too, Lew Kwin. This is where my heart is. There has to be a frontier.'

Lynch and Leer

When the brothers woke up in the night they tried to guess where they were. Leer rolled out of one side of the bed and felt not the warm earth break his fall but the bevelled slats of Fuege wood, and when his hands reached out in the darkness it wasn't the mosquito net or the rough branches of their home on the run. He touched icy metal and recoiled. Lynch sat up in the fluffed up bed with its two duvets, two blankets and more pillows than he had heads and when he put his arms out in front of him it was like he was still slipping and sliding with his brother, all over again, tumbling like they had in the mud, in the heat, in the forest.

It was too dark. Always there had been the sky, its stars or moon, lighting their village. Even in Mae Rot there had been the burn of yellow lights behind old smoked glass and in the Clinic grounds there had been the constant glow from someone's fire. But not here in this cold, strange room. From either side of the bed their signs were no use: all the lights of the house had been turned off and the small window they had looked out from earlier was just a black hole. Lynch laughed as he held his hand in front of him and couldn't see it. Leer hissed his frustration at not being able to find his gun. Lynch slid down the luge of white sheets and knocked the bed's metal frame and Leer answered twice from where he knelt and kept knocking as he made his way to the end of the bed to meet his brother. They smelled each other at first and then finally used their hands to touch mouths and flick noses; Leer twisted ears while Lynch pinched a cheek. They tussled quietly and were relieved when, looking up at the window, they saw some night sky now that their eyes were becoming used to the dark.

Climbing on to the chest of drawers in front of the window they watched the snow for a long time, waiting for the moment when it would finally stop, timing their sleepy gaze so that they would witness the storm reduced to flurries and then to flakes again, just as it had started. They did not know this view but then it had been some time since they had woken in their own beds to something they knew. Such were their waking thoughts. What they saw was glazed by what they had seen.

They knew they were far from the forest, their forest, far from its humid embrace, their play with Salva in the muddy water, their running battles with Jel Unw and his teasing, the sombre tones of Verlaine's stories told to them like this, side by side but not here, not this side by side. They were far across the mildewed world of Lawe's map; the same map they had torn they had now traversed. Cold air had changed everything, from their escape in the rain on the Papen Hills to their cushioned flit in the car, with clean air from a machine that sighed like the ghost they sometimes heard close to their ears. Since then heat hadn't touched them – they had to be wrapped in extra blankets on the plane because they shivered so much and in Bente they had become not boys but layers of protection.

In the quiet house with its creaks and groans they cocooned themselves on the windowsill in a world of soft cotton, watching, waiting for the first glint of sun to silhouette the tops of the old compound trees. They gasped and gripped each others' hands when they saw the jagged wings of a large Crelaw gracefully emerge from the white canopy, and when Leer caught sight of its beating wings, its powerful ascendance into the dawn sky, he aimed and fired without his gun.

Acknowledgements

P 16 -

Research for this novel involved reading and watching many accounts of the life and work of those who intervene in the suffering of others. There are many NGOs directly involved in the lives of IDPs often at great risk to themselves. There are many committed individuals armoured with belief and sustained by hope trying to make a difference to lives blighted by terrible circumstance.

With regard to political intervention I'd like to acknowledge the Human Rights Watch publication *My Gun Was As Tall As Me: Child Soliders in Burma*, authored by Kevin Heppner, edited by Jo Becker and others at HRW. This thoroughly researched report details the harrowing and malicious use of children as coerced actors in the theatre of war. In addition I'd also like to acknowledge the following writers, filmakers and organisations who helped, diversely, to give me a deeper understanding of struggle and survival; Edith T Mirante, Norman Lewis, Jason Bleibtreu, John Boorman, The Burma Campaign, The Irrawaddy, The Mae Tao Clinic.

I'd like to express my appreciation to Adrian Searle for his intervention, encouragement and belief; to Helen Sedgwick for intuitive, meticulous editing; to the early readers of the novel, Mark Waddell, Margaret Blythe and Frances McKee and to my wife, Kate Orson, and daughter Ruby for everything else that matters.